The Kingdom of Saudi Australia

By Oskar Zimmerman

The following people deserve to be thanked here:

My family, for their support - well beyond the call of duty,

Michael & Marion, for ongoing advice, help and constant encouragement,

Steven, for your excellent military advice.
Any inaccuracies are my own work, usually against his advice and are done purely to serve the plot or protect sensitive details, and should not reflect on the excellent advice I received.

"If you know an author, never underestimate the value of your encouragement"
– Matthew Reilly

Look at your young men fighting
Look at your women crying
Look at your young men dying
The way they've always done before

Look at the hate we're breeding
Look at the fear we're feeding
Look at the lives we're leading
The way we've always done before

My hands are tied
The billions shift from side to side
And the wars go on with brainwashed pride
For the love of God and our human rights
And all these things are swept aside
By bloody hands time can't deny
And are washed away by your genocide
And history hides the lies of our civil wars

Look at the shoes you're filling
Look at the blood we're spilling
Look at the world we're killing
The way we've always done before
Look in the doubt we've wallowed
Look at the leaders we've followed
Look at the lies we've swallowed
And I don't want to hear no more

My hands are tied
For all I've seen has changed my mind
But still the wars go on as the years go by
With no love of God or human rights
'Cause all these dreams are swept aside
By bloody hands of the hypnotized
Who carry the cross of homicide
And history bears the scars of our civil wars
-   'Civil War' by Guns N Roses

A Warning and Disclaimer:
From Unintended Consequences by John Ross

History has shown us that government leaders often ignore the fundamental fact that people demand both dignity and freedom. Because of this disregard, these decision-makers then initiate acts that are ultimately self-destructive. To illustrate this point I will remind the reader of the origin of two of modern history's most destructive events, and of all the warning flags that were frantically waving while the instigators rushed headlong towards the abyss.

In the late 19th and very early 20th centuries, European leaders formed two major alliances. Germany, Austria, and Italy comprised one coalition, and Britain, France, and Russia the other. Belgium remained neutral per an 1839 treaty signed by all of these nations except Italy. The smaller European countries became indirectly involved in the two aforementioned alliances. One such example was Serbia, a country Russia had pledged to aid in the event of war between Serbia and Austria. Despite Russia's presence, Austria annexed a large part of Serbia, a province called Bosnia, in 1908.

Few people remain emotionally indifferent when their culture and country are taken over by an aggressor, and the Bosnian Serbs were no exception. Many Bosnians despised the government that had chilled their independence. In spite of this obvious fact, the Austrian leaders sent an archduke to the capital of Bosnia to survey the people Austria now ruled. This archduke was resplendent in full military ceremonial dress, festooned with medals and other military decorations, and accompanied by his elegantly-dressed wife. An objective observer might at this point have said, 'Stripping motivated people of their dignity and rubbing their noses in it is a very bad idea.'

Archduke Ferdinand and his wife arrived in Sarajevo in an open vehicle, and the only protection either of them had was their chauffeur. This man was expected to drive the car and at the same time protect the Archduke and his wife with only a six-shot revolver he carried in an enclosed holster, and no spare ammunition. Our theoretical observer might here have said, 'This is a recipe for disaster.'

Almost as soon as the Archduke and his wife arrived in Sarajevo, a Serbian National tossed a bomb under their car. Its fuse was defective and the bomb did not explode. Here, our observer might have advised, 'A miracle happened. Go home. Now. Immediately.'

Despite this obvious wake-up call, the Royal Couple shrugged off the assassination attempt and continued their tour of the Bosnian capital. Later that same day, a second Serbian National shot them with his .32, killing them both. The Austrian leaders blamed the Serbian government for the assassination and demanded a virtual protectorate over Serbia, issuing Serbia a list of demands. Serbia acceded to all but one of Austria's stipulations. Here, our observer might have said to Austria's leaders, 'Russia has pledged to aid Serbia in any war with you, and Russia has both powerful allies and powerful adversaries. Serbia has agreed to almost everything you demanded. Settle, and avoid a world war.'

Instead, Austria shelled Serbia's capital with artillery fire.

Our observer might here have told Russia's leaders, 'Serbia is not worth starting a world war over,' but Russia honored its commitment to Serbia and mobilized its army, sending troops to the Russian-Austrian border. Since this left Russia vulnerable to attack from Austria's ally Germany, the Russian Army mobilized against Germany as well.

This forced the German Army to mobilize. Since France was allied with Russia, the Germans feared an attack by France in the west while German troops went east. So Germany decided to invade France immediately, VIA Belgium. Here, our observer might have said, 'Saying this is your 'destiny' is not going to be good enough, Germany. When you invade a neutral country and rape their women and slaughter their livestock and burn their houses, Britain is not going to just look the other way.'

When the Germans invaded Belgium, Britain honored its commitment to defend Belgian neutrality, and declared war on Germany. Every major country in Europe was now at war.

Four years later, over thirty million people were dead, half of them killed directly in the war itself, and the rest so weakened through shortage of food and medicines that they succumbed to the influenza epidemic. In addition to the lives lost, the war's monetary cost in 1918 was almost three hundred billion dollars.

No sooner had the war ended than the victors demanded their pound of flesh at the Treaty of Versailles.

The treaty required Germany to accept sole responsibility for causing the war. It dictated that German military leaders were to be tried as war criminals. It prohibited the German army from possessing heavy artillery. It abolished the General Staff and the German air force, and prohibited Germany from producing military aircraft. As in 1914, our observer might have said, 'Stripping motivated people of their dignity and rubbing their noses in it is a very bad idea.' But if such words were in fact uttered, they fell on deaf ears. A humiliated Germany was ripe for the nationalist message of Adolf Hitler, and in this fertile soil were planted the seeds of the Second World War.

Today in this country, honest, successful, talented, productive, motivated people are once again being stripped of their freedom and dignity and having their noses rubbed in it. The conflict has been building for over half a century, and once again warning flags are frantically waving while the instigators rush headlong towards the abyss, and their doom.

It is my hope that these people will stop and reverse their course before they reach the point where such reversal is no longer possible.

John Ross - 'Unintended Consequences'
September 1995

The Kingdom of Saudi Australia

Aftermath

December, two years from now

Bilal sat on the concrete steps of the bombed-out unit block facing Punchbowl Road. Midnight was long past. With the coming dawn a light rain was beginning to fall, shimmering in the dancing light from the burning cars and washing the smell of dust, smoke and blood from the air.

Head resting in his hands, Bilal sobbed uncontrollably as his brain tried to process the events of the past few hours, weeks and months. Sydney's Caliphate was over, gone, blown apart from without and betrayed from within. The burning desire of their cause, the sure knowledge that they were right and destined for success was gone, replaced instead by a cold, hard doubt that spread from his guts up towards his heart. A deep sorrow fell over him, draining his strength and feeding a great sense of shame and defeat. Despite hundreds of true believers fighting hard, it appeared that God had abandoned His latest possession, and half of Western Sydney lay in ruins as a result.

The lively hopes & dreams of his friends lay strewn in the rubble beside their corpses, the holy dream they had trained and fought so hard for. Their promised land, a 'Caliphate between two rivers,' wrenched out of their grasp by infidels without and treachery within their own ranks. How could they come back from this defeat? Without a sure sign of success, the necessary funds, fighters and equipment to rebuild the pure Islamic state would not flow in from overseas, support which had flowed so thickly in the past 12 months would dry up, as their King and Princes' interest moved on from what now appeared to be a lost cause. His hope of reigning as a Prince was as dead as the bodies in the road in front of him.

Aching muscles protesting, he turned his head to the right and looked east along Punchbowl Road towards the Lakemba Mosque – or what was left of it. Even from this distance, the damage was obvious. The normally floodlit spire was missing from the skyline. A thick pillar of smoke rising into the rain clouds, silhouetted by the leaping flames around told him everything he needed to know and washed him with cold waves of despair. '*Inshallah*, no help from that direction', he thought, and realized that he was on his own.

He knew it would be a few seconds before he was able to stand, so he used the time to take stock: his normally white *dishdasha* was filthy, bloody and shredded in places but the pants, long shirt and his precious leather boots seemed intact. He couldn't see his rifle or his pack, but thinking about them brought back the events of the past hour in a series of disorienting, violent flashes behind his eyes. Suddenly he remembered the barricades, falling bombs screaming out of the sky, the wave of infidels attacking their section, a white searing flash that blinded him, hands grabbing at his arms and shoulders, dragging him away as he fell into darkness – but nothing after that.

The fact that he was still alive told him he hadn't been captured by the infidels – surely they would have killed him on the spot, so he must have been knocked out and dragged to safety by some of the *Shaheed* – the lions prepared to be martyrs - beside him. They must have done what they could, then taken his rifle and pack and gone.

Fled, or died fighting?

He didn't know and felt sick when he realized that he may never know. These young men and women were his family in the most basic, fundamental meaning of the word – his family of God, and now he was alone. His feelings twisted and burned like the flames and smoke drifting through the air.

Grasping the stair's handrail with a burned and blistering right hand, Bilal levered himself upright, holding tight while the spinning in his head slowed. He moved off the steps and turned left, down Punchbowl Road then left again into Colin Street and headed towards Lakemba Train Station. Surely there would be someone there who knew what was going on.

Hunched against the rain, his thoughts ran again through the past night's events, trying desperately to piece together what might have happened.

'Fuck this!' he thought. 'You dumb shit, how did you end up like this?'

It was a big story, he knew. An epic. But his own part in it started just after he left school two years ago.

Chapter 1

November of this year

It was perfect weather for early summer in Western Sydney as Bilal's school education came to an end in a haze of parties, burnouts in their parent's cars and lazy afternoons at the Westfield's Food Court. Like most of his classmates, Bilal's parents had come to Australia in the 1980s as young refugees from Lebanon's civil war. His father had trained as a real estate valuer, and soon found work, connections and opportunity in the booming economy of Sydney during the 1990s.

Bilal was born into this bustling wave of rising wealth, living comfortably with his mother in a two-bedroom unit in Lakemba. The unit and family it contained was similar if not identical to thousands of others in the same area – a moderately successful businessman or taxi driver with (now) several wives and their children scattered about the area. Bilal knew his extended family pretty well, although like most second-generation Australians, his own culture was complicated. A mix of Old Country, American media and the local teen culture that evolved its own expression of identity that changed on a weekly basis. Much of their daily conversation, words and expressions were drawn from the dialogue in Grand Theft Auto.

Although some of his friends took their education seriously and studied hard for their exams, Bilal and most of his class weren't bothered with the Western education system, particularly its obsession with university qualification and corporate life. Bilal knew from experience that the real world was different – connections, power and money were what mattered, and a man's social standing was far more important than owning a house, nice car and an investment portfolio.

What really mattered were connections, being able to do favors for people, help them out, to be the man they came to

4

when they needed a match for their daughter, smoothing over an obnoxious council building or heath inspector, or organizing the 'right' valuation on a real estate deal.

For almost a year, the deputy Mayor of Auburn council had been a role model for exactly this kind of connected, wealthy, fast living community icon. Even when he got into trouble with the law, thousands of Auburn residents had turned out in support of him. They recognized the pattern and knew that if they supported him and he managed to avoid losing his power, they would then be able to call in the favor when they needed it. If he fell from grace, no harm done – they would simply shift their support to the next likely power broker who arose. It was how the world worked, and had worked for ten thousand years. Modern laws and technology didn't change human nature, and humans inevitably either took power or gravitated towards those who appeared to have it.

To most Australians, the case was simple: the Deputy Mayor had broken the law, and must be punished. But to a culture that pre-dated the written word, one that had survived in one of the harshest environments in the world, the clan or patriarchal system simply worked. It may not be perfect, but it had held society together from Morocco to the Indus River since before humans started living in villages.

Although he had never specifically put any thought into the differences between the two world views, he had absorbed enough from his own family life to know that if you could do favors for people, if you were 'the man' that people turned to if they needed something, that was a man who was successful.

Bilal's father provided funds to all his wives for raising the children, and the Centrelink single parent, education and disability benefits that they all claimed gave them an excellent standard of living, compared to anywhere else but a few select places in the world. Growing up in modern Australia, Bilal had no idea how confusing it had been for some of the new arrivals to learn how the country operated. In many of the places they came from, the government or head of the family provided everything you needed, and all one had to do was a little side operation if you wanted extra money. The patriarch of the area held all the authority and one went to him for permission to marry, start a business or buy property - usually building a cut for the patriarch into the deal.

To be a patriarch was a complex, often difficult job, distributing the income from family businesses to a tangled web of family members, rivalries and egos while at the same time keeping enough cash on hand to give to the poor as you passed them on the street or at prayers. The greatest honor was to receive the praise and thanks of those whom one helped, and this principle existed in every tribal community from London to Sydney.

Bilal had already asked his father to get the name of a doctor who could write a letter and get him a disability pension as well as the unemployment benefits. This small but steady cash stream would be enough to pay for Adidas clothes, jewelry and his phone credit.

Having no specific plans about the future, his role models usually lived at home until they got married for the first time, and then moved in with wife number one while working or growing a business. As success came and he could afford more wives, these would be housed in a rented flat of their own. His vague plans were simply drawn from those of his extended family, his community and hours spent playing Grand Theft Auto.

While Bilal saw the advantages in a life on unemployment only, he had also learned from his father and uncles that success in any form would still take work. Sitting with him at a white Formica table in the Bankstown Westfield's Food Court were three of his closest friends – Mahmoud, Victor and Ibby. Victor was stuffing KFC into his mouth while talking non-stop about his recent troubles.

'Mum wants me to get married, now school is over'. The other three laughed aloud, spraying tiny chunks of chicken and chips into the air.

'Fucken A bro. Git some ass twice a day guaranteed!' Ibby said grinning like a chump and bumping his fists together to mimic some kind of sex act. He slurped down a large gulp from his caffeinated energy drink and moved his hips back and forth on the seat.

Victor wasn't so sure it was a good idea. 'All mum wants is to dump the housework onto someone else. 'Sides, look around bro - which girl our age wants to get married, load up on mum's housework and never leave the house without hijab ever? Bitches be clubbing, not baby factories anymore.'

The others looked at each other and shrugged. They did know a fair few girls, either at school or a range of close and distant cousins, most of whom were doing their best to imitate the Kardashian women. Like most of their demographic, few were religious or interested in living their lives according to tradition. As far as they were concerned, Australia was 'under new management' and they could live however they wanted - money permitting.

And right now, marriage was the last thing on Bilal's mind.

'Fuck that' he said. 'Imma get some money and status first. Gotta get a job, find some work.'

'Work?' Mahmoud smirked, and the line from GTA rolled off his tongue 'Yo couldn't work a fart outta dat ass o yours'

'Fuck you homie' retorted Bilal. 'When there's some shit to be won, Goddamit, I want it. I don't give a fuck what it is. You know what I'm talkin' about? Take no prisoners. I go hard doing that shit. Big dog. Big nuts. When names is on a motherfucking board, I wanna see MY name at the top of that motherfucker and next to it, it needs to say 'Winner'.'

They all laughed as he parroted the lines from GTA5 word perfectly, but Bilal's laugh rang a little hollow - he knew it wouldn't be easy to get ahead. 'Fuck it' he thought, drinking the last of his Monster drink, 'call him tonight.'

That evening, Bilal sat on his bed, considering his options. Having treated school as a necessary interruption to his routine entertainment, he knew there was no point looking on a job website or attending interviews set up by Centrelink. No, he had to get his start by working contacts within his community. Since he lacked any contacts of his own, this presented a serious problem.

'Fuck it' he thought, thumbed away from the internet on his phone and called his father.

'Marhabaan 'abi' he said, trying to sound as casual and confident as possible. 'Hi Dad.'

'Marhabaan aibnih' said his father Rafik. 'Hello Son' – then added in English, 'Wassup?'

Bilal rolled his eyes at his father's attempt to sound cool. But he needed help, and a smartass reply would only make his father angry.

'I, um, well... I'm looking for a job now' stammered Bilal. 'Could you...umm... do you know anyone...,' his voice trailed off as he was embarrassed to ask.

There was a short pause, then his father's voice said 'Maybe I do. Meet me before prayers on Friday.'

Bilal's heart sank, and he rolled his eyes, without making any sound that his father might hear. That meant going to the mosque instead of meeting his friends. F'kn boring. No, he realised, not just boring, it was just a part of his culture that he had never felt comfortable with. The kneeling, chanting, all the memorization, plus the Australian media kept on about Terrorists, Islamophobia and hate preaching. It just wasn't something he had been around. Growing up in Sydney had given many young people his age the option of not being

8

religious, and as far as he was concerned he was as un-religious as it was possible to be.

Bilal's normal Friday afternoon routine involved going to the gym with his friends, doing a heavy upper body workout to pump up his muscles as much as possible, then a quick spray of deodorant and heading out to meet up with other partygoers and see what shenanigans they could get up to. Chasing girls, spraying graffiti, tuning and racing cars, living life to the fullest. It seemed to Bilal this was about to change.

In every culture, the children of strict parents often choose a different path to what their parents would prefer. That didn't stop many parents from taking advantage of any situation to push their influence onto their offspring, and Bilal's father knew that he wouldn't be able to say no.

'Okay, I'll wait for you outside' he said respectfully. 'Shukraan 'abi.'

Ending the call, his news feed briefly flashed up a headline from one of the news media sites. Bilal had no interest in the news, and something about "Coalition Collapses – new elections in December" didn't register as important. He thumbed away, looking for something about fast cars or bodybuilding.

It was still broad daylight when Bilal walked from the bus stop to the Mosque. In the broad open area in front of the doors, a crowd was already forming. Not really a crowd, thought Bilal, but several groups of men talking with each other. It was obvious that there were cliques and existing friendships, and people were catching up on news and sharing gossip about neighbors. Bilal didn't know any of these people, and felt uncomfortable, an outsider unable to break the ice and join any of the conversations.

Instead, he swiped on his phone and scrolled through his news feed. Nothing of interest from his friends, and the news headlines were only going on about the vote count and how the racist party seemed to be well in front.

ISLAM INQUIRY SET TO GO AHEAD

MORE ELECTION CANDIDATES DENY RACISM

CALLS FOR TOLERANCE AMID GLOBAL TERROR ATTACKS

Since there was a lot of news about Islam, he was starting to pay more attention to it, even though he didn't see what effect any type of government would have on his life – he was just insignificant in the overall picture.

On the other side of the square were the women's groups, dressed in a wide variety of coverings. Some of them wore the classic black chador – which left the face open, and a couple even wore a niqab or burqa to cover their faces. Mostly however, they wore a coloured hijab, which was more like a scarf that covered the hair and shoulders.

Bilal must have looked for too long as he felt a sharp slap on the back of his head and heard his father's voice say 'Haram!' Whirling around, he saw his father's disapproving look, and the grins on the faces of some of the other worshippers who had noticed. Then Rafik grinned as well, winked and said, 'pull your tongue back in and come with me.' Bilal blushed and shook his head but greeted his father politely.

Leaving their shoes at the door, they entered the Mosque and Bilal gasped. It had been a long time since had been inside and he had forgotten the majestic sense of space and light that it conveyed. Dominating the ceiling was a giant blue dome covered in mosaic tiles in a pattern of yellows, orange and light blue. The setting sun was shining through the arched windows around the middle, creating a unique sense of light and space which Bilal thought must be what heaven looked like.

In front of their feet, the purple carpet was marked off with light brown stripes as a reference point for worshippers to pray in lines without crowding each other. Rafik looked around, and led him over to a group of men clustered around listening to a taller man speak. Dressed in a perfectly white dishdasha, a long sleeve shirt that fell all the way to his ankles, the man was speaking quietly but with great emotion, his face and hands moving but Bilal couldn't hear what was being said.

Approaching the group, Bilal's father was greeted by one of the men who had been listening, seemingly eager to get away from the emotional exhortation. They embraced in the traditional way, kissing each other's cheek, then spoke quietly for a few seconds. The man looked sharply at Bilal, who straightened up and tried to look respectable. The two men came over and Bilal's father said 'Mr. Mohammed, my son Bilal. Bilal, this is Mr. Mohammed. You will work for him, understood?'

Bilal had no idea what was being planned but he just nodded and kept a respectful silence.

Mr. Mohammed looked past Bilal's shoulder and beckoned to another man who had just entered. The man was younger than Mr. Mohammed but older than Bilal by a few years, with closely cut hair and a large bushy beard. As he came closer, Bilal saw that the man's upper lip was shaved, so the beard only covered his cheeks and chin.

'Sargon, this is Bilal' said Mr. Mohammed. 'He will be riding with you to help the deliveries. Start tomorrow.'

Sargon looked at Bilal and nodded 'Ya ok,' he said. His eyes narrowed, 'whassa phone numbah?'

Bilal and his new boss exchanged phone numbers, just as the PA system gave a click and the Muzzein began the call to prayer:

'Allahu akbar' – God is the greatest

'Ash-hadu an-la ilaha allah' – I acknowledge that there is no god but Allah

'Ash-hadu anna Muhammadan-Rasul ullah' – I acknowledge that Muhammed is the messenger of God

'Hayya'alassalah' - 'Hasten to prayer'

'Hayya'alal-falah' – Hasten to success'

'Allahu akbar' – God is the greatest

'La ilaha illa-Allah' – There is no god but Allah'

The formal call completed, it would only be a few minutes before the Muezzin made the iqama, the second call for worshippers to line up - the beginning of the ceremony.

Bilal didn't know what to say, so he just stood there, feeling awkward, until his father turned to Sargon and said 'hey, keep him out of trouble, okay?'

Sargon just shrugged but Mr. Mohammed said, 'Don't worry – there's a different kind of trouble, and we're all in it.'

Bilal's father raised his eyebrows and tilted his head at the group they had recently left. The unspoken implication was understood by the other three.

Mr. Mohammed nodded. 'Troublemakers. Wealthy troublemakers from overseas'.

Bilal waited for the older man to continue but the conversation was cut short by the Muezzin starting the service.

Chapter 2

December

Bilal was already awake when his phone buzzed and the SMS glowed green. It was Sargon.

'5 MIN' was all it said, but the meaning was clear. Pulling on his Adidas track pants and hoodie, Bilal moved through the silent apartment, eased open the door and went downstairs. Even though dawn was an hour away, the city traffic had started moving, a constant restless hustle in the background. Trucks and cars roared on the main roads nearby, but in their little side street the air was calm.

Bilal had no idea what to expect, so he just stood outside the block of flats, thumbing through the updates on his phone. He had no interest in politics, but the news headlines screamed a combination of 'Racism' and 'Islamophobia' as the different parties campaigned towards the mid-December election date. He was about to read more when a medium sized delivery truck pulled up in front of him and Sargon opened the passenger door. The truck body was square, about the size you would use to move furniture, but painted on the side were the words 'DIMO: Halal Food Supplies'

Climbing into the cabin, Bilal shifted a clipboard stuffed with papers off his seat, and clipped into the seatbelt. His stomach growled as he saw Sargon gulping down a Mother energy drink and he mentally smacked himself for not preparing the night before.

Sargon put the truck in gear and moved off, pausing at the end of the street to turn into Punchbowl Road, and heading towards the city. He gestured to the sheaf of papers in the clipboard and said, 'find the first address.'

Grateful to have something to do apart from trying to make small talk with the older man, Bilal leafed through the pile of delivery orders, noting the addresses and suburbs, he shifted them around until they formed a decent route across the suburbs, without doubling back too much. 'First stop is in Belfield – cross the train lines, then turn right.' He squinted as the rising sun dazzled into the windscreen, trying to make out the details of the other address.

WHITE BAY CRUISE TERMINAL

'Fuck's White Bay?' he asked Sargon.

Sargon glanced at him, 'Shut up, watch, learn. Do what I tell you.'

Bilal felt the anger rising inside him – nobody had ever spoken to him like that. He was about to tell Sargon exactly what to do but was forced to shut his mouth when Sargon slammed on the brakes outside a small restaurant. Their first delivery. They both went to work unloading the various boxes, checking off the list and running them inside.

By the time he was back in the truck Bilal was a little out of breath so rather than talk he got back on his phone, scrolling through his news feed again. He didn't know what BREXIT and GREXIT meant so he just scrolled past, looking at the latest memes and videos his friends were posting.

The delivery truck worked its way across Sydney's suburbs, as the sun worked its way across the sky and by early afternoon they were in Rozelle, down by the docks in the inner west. Bilal had never been this far from home before, and was amazed at the blocks of large houses, spacious lawns and decrepit industrial estates. He wondered about the people who lived in these houses, driving nice cars, having the respect of their neighbors. He felt jealousy stir inside him.

Sargon drove past a long chain link fence that separated the road from the grey, oily water and pulled up at a small white booth in the middle of the road. A boom gate blocked their forward progress. Sargon grabbed the clipboard as a security guard came out of the booth and eyed off the signs plastered to the side of the truck. Looking at the paperwork, the guard looked up at Sargon and smirked slightly, 'Can't go in yet, Customs still checking off the passengers.'

'Fucken fine, first prize for being early,' grunted Sargon under his breath then said aloud, 'can we park here until you ready?'

The guard just shrugged and went back into the booth. Sargon pulled the truck over to the grassy verge and shut off the engine.

The sudden silence, broken only by the metallic ticking of the cooling engine made Bilal uncomfortable. He risked Sargon's anger by asking a question, hoping it would be interpreted as Bilal trying to learn as much as possible about the job, rather than being a smartass.

'Fuck we have to wait for?'

Sargon didn't even turn his head. 'Dere a cruise ship up dere, beyond that cargo ship. Passengers get checked off by customs, make sure dere no illegals snuck on board. Once they finish, dey go to lunch wid the crew. Dose hot hostesses....' Sargon sighed and continued, 'once customs gone, we drop off the Baklawa and date Kaak for de next cruise. Den we go home'

'Huh' grunted Bilal. That kinda made sense.

'Watch. Listen. Learn' said Sargon, emphasising his earlier lesson. 'No madder what you see or hear, doan say nuthin to nobody. Evah. Unnerstand?'

Bilal looked at the floor and nodded.

'You see or hear anyting, you ask me, only me, unnerstand?'

'Okay, okay' stammered Bilal, causing the older man to glare at him. Bilal saw him evaluating whether Bilal was serious or mocking him, and was relieved when Sargon appeared satisfied that he was serious.

Fifteen minutes ticked by, and Bilal surfed the internet on his phone while Sargon sat almost motionless beside him. Bilal couldn't tell if Sargon was awake or asleep, and thought it best to keep his mouth shut. This was an almost impossible task, since he was used to running his mouth with whatever came into his head. But he really wanted this job – no, not really - he corrected himself. What he really wanted was the respect that money and connections would bring – and this job was the first step along that path.

Idly pulling out his phone, Bilal flicked past the news headlines:

ELECTION CAMPAIGNS HIT FULL SPEED

MELBOURNE VIOLENCE DRIVES GREEN VOTERS TO HANSON

He was looking for something interesting, but his mind kept going back to the Friday in the Mosque. He remembered the way the worshippers behaved around the Imam, the speakers and VIPs. He knew very little about the Koran or Islam in general, but he saw another form of power there – the respect of the people for their Mayor, Priest or Rabbi. The religion and title did not matter, because the community's respect came from the conduit that the person represented. Regardless of the God, the conduit represented power.

Bilal's thoughts were interrupted by the truck engine starting. Sargon acknowledged the guard's wave and nosed the truck down the driveway towards the docks. They turned a corner and the stern of the giant white cruise ship came into view. Clustered around it were a dozen trucks of different sizes, and forklifts swarmed like cockroaches, unloading and stacking pallets of food before shoveling them into a hatch on the side of the ship.

Finally, their deliveries were finished, and the truck was heading into the early afternoon sun. Squinting in the glare as the truck turned right onto Georges River Road, Sargon turned to Bilal and asked, 'you going home, or gym?'

Bilal really wanted to go home but he made a split-second decision, nodded and said 'gym.'

He had no idea of the way this decision would change his life.

Chapter 3

January of next year

Bilal had barely noticed the election passing, most of his days alternating between deliveries, the gym and the mosque. He and his friends made a big deal of voting for the Help End Marijuana Prohibition party – against the instructions of their community to vote Liberal, but overall, they felt that politics didn't affect them. It was just one of those things that happened around their lives, without having much effect, regardless of who was in power.

Bilal only paid attention to the news headlines when they triggered something he was interested in:

ONE NATION CONFIRMS ISLAM INQUIRY IF ELECTED

AJP DEMANDS PIG FARMING BE PHASED OUT IN TEN YEARS

CRIME: NEW POLICE MINISTER PROMISES 'ACTION'

At least twice a month, old Mr. Mohammed who owned the business would catch him at evening prayers, asking about how he was feeling, how the job was going. At first, Bilal was uncomfortable in the old man's presence, then after a few weeks he got used to it. But it didn't take long for the questions to feel a bit like harassment, and Bilal wasn't sure what the old man knew – if anything, or if he suspected there was more going on behind his back.

Several times, he felt tempted to ask the old man about Sargon, some of the strange things he had noticed that Sargon was obviously trying to hide from him. Several times, Sargon had come back from a delivery with a backpack on – a backpack that he hadn't had earlier in the day. Other times, they stopped at a Post Office or PO Box that wasn't on their scheduled list.

Bilal wondered if Sargon was running his own business as well, but then shrugged because although it may have been dishonest and maybe illegal, it was ultimately between Sargon and old Mr. Mohammed, and two prime things kept his mouth shut. The first was the knowledge that everybody had their own little thing going, and he was on the lookout for opportunities himself.

But the main reason for his silence was the expression on Sargon's face that first day in the truck.

'No madder what you see or hear, doan say nuthin to nobody. Evah. Unnerstand?

'You see or hear anyting, you ask me, only me, unnerstand?'

There had been something in his voice, something in his eyes that told Bilal that the punishment for breaking Sargon's order would be far longer and painful than anything he could imagine.

So, he told the truth – most of it, and kept Mr. Mohammed advised that the delivery work was fine, he was able to lift the boxes and he was looking forward to more work if the opportunity – he made sure to emphasise the word – arose. Mr. Mohammed appeared pleased with the way things were going, even if he was ignorant of Sargon's extra activities.

Besides, Sargon and the other four they worked out with were solid guys. Sure, they joked and teased each other, but that was just normal. Bilal remembered meeting them for the first time, on his first day at work with Sargon. He had acted cool, since he knew his way around a gym, but the first joke was definitely on him.

Sargon had introduced him to Ninos, Abdul, Ghulam and Amal, and he noticed that while they all wore different clothes and were obviously not related, they had all grown a large, bushy beard but shaved above their top lip. He had noticed it because it looked a bit like a uniform, a badge of common identity but he didn't know what it meant. He didn't have time to ask because they had gone straight to the bench press equipment and started working out. Sargon had said 'Spot me' as he loaded up the bar, swung his arms in circles for a few seconds and then lay down on his back to push.

Bilal counted off ten reps and then helped Sargon aim the bar back onto the rack. They swapped positions and Bilal gripped the bar and pushed with all his strength.

It didn't move.

He was able to lift it enough for it to roll on the rack, but he couldn't even get it off the frame and into the air above his chest.

The others roared with laughter, and gave high-fives all around. Ninos said 'urgggg' and strained his face in a parody of Bilal's effort, which made the other three laugh even harder.

Bilal had sworn a lot, with words that he no longer used, since the Mullah had started educating him about how a true Muslim should act and speak. Still grinning, Sargon had told him to wait while he removed a few plates, then he started again.

This time, the bar was much lighter, and he could finish ten reps without feeling like he was about to throw up. Sargon nodded approvingly and said 'Good – go heavier and we git you stronger, very quick.'

For the next hour the six men worked out, joked and got to know each other. Bilal learned that they were all born in Australia except for Ninos, who had come from Greece with his parents in the late 1990s. Ninos' father had gotten in trouble with Jordanian Police, and fled to Europe with his wife, then came to Australia with Ninos as a baby.

Asked about his own life, Bilal shrugged in reply. 'Fuck all' he said. 'Born here, Lakemba High, then I got this job with Sargon for Mr. Mohammed.'

Ghulam shook his head. 'No no, I know you – Maryam is your sister, yes?'

Bilal nodded. 'Yeah, so? She's a year older than me' he confirmed. 'Where you know her from?'

'My sister - in her law class at Uni.' Ghulam said in between slurping from a shake bottle. Bilal nodded and went over to the free weights as the conversation drifted to cars, music and arguing over the correct movement technique for the exercises.

By the time the workout was over, Bilal could hardly move and was worried about being able to work the next day. As they climbed back into the truck to go home, Sargon opened his gym bag and took out a plastic lunch box that contained many different pills, in various bottles and blister packs. He eyed off a few of the options, glancing at Bilal then back to the pills as if doing mental arithmetic. Then he shook out five different capsules into his palm and handed them to Bilal.

'Take dese, drink lotsa water' he said.

Bilal looked at the handful of pills dubiously. 'The fuck is this?' he asked, as Sargon sorted out a similar dose for himself and downed it with water from a bottle.

Sargon smirked, 'Testosterone Cypionate, Anadrol, Durabolin. Steroids.' He looked at Bilal. 'Dese will help you recover fastah, much fastah. You be able to lift more at work, too. Get strong, get huge.'

'Fucken make my balls fall off, too, huh?' asked Bilal. He had heard bad things about steroids.

'Not any moah' said Sargon. 'Dese new pills from Europe, new formula. All good, all safe.'

'Fuck it' thought Bilal as he swallowed the pills and took a drink of water. Sargon seemed to have it all together – a decent job and a side business, incredibly strong with a good group of friends. It was exactly what Bilal had been looking for and he knew that he needed to keep up if he was to earn their respect.

It was now the last week in January, and Friday afternoon prayers were finishing up at the Mosque. Bilal waited around longer than usual, because Sargon had told him there was someone he should meet, but now he had disappeared. Although he was now a regular at prayers, he still didn't know many people and felt left out of the various conversations going on around him. He wasn't confident enough to just walk up to a group and introduce himself, so he stood awkwardly, looking around and desperately trying to appear uninterested.

Finally, he felt a touch at his elbow and turned to find Sargon standing there. Beside him was the tall man that Bilal had noticed when he first came to the Mosque with his father. The man that Mr. Mohammed had called a "wealthy troublemaker." Bilal was stunned, not sure what Sargon was doing with this guy, but then he thought maybe Mister Mohammed was wrong about him.

Sargon said, 'This is the Melbourne Mullah.' Bilal thought it was a funny name, more like a title. No way on earth was the man called that when he was born. Bilal knew what a Mullah was, and the man could have come from Melbourne. But who was Bilal to judge? If the Mullah wanted to keep his real identity private, that was up to him.

The Mullah greeted Bilal formally. 'Peace be upon you' and Bilal responded, 'and upon you.' The Mullah's English was perfect, although his accent showed that it wasn't his first language.

'So, this is the young man you have told me about' said the Mullah, his face and eyes smiling at Bilal. 'What is your name?'

Bilal introduced himself, but didn't know what else to say, or if he should ask the Mullah anything. It was difficult to watch his language as well, since he knew the Mullah would be offended if he spoke in the way he normally talked to his friends. To his relief, the Mullah asked about his family, his job, what he wanted to do in the future. Bilal spoke about how happy he was with the work opportunities and Sargon's friendship. Life was good, and he was looking forward to starting his own business so he could help others in the community.

'And are you a good Muslim?' asked the Mullah.

Bilal was caught. He didn't know what to say, because he knew that the Mullah's view of what made a good Muslim was different to most of the people he knew, certainly different to most of the Muslims in Sydney. 'Ahhh, well.... I'm learning a lot' he stammered. 'And I'm trying to follow the example of the Prophet, peace be upon him' he ended lamely. Sargon's approving grunt told him that he had made a good save.

The Melbourne Mullah smiled as well and nodded approvingly. 'Good answer, young man. I see very important things in your future, great things, and I would like to help you. Will you learn from me, and permit me to guide you?'

Bilal's agreement was immediate. If Sargon knew this Mullah, and the Mullah had the overseas and social connections that Bilal thought, then this was a once-in-a-lifetime opportunity. For a moment that old but iconic Eminem song flashed into his mind:

'You only get one shot, do not miss your chance to blow
This opportunity comes once in a lifetime.'

Bilal shushed his brain, and listened to what the Mullah was saying. His voice was deep and soft, and Bilal had to concentrate to follow along.

'We have been looking for strong men, men who are willing to become great by doing the will of Allah, the gracious, the merciful. To right the wrongs of these infidels. Will you answer the call of Allah, the merciful? To secure a safe place for our families, our wives and children.'

'And our businesses' said Bilal, hoping to indicate the direction that he wanted his life to go.

'Of course,' said the Mullah emotionally, passionately. 'It is God's will that you become the most successful that you possibly can, to become a great leader in the community, am I right?' He moved his arm to indicate that they should move into a side room to continue the conversation in private.

Bilal was very hopeful that he had made a good impression. This discussion was exactly what he had been looking for, and the patronage of a wealthy and powerful Mullah would be essential to growing his reputation and his own business.

-

Busy with work and learning the ways of the world, Bilal had no time for politics. Unfortunately for him, he was living on the edge of a great upheaval, and the two worlds were about to clash.

The results of the Federal election stunned everyone – even the winners.

The media had run a vicious campaign in support of the three major parties against the minor parties – of which One Nation were increasing their vote all over the nation, but especially in Queensland. In the 2016 Federal Double Dissolution election, One Nation had smashed all expectations, winning five seats and dominating the coalition – until the government had collapsed a few years later.

So, the media had ramped up the opposition, pushing opinion pieces, articles and surveys all attacking the party and accusing members of ignorance, racism, creating division and fostering intolerance. However, in reality, the increase in support for the party was from Australians who were not racist, divisive or intolerant. They were simply sick of being ignored by the major powers and preached to by a hypocritical media who seemed intent on serving their corporate masters instead of reporting actual news.

The population were getting sick of fake news. And it showed in every pre-poll survey, in every capital city.

Desperate times drive extreme people to extreme ends, and the media and those who control it were no different. Sensing a seismic shift in Australian politics, they had tried desperately to stop the tide, but even now refused to see it had had the opposite effect. The more the media attacked the minor parties, the more popular they became. The more the established parties spoke, the more out of touch they appeared, and lost increasingly more votes as they became more desperate and shrill.

Instead of learning from their mistakes, the Australian media followed the same path as the American anti-Trump media, doubling down and increasing their rhetoric to nonsense levels.

It didn't help that a weak approach by Government and police to immigration concerns and their inept handling of the rising crime waves belied their rhetoric about making the country safer. They also refused to allow citizens to patrol their own neighborhoods where crime was out of control, leading those people to warn others on social media and in the mass media. Once people stopped trusting the government to keep them safe, they also looked at the long list of broken promises and decided they did not like what it amounted to.

By the time the results were in, checked and all the preferences accounted for, the Australian parliament looked nothing like it had since Federation in 1901. The idea of a single party holding the majority or a coalition of two parties forming a majority had been blown out of the water. The major parties – Labor, Liberal and Greens had held onto one or two seats in Victoria and New South Wales, largely due to the massive support they had in the inner city, 'trendy café voters.' But they were annihilated in the rest of the states, in particular losing all their seats in their original stronghold of Tasmania.

Labor and Liberal, the two main parties which had governed Australia for over a hundred years, also lost most of their seats to a wide variety of minor parties and independents representing an equally broad spectrum of issues. It was as if most of the nation's voters had reached a breaking point and snapped all at once, taking out their anger and frustration at the ballot box.

Not only did the 'larger' minor parties like One Nation, Christian Democrats and Katter's Australia Party storm in with a dozen seats each, the election also saw tiny parties like Help End Marijuana Prohibition Party, Liberal Democrats and the Motoring Enthusiasts Party each take several seats between the House of Representatives and the Senate. Several of the parties had to scramble to find representatives to fill the number of seats they had won.

Capitalizing on their success in the earlier 2016 election, One Nation had campaigned cleverly against a bitter media campaign, and had stuck to their policies in the face of increasing accusations of xenophobia, racism, division and hatred, driven by the media. All the hysteria about racism and hatred became clearly revealed for the manipulative spin it was, as more people suffered from rising crime, reverse discrimination and ever-tightening government policies that took ever more away from the people who had voted for them. As reality intruded into their lives, they woke up to the lies they had been sold and once that happened, the propaganda had the opposite effect, further hardening their minds against the current regime.

The media were convinced by their own ideology and pay-cheques that they were fighting the good fight. Blind to the swing in public opinion they learned too late that they had overplayed their hand. If they had ignored One Nation, or at least been less virulent in their opposition, their claims may have appeared more reasonable to more of the population.

But now it was too late. The damage was done. Enough voters had rejected the hype and voted for conservative, minor parties. The balance of power had shifted.

Chapter 4

February

Lakemba Mosque

'You keep saying 'good Muslim' – like 'a good Muslim does this' or 'a good Muslim doesn't do that" challenged one of the men in the discussion group the Melbourne Mullah was leading. The dozen others looked at him, respectfully waiting for him to finish. The man was short and plump, and had begun sweating under the stern glare of the Melbourne Mullah.

'Perhaps there is a difference between what is a good Muslim in one country and a good Muslim in another?' He paused, 'All of us here are good Muslims, we pray, we preach, we look after our families and each other.'

'No, The Holy Quran and The Prophet, peace be upon him, clearly say that is not enough' replied the angry Mullah. *'Whosoever turns from my sunna is none of mine.'* 'Any Muslim who does not follow the example of the Prophet, peace be upon him, is apostate and must suffer the penalty!'

Another man spoke up softly 'The prophet, peace be upon him, never broke his arm, so if I was to break my arm, or get diabetes, or measles, or anything that is not recorded, there is no example for me to follow.'

A third man asked a pointed question directly at the Mullah. 'You flew here in an airplane, and you have a credit card, yes?' The Mullah scowled, but did not deny it. The speaker continued, 'The Holy Scriptures and The Prophet, peace be upon him, are from a time before these things existed, so you yourself are breaking your own requirements. Are you a hypocrite, then?'

'You dare question my authority?' demanded the Mullah. 'I have completed the Haj!'

'I have done the Haj three times' replied the second man calmly, almost lazily. 'Yet I do not insist that others be put to death just because they disagree with me.' He shrugged, 'you cannot deny that there are areas in life that cannot be completely explained and directed by the Holy Scriptures and the *Suras*. In these matters, there is proof that each man must live in accordance with his own conscience in the sight of Allah.'

'Lies' snarled the Mullah. 'Anyone who turns his back on Islam is to be slain – 4:89. Repent, or I will kill you right now.'

'Nobody will be killed – and surely not inside this Holy House' boomed a loud, clear and authoritative voice from behind him. The Imam had approached quietly, and listened to the conversation flow until he heard something that had to be stopped. 'If the only way to refute a statement is to kill the bearer, then the killer lacks understanding, and is as an unclean animal. The truth of Allah's words will overcome all enemies. It is with words and reason that we declare the truth, not with the sword.'

Caught off-guard and outranked in the other man's Mosque, the Mullah struggled to control his emotions. 'But Sayidi, Imam Malik 36.18.5 requires that if someone changes his religion – then strike off his head.'

'Nobody here has changed their religion' responded the Imam. 'Every man applies the truth of the Holy Scriptures and the example of the Prophet (peace be upon him), according to his understanding. Would you kill a child because they cannot recite or pray? Of course not, the requirements for a Muslim change over the course of their lives. So, in the same way, the requirements for a Muslim change with the country they live in.'

'No, no' returned the Mullah. 'The will of Allah is absolute. The whole world is the realm of Allah, polluted by infidels, sin and drunkenness. Those who practice sin must convert or be eradicated until the peace of Islam rests on all the lands, including this one. This is the true meaning of *Salaam*.

'The only reason that the infidels have not killed of enslaved you all is that you are bad Muslims. You follow their laws, even if contrary to the laws of Allah. You allow them to prostitute their women, almost naked in advertising and on television. You can tell that the women on TV are all prostitutes because they do not cover their heads. It is sinful, and it must stop, Allah commands it. A good Muslim would fight against such evils, no matter where they live.'

'So, if you were to discover that your life contained an error, would you cut off your own head?' mocked a younger man at the back of the crowd. 'What about words that have changed their meaning over hundreds of years – your understanding might be different to what the Prophet (peace be upon him) intended. How would you know?'

Another man interjected, 'I have a question, hear me out' and paused for a moment to collect his thoughts. 'We know that animals such as bats, horses, dogs and whales can hear sound that is too high or low pitched for human ears.' Several men in the group nodded, and he went on. 'Your broken arm was healed by doctors using an x-ray image, so we know there is a light spectrum that we can only see a small part of – there is ultra violet and infra-red, to name a few.'

'So, there are many things that Allah the merciful, the all-knowing has made, which we cannot perceive with our senses. Who knows what other discoveries science will make in the future? And the seasons - they are reversed in the hemispheres; there are 4 seasons – all different yet all equally important to the farmer. The differences are important and created by Allah, blessed by him. Is it not so in our religion also?'

The Mullah had to watch his tongue and his temper, so he prepared to leave while he still had some dignity and credibility. 'Perhaps there is more to discuss,' he said. 'I will see you next week.'

Bilal and Sargon walked in just as the discussion was wrapping up. Sargon caught the eye of the Mullah and they joined him as the crowd dispersed in twos and threes, most of them continuing the discussion about what it meant to be a 'good' Muslim. The two younger men had been meeting regularly with the Melbourne Mullah for religious instruction, receiving his opinion on scripture, world events, politics, humanity and sociology in a sequence of hour-long classes.

The three moved into a side room and the Mullah began. 'Great news, my young lions. Truly Allah is merciful and just.' Bilal and Sargon looked at each other, waiting for him to get to the point.

'For too long, these lands have suffered under the cruel and sinful hand of the oppressive infidels. Worshipping false gods, electing corrupt men to govern them, who pass unjust laws and send armies to fight illegal wars in our homelands.

'Their media constantly attacks us, calling us terrorists, while they parade whores and prostitutes around with uncovered heads, deliberately stoking the fires of our lust.'

Sargon shrugged; there wasn't much they could do about it than look away. Or was there? Was there a way to live a pure life of peace and success, as the Melbourne Mullah had been teaching them?

'I have received great news. News that will change the world. But first we all must swear to secrecy. The Prophet, peace be upon him, did not immediately attack Mecca when he received the call of God, did he? No – he gathered his army, his resources and secured a base from which to liberate the Holy Land'

'Our lands here in Bankstown have been selected, honored above all others - apart from the Holy shrines. In this land, King Nayef will build his palace, his court and his emirates.

Bilal was stunned at what he was hearing. He opened his mouth but all that came out was 'what??'

The Melbourne Mullah nodded, giving it time to sink in, then confirmed it.

The head of our religion, King of Saudi Arabia, Nayef, will be moving his court, his house, everything away from the dangers of war and pestilence in Riyadh.

'He has called upon a few of his most trusted to start the work of building the pure state for him to take and possess.'

'The most honor goes to those who volunteer first.' He continued, cunningly appealing to all aspects of their desires, religion and self-interest. 'Will you answer the call of Allah? Will you join the other lions in creating a safe home for all Muslims in this city?'

Bilal paused. He wasn't sure if this was something he really wanted to get involved with. It seemed very political and he was more interested in using politicians to help make him powerful in his own community, rather than becoming one himself.

'Honor awaits those who help' encouraged the Mullah quietly, addressing his fears and appealing to his pride and self-interest. The greatest share of the spoils, the greatest honor and influence belongs to those who step forward first.'

Sargon looked at Bilal and nodded. 'I'm in' he said. 'I will lay down my life for the prophet, peace be upon him, if necessary.'

Bilal desperately wanted to stay friends with Sargon so he nodded as well. '*Inshallah*, we will both become princes in this land.'

The Melbourne Mullah smiled and blessed them both. 'Continue your studies, say nothing to anyone about this honor,' he commanded. 'We will soon begin preparing you for glory.'

Then he turned on his heel and left the room, as Bilal felt a surge of electric excitement shiver through his whole body.

Chapter 5

March

The painters had left a nasty smell in the PM's office, so she sprayed a few squirts of air freshener around because the windows didn't open, and the air conditioning wasn't coping.

Pauline Hanson had been the very visible face of One Nation for over a decade, acting as a lightning rod for every journalists' scorn and vitriol. Since her term as Federal Senator was cut short due to the collapse of the government, she had taken the advice of expert advisers and made the difficult decision to become Deputy Prime Minister when re-elected.

To the nation's surprise, she turned down the top job and asked one of One Nation's younger female members to become Prime Minister.

Although Pauline had undertaken a lot of training in the ten years leading up to 2016, she recognized talent and a media darling when she saw it - and besides, as Deputy PM she would literally be the power behind the throne, without the intense media spotlight on her literally every waking hour. She had argued it all over with her advisers, going over all the issues several times, and at the end she agreed it was the best way to proceed for the party, the government and the nation.

Now, she sat facing the new PM who was in the large black executive chair behind the desk. She cocked an eyebrow and asked 'comfortable?'

The PM laughed. 'Deliciously - but don't tell me you didn't sit in it yesterday, just to try it out?'

Hanson grinned and feigned innocence. 'How could you accuse me of such a thing?' Then she became serious. 'First Hundred days – where's our policy plan at?'

The PM flipped open a manila folder on her desk and scanned the contents.

'We've filled all the ministerial positions and are almost finished replacing the advisers and wonks who either didn't want to stay or were deemed unsuitable to stay in their jobs. We all knew it would take time to clean out the dead wood, but we've finished the first step.'

She raised an eyebrow. 'Save a fair bit on the salaries and entitlements in the next budget too – can't hurt.'

'All immigration & refugee processing has been put on hold until we can get the new regulations through Parliament. Approved visas will be honored but no new ones will be issued until the new system comes online.'

'Norfolk Island have replied to our invitation – they are glad we've reversed the previous government's annexation and are willing to discuss recognition, trade, a whole raft of things. We really need to spoil them, or they'll be China's next military base – right in our front yard.'

The Deputy PM nodded, the whole Norfolk Island debacle had been an incredibly stupid move, done by a blind and arrogant government that was now, thankfully, in the dustbin of history. Now, the hard work to repair the damage would have to begin.

The PM took a deep breath. 'And the big one. The inquiry...' her voice trailed off as she looked at her colleague. This was one of the issues that the media had blown out of all proportion and twisted out of shape.

Hanson sat up straight in her chair. 'Despite the media, or maybe thanks to them, this is why we got elected. The people want action. They want results. They want a firm hand. And we are going to give it to them.'

'However... nobody needs to lose their head...literally or figuratively.' She thought for a moment, and then chose her words carefully.

'At the moment there is a large amount of uncertainty, emotional rhetoric, deliberate misinformation and hidden agendas with relation to Islam in Australia.

'We've all seen how quickly the comments on Facebook or a newspaper article degenerate into trivialities, blind emotion and personal attacks whenever this issue is raised. The media are no help, since their existence relies on controversy.'

The PM nodded. 'Any attempt at rational, logical conversation just dissolves into different groups who refuse to follow the rules of debate – most of them are unable to agree that opposing viewpoints may have some validity. It only takes a few moments reading through the comments to make my head hurt. There is absolutely no way we can have an intelligent debate on an issue as thorny as this.'

'We need a neutral forum where all interested parties can submit evidence, which can be assessed by a group of people who are trained and experienced in weighing that evidence. No member of the public can conduct a reasoned debate, free of emotion.'

'We need to clear this up once and for all. Since followers of Islam come from pretty much every country and ethnic group in the world, Islam cannot be described as a 'race of people' – a person who opposes Islam is regularly attacked as being racist, and we need to stop that - permanently.'

'We need experts to review submissions, independently, and make a decision that we will abide by.'

The PM nodded. Inviting anyone who wished to make a submission was a good way of avoiding accusations of bias or preference, and appointing a panel of judges would move the debate out of the depths of fear and bigotry – on both sides.

'Any ideas on who we should invite to the table?' She asked.

Hanson shrugged. 'I think we need either three or five – that way we get a majority decision no matter what. I'll talk to the others and draw up a list.' She stood up and said 'I'm going back to Brisbane. Call me if you need anything'.

The PM nodded. 'Goodnight' she said as the party founder left the room.

Chapter 6

April

The meeting took place in a private suite at the Intercontinental Hotel in Double Bay. One of the largest investment banks in the world kept the suite rented year-round as a secure pad for travelling executives, hosting of parties and brokering deals when the circumstances required complete discretion and suitable luxury.

While waiting for the rest of the attendees to arrive, the three VIPs stood on the balcony, drinking coffee and admiring the view as the morning sun moved across the forested hills and sparkling waters of Sydney Harbour. The Englishman looked at his companions and smirked, 'And to think we sent you bastards here as punishment!' The two Australians grinned, raised their cups in salute to the perfect autumn weather.

'Beautiful day' agreed the taller Aussie 'but I'm not so sure about this proposal. Are you absolutely positive it is feasible?'

'Fret not, gentlemen' assured the Englishman with a flair of condescension. 'The British Empire has been making and breaking kings for almost a thousand years. The current century's political and economic development simply would not have been possible without our funding of Ibn Saud against the Hashemites and Rashids in the early 1900s. Without a fractured Middle East, giving us – and then the Americans – relatively easy access to their oil, all of us would be stuck – economically – in the 1920s. Without cheap oil, there is no economy.' He shrugged 'Rest assured, we know what we're doing.'

Overachievers, driven to the point of obsession, they had all woken around dawn, dealing with a few urgent messages and emails from around the world before working out in the hotel gym, then showering and presenting their credentials to the private security at the suite's doors, making sure they arrived at least 5 minutes before the meeting was due to start.

Just on 9.30am, the suite doors swung open and the security detail for the Prime Minister came in, followed by the PM herself and the American delegation. Courtesy introductions were made, some of the attendees knew each other from previous dealings shook hands as the meeting began.

The Englishman represented the largest private bank in the world, routinely closing infrastructure and trade deals at the highest levels of government.

The two Australians represented the largest media and insurance conglomerates in the country.

The American represented a joint venture of American and European influences, corporations and banks, funding government projects, wars and regime change all over the world.

They seated themselves comfortably on the sofas surrounding a central coffee table in the middle of the room, and the PM began.

'Thank you for inviting me.' She said calmly. 'I've been told who you all are and what you do, what is the problem and what are your proposals for resolving it?'

The Englishman cleared his throat, 'Prime Minister, as part of your background briefing, you would have been advised that ASIO has been fully briefed on the experiences MI5 has had with similar problems in London, and the DGSE in Paris.' She nodded.

'Since we won World War 2, immigration has been used as a powerful tool to keep our economies strong and growing. Cheap labour, increasing demand for goods & services have been a bonanza for every sector in the economy.'

'Through the 70's, 80s and 90s, the good times rolled. A rising tide that lifted all boats, so to speak. But now the wheels are starting to come off, the tide is going out. The economy has tanked, immigration patterns have changed, and London, Paris and Sydney all find themselves with enclaves, populated by immigrants who often refuse to integrate.'

The PM nodded, her short blonde hair bobbing. 'I know that, why do you think I was elected?' she snarled. 'What are we going to DO about it?'

It was the American's turn to speak. 'It gets worse. Our contacts at Parsons indicate the Saudi Royal Family no longer feel safe in their kingdom.'

'Parsons?' asked the PM.

'OK, let's have a quick background sketch' replied the American. 'After World War 2, American assets worked with the Saudi's to develop their oil reserves, infrastructure, military, civil administration, sewerage, the whole thing - all funded by sales of oil in Petrodollars.' 'One of these assets – the main one - was a consulting company called Chas T Main. In 1990, Main was bought by Parsons engineering, but the special advisory department remains there, and our links and co-operation remains as close as ever.

'These men are among the personal advisers to the King, princes, ministers, everyone at the top levels. The information we exchange is extremely profitable to both sides, but with oil production flat for the past 10 years, the kingdom will soon be unable to continue in its current state. They have been buying security with oil money for as long as the oil has been flowing. Now that it is slowing, they can't fund their security AND lifestyle budgets for much longer' he concluded.

'But my main point is, the Saudi Royal Family are leaving Saudi Arabia. They plan to set up in a new Caliphate, away from the problems of their old country and region.'

The PM wasn't really following. 'OK, what does that have to do with us?'

The American dropped his bombshell 'They plan to set up a Caliphate in Sydney'

For a full minute, there was silence in the room. The PM closed her eyes, trying to visualize what this meant in its full implication. 'You cannot be serious' she murmured.

'We know that many princes have already immigrated to Canada' drawled the Australian Media representative. 'They have already started lobbying to have the laws against polygamy overturned – with some success, I might add'

The PM's face set like stone. 'NO. FUCKEN. WAY.' She spat. 'The people elected me to stop this rot, not let them steal half the city from under us'.

The other Australian rolled out a map of the city and drew his finger across it. 'Our sources indicate the most likely area claimed would be between these two rivers. The Cooks River flows to the Airport from Strathfield, and Salt Pan Creek – it flows into the Georges River.'

'The area we are looking at includes the suburbs of Campsie, Belfield, Greenacre, Lakemba, Wiley Park and Punchbowl' he went on. 'Based on demographics, the main core would be this stretch between the Cooks River, the M5, King George's Road and George's River Road to the north. South of the M5, the suburbs of Rockdale, Kogarah, Hurstville and Mortdale don't have nearly the demographics of Campsie/Lakemba. Any non-Muslim in those areas would basically be fucked, of course, should the northern crescent be secured by the insurgents – they would be cut off from their jobs, supplies, they would have two simple choices – pay the Dhimmi tax or try to leave.'

The PM shuddered at the thought of Australians becoming refugees in their own country. The irony of the situation made her angry, then her anger changed to calm resolution. She nodded, and the media rep went on:

'All told, this area contains almost half the mosques in Sydney – which we believe would be the main command centers for their operation.

'The population of the core Caliphate would be about 150,000 people; the whole at-risk area contains double that. Of this, we estimate they could raise, train and arm no more than 15,000 militia fighters.'

'Fifteen thousand fighters – but how many of them are trained properly?' she wondered aloud.

'Based on our intelligence, about a thousand – give or take' replied the Australian Banking & Insurance rep. 'We have been monitoring Persons of Interest, travel made, phone calls, and money transfers. The biggest challenge they face is keeping their training secret. Any big group of men doing military training would immediately raise suspicion. So far, we haven't been able to identify anything.'

The PM wasn't impressed. 'Even so, even if they have a dozen trainees for every decent fighter – all they have to do is put up road blocks and the whole area would be sealed off. A quarter of Paris is like that already, and London is heading that way.'

'Opposing this would be – what?' she asked, her head spinning. 'What troops do we have available to go in and stop this…this…terrorism?'

'Two battalions of Army regulars coming off training exercises in regional NSW. That's about five thousand men, but not all of them are trained combat troops. A lot of them are engineers, communication specialists, supply clerks, cooks & laundry personnel. Call it two thousand combat troops - trigger pullers – at the very most.'

'At Holsworthy there are Black Hawk and Kiowa helicopters, but these are just transport and surveillance assets, not gunships. The Tiger attack helicopters are in the process of being retired early because the French software won't talk to the American weapons we want to fire from them.'

'There are some artillery howitzers at Holsworthy, and we can bring more in from Enoggera and Palmerston in the NT but that will take a while. ADF Reserves would add about two thousand more rifles, but sustained operations would put a lot of strain on the economy, having that many people off work and away from their families – I wouldn't count on using them for more than a week at the most.'

The thought of a week-long military action on Australian soil brought a harsh, coppery taste into the PM's mouth. 'Mother of God' she thought, 'what the fuck have I gotten into?'

'Scraping the barrel – we could add five thousand Army cadets – mostly teenagers.'

'Mostly cannon fodder' she gasped. 'I will not send children into combat, no matter what the risks'.

'If it's the media you're worried about, don't' emphasized the Australian Media rep. 'We can spin the war so you smell of roses the whole time.' His oily smile and apparent glee at the topic bothered her - a lot.

'That's not my concern' the PM responded. 'I have a mandate to stop immigration problems and get the economy back on track. A few inner city NIMBYS writing letters to the paper don't count for shit against five million primary votes. NO, this is going to be done properly; I will not get sucked into another Vietnam – not in my own country.'

The Englishman nodded. 'Absolutely agree. Now, there are some concerns that we have identified and would like to suggest solutions' The PM sat back and stared at him.

'First, property damage. In any MOUT – that is, Military Operations in Urban Terrain - this tends to be extensive.' He nodded towards the insurance rep and continued 'naturally, most insurance policies explicitly exclude cover for any act of war. Some are covering terrorism damage, but an act of war is specifically excluded. So, the insurers are off the hook for any kind of insurance claim.'

'Loss of life falls into two categories' he continued, as if reading an audit report or shopping list, instead of describing lives lost and families torn apart. 'Casualties outside the Caliphate would be light, limited only to Australian forces and any collateral damage from insurgency operations or accidental misses by Australian assets. Inside the Caliphate however, we would suggest you prepare for 50% of the rebel fighters to be killed and 30% of the entire population – as a general guideline'

The PM felt the bile rise in her throat – she couldn't imagine how this man could remain so cool and calculating and felt compelled to ask, 'and where did this …general guideline' come from?'

'The closest real-life scenario we have would be the second battle of Fallujah, in 2004' he replied, warming up to the topic and mistaking her question for interest, rather than disgust. 'Thirteen thousand allied troops liberated the city from about 4,000 insurgents. They captured about 1,500 and killed the rest.'

The PM's voice dropped to a whisper. 'What about civilians?' she asked.

'Actually, those figures are unknown. Most of the population fled before the battle began, but of the 30,000-odd people left in the city, probably half were killed or wounded' he answered.

The PM's brain whirled. The population of the Caliphate's stated area in Canterbury & Bankstown was about 350,000 people, so the comparison made sense. Was it even possible to destroy an area of Sydney the size of Fallujah?

'Anyway, back on topic' the Englishman's manner became businesslike again. 'Should the Australian Government seek to destroy the Caliphate, it is reasonable to assume that several suburbs of Western Sydney will be largely destroyed. Without insurance cover, the property owners will not be able to afford to rebuild the homes – mind you, half of the homes won't be immediately necessary.' He paused, smirking at his little joke.

'So, to summarize, the option we recommend is as follows: you raise and train a suitable armed force, while buying time and placating the Caliph as much as possible. When the time is right, you seal off the area, attack from three directions under cover of air and artillery bombardment and wipe out the insurgency.'

He looked around at the other men. 'Our combined resources will be used to maintain positive media spin, and ensure that the underwriters stay calm. Once the dust settles, we will provide a reconstruction loan to the Australian Government, with which you can pay developers and builders to start again. Instead of a thousand medium density unit blocks, randomly scattered around the suburbs, linked up with congested little streets, you can properly plan for combined developments – transport hubs, commercial offices and shops with thousands of unit blocks on top.'

'With one stroke you can eliminate this terrorist threat from your living room, send a clear message to your supporters that you mean business, and provide thousands of construction jobs for the rebuilding work. The GST on the building materials sold will more than pay for the interest on the loan.'

'Before your first 4-year term ends, this whole part of the Sydney basin could be transformed into a properly planned urban center, with extensive public transport options, walkable communities and brand-new infrastructure for business, commerce and industry.'

Normally gifted with knowing what to say at any time, this time the PM was actually speechless. They had thought this through and managed to spin the concept that a civil war would be a good thing for the economy.

Head reeling, the PM frantically tried to think of objections. 'But there are too many of them, don't we need something like three-to-one if attacking a defended position? Plus, it's their home ground, so they know it well and could booby trap every street and house. It would be a nightmare.'

'Ordinarily, yes' said the American. 'We have two suggestions that would offset the defenders advantage. First, we can use artillery and air assets to break up the infrastructure, deny them water, power, shelter. For this first phase, the nation's troops will only be needed as a cordon, to prevent any insurgents from escaping. Minimal casualties expected.'

'Secondly, remember the objectives here. We are not trying to simply kill everyone in the area. That would be a bonus, mind you, but not necessary to preventing the Caliphate. All we need to do is render the area uninhabitable. Then, re-locate any remaining residents and the site is ready for re-development. Think about Europe's beautiful cities: Rome, Dresden, Hamburg, and Budapest – these were largely bombed flat during WW2, but we've rebuilt them even better than before. The plumbing, electricity, public transport was all improved far beyond the original, and it gave work to millions of people - and made billions in profits for the contractors and banks involved.'

The American paused to let his pitch sink in. 'Finally,' he said, 'we propose that you add to the trained military troops by establishing an auxiliary force.' He passed around a sheet of paper and they all looked at it. The main image was a picture of a man in a Redcoat uniform, the iconic British military uniform of the 1700s. White pants, red coat and a black hat, holding a musket that was almost as tall as the soldier.

'The New South Wales Marine Corps' he said proudly. 'This was the first regiment established in the colony, it served the governors until 1891 when it was replaced with the infamous Rum Corps. To raise the largest number of troops in the fastest possible time, at the lowest cost, we propose that you re-activate the NSW Marine Corps and call for volunteers from the population.'

'Fuck off' spat the PM. 'We can barely train our own officers and troops for your wars in Afghanistan & Iraq. The ADF has been crippled by political correctness for decades, so how the hell are we supposed to turn civilians into soldiers in time to stop this insurgency?'

The American simply beamed, and with the shit-eating grin on his face, turned to the security detail and said, 'show him in.'

The door swung open and the PM involuntarily gasped. Striding into the room was perhaps the most perfect example of a man she had ever seen. Almost six-foot-tall, his broad shoulders tapered to a narrow waist and his perfectly fitting blue uniform seemed to radiate pheromones. The PM's eyes rose from the perfectly shined black shoes, the razor sharp creased pants, white belt, and deep blue jacket covered with colored pins, and lingered on the face. Late 20's, his tanned, taut skin was chiseled over a jaw that reminded her of the cliffs near her office in Brisbane. The stone-grey eyes did not blink as the man walked a few paces into the room, swung his peaked cap under his left arm and saluted.

'Colonel Mason, 1st Battalion, 1st Marines from Marine Rotational Force, Darwin.' Col. Mason's voice was deep and clear, his speech precise and confident.

The PM shifted her hips in the seat. Dear God, he was attractive.

'Another American?' were the only words that came to her mind, still trying to process the raw masculinity and animal magnetism radiating from the Marine. She had no idea what all the little flags on his chest were for but damn they were impressive. The man was hard, confident and had an energy that acted like a bar heater in a cold room.

'Yes Ma'am. There are eleven hundred Marines in Darwin at this time' he replied, his eyes fixed straight ahead on the horizon. 'Every single one of us would be honored to train your Auxiliary forces to fight these terrorists.'

The PM's eyes narrowed. As far as she knew, US Marines ranked very highly in the world's best small unit fighting forces – quite possibly the best, given their decades-long experiences in the Middle East and Africa. 'What would be involved?' she asked. Then, waving towards a seat, she said 'For God's sake, sit down'.

In one fluid motion, the Marine sat, placing his hat on the space beside him, and continued.

'Ma'am, I and four other Marines in the battalion are qualified recruiters. We can easily work with your own resources to process applications – which based on your election results should be sufficient. The general population supports what you are doing, and once they know what's going on, we should have plenty of volunteers. We generally eliminate almost half of our applicants because they don't meet entry requirements – tattoos in the wrong place, serious criminal history, or they fail the academic tests. But if you need lots of bodies, you could consider a waiver for certain categories if they don't render a recruit dangerous to themselves or the country.'

'Marine recruits generally don't fail once we they start basic training' he continued. 'We might recycle recruits a few times if they need to improve in some areas, but in this situation, we aren't training full Marines. The auxiliaries need to know how to follow orders, handle a rifle and a radio and perform combat first aid, not much more. We can modify the 12-week Basic Training course and probably have the first companies ready in 9 or 10 weeks.'

'What are they going to train with?' asked the PM. 'We scrapped all our old defense hardware in the 80s, and our rifles look different to your American ones.'

'No problem, Ma'am' replied the Marine. 'The rifles use the same ammunition, which can be shipped here from Hawaii in a week plus a few days. We can use what you have right now for the first few recruit training platoons, and build up as more supplies arrive. Some platoons might end up with a mix of M4s and Steyers, but that's nothing we can't handle with good training. Your Hercules transports from Richmond can bring everything we need down from Darwin within a week.

'There's plenty of land at Holsworthy for training, staging and warehousing. We would request that you set up a JC2 – a Joint Communications Centre - there as well, staffed from all necessary areas of the ADF: Artillery, supply, recon & surveillance, air support. That way we can co-ordinate everything we need through a single hub - for training and once combat operations start.'

This was looking like a definite possibility, thought the PM. These Marines really knew their stuff, and if they could ramp up training as more resources became available, they just might be able to stamp out this cancer once and for all. If the media held up their end of the bargain, an early victory could set her career for life.

'Okay, let me see if I understand this…proposal' she said.

'You will recruit and train a force to deny a suitable area for this Caliphate. Then fund re-construction of the area once the fighting stops and everyone goes back to work. How are we supposed to pay for this?' she asked.

The Englishman waved his hand dismissively. 'A minor consideration, Prime Minister. 'Priority access to your natural resources – especially that natural gas – should fund the interest payments' he said. 'The only other favor we would ask – and this one we must insist on, I'm afraid – you would vote on certain issues in the UN Security Council according to our suggestions…'

'Fine by me' agreed the PM. 'PM&C will contact your local assets to start the paperwork'. She turned to the media representative and said, 'get your people working on making sure NONE of this sticks to me.' She looked around to close the meeting, inviting any further comments or questions.

'One question, Ma'am,' Mason fixed his eyes on hers. 'Chain of command – who do we report to?'

The PM smiled evilly 'Oh, I know just how to arrange this. US Marines are a department of the Navy, aren't you?' The Marine nodded.

'So, we will do the same thing – create a department of our navy called the Australian Marine Corps. We have a female Muslim Captain in the Navy – wears a hijab and everything. I'm going to promote her to Commodore and put her in charge of the training phase. Hopefully she will be targeted by these...insurgents: that would give us a clear declaration of war and get rid of her as a bonus – two birds with one stone.'

'Operationally, I'm going to pull Peter Cosgrove out of retirement and get him to head up the whole thing. He's manifestly more qualified to do it than anyone else, and he knows how to handle the media as well.'

Impressed with how quickly the PM had accepted their idea, the men stood to leave.

As they filed towards the door, the PM waved her hand dismissively at the security detail. 'Colonel, please stay – I have some further questions for you...'

As the door closed, leaving them alone in the room, the PM stood and gently pushed the Marine back onto the sofa. 'You're required to help improve diplomatic relations with our nation' she said huskily, climbing onto his lap and unbuttoning her top.

-

Sargon was giving Bilal a tour of Mr. Mohammed's main business site. The food supply truck was only a minor side business to the main import company, DIMO Furnishings & Flooring.

They had driven out near Bankstown airport, parked in the street and walked inside the factory complex. At the rear was the main receiving yard, where metal shipping containers were lined up and a small team of men were unloading carpets, rugs and cardboard boxes for storage inside the warehouse. Shelves up to the ceiling held piles of goods that had been imported from all over the world, and were being shipped out to a range of wholesale and direct outlet customers all over Sydney.

They watched the forklifts emptying the shipping containers and stacking the contents in the metal shelving, then went upstairs to the office. Sargon pushed the door open and stepped inside, greeted by the plastic-and-stale-cigarette smell common to all factory offices everywhere. Bilal looked around and noticed that the office area was divided into two sections. The main section contained the reception area, where they stood, with several desks scattered around, almost buried under piles of colored paper, brochures and manila files. At the other end, behind a dividing wall, Bilal could see an office, with a leather chair and a dark timber desk visible.

There was only one person in the office, and old man with a narrow face and a big nose, wearing thick glasses and an old-fashioned sports coat over a white buttoned shirt. He nodded to Sargon and Bilal as they came in greeting them warmly in Arabic.

'Peace be upon you.'

'And upon you' they responded. Sargon introduced Bilal to the man, whose name was Akram.

Sargon explained that the other desks were for the sales clerks, who placed orders with suppliers overseas. Akram's job was to monitor the orders as they were completed and ready for shipping. He would then arrange for drugs, weapons, cigarettes or other prohibited and therefore profitable items to be included in the shipping containers and transported to Australia. He also tracked the shipment identification numbers, matched them to the ships they were on and logged the date they would arrive in port. Once the arrival date and dock number were known, the transport company would collect the containers and deliver them to the warehouse.

Sargon pointed to a list of phone numbers taped to Akram's desk. 'Dis de most important part of 'is job. Our customs officers – well paid to keep our containers away from de scanners and sniffers.'

Bilal realized the extent of the operation. 'Fffff.....So we can import whatever we want, and these people, on this list, will make sure it isn't inspected?'

Akram smiled 'Yah. Less dan ten percent of imported containers can be inspected. So, we just tell dem which numbers are ours and dey makes sure dey don't get scanned. We bring in lotsa tings that many people want, but the govmint tries to stop dem having.'

Bilal was stunned. 'So, all these drug laws, gun control laws, prohibition, import taxes...'

Sargon laughed. 'We love gun control laws. Makes our business so much more profitable...

'I always laugh at dat woman...Samanta Lee, on the Tee VEE' he rhymed. 'But I love her work. Keeps de police busy chasing ordinary hunters, so dey have less time to chase us or our customers!

He frowned. 'She should cover her head, though. Shameful to be seen in public without a covering.'

'Also, de gun laws keep supply down, so da price is higher. If drugs and firearms were legal, we would be outta business.

Bilal nodded as he appreciated the scope of the business operation, then Akram went on.

'Straya used to have a big firearms industry, made rifles dat won World War 1 and World War 2. But after dat dey shut most of it down, den more and more restrictions and laws made business much better for us.

Bilal nodded, impressed. 'I thought most criminals stole guns from legal owners.'

'Nahh, too risky. You bin listening to Samanta Lee too much.' said Sargon. 'Even though we got the list from the registry, we don't really need it. Only if there's something really valuable or someone places an order and we want to keep 'em happy. De shopping list is mostly used by small timers exporting to places like China.'

'Cheaper to buy from us, the importer - less hassle and dey know we aren't gonna get investigated by de cops'

'Do you seriously have a list from the registry?' asked Bilal.

'Sure' said Sargon. 'We got it from some bikers – dey got even more people inside de police than us. Guys who owe dem big favours – owe dem for a long time, officers, high up guys. Get lotsa money to look de other way, help out where dey can.' His brow furrowed as he searched his memory for a name. 'Who was dat other guy, dat cop selling fake IDs…Gary, Garis, Jeff Garis? Wanna bet he was also selling de firearms registry to anyone who had cash?'

'But I heard on the news, there's lots of farmers getting guns stolen.' Bilal objected.

Sargon laughed. 'I reckon most of dem are neighbours, doing de right ting.'

Bilal raised an eyebrow. 'Whaddaya mean?'

Sargon looked at him as if he was simple. 'Tink about it – farmer goes away for a few days. Neighbour breaks in, breaks open de safe and takes de guns. Leaves everyting else. Den de farmer gets back, reports guns stolen to police and claims on insurance. Buys new legal guns and collects his old ones from de neighbour – puts dem in de roof or de barn. So now he has guns dat cannot be traced, seized or stolen because dey are removed from de registry.'

They both laughed at the idea of a registry stopping gun crime from happening. They didn't know for sure, but official figures confirmed that the registry has never solved a single crime. Despite what TV shows said about 'ballistic fingerprinting' and 'matching bullets to a gun', every bullet deforms when it hits something, so trying to match a fired bullet to a particular barrel was extremely difficult. Besides, in the rare instance that a criminal actually had to shoot someone, the gun usually ended up in the Georges River or Sydney Harbour ten minutes later. To the criminal, a gun was much more useful as a threat than an actual tool of violence.

It was obvious to Bilal that the people running the registry were benefiting from keeping the population disarmed. They were well paid to do a little paperwork in a comfortable office and in absolutely no danger of repercussions from stopping criminals from getting their hands-on firearms. Meanwhile, shipping containers full of pistols, ammunition, explosives, drugs and precursor chemicals were flooding in through the ports and marinas. Under the laws of supply & demand, banning something never stopped the demand for it, all it did was increase the price for the importer and the profits for organized crime.

Bilal thought about it. Corrupt cops and customs officials, useless government bans pushing up the price of illegal items, a gun control lobby that was actively assisting organized crime – this city was full of opportunities. He could barely stop dancing on the spot at the ideas that were bubbling up in his brain.

He reflexively pulled out his phone and scrolled through the news headlines:

PREACHER SEEKS PEPPA PIG BANNED FROM TV

100 HOMES BURGLED IN 1 DAY

HOME BUILDING APPLICATIONS SLUMP – CRASH LOOMS

EXCLUSIVE - BANKS FEAR SLOWDOWN IN LOAN APPLICATIONS

He scrolled through a few of the comments on each article, shaking his head at the stupidity of the masses until Sargon had the car unlocked and he climbed in.

—

Sargon dropped Bilal home, but he knew that he was expected at the Melbourne Mullah's house for lessons, so he walked towards the mosque for a few minutes, then turned into the driveway of the house nearby. As he kicked off his shoes and opened the door, the Mullah met him.

'Bilal, peace upon you' he said quietly but intensely, hugging Bilal and then stepping back inside the house to give his guest room to enter.

'And upon you' responded Bilal hesitantly. He wasn't sure what he should do, but again the Mullah set his mind at ease by saying 'please follow me' and moving into a side room. The room was large and had several rugs on the floor with cushions scattered around. Bilal wondered at the size of the room, then realized that there was no furniture around the walls or in the middle to take up space. It was an optical illusion that made the room appear larger than similar ones full of Western furniture.

The call of the Muezzin sounded from the Mosque up the street as they entered the room, so Bilal looked around the ceiling and spotted the mark that indicated the direction of Mecca. He and the Mullah stood side by side, facing the right direction, and began to pray in Arabic, the Mullah louder than Bilal, who still wasn't quite sure he had all the words right.

Once the prayers were finished, the two men sat and Bilal's lessons continued. His Arabic was improving, and he could maintain a basic conversation with the Mullah.

Next came religious questions about events and people from the life of the Prophet, peace be upon him. Bilal had the most difficulty with history because it felt so foreign, so irrelevant. He expressed his doubts to the Mullah, who nodded.

'Understandable. Things happened long ago, far away. This is true. But several things remain constant, no matter where or when a man lives. The first is the true path of Allah, the path of Jihad within and Jihad without. 'The words of the Prophet, peace be upon him, remain true forever.

'The second thing, which never changes, is the human nature of those infidels who oppress. Greed, lust, power – these things all remain the same. The stories of old, the history of the world – can be easily understood once you understand the nature of the oppressor and those they oppress.'

'The lessons are plain. Those who are prepared to fight for what they believe in with a pure heart will always be successful. Those unable to kill will always be slaves to those who can.'

-

An hour later, the lessons were finished, and Bilal said goodnight to the Mullah. He put on his shoes and began walking towards his home, thumbing through his phone again, checking the news feed.

YOUTH MURDERED IN NIGHT VIGILANTE ATTACK

The sensational headline grabbed his attention, but upon reading the article he learned that the teenage gang member had been caught stealing mail from the mailbox in a large strata scheme.

Several residents had held him and called the police, but during the struggle the thief was put into a headlock and suffocated. By the time the police arrived, there was nobody around and neighbors said they hadn't seen who was involved. With his new knowledge and understanding gleaned from the Mullah, Bilal could see how the reporters had twisted the facts, and the misleading headline gave the impression that the residents were to blame, when in fact it was the criminal's fault for committing a crime in the first place.

He felt good that he was able to detect the bias in the media, but then he also realised something. If the media was so eager to pardon the real criminal and blame his victims, then he could play on that bias as well.

He filed that idea away in his mental notes for later improvement.

Chapter 7

May

Villawood Immigration Detention Centre

Deng sat on a hard metal seat, his back resting against the wall and his legs stretched out in front of him. A few kids were playing on the equipment across the yard, and the early sun was shining over the whole scene, warming the air and his spirits. It had been a difficult journey to Australia, but the Villawood Detention Centre was quite comfortable when compared with many places he had lived, and surely the day would soon come when he was free and able to continue the will of God - Inshallah. He had just met with Sargon, a good Muslim who regularly visited him with news, toiletries and a few items to help pass the time. The news this time was particularly good, and Deng was pleased to receive instructions on how he was to be released.

With his body enjoying the sunshine, Deng's mind was free to roam, away from the infrastructure of the Immigration Detention Centre around him, drifting to his favorite verses of the holy book, long sermons committed to memory, some of them delivered to audiences seated in mud huts or in grassy fields, chemical and electrical formulations which formed the tools of his trade.

His thoughts drifted to the path that had led him from his childhood home in the rocky foothills around Yemen's capital Sana'a, across the Red Sea into Somalia, Sudan, Libya, back into Sudan and now to Sydney. Inherited from his father and grandfather, Deng's life was that of a warrior.

Born into a conflict as old as the desert sands, Deng had been trained from a young age in the arts of war, learning hard lessons fighting oppressors – firstly local bandits and enemy tribes, then uniting with many of these former enemies to fight the growing power and decadence of the Royal House to the east.

Deng only knew a little of the history of the region, all he had been taught was that the Saud families' lands were filled with oil, which had made them fabulously wealthy as the infidel's machinery and technology required ever increasing supplies. So, for the past hundred years a small group of rulers had amassed a wealth in the trillions but instead of using it to help others, as the Quran instructed, they had kept it for themselves, purchasing domestic peace by lavish spending, vain infrastructure projects, and a massive security & intelligence force to ensure they stayed in power.

Deng's religious beliefs were technically similar to the Saudis - they would both be classed as Wahabi by any scholar - western or Islamic. But as far as Deng and his fellow believers were concerned, the ruling classes in most Islamic countries were corrupt, decadent, having been seduced away from the true path by wealth, pleasure and politics. As far as he was concerned, there were only two ways to resolve this problem: destroy these ruling classes and free their people from oppression, or create a new, pure Islamic caliphate where true Muslims were free to practice their faith as Mohammed had intended.

Reflecting on their successes and failures to date, Deng knew it was a work in progress. Somalia, Libya, Egypt had started the birthing process, experiencing the contraction pains as the old regimes struggled to retain power against the rising tide of true believers. Iraq and Afghanistan were proving difficult, the Great Satan had so devastated their peoples, cities and infrastructure. Deng thought that unless the wars were stopped, and a strong Caliph or Ayatollah united the peoples, they would end up like Palestine - a nation of mentally damaged people, crippled with Post Traumatic Stress, giving birth to another generation afflicted by the same thing. The cycle would continue unless a place could be found, free of war, where true Muslims could submit to the will of Allah in peace.

Which was why he had been sent to Australia.

Deng had fought wars and skirmishes from Yemen to North Africa, and had long experience not only in combat, but also fundraising, teaching, training, logistics and communications. A genuine all-rounder, he had been honored with instructions to start the creation of the Caliphate.

His instructions were simple, and he knew better than to ask for more information. So he did as ordered, flying to Bali via Jakarta and then making his way to the boat that would take him through the Savu Sea then east towards the patrolling Australian navy. Once on board the small fishing boat, he had dumped all his identification so that when the boat was intercepted, the immigration policy of the time landed him right in the Caliphate's back yard, Villawood Immigration Detention Centre. He waited patiently while Immigration officials attempted to confirm his story and determine his refugee status.

What he did not know was that the Saudi's had seen their oil production rates slow down, as the pressure from the vast reservoirs could no longer lift the valuable liquid to the surface. Immense amounts of money were invested in technology to increase the flow rate, but they only helped a little. In 2005, what had been an ever-increasing supply to an every-hungry world stopped growing, and production basically remained flat for the next 10 years, despite billions in investment, exploration and injecting nitrogen or sea water into the wells. There was plenty of oil in the ground, but it simply couldn't be extracted at a price that the world could afford.

Fortunately for the global economy, experts at the International Energy Agency, International Monetary Fund and the World Bank had foreseen this as far back as the 1970s. Plans that had been regularly updated were now implemented. To soften the impact on markets, 'oil production' figures were combined with other categories that technically weren't 'crude oil', but served to make the production figures look higher than they were. Non-Gas Liquids, refinery gains, tar sands, tight oil - all these were combined into 'oil production' in order to avoid spooking the markets.

But oil supply itself was only part of the problem. It only represented cheap energy - an essential input for a global economic system built on debt, which requires an ever-increasing creation of value to pay back the debt plus interest. Without cheap energy, everything created by the economy was more expensive, cutting into profits, debt repayment and interest.

The first crisis hit in 2008, but by throwing ever more money at the problem, the gurus in charge managed to calm the markets and extract even more money from the system. Labor costs were cut by shifting factories from China to Africa, automation boomed - making its way from factories right into the everyday shops in the form of self-checkouts and console ordering systems in McDonalds.

But the energy problem was just too big to handle. For a global economy created to run on cheap and plentiful energy, the crisis was unsolvable. Tinkering around the edges with alternative energy and efficiency gains did nothing to solve the energy elephant in the room. There wasn't enough energy to go around, at a price people could afford to pay. Something had to change, drastically.

While Deng was fighting actual wars in Somalia and Libya, men in $5,000 suits were fighting an increasingly desperate war against declining energy supplies and the inevitable changes - and losses - that were the natural consequences. But the increasing wealth in developing nations exacerbated the problem - as more and more Chinese and Indians were lifted off the poverty line, they purchased phones, cars, computers, and meat, and medical care, clothes - consuming further resources and compounding the scarcity problem. Oil prices fluctuated wildly as different methods were tried to calm the situation, but it became clear that oil below $80.00 a barrel destroyed the producers, and oil above $40.00 destroyed the consuming economies.

The ruling houses of the oil producing nations were in a desperate bind. Without a steady supply of petrodollars flooding into the country, they would be unable to pay off the massive, angry population and keep it pacified. The only way they had held on to power this long was by bribing the population, importing thousands of foreign workers to do any kind of work, and ruthlessly suppressing any voice that spoke out against them. But without the incredible wealth necessary to maintain such a nation, the question became ever more urgent: What can be done?

By 2016, the issue had become pressing but the 80-year-old King Salman's health was declining, and he had no time or interest to discuss options. Salman saw his role as protecting his kingdom, routinely executing opponents and involving the country in a full shooting war in Yemen. Believing that he would always be able to rely on American military assets to retain power, he could not comprehend a situation where declining oil output would threaten his family's hold on power.

Muhammed bin Nayef had been named as the King's successor in April 2015, and having spent most of his career in the Ministry of the Interior, counter terrorism and chair of the Council for Political and Security Affairs, he was privy to information that nobody dared bring to the attention of the King. While Deng was waiting in Australian detention, Nayef was in his office in Riyadh, waiting for a Skype call to George to go through. As the computer whirred, Nayef's mind wandered over the path that had brought him to this point.

An experienced businessman, diplomat and strategist, he agreed with his adviser's assessments that the writing was on the wall for his Kingdom. Hostile forces within and neighboring the area were growing stronger each day, and the kingdom was pumping oil flat out, using every available technology to produce oil – and constantly evading accusations that the production figures published were inaccurate. But the supply refused to nudge over 12 million barrels per day. Sure, the published figures were more than that, because they included the energy equivalent of gas produced alongside the oil. But the global economy didn't run on natural gas - the plastics, medicines & chemicals that were essential to modern life were rooted in an economic model that required cheap light sweet crude oil.

While there was no danger of 'running out of oil', the simple economic fact was that few producers could sell oil profitably for under $80 a barrel any more.

Nayef had read the Club of Rome's report 'Limits to Growth' in the 1980s, and in the ensuing 30 years had been impressed to see that despite sustained and hysterical criticism, the Club's assessment had largely been correct. As the population had grown and become wealthier, several factors started to kick in which started a Feedback Loop. Oil wealth was spent on luxuries, travel, cars, planes, buildings and streets – all of which consumed energy not only to create but to maintain. The vast population of the kingdom, no longer a simple town on the desert coastline but a sprawling metropolis required vast amounts of oil to make and maintain the roads, plastics, medicines, computers, clothes, not to mention the transport of all of the items into the country.

Oh, there was plenty of oil there, but getting it out – at a price the world could afford? He shook his head at the thought. To make matters worse, the early kingdom had been able to sell almost 100% of its oil production to the West at a good price, but now, their own infrastructure required an increasing share of not only the crude but the profits that flowed from its sale.

Economists called this the 'Export Land Model' but Nayef like the more poetic phrase 'going back to riding on camels'.

Nayef also had a great deal of experience with the British and Americans. He was under no illusions that once the kingdom was unable to supply an increasing amount of oil for their economies – addicted to cheap energy and utterly unable to cope with prices over about $50 a barrel – when that time came, the Americans would be gone faster than one of his several Ferrari's.

Very quietly and discreetly, Nayef had started investigating the options available to the Royal House. Solar and Geothermal infrastructure received massive investment, and discussions were started about changing the wasteful and obscene manner of patronage, where thousands of Saudi family members were well paid to do nothing at all.

But he quickly learned that nothing was going to be enough. Once the tipping point was reached, American help would vaporise and the angry, starving hordes would overwhelm the elite's personal security. Nobody knew when that tipping point would be reached, but within six months, the cities of Riyadh, Dubai and their sisters would be torn apart before crumbling into dust.

Perhaps it was fitting, in some philosophical way, he thought – after all, the cities existed because of the oil that came from the desert, so in a sense they were an aberration, and the desert simply waited to reclaim what belonged to it, merely transformed from oil to skyscrapers, then dissolving back into the desert sand.

No, his family line would continue for generations but not in this place. Like the earlier generations of Bedouin tribes that he was descended from, he would relocate, seeking more favorable conditions now that changing circumstances demanded it. The plans he had put in place were taking shape – hundreds of Saudis, some students, some princes and their families – had already moved to Canada. Others had gone to London, Switzerland or other central European countries.

But Nayef had looked further afield. Even before the mass immigration to Europe had hit the news headlines, his intelligence assets had made him aware that Europe faced major challenges from millions of immigrants who were ideologically and economically opposed to his family's existence. So, Europe was out of the question, Canada and North America had their own problems, the pacific islands suffered from long supply lines and unstable politics.

Australia featured highly on the short list of suitable countries. Technologically advanced, politically stable, self-sufficient in food and energy and with a long history of positive relationships both with Muslims domestically and in international affairs. True, there had been a race riot in Sydney a decade ago, but the reports stated that this was a result of specific conflicts which had since been largely resolved. The media in Australia was strongly pro-Muslim, leftist and dominated by friendly media barons based in America and Europe.

Over the course of several meetings with Parsons' Executives, Nayef had covered a range of concerns and received pleasing assurances that a plan to annex a section of Sydney was achievable. By the end of 2014 and early 2015, he was confident that the Australian government and media were actively preparing to make his dream a reality. News – both online and print – were consistently pushing pro-immigration and pro-Islam stances, and actively branding anyone opposing these ideas 'racist', 'xenophobic' and 'intolerant'. Nayef was pleased to hear the assessment of his advisers. In their opinion, daytime infotainment shows employed some Muslim and many pro-Muslim infidels to push political correctness into the population. Opinion pieces insisting on 'tolerance' were increasingly being used to suppress anyone who spoke out against the process.

Nayef chuckled at the thought of using the media instead of prisons to silence rivals, but then again, patience was required for a successful colonisation. Once he was established as Caliph, he would be at liberty to make the necessary changes to ensure his rule was as 'peaceful' as possible.

He trusted the Parsons men, since he knew of their extensive experience with top level politics and economics around the world. If anyone could help him create a safe place for his family, it was the same group who had looked after them for so long.

The computer screen blinked, and his old friend George's face filled the screen. The light from George's own screen reflected off his glasses, but as he took them off Nayef couldn't help thinking that he was looking at Jabba the Hutt, from the Star Wars films he enjoyed so much.

In fact, George Soros looked ill. His silver hair had receded in the weeks since they had last seen each other. Thirty years older than Nayef, George's sagging cheeks and the deep bags under his eyes gave his pasty face an eerily reptilian appearance. The fact that it was almost 3am in Davos and George obviously hadn't slept much increased Nayef's concern for his friend and mentor.

'As-salamu Alaykum' said George. 'How are you, young terrorist?' His thin lips twisted in what Nayef interpreted as a smile. Truthfully, Nayef thought it looked like a toad being strangled.

Nayef laughed aloud and gave the accepted reply 'Wa'alaykumu s-salam.' 'I'm merely thy humble student' joked Nayef in return, knowing full well that George had caused more damage to the global economy, causing more suffering and indirectly – more death, on a single Wednesday in 1992 than any of the orders Nayef had given in his career.

That Nayef was born a Wahabi Saudi, and George was a Hungarian Jew made no difference at the levels these men operated at. Any sort of ancient or modern feuds had been set aside long ago, as the pursuit of wealth and more importantly, power took precedence in their lives. More often than not, the two men and the others like them – truly 'internationals' whose business empires and lives spanned the globe - used, stoked and sometimes even started feuds and conflicts to sell weapons, secure or deny access to resources, or simply to show off to the others. They all knew that power was the true currency, religion and means for existence. These men at the top of the tree used currencies, religions and governments to play their own game of global domination.

George had made a billion dollars in profit from a single operation that broke the Bank of England in 1992, and he had invested that wealth through various foundations that created incredible influence at all levels of society. Partnering with Nayef and others like him as the need arose, George and his various foundations pretended to champion environmental and human rights causes, while the bulk of their investments were directly aimed at securing total control over the world's population. Like chess pieces on a board, the UN, IMF, World Bank and the various central banks of the world's nations were played off against each other.

Straight to the point, George asked 'So, you have decided to move?'

'Indeed, we must' said Nayef. 'We can calm the markets for maybe a year longer – any more would be completely in the will of God.' Any collapse in the energy markets would be catastrophic for a global economy that had barely recovered from the Global Financial Crisis and Great Depression.

George grunted. 'God is a useful control for the masses, but he doesn't make business decisions, and he certainly won't keep your family safe'. For the briefest moment, his mind brought up a distant memory from his childhood, of the prayers made by local Jews as he helped the Nazis round them up and ship them off to the camps. None of those prayers were answered, and George knew that he alone was responsible for his life and the consequences of his actions.

Nayef nodded. 'The preparation and propaganda are almost finished, and messengers have been sent to Sydney to start organising a governing body. They have identified some who can be trusted, and who will need to be removed. But soon they will need weapons and equipment to form a defensive army.'

'Already arranged' replied George. 'We're using the same setup as we did with the RPF in Rwanda.'

Nayef was concerned. 'Is that wise?'

'Don't worry' soothed George. 'We got away with it then, and we will achieve success this time as well. I'll handle the UN side of things and make everyone believe that it's a natural evolution in the democratic process. Immigration, then a democratic expression of the immigrant's rights. They'll love it when I put it that way.'

'Thank you, my friend' said Nayef. 'I will send you the reports from Sydney when they arrive.'

'See you in New York' George ended the conversation and waited for the connection to close.

Then he made another call.

'He has swallowed the bait' he said cryptically. 'Tip off ASIO but make sure nobody can trace the intel back to us.'

'The French are going to raid another lot of Mosques next week' intoned the voice on the other end of the line. 'I'll make sure one of the kids overhears something the day before'.

Chapter 8

June

The Villawood Detention Centre is a sprawl of drab brick buildings and metal fences, all surrounded by a high security fence. The security fence is mostly steel mesh, interspersed with concrete sections and separated from the fenced-in living and activity areas by well-lit grass areas and driveways. There is no cover near the fence, making it impossible for anyone to hide or cross it.

Until now.

One of the outer fence panels was missing, and the stolen car Xanthe has driven through the gap had crashed through the inner fence of Deng's enclosure, opening a clear path for him to escape.

Driving in had been an exhilarating rush, but now Xanthe was running for her life.

Heart pounding and lungs rasping in her chest, she sprinted across the grass between the two walls of the Villawood Detention Centre. Getting in had been simple, and Deng had been exactly where he was supposed to be, but as they raced back to the hole in the outer fence, the much older man was several meters in front and leaving her behind. Terror at what would happen to her if she was captured drove her legs. She dashed blindly across the open space between the two fences, over the crumpled section of metal fence that now lay on the ground between two concrete wall sections, and into the paved yard of the DIMO WASTE SERVICES compound.

In the compound waited a white delivery van with the engine idling. By earlier agreement, the owners of the vehicles were only reporting them stolen at this moment– to minimise police attention for as long as possible. Two other men, the driver and a passenger slid the door shut, climbed into the front and planted the accelerator. The van shot down the short driveway, onto Birmingham Ave, then turned right onto Christina Road. Lying on rugs and carpets covering the metal floor of the van, Deng and Xanthe instinctively spread their arms and legs to prevent being slammed into the walls by the sharp turns. Still gasping for breath after her sprint Braced against the centrifugal force, Xanthe tried to breathe but all she managed were some shallow gasps. Speeding parallel to the train tracks, they raced underneath an overpass, then lurched right, across two lanes of traffic and up the 'on' ramp, heading north up Woodville Road.

Barely slowing and weaving through traffic, the van passed a car dealer, a petrol station and crossed over the metal pipes that were used to supply water to the city. The driver moved into the left lane and slowed, preparing to turn into a side street. Itching under the hot synthetic balaclava, Xanthe used one hand to pull it off, shaking out her short, blonde hair before bracing again as the van turned left.

Immediately after turning left off Woodville Road, the van lurched right, into the driveway of a unit block, rushing down the concrete ramp to the underground basement car park. Pulling into a marked Visitor car space next to two other small passenger cars, the driver shut off the engine and everyone exhaled. They all felt as if they had held their breath for the entirety of the jailbreak, and now they laughed nervously, shaking their heads and unbuckling seat belts, discharging the nervous energy from their bodies.

Getting out of the van, Xanthe threw her arms around Deng and hugged him gleefully. Their daring plan had worked. Xanthe was passionate about social justice and so infuriated at the detention of innocent refugees that she had jumped at the change to strike back at the evil government and its inhumane program. She was amazed at how alive she felt, so relevant, making a clear statement that her people would no longer tolerate inhumanity, no matter if it was done by a legitimately elected government. Graduating High School last year, she had done less than a semester at university, but had thrown herself into every cause possible. Social Justice, equality, refugees, economic socialism, she took any opportunity she saw to advocate and fight for those she saw as voiceless, defenseless, exploited by a system that had given her so much privilege.

Xanthe let go of Deng and continued to dance around the bare, dusty car park. She felt like a messiah, pivotally important in the salvation of others. Desperately trying to purchase atonement for the unequal privileges she had innocently enjoyed as a child, by emancipating Deng, even if that involved breaking the law. To her mind, if she felt a law was morally wrong, then it was okay to break other laws to overthrow the injustice. The feeling was intoxicating. She felt energized, powerful in the most basic, electric meaning of the word.

Interrupting her moment of celebration, the nameless driver took off his mask and said 'Not over yet. Go get your phone, meet us with Maryam.' Then he bundled Deng into one of the small cars and drove slowly out of the garage.

Xanthe and the van's passenger got into the other car and followed, turning left out of the building and then left again onto Woodville Road. In silence, they continued north into Parramatta, and a short time later Xanthe was dropped outside the main shopping center. Entering the food court, she found her friend Maryam reading a book at a table, an empty coffee cup and plate in front of her. Maryam closed the book and stood up quickly, straightening the chador that covered her face.

Brimming with excitement, Xanthe hugged Maryam and almost danced a little jig on the spot. Her eyes shone with delight at the experience she had just had, and she desperately wanted to tell her friend all about it.

'Ready to go home?' asked Maryam with a smile. She took a phone out of her bag and passed it to Xanthe. Thumbing it open, Xanthe saw she had no messages or missed calls.

The two young women left the shopping center in Maryam's car and headed south-east. Maryam handed over a list of the shops she had visited with Xanthe's phone in the past two hours and Xanthe looked over it, committing a few to memory so their alibi stories would match if they were ever to be caught and interrogated.

While driving towards Bankstown, Maryam listened to Xanthe telling her about the raid and how it had gone exactly as planned.

'I followed the van into the DIMO yard – their back fence is the exterior security fence of the centre. The other two from the van hooked up cables to the tow bar, and then clipped them to the fence right where the metal sections joined the concrete parts. They got back in the van and floored it; the cables ripped the whole metal section of fence right off the wall. The bolts just broke out of the concrete and it went sliding along the ground.

'I drove straight through the gap, across the grass and into the interior fence. I was afraid it wouldn't bust through, but we did, and Deng was standing RIGHT THERE. You shoulda seen the look on his face!' she giggled at the memory.

'Soon as the car stopped we were both out through the hole in the fence, bolted to the van. By that time the others had unhooked the cables, we got in and we were off – bam'. Xanthe swept one palm across the other to express the speed of the van. 'We swapped cars in the car park, then they dropped me back to you' she concluded, then smiled. 'And I got an alibi, I can prove I was with you the whole time, my mobile phone tracked me around the shops.'

Maryam smiled, briefly taking her eyes off the road. 'I'm so glad everything went as planned. I couldn't live with myself if anything happened to you.' She paused, then asked 'are you going to stay for dinner?'

'I'd love to' nodded Xanthe. She loved Middle Eastern food and her new family even more. She felt so alive, as if she had stepped through a metaphorical doorway into a brand-new life, one where she made the rules, where she was in control. She felt so mature, like a movie hero in real life.

The two young women drove parallel to the M4 motorway, staying away from the toll points that would register the location of the vehicle on the tag glued to the windscreen. They turned south in Auburn, went through Berala and arrived in Lakemba about ten minutes later. Maryam parked in the street outside their unit block, right behind Xanthe's own small hatchback.

They got out of the car and went inside the first-floor unit, greeting the small crowd in the living room and being greeted like heroes themselves. Everyone was cheering, hugging and some were even crying, relived that their little rescue operation had been successful. Xanthe saw Deng across the room, talking with the driver and some other men she didn't recognize, and then she was mobbed again by a pair of older women who hugged her tight.

Eventually, everyone started to calm down and some of the elder women started shooing people away from the middle of the room. They set up several small tables to make one large one and spread out brightly colored cloths over the whole thing. From the kitchen they produced a steady stream of cooked foods: spicy lamb & chicken, rice, flat bread, vegetables and more – set out in several places so they were within reach of everyone regardless of where they would be sitting.

Xanthe stayed by Maryam's side, watching and waiting to be told where to sit. First seated was a tall, thin man with a full, grey beard. Seeing him seated first told Xanthe that this man was extremely important, probably the head of the family that lived in the unit. He would have other units, housing other wives and children – some of whom may even be here at the party, Xanthe had no way of knowing without asking Maryam, and she didn't want to be rude.

The older man then indicated Deng to sit next to him, indicating that Deng was an honored guest. Then the driver and passenger made a little group around Deng. Xanthe knew enough about dining etiquette to understand that these were the places of honor. Next would be the male family members in order of age, thought Xanthe; finally, the women would be seated.

She gasped aloud when the host looked directly at her with a wide smile and said 'Zantee. A daughter who is a warrior like any man. Please...' he indicated a seat next to Deng, inviting her to sit.

Xanthe couldn't believe that the host had broken with tradition to honor her in this way. She bowed her head to acknowledge her gracious host and moved across the room, sitting as quietly and quickly as she could. The rest of the young men waited awkwardly, then moved as indicated by their host. While somewhat confused, they knew that it was his table, and he could seat his guests at his own discretion – within reason. Once the men and older women were seated, Maryam took the empty seat next to Xanthe.

Looking around, Xanthe noted the skill of her host. He had balanced the table, respecting his male guests and relatives and seating Xanthe and Maryam with the rest of the women, but closest to the male end of the table. It was a neat way of honoring her while at the same time, maintaining tradition and a family structure that everyone understood. Putting it in perspective, and given her contribution to the rescue was far more than any of the younger men, it made sense for the host to break with tradition in this way. It also sent a subtle message to the entire family: participation and results were recognized and respected. If you didn't participate, you were demoted in favor of those who did – regardless of their gender. Xanthe knew this was a bold statement, indicating their host was setting out to make his own rules. She wondered what other traditions might be altered to suit their new homeland.

The meal began in the same order. Xanthe knew to keep her left hand at her side, only eating or passing food to others with her right. Several conversations were going on at once, ebbing and flowing in a mixture of English and Arabic as vibrant and exotic as the food on the table.

Once the eating had slowed, the conversation continued until it was interrupted by the host gently clapping his hands. He looked around at the group and welcomed them all.

'Peace be upon all of you' he began.

'Today, we have won our brother's life from the jaws of Satan himself.

'Today, we have declared with our actions that we can and will, act. We will secure our lives, our lands and our families.

'Today, we have gained our brother, and tomorrow we will declare to all that we will possess our lands, we will serve Allah, the merciful, and we will bring this land under His peace and His law, *Inshallah.*'

The group nodded in agreement and most of them murmured *'Inshallah'* as well.

He then turned to Maryam and said 'Maryam, would you and Zantee please tell us what happened?'

Xanthe appreciated what he was doing. It was unthinkable for the host to communicate directly with her, a female who was not a direct family member. So he had obviously and cleverly asked a directly related female family member to act as a liaison.

Maryam began telling their story. She alternated looking at Xanthe and her host, avoiding eye contact with the other men at the table.

'Well, Xanthe and I have been friends for months. We're in all the same classes at Uni – we're both passionate about social justice, opposing intolerance and fascism.'

Xanthe continued, making sure to speak to Maryam, but loudly enough that everyone in the room could hear. 'We've done a lot of activism, marches, Antifa rallies, putting up posters. We both volunteered for the Greens at the election.' She paused, a little sad that the Greens had lost almost all their seats in parliament at the recent election. All that effort had basically been wasted.

Maryam nodded. 'So I overheard Sargon talking about the Villawood Detention Centre. It's such an evil place, a symbol of the corrupt government, the torture of innocent people. Everybody deserves a home, and we are such a rich country, we owe it to humanity to give a home and food to anyone who wants it.'

'It was mostly Xanthe's idea. She and I drove around the centre to get an idea of the place and we memorised the layout from Google Maps. Sargon had told us what area Deng was in, how important he is, and when we saw there were two walls, I thought it was impossible.'

But Xanthe looked at the walls up close, and had the idea of pulling down the outside section, then driving a car through the gap and into the inner wall.'

'Punching two holes' explained Xanthe. 'It meant that we had to leave the second car in the fence, but since it was stolen anyway, there's no way of tracing it back to us.'

'Sargon arranged for two others to help us out, and we arranged for Maryam to stay at the shops with my phone, to create an alibi, just in case. The four of us went over the plan every day for a week, then did a dry run yesterday, to get used to the road, turns, everything.'

So this morning, it all went as planned. Even though Sargon had a key for the gate, we cut the lock off, then the van went in and they hooked up steel cables to the metal fence – it's there in sections – bolted into other parts of the wall that are concrete.

The van drove off and pulled the whole metal section off onto the ground. I drove through the opening and smashed the car into the inner fence. That's what made the hole big enough for Deng to get out. We ran back to the van and got away.' Xanthe was smiling and wiggling around on her seat as she relived the excitement.

'Then we switched cars in a unit block basement nearby, and then they dropped me back at the shops where Maryam was waiting.'

Everyone else at the table had been listening with great attention, and now smiled, nodded and clapped to show appreciation of the planning and execution of the escape.

But none of the smiles were wider and warmer than their host's.

'Well done. A bold but simple plan,' He nodded again. 'And we are very pleased to have our honored guest with us safely. Truly Allah is merciful and gracious.' He paused, then went on.

'Both of you have brought great honor to our family. Thank you and bless you.'

He turned to one of the younger men sitting at the table near him.

'Bilal, would you please call Mullah Melbourne and arrange for Zantee to join your classes? I believe she has the makings of a great warrior for Allah.'

One of the young men about her age blushed, and then nodded. The older man saw it, laughed, and said 'perhaps we should marry you as well!' Bilal's eyes nearly fell out of his head, and Xanthe laughed aloud at the idea. It was absurd.

But their host's eyes narrowed as he thought about it. 'Maryam, can you tell me who Zantee's father is?'

Xanthe shook her head. 'Both of my parents are dead, I was raised in a foster home and once I turned eighteen, I was on my own.'

Maryam put her hand to her mouth as she learned this about her friend. 'Oh – I had no idea…'she said but Xanthe smiled at her friend and shook her head slightly, smiling to show she was not upset.

'It's just a part of me, and my life's story, no big deal. There are many more people less fortunate than me – maybe it's why I feel so strongly about helping people.'

One of the other men at the table tilted his head to the side as he asked the host a question. 'If a young woman has no father, no male authority, how then can she be married? Who can vouch for her?'

The host smiled 'Truly Allah is merciful, and has provided all things for us. If a woman is to be married, and has no male relative, then the Imam can take the place for her.'

Xanthe looked at Maryam, somewhat alarmed. 'I do NOT want to be married right now.' She paused, 'One day, yes, but not right now.'

Their host nodded and stroked his beard as he entertained the idea of marrying this woman who had a lion's heart to one of his strongest warriors – maybe Sargon would be a good husband for her. Surely their children would have the strength of a hundred men - like the Prophet, *peace be upon him*. Then he laughed with the others, waved his hands to dismiss the idea, and went on with the last of the meal.

When it was time to go, Bilal offered to take Xanthe to meet the Melbourne Mullah. Their host asked them to take Deng as well, since he was going to be working for the Mullah. Bilal nodded and gestured for Deng and Xanthe to follow him. She wrapped a scarf around her head as she went out the front door, down the steps and climbed into the EVO, Xanthe and Bilal in the front and Deng in the back. Bilal fired it up and roared off towards the house near the Mosque.

As they drove, Xanthe turned to Deng and smiled, the relief of the jailbreak bubbling up inside her again. 'How are you feeling?' she asked him. 'Do you need anything?' Given he had run out of the detention centre with nothing but the clothes on his back, it was a reasonable and thoughtful question.

Deng looked at her for a moment, his mind weighing up whether to respond. She was a non-relative, a woman, but then again, the host had honored her highly, and he was in a foreign country, with a specific mission, and he needed to learn more about everything before he would know who was to be obeyed and who could be ignored. Best to show minimal courtesy but be polite to everyone until he knew more.

He didn't smile, but he said 'Thank you, no. The Mullah will give me what has been provided, *Inshallah.*'

'Fuck yeah I'm interested,' drawled one of the wealthiest property developers in Australia. Despite a net worth well over $2 billion, he still spoke and thought like a Western Sydney bricklayer. Harry leaned forward in his chair at a private table in the Mosaic restaurant, part of the exclusive Westin Hotel in Sydney's Martin Place. He scrawled his signature on the Non-Disclosure Agreement and tossed it across the white tablecloth towards his host. Anything that required a contract of secrecy would be profitable, and he loved being in on the ground floor of any development enterprise.

'Ahem' said the Englishman, clearing his throat and sipping on iced water. He was having difficulty reconciling the wealth, power and dress of the man with his crude manner of speaking. It was incongruous in the extreme, particularly when contrasted with the style and eloquence that normally frequented the Westin Hotel in Martin Place.

The Englishman steepled his fingers, resting his hands on the white tablecloth while he chose his words carefully.

'Harry, the interests that I represent have come into some information…that indicates…major reconstruction and development works will be soon required…in South Western Sydney…'

Harry looked quizzically at the Englishman. 'I know about the fucken Caliphate, mate. What, you think they're going to want us to build their Taj Mahal?'

The Englishman shook his head, 'Well, no – the Taj Mahal is Indian – but that's not it at all.' He shook his head and quietly continued.

'My clients believe the Australian Government will not allow the Caliphate to continue for more than six months. They are quietly gathering forces to evacuate, surround, secure and clear the Caliphate of all extremists.' He considered Harry's eyes, and saw them widen in disbelief, then narrow as the implications – and profits – became apparent.

'They're gonna destroy the joint!' Harry gasped.

The Englishman breathed in, then said quietly 'Using a combination of air power, artillery and some ground forces.'

Harry leaned back in his chair, fixing the Englishman with a piercing stare as his brain worked. Finally, he uttered two words, in a question: 'Seven suburbs?' His bushy eyebrows arched over his hawkish nose as he contemplated the loss of life and property involved in what was being proposed – as well as the incredible profits for those involved in reconstruction…

The Englishman cocked his head, 'well, not all of those suburbs will require…complete… rebuilding, but essentially that area of land will need to be completely re-developed, much like Berlin or Tokyo after World War 2…'

Harry shook his head. 'No, that won't work.' The Englishman started to contradict him – worried that Harry was concerned about civilian casualties – but Harry held up his hand to request patience.

'There's no point just rebuilding more houses' said Harry slowly. 'We need to start below ground, put the trains and busses in tunnels.' He held out his hand flat, palm down, indicating a strata level below ground, and then lifted it a little higher. 'Above that go the services, water, electricity, and communications.' He lifted his hand a little higher: 'Then, at ground level you put in transport hubs, warehousing and distribution, shops and restaurants.'

The Englishman nodded, pleased that Harry had grasped the scope of the idea but believed it to be his own. He was man enough that he didn't need everyone to think he had all the ideas. If his client's proposal was implemented, that was all that mattered.

'Above that, you have a couple of levels of offices, then your residential towers,' finished Harry, as his hand swept up from chin level to above his head, indicating the amount of residential he foresaw.

Then his eyes narrowed, and he scrutinized the Englishman's face again, looking for any wavering, any hint this was not serious. He saw none.

'What about the government?' he asked. 'Something like this would take years to get through all the planning departments – just look at Barangaroo...' his voice trailed off as he noticed the Englishman's Cheshire grin.

'Fear not,' the Englishman chuckled. 'My clients have made sure that both the Federal and State governments understand that this is being done under Emergency powers. Do you think you can accomplish a project of this size?'

Harry had already figured out who he would involve, and who would be shut out of the deals to come. 'Sure' he responded, 'I've got everyone from demolition, excavation, construction – and every fucken strata manager and real estate agent in New South Wales is going to be lobbying for a piece of the sales and management – fucked if we can do it all, so lucky for them!'

'You're not worried about…casualties?' asked the Englishman.

'Fuck no,' replied Harry. 'Anyone with any brains will get the fuck outta there as soon as they can. Those who stay deserve what's coming to them.'

The Englishman picked up the secrecy contract that Harry had signed to finalize the meeting. 'Then we're done, I'll leave all the administration and organization to you. Have a think about setting up a working group to liaise with the necessary people in State and Federal circles when the time is right. Develop a list of any questions about infrastructure you'll need answered once those secrecy requirements expire.'

Harry stood to shake hands, and said 'What about local government? What about council? Who do we talk to about local logistics and waste?'

The Englishman just laughed quietly as he equaled Harry's firm handshake. 'You write your own rules for now. Local councils will be abolished by the Caliphate, so once they are gone,' he shrugged, 'those who get out early might be able to stand for new elections once the dust settles.'

'But by that time, we'll both be rich, and I'll be long gone…'

-

Twelve hours later, on the other side of the world, the sun was beginning to set in Paris and Muslims from every quarter were on their way to Friday evening prayer. Philippe had arrived earlier than most, and had started the ritual washing in the men's room. He was almost finished when two more men entered, talking loudly, almost arguing. Philippe didn't mean to overhear but he gathered that they were talking about Australia.

'I don't care if you don't believe me, I'm telling you, it's happening,' said the first man.

'A Caliph?' said the second in disbelief. 'None of the Caliphs have enough money to buy that kind of land.'

'No, no, I'm not talking about the Jordanians' replied the first man. 'It's the Saudis – the new king doesn't feel safe anymore, not in Arabia, not in Europe. They are starting a whole new Caliphate and he will be the Caliph!'

Philippe didn't hear any more, since his business was finished, and he was focused on prayers and the evening ahead. He entered the main area of the small Mosque and completed his prayers with about a dozen others. He stood up just as the doors burst open and black-clad figures rushed in screaming 'descendre' in French and 'nankab' in Arabic. Philippe saw that some were ordinary National Police, their clothes had POLICE written in English – but others were more like commando soldiers with GIPN on the back of their jackets. All wore body armor, black helmets and carried small rifles. Philippe realized that his dinner plans didn't matter anymore, and if he was lucky he might be able to get to work on Monday.

The intruders pushed everyone to the floor, used cable ties to secure their hands and feet, and then left them on the ground while they searched the Mosque.

Since Philippe was lying nearest the doors, he heard the team leaders reporting back to the commander. They had been looking for weapons, explosives and computers but hadn't found anything.

'Pack up' he heard the commander order. 'Get this lot back for interrogation.'

Philippe was hauled to his feet and the cable ties on his ankles replaced with shackles that allowed him to walk. He was bundled into a police van with the rest of the worshippers and the van drove slowly through the crowded Paris streets. The van had no windows, so Philippe guessed that they had only moved a few districts when the van stopped and the doors opened, revealing they were inside what looked like a police garage. The walls were concrete, same as the floor, and there were other vans and police cars parked in rows.

Still shackled, the prisoners were led through a door into a reception room where their personal items were taken, sealed in plastic bags and registered in a computer. Then they were led into a long corridor, which had many glass doors set into it on both sides. These turned out to be interrogation rooms, containing a metal table and four chairs, all bolted to the floor. Philippe was pushed into the first one and left alone as the door clicked locked. Through the glass, he saw the rest of the worshippers shuffling down the hall, each being allocated a room. He sat in a chair, rested his arms on the table, put his head in his hands, and began to wait.

He was mentally prepared to spend several days in this room, but was surprised when less than ten minutes later, the door opened and two plain-clothes investigators came in. One was blonde, the other had red hair. Both men were tall and thin, pale from spending too much time indoors. They didn't introduce themselves, and Philippe didn't speak either. He was sure they knew who he was because they certainly would have examined his belongings, wallet and ID as soon as they were recorded in the computer system.

'Philippe Brulee' began the redhead. 'Thirty-two years old, you live in Saint-Denis, you teach law at the 13 University.' Philippe spread his hands in a gesture that acknowledged the man had spoken, but remained silent. They hadn't asked a question yet.

'What do you know of the reasons you have been arrested?' asked the blonde man. Philippe chuckled inside – he recognized the Good Cop – Bad Cop routine right away, but decided to play along.

'I am not aware that I have been arrested,' he said calmly and slowly. The last thing he wanted was to upset these investigators and turn his life into a pissing contest. 'I understand that I have been brought in for questioning, but nobody has told me that I'm under arrest.'

The two interrogators looked at each other. Despite their power, they knew they had to tread carefully. This guy was a teacher at the same school that the Mayor of Paris taught at, and undoubtedly moved in the same circles. Any abuse of their authority may come back to bite them – hard, particularly since nobody knew the future and who might be in control of their budgets in five or ten years' time.

The redhead cleared his throat. 'Correct. We had a tip-off that the Mosque was being used to assemble and store weapons for a future terror attack. Do you know anything about this?'

Philippe honestly replied that he had no idea what they were talking about. Yes, he lived in a terrorist stronghold - that was a fact. But just because his part of the city had become a war zone didn't mean he was involved. All he wanted to do was be left alone to teach his classes and climb the bureaucratic ladder in the university. He racked his brain to try and figure out a way to convince them he was just a public servant who happened to be a Muslim. Then he remembered.

'All I can tell you is what I heard in the wash room.' The two men stared at him, the redhead started writing in a notebook.

'Two men came in. I didn't see their faces because they were behind me. But they were talking about Australia.

'Australia?' asked the blonde man. Philippe paused to search his memory to make sure the words he used were clear and couldn't easily be twisted against him.

'One man was saying the Saudi King is moving to Sydney. He doesn't feel safe in the Middle East or Europe, but they are preparing a place in Sydney – a Caliphate.'

The redhead stopped writing. 'You can't be serious.'

'That's what the other guy in the washroom said,' replied Philippe. 'I'm not saying I believe it, I'm just telling you what I heard. Sorry, but I don't know anything else.'

The two interrogators looked at each other, then back at Philippe. They seemed at a loss for words, then the redhead asked, 'and there's no way you would recognized them again?'

Philippe shook his head. 'My back was turned, that's all I heard. Sorry I can't help you further.'

'Have you noticed or heard anything else? Even if you don't think it's important.'

'Look, gentlemen,' he pleaded. 'Every religion has its extremists, and there are morons everywhere, right? Even *WE* had Vichy, didn't we? I believe in the rule of French law. I teach it for God's sake. I'm not a criminal or a terrorist, my family goes back to Charlemagne.'

The blonde nodded slowly, his mouth twisting to express reluctant agreement.

'Looks like you were in the wrong place at the wrong time.' Philippe breathed a small sigh of relief.

He sensed they wanted to check his story with the other worshippers and decided to put a little pressure on – see if he could still get home in time for dinner.

'Look, you know who I am; you know I'm not going anywhere. I've co-operated, told you everything I know. Can I go home?'

The redhead stiffened in his seat. 'That's not up to us. We need to check a few things.'

They stood, collected their notes and left him alone.

But Philippe had the last laugh, because it was only a few more minutes before the door unlocked again, and another police officer came in. This was an old man, dressed in a normal police uniform. Philippe immediately sensed this guy was close to retirement, and worked in administration, not front-line police work. The man checked a file in his hand and asked 'Philippe Broulee?'

Philippe nodded, and the man said, 'You are free to go, please come with me.'

Going back to the reception room, Philippe collected his wallet, phone and keys, signed the paperwork and walked out into the night. He made a phone call, explained his disappearance and was pleased to hear his dinner plans were still valid.

It would be months before he learned anything about what was going on in Sydney, or what his unwitting actions had unleashed. He had no idea that his report had been included in the joint Interpol data sharing network and picked up by ASIO clerks. The intel was routed upwards and included in the PM's daily Threat Assessment Brief.

-

Bilal was tired but focused on what the Mullah was saying. The group lessons were held several times a week, and Bilal had learned a lot – his Arabic was conversational now. Although he was tired, he was looking forward to the end of the lesson because he had a special surprise planned for the Mullah.

Bilal waited patiently while some of the slower learners got individual attention from the Mullah, then sat up a little straighter as their teacher went to the front of the room and sat down. 'Inshallah, that's all for tonight,' he said, smiling at his students in turn. 'Anything else before we all go home?'

Bilal cleared his throat and raised his hand, waiting for the Mullah to give him permission to speak. Receiving it, he held up a small bag he had created and proudly explained his idea. 'It's called a Faraday Bag.' He began. 'Two zip lock bags with a foil layer in between. You've taught us that the infidels can access our phones even when they are turned off, but... I thought... if you block the radio signal completely, they can't get anything...' He was extremely pleased to see the other students looking at him admiringly and finished in a rush. 'It would mean we can keep our phones with us, but invisible to the infidels...'

The Mullah looked at Bilal with a smile on his face. A warm, enthusiastic smile that gave Bilal a rush of power and joy. Perhaps he had shown the all-wise, worldly Mullah something new, something he hadn't seen before. The Mullah stroked his bearded chin, and nodded appreciatively.

'Well done, Bilal. You are thinking, testing, that is good. Let's test it, shall we?' Bilal's heart froze a little at the idea. He hadn't tried it yet and he wasn't even sure how his idea might be tested.

The Mullah nodded to Bilal. 'Put your phone in the bag. Make sure it is turned on and the ringer isn't silent.'

Hands trembling, hoping against hope that he was right, Bilal complied. A few seconds later, his phone was securely wrapped in the foil bag. Slowly, almost theatrically, the Mullah pulled out his own phone, an ancient Nokia 3330, scrolled into the menu then hit the green phone key.

The nervous energy in the room climbed exponentially in the two seconds after the tinny BEEP sounded, as if the old phone in the Mullah's hand was radioactive. Then Bilal's world imploded.

The familiar trilling of his own ringtone filled the room, and all Bilal's pride and excitement evaporated as the rest of the students burst out laughing. Bilal was about to yell at them to shut up when the Mullah did it for them.

'Silence' he bellowed, and the room instantly hushed. Nervous eyes locked onto the Mullah, shame creeping across some of the faces as the owners guessed the lesson they were all about to learn. The Mullah glared at them all. '*Inshallah!*'

'None of you had any original ideas. Bilal has learned an important lesson, as I hope you all have. No physics or electronics training, yet he has brought up a valid idea. I praise his ideas and initiative; I want to see more of it.'

The older man turned to Bilal. 'A layer of tinfoil will not insulate against the radio signal from your phone. Solar radiation, yes. EMP, maybe. But the tinfoil you buy in a supermarket is not sufficient.' He paused to make sure Bilal understood that he wasn't being scolded or mocked, then went on. 'You will need to find a more effective insulator. It may simply require more layers, it may need to be a metal box with soldered sides. This is a good project. Do more research and give a report next week. OK?'

Bilal nodded, swallowing his pride and grateful that the older man had defended his ego from the others in the class. He would get onto Google as soon as he got home.

Mario was so average he could have been a stereotype. Stocky and dark haired, he had average looks and he lived in an average fibro house in Western Sydney. Like a lot of almost-forty-year-old men in his situation, he lived alone, sharing the care of two teenage kids with his ex-wife.

Like most average Australians, Mario worked hard, earned decent money and saved up his annual leave so he could take a week off at a time. His lifetime passion was hunting with a bow, and he would finish work about 4pm on a Friday, dash home, finish packing his Land Cruiser and then head out to one of the hundreds of State Forests in country New South Wales. There he would set up camp and hunt for several days and nights, stalking the feral goats and deer that made excellent organic, free range food. While he absolutely preferred to eat what he killed, he had no issue shooting feral dogs, cats, pigs and other predators that were destroying the native plants and animals at a rapid rate.

Earlier in the evening, his small lounge room had looked as if a hurricane had hit a camping store, but now all the pieces of equipment were organized, pack and loaded into the Cruiser. Tent, stove and gas, clothes, food, water, batteries, lights, butcher knives, baby wipes... A dozen other items to make camp life a little more comfortable and help preserve the meat he hoped to take.

Now, it was close to midnight and he was ready to leave. The house lights were all off except for a small desk lamp in the study where he had gone over the maps one last time, and he was in the process of checking over his bow before he left for his hunt. It was important to check all the moving parts, the cams and strings for cracks, wear or other damage that could cause it to fail. While he did carry spare parts, it was best to check it while repairs could be done at home – much more comfortable than trying to work on it in the field.

The house was quiet, almost resting after the bustling teenagers had been causing constant noise for a week. They had gone to their mum's house after school on Friday, and now there was no music, no electronic entertainment, even the WIFI router was switched off. Mario's mind was approaching a state of Zen as his eyes and hands worked around the familiar shape of the bow, evaluating the components and comparing what he saw to what should be.

The bow was a perfectly proportioned creation of carbon fiber, steel and rubber. It flexed gently under his hands as he ran his fingers over the surface, checking for cracks, lumps or imperfections that could indicate damage. He touched the bolts that held it together, the cams that tensioned the string and then ran his fingers over the string itself, making sure it wasn't twisted, knotted and sat correctly in the grooves.

Fixed to the top of the bow, a quiver of arrows lay vertically opposite the grip and sight, with four razor-sharp broadhead arrows secured into the rubber rack. The arrows were clean, sharp and virtually identical, free of variations that could affect their flight to the target.

He was completely relaxed and about to take the string off the bow when he heard glass breaking from the rear of the house. Startled, he forgot about the bow in his hand as he stood up and eased his body into the doorway, peering down the central hallway that ran from the front door, past three doorways – including the one he occupied – and ended at the kitchen on the back wall of the house.

The house was pitch black, and his night vision hadn't recovered from the desk lamp he had used a moment earlier, but a rising moon shone enough light outside to shadow the figure that had broken the window in the back door, and was now reaching through to unlock it.

Mario's breathing stopped. He was terrified. Blood was roaring in his ears and he tried to comprehend what was happening and what he could do – but nothing came. His brain felt paralyzed, and he stood, frozen, watching as the lock clicked and the door swung open.

The shadowy arm moved again, towards the wall and with a softer click the hallway light came on, startling Mario but his brain stubbornly refused to help him. He stood stiffly, looking at the intruder less than ten meters away – blue overalls, black nylon jacket, no mask or face covering. Mario saw a man, mid-20s, with a narrow, emaciated face and deep sunk eyes. The dark hair was long, tangled and greasy and Mario could see tattoos on the man's neck and face.

The terrified home owner's brain screamed 'JUNKIE' as Mario's eyes moved to the gloved hands and fixed upon the gleaming knife blade that shimmered menacingly in the pale light on the ceiling. Mario wanted to scream out, to threaten the intruder, to drive them off, but nothing happened until the burglar took a step into the hallway and saw him there.

Mario's heart and lungs started working again, but his throat couldn't make a sound pass into his mouth. All that came out were a series of squeaks like a mouse might make, until the intruder took another step and he was able to cry 'Get…out…' To Mario, it sounded like a ten-year-old boy trying to stand up to a schoolyard bully, and the intruder simply laughed. A deep chuckle that seemed to swell from hell itself, up through the floor and into the man's body. Mario seemed hypnotized by the knife as the man stepped towards him again, twisting the knife in the air.

'Too late cunt' hissed the burglar. 'Seen my face, I gunna cut you up.'

As the words registered in his brain, Mario felt the terror in his body washed away by an overwhelming feeling of calm. He was as good as dead. Messed in the head by who knows what kinds of drugs, for how long, this junkie would have no trouble slitting his throat before stealing whatever he could. But then Mario's brain jumped to the next logical conclusion, the criminal would also be free to rob, rape and kill his next victim, then the next and so on.

By the time these thoughts had gone through his brain, Mario found he had stepped out into the hallway and turned towards the intruder, bringing up the bow and nocking an arrow into the string. He had no memory of the movements, everything was flashing by so quickly, but his eyes focused on the broad-head hunting arrow, reflecting the same light as the attacker's knife.

Mario's throat twisted again, and he managed to croak 'no, get out' as he drew the string back and locked his fingers in next to his cheek. In a confused mass of jumbled images, the man sprang towards him, lashing out with the knife and Mario jumped back, losing his balance and reflexively releasing the bowstring at the same time. His head struck the inside of the front door and he slid to the ground, seeing stars for a full five seconds.

Opening his eyes, shaking his head to clear it, Mario saw the intruder lying in the hallway, halfway to the back door. Body trembling with the aftermath of the massive adrenaline shock, he crawled to his feet and moved closer. The burglar was lying on his right side, head towards the door with the arrow embedded in his chest. Mario shuffled closer, there didn't look to be any blood on the carpet – could the man still be alive?

Reaching the body, Mario saw that he was indeed dead, the arrow had struck right in the heart and stopped it instantly. With the heart stopped, the dying man had been able to take two or three steps – purely on reflex, before crashing to the floor. The hydrostatic shock of the impact in the heart would have overwhelmed his nervous system instantly, shutting down all conscious thoughts, although the subconscious reflexes remained active for a second or two more. In short, the burglar was dead before he hit the ground. Because his heart had stopped instantly, only a small amount of blood had leaked from the wound, and remained trapped inside the jacket - Mario saw it as he gently touched the end of the arrow pointing grotesquely up in the air.

Mario dropped the bow and collapsed into a chair in the kitchen as the stress reaction kicked in again. His hands shook violently, his head spun, and he felt like he was going to throw up. Dropping his head into his hands he moaned weakly, an audible expression of the nervous energy pouring through his body.

After a few nerve-wracking minutes, he began to calm down and think clearly. He involuntarily grabbed his phone to call the police, and then thought twice. A proverb his mother had often repeated came into his mind, and he smiled at her ancient wisdom: 'If you have an intruder in your house, then you have a problem. If you call the police, then you have two problems.'

No, the police would be almost as bad as the burglar. They would certainly snoop around and see if they could find what the burglar was looking for. They would question him for days – he could kiss his camping trip goodbye. Then there would be media attention – the last thing he needed was for his wife and kids to find out about this on TV.

Absolutely not. He would need to take care of this himself.

Mario crossed himself, closed his eyes and whispered, 'Bless you Mama'. When he opened his eyes, there was something different in them, a hardness; a bitterness. The set of his jaw was resolute. He had an ugly job to do and was resigned to seeing it through.

He realized exactly what he had to do, and he most certainly did not like that knowledge. Steeling his nerves, he went into the garage and brought back a blue tarpaulin, opened it on the ground next to the corpse and then moved the feet onto it. Moving around to the head, he grabbed the jacket shoulders and used them to lift the torso off the ground and onto the tarp. Then he knelt, grabbed the arrow shaft and began to screw it off the head, still buried deep in the corpse.

After several turns, the arrow shaft popped free and he jerked it out of the corpse. Mario shuddered involuntarily as the horror of the whole situation crashed down on top of him. 'Get a grip, mate,' he admonished himself and rolled up the tarp to completely cover the body. Using the tarp as a sled, he dragged the corpse into the garage, stopping several times to catch his breath. It was heavier and more difficult than it looked in the movies.

Leaving the garage lights off, he opened the garage door and reversed the Landcruiser inside, then shut off the engine. He closed the garage door, then went around to the back of the vehicle and opened the rear doors. He spent a few minutes re-arranging the camping gear in the back and then, with great effort, managed to get the body in as well. He covered the tarp with camping gear and slammed the doors shut.

The sun was almost rising as he pulled the Land Cruiser out onto the road and started heading west. He had patched the broken glass pane in the back door of the house, retrieved the rest of his gear & maps and then locked up the house as he left. Now, as the tyres ate up the black roadway illuminated by the headlights, he had time to think, to plan. He blasted the air conditioner as cold as possible and tried to get his thoughts in order, to categorize options as 'workable' or 'not' and eliminate the unworkable. He was on the M4 approaching Penrith when he settled on a plan that was 'workable' in all elements.

He pulled off the freeway and made several turns, finally pulling into the car park of a giant Bunnings hardware store. Turning up his coat collar and settling a hat low over his eyes, he entered the store just as it was opening. He knew enough high school chemistry to understand that it would take weeks for acid to dissolve a human body, but his plan didn't need to dissolve the body, just make it unrecognizable. He bought several PET plastic tubs, aluminium foil, a selection of bricks & pavers, protective equipment and some pool chemicals. Now that he was committed, Mario's mental process was remarkably clear. He ticked off the items in his head, adding in the equipment he already had in his car, paid cash and then exited as calmly as he could.

The Land Cruiser crossed the Nepean River, climbed the steep ascent at Emu Plains and Mario mentally cancelled his planned breakfast at McDonald's. He just didn't feel like eating.

At each of the towns strung along the railway line through the Blue Mountains, he stopped in at pool shops to buy an extra drum of pool acid, paying cash and taking precautions to avoid CCTV without being noticeable. He spread out his purchases through several shops, just in case somebody tried to put together a trail of evidence. Traffic was slow, but he eventually reached Lithgow and dropped down off the Great Dividing Range, and out of mobile phone reception as well.

Steering with one hand, he turned off his phone, then wrapped it in several layers of aluminium foil to completely block any signals it might be displaying. Then he opened a metal .50 caliber ammunition box and stuffed the foil-wrapped phone inside. For anyone tracking his movements, or going back through the location data stored in the phone memory, there would be no indication as to where he had been since leaving Mt York.

He turned north off the Great Western Highway onto State Mine Road, heading deep into the Newnes State Forest. Heavily logged for decades following the collapse of the kerosene shale mining industry, this wilderness was crisscrossed with logging tracks, dirt bike ruts and fire trails. This maze of paths could disorient even an experienced local, but Mario wasn't interested in keeping track of his movements. He planned to find the most remote camping spot he could, do what had to be done and then head east until he hit State Mine Road again. It didn't matter where he got onto that road, he could just go south until he arrived back in Lithgow.

Six days later, Mario arrived back in Lithgow and ate breakfast at McDonald's, refueled the Land Cruiser and headed back towards home. He had unwrapped his phone on State Mine Road, leaving behind a burnt-out fire pit, some crushed grass but otherwise no indication that he had dismembered a body, burned off the fingerprints, face, tattoos, teeth & eyes in acid and then buried the remains under several layers of bricks to make sure the predators couldn't dig it up. He had done his best, and to the best of his ability, nobody would ever find the body or be able to tie him to it if they did.

Mario focused on these positive thoughts, and boosted his spirits even further by thinking about several kilograms of goat meat cooling in his Esky. Mario loved goat curry, made in his slow cooker, and several days' hunting had ensured he would be eating quality, free range, and organic meat for weeks.

Chapter 9

July

'I don't get it, homie' said Bilal's friend Mohammed. 'Why you wanna fight to bring Sharia law into this country? If you wanna live under Sharia, why not go to Iran or Dubai?'

'You don't understand' replied Bilal calmly. He was confident because this was one lesson that the Mullah had spent a lot of time on. He was educated now, his eyes opened to the reality that had been concealed, drowned out by the infidel distractions of television, internet and advertising.

'The whole world belongs to Allah, the whole world desires to be free to live according to his mercy. Some, many, may not know this, but subconsciously, they do. Sadly, many parts of it suffer darkness, blindness and the oppression of the infidel. But now, the balance is changing.'

'It makes no difference what the people in any land want. It is the will of Allah. The whole world will submit, and we will be the ones to do it. Inshallah'

Bilal took a sip of bottled water and went on to describe the Arab Spring sweeping across North Africa and the Middle East. Millions of believers freed from the yoke of colonial oppression, free to reject the sinful, sexualized advertising, the corrupt and extractive corporations, taxes that supported foreign invasions and regime changes that only suited the global elites. He spoke about corrupt Western governments stoking sectarian divisions and strife, maintaining factions that prevented nations from coming together in unity.

'For the first time in a thousand years, we have a chance to fill the whole world with praise to Allah.

'Shit bro' scowled Mohammed 'if it gets serious, it's not like Battlefield 4, you're dead. Ended.'

Bilal's smile widened and he stroked the thin, wispy beard that was starting to grow on his chin. 'And if Allah does take me on the field of battle, then what awaits the pure soul is truly better than our mortal minds can understand.'

Mohammed shook his head again. 'Life's good HERE, bro. Big risk - for what?'

'Yeah, life has been good – for the infidels. But what of the true Muslims? Harassed and targeted by police, Halal opposition, fascists, constantly accused of terrorism – it is truly evil to oppose an entire group of people based on the actions of a few. We must, all of us, make a stand against evil.'

'Besides, times are changing.' Bilal's voice had changed in the past few weeks, along with his speech. He rarely raised his voice any more, adopting the softer, more expressive tones of the Mullah and the Sheikhs. 'You been following the elections? The government is a mess, the people are upset, and this is the perfect time.'

'Perfect time for what?' asked Mohammed.

'Perfect time to fulfill our destiny!' preached Bilal quietly. 'To become princes in our own land. To make our own laws, collect our own taxes. To become the heads of our own families'

'Look around you, everywhere the peace of Allah is under attack from infidels. They control the economy, the military, the water and food supplies, the law, the media. Every day the media attacks us directly, calling us terrorists, promoting sin and corruption. There's more Muslims in prison than any other religion. Ask yourself, have you ever felt truly happy and free?'

Mohammed thought for a moment. 'Shit bro, I never… maybe…when I was little. But now, even with decent clothes, work, money, shit. I got what I thought I needed, what should make me happy. But no, I'm not happy.

Bilal nodded, 'That's exactly what I said when the Mullah asked me.'

'We never knew how badly our true way of life was under attack. They're just using us for our labor, taxing our money right out of our pay, before we even see any of it. And what do they do with our money? They give it to young women to have babies, they send soldiers to the Middle East to steal oil and opium. They pay judges to put us in prison – for what? Being Muslim? It's not right.'

Mohammed was beginning to agree that life wasn't as good as it appeared on the surface. 'But still, shit – starting a war? That's extreme, bro.'

'I'm not starting anything' retorted Bilal. 'THEY started it. They continue it, snooping in our homes using our own TVs and laptops, passing laws that make us guilty before we even did anything. We live in a comfortable injustice, a comfortable cage; but the comfort is failing every day, more and more people are waking up and realizing the prison we are all living in. We deserve to be able to live in this country, without living in a social prison.

'All we want is to live in the way we choose, just like everyone else wants to. But if the oppressor's hand weighs too heavily upon us, it is our duty to strike back, to kill, conquer and create a safe land, a sharia land.'

Mohammed shrugged again, and shook his head 'Fuck no. Crazy talk bro.'

Bilal recalled the words of the Mullah: 'If they will not hear immediately, do not push too hard. Plant a seed in their mind, and water it regularly, then when it grows, it will change their mind for them.' He decided to back off. Perhaps his old friends could be useful in other ways.

'OK, I get it' he held up his hands, palm out in appeasement. 'Forget it. Change the subject. You know when we played soccer, those hot/cold packs they used?'

Mohammed screwed up his eyes to help him think. 'Maybe.'

'The Mullah is starting a sports club, needs as many as he can get. So if you see some in the chemist, do me a favour and buy em?' Mohammed was glad that his friend was talking some sense now, hopefully getting involved in sports would channel his energy away from the religious stuff.

'Sure bro, my sister works at Priceline now, I'll see if she can hook you up with a carton.'

Bilal smiled. The Mullah and Deng would love that.

-

The next afternoon found Bilal back in the DIMO truck, waiting for access to another cruise liner at White Bay. As was his habit, he scrolled through his news feed, but paid more attention to the news headlines these days.

VIGILANTE VIOLENCE INCREASING

MUSLIM LEADERS DENY TERROR ACCUSATIONS, CALL FOR CALM

PM ANNOUNCES NEW JOBS INITIATIVE

He sensed that there was more to it than simple sensationalism, but all he knew was that he didn't know anything about psychology, propaganda or mass media. Shrugging, he flicked off his phone, closed his eyes and bent his mind in submission to something he could understand:

'In the name of God, the Gracious, the Merciful.
'Praise be to God, Lord of the Worlds.
'The Most Gracious, the Most Merciful
'Master of the Day of Judgement.
'It is You we worship, and upon You we call for Help.

'Guide us to the straight path.

He repeated the opening words of the Holy Scriptures, clearing his mind and calming his breathing. The peace and calm radiated from the words through his entire body, relaxing his muscles.

He opened his eyes just as the guard was waving them in, and the truck shuddered as Sargon started the engine. The same routine played out as it had several times earlier, however once the truck was unloaded Sargon said 'wait here, one minit, grabbed a daypack from behind the driver's seat and disappeared into the maze of shipping containers, forklifts and delivery trucks.

Bilal sat in the passenger seat and watched the commotion as tonnes of food, alcohol and supplies were shoveled into the ship. His interest was interrupted by Sargon's return, stuffing the bag back behind the driver's seat and getting the truck moving. Bilal gave no indication that he had noticed anything, and was relieved when Sargon asked 'Gym?' and their normal routine continued after the irregularity.

-

On Friday, Bilal's delivery schedule ended at the Lakemba Mosque for prayers. As the worshippers were milling around afterwards, the Melbourne Mullah found Sargon and Bilal and introduced them to another man, dressed the same in a clean white dishdasha with a small white *Taqiyah* – a prayer cap - on his head.

'Here are the two young lions I was telling you about,' he said, indicating Sargon and Bilal with a sweep of his hand. 'Sargon, Bilal, this is my old friend and associate, Sharik Eamal. We call him the Sydney Sheikh.'

The three men greeted each other formally and respectfully. Bilal looked at the Sheikh, sizing him up and trying to get a feel for where he fit into the community. He saw a tall, thin man with dark, freckled skin and black eyes which were studying him carefully. Then the Sheikh spoke fast, in a deep voice that resonated with authority.

'Very impressive. You young men are part of a great destiny, a calling. Very special.'

Bilal thought this sounded good, but wanted details. Everyone seemed to be talking about a great mission, but exactly what kind of greatness awaited them seemed to be vague.

The Sheikh must have sensed Bilal's thoughts, because he smiled warmly and clapped him on the shoulder. 'Soon, soon – all your questions will be answered. Inshallah, our descendants will write and sing of your deeds for generations to come.

And your family will be wealthy and powerful, long after Allah has received you into heaven.'

Now that was exactly what Bilal wanted to hear.

Chapter 10

August

'You've already passed a test that you are trustworthy, and know how to keep your mouth shut' intoned the Melbourne Mullah. 'Now you are required to be silent even to yourself. Nothing of what we are about to do can be whispered outside these walls. Inshallah, the success of our caliphate is surely won through our silence.'

His audience of five young men and Bilal were kneeling on the carpeted floor of the house just down from the mosque. Friday evening prayers had finished, and the latest batch of recruits were being given their first lessons.

'No phones, no email. The infidels invented those things and they know every word that is sent through them.' He went on, describing the Five Eyes and Carnivore programs that copied every electronic transmission from anywhere in the world, sifting for keywords and then filing it in the giant data warehouse in Utah. 'From now on, your phones will only be used as a weapon against the infidels.'

'You have been given a roster for the week of where you are to work, and where you are to learn.' Bilal looked at the sheet of paper; it reminded him of his High School class timetable – each day of the week was broken up into morning, day, evening and night – each delineated by the five-required prayer-times. For the current week, Bilal's schedule was like his regular work week – except for added prayer times. He felt angry, insulted to have been excluded from more glamorous things – religious or military training, logistics, anything but helping Sargon in the delivery route. He was about to say something, anything, when a new thought entered his brain, as if dropped from the throne of Allah in heaven itself.

It simply said, 'Is this another test?' The thought was so clear, sudden and sharp that it immediately cooled his rising anger.

Hmmm...What if it was? Another test of his patience and ability to keep his mouth shut? Bilal frowned and concentrated on the rest of the lesson.

The Mullah continued 'Stay off your phones at all times. Any time you are NOT doing your *Taqiyyua* - your normal job and tasks to deceive the infidel - your phone will be switched off and left in your bedroom. That will stop the infidels from listening or watching.'

One of the younger volunteers asked, 'but if the phone is off, how can they listen?' One of the other students nodded in agreement.

'Young fool, child' scolded the older man. 'The infidels built these phones so that even though they appear to be off, the camera and microphone can be turned on by remote control - even if the screen remains blank. You MUST assume they are ALWAYS listening, and watching through the camera. The same thing with any electronics - consoles, TVs, laptops. Anything with a microphone or camera, anything connected to the internet – you must be aware that these things are always watching, always listening. Their computers are always recording, indexing, snooping.'

Bilal felt ill. The things he had said while on the phone, or while playing his X-BOX ONE would be stored on the infidel's data servers. He thought about the gigabytes of porn on his laptop and felt even worse. He would have to smash it, burn it and buy a new, clean one. Start a new online identity. He hoped that these new ideas for keeping secrets, tested and proven all over the world, would help in his own business plans, as well as his Holy Jihad.

'Now, nobody can survive in society without a phone, and a young man without a phone will immediately raise suspicion. So, get a decoy phone, one you take with you any time you are not on jihad training. Make sure it is different, so you can tell the difference. The punishment for losing them or getting them mixed up will be severe.'

'Email,' continued the Mullah. 'Any instructions or information will never, ever be sent by email, as every email is automatically saved, scanned and filed by the spy agencies.'

The group was shown how to log in to web-based email servers, using the 'draft' folder to leave and receive messages from operatives around the globe, logging in with the same credentials, then changing the password according to pre-arranged schedules. By saving a message into 'draft', the next operative could read it and delete it without ever sending it through an email server.

'Remember, above all' said the teacher. 'We use the enemy's technology against him. Just because smart phones track your location wherever you are – even if they are switched off – does not mean we cannot use them as a weapon. In 2007, we hid some army rocket launchers in the Royal National Park, but do you think we went straight to the location? NO!'

'Instead, everyone left their phones with a decoy. He walked around in circles for an hour, while the others took the weapons further on, and buried them safely. Surely, when the police arrested everyone and examined the phones, they dug holes in the park for weeks but found nothing! Because they were digging where the decoy walked, not in the true hiding place! Nobody could be charged because there was no evidence!' His laugh filled the room and Bilal with hope. Truly, this man was wise and experienced.

The students nodded, understanding the lesson. Every technology had both advantages and disadvantages to the operator, and the tables could be turned if one understood the implications.

The rest of the evening passed with instruction in Arabic, codes, counter-surveillance and operating the radio. Of the group, Bilal knew the most about computers so he was asked to set up social media accounts for the Mullah, and begin ramping up a propaganda campaign to gather and educate followers.

Before they left, the Mullah passed each of them a plain envelope stuffed with $50 and $20 notes. 'This is to help you buy a copy of the Noble Quran, pious clothes and halal food. Make sure you clean it properly before you use it' he added, referring to laundering the money.

As a group, they went to the local RSL club and each put over two thousand dollars into the electric poker machines, then immediately pressed the button for a payout, making sure they avoided the other buttons because they considered gambling a sin. The machines printed a ticket, which they took to the cashier and got their money back, with a receipt. They filed their receipts carefully to justify their income to any government tax or investigative agency that came sniffing around. In this way, foreign funds were made legal inside the country, and used to fund the growing security and recruitment efforts of the Caliphate.

During one of the earliest lessons, Bilal had asked the Mullah where the money came from, and how it got into the country. The Mullah smiled graciously and complimented Bilal on his curiosity and quick learning.

'Hawala,' he began. 'Truly, there is only one true currency. There is only one basic, fundamental measure of value. It is trust, honor. A man may own much property but without honor, nobody will befriend him or do business with him.'

'But we do need to use symbols of value, money, currency to carry out trade around the world. Money, gold, computer symbols – all these occupy a different level, a much lower level, to the trust and honor that a man has in his own community.'

'There are many people who wish to see our efforts succeed. While many of them are very poor, there are some who are very wealthy and have been blessed by Allah the merciful. These men are happy to provide funds for our cause, and it uses the Hawala system.'

Bilal's confused look encouraged him to continue. 'Hawala is a network of brokers all over the world. Some of them operate inside the formal banking system, but many of them are traders, merchants and the like, in every city and town all over the world. You will find a Hawala dealer or sub-dealer in every Mosque in the world.

'So, let us say that a wealthy man in Geneva wishes to send you money' he went on, pointing at Bilal. He sends you a message with the amount of money in your local currency, the details of the broker, and a password. This can be done over the phone, by mail, by courier, any way you like. Most of the transfers I use are done on the Gmail account, saved as a draft but never sent.'

'So you go into the Hawala dealer, and you give him the password and the amount of money you need, and he hands it over. Very simple, but you need to be able to explain the money to the kaffir officials, so we use their own systems of gambling and sin to make it legal in their eyes.'

Bilal understood the process now, but it still didn't make sense. 'But how does the Geneva man know that the local man won't rip him off?'

The Mullah laughed. 'That is the basis of the whole lesson. The world is ruled by trust, and every Hawala dealer is a trustworthy member of the community, with many connections. Can you imagine to a dealer once word got out that he was a cheat?'

'What would you do if you were cheated by a Hawala dealer?'

Bilal thought about it for less than a second, the answer was already moving off his tongue. 'I'd kill the ffff….. dealer.' He stammered, acutely aware and embarrassed that his emotions had boiled up for a second. He knew the Mullah would not tolerate curse words or swearing – they were as *haram* – forbidden – as alcohol or gambling.

The Mullah shrugged, 'That may be a lesser punishment than being an outcast. Once broken, trust can never be established again.' He shook his head. 'It is not like this government, who makes agreements and then breaks them at will. They get away with it because they do not know the people who they are harming. Small business owners, families, and babies - the unjust system only exists because it is an extremely wealthy and disconnected society.

'Once the oil supply slows and the economy crashes, everyone will need to develop trust with their neighbors again. And where neighbors trust each other, it is difficult for a foreigner to impose his will upon them, for they will fight for each other, their clan, against the invader.'

Waiting for his friends at the Westfields Food Court, Bilal was scrolling through his phone, searching for a car to buy. Mister Mohammed was paying him in cash every week for the delivery run, and he was also laundering several thousand dollars per month from the Melbourne Mullah. With only his mobile phone bill, clothes and jewelry to spend money on, he had rapidly saved up almost twenty thousand dollars. For a young man in Sydney, the next logical step was to buy a suitable set of wheels.

In seventeen years, a high proportion of his waking hours had been spent reading about, talking about, arguing about and working on cars – the faster the better. He had routinely passed hours with his friends, arguing over minor details that made one vehicle superior to another. He knew that he would love to drive a Ferrari, but that wasn't going to be happening immediately. One day, but not right now.

He looked at a couple of cars, mentally comparing them to the various 'ideal' cars that he had argued with his friends about. He knew his price range excluded anything over about $25,000 – he didn't just have to pay for the car but there was also registration, insurance – even with his mother's disabled pensioner discount, it all added up.

He had narrowed down a short list, regretfully excluding nice cars that were in other states or out of his price range when his eyes fell on a yellow Mitsubishi EVO III. Sure, it was 10 years old and had done 100,000km but it was perfect: Dandelion Yellow, black interior with a 2.0l turbo intercooled engine. Factory tint, heavy suspension and 17-inch alloy wheels – his eyes ran down the list of features, absorbing the details and making comparisons, judgments and evaluations.

Bilal heard his friends approach across the food court before he raised his eyes and saw them. Joking, laughing, shoving each other and generally being as obnoxious as teenagers could possibly be. They collapsed into the other 3 chairs at Bilal's table and greeted each other with the usual insults and penis jokes.

'Are we even eatin?' asked Victor. 'I not hungry.'

'Not yet' said Bilal. 'I'm thinking of buying a car.'

'You're a dick' said Mahmoud reflexively. 'You'll pay too much'

'Fuck you' retorted Bilal. 'You haven't even seen what I'm lookin' at.'

He put the phone on the table and the others flicked through the details, looking at the pictures.

'Looks neat bro' said Ibby. 'You need to change the rims though. My cousin can hook you up.'

'It's too much car for you' Mahmoud went on. 'You can't even control that kinda power.'

'Piss off' said Bilal. 'You haven't even got your Ls, and I beat you on Grand Turismo every time.'

'Asshole' said Mahmoud. 'It's not the same.'

'Fuck you' returned Bilal. 'Even my sister can beat your high score'

Chapter 11

September

The Chief Justice's hour-long statement was cut down to just 15 seconds for the TV news. A 3-month Federal inquiry into Islam and its place in Australia was under way.

'We welcome all submissions into this Inquiry, however we must insist that only submissions that comply with the terms of reference will be considered.'

The declaration flashed like a bolt of lightning across the country, electrifying and dividing communities, suburbs and families. The talking heads on TV immediately began speculating on what the effect would be – on tax policy, foreign affairs - possibly even domestic unrest.

Facebook memes began hitting news feeds, pushing every angle from anti-immigration to anti-islamophobia.

The PM scheduled a press conference at 4.00pm – leaving all the media organizations plenty of time to spin the story right for the 5pm news. In front of Parliament house, surrounded by cheering crowds, the PM played to the cameras and the electorate.

'I welcome the clarification that this inquiry will deliver' she said smoothly. 'For too long, this country has been subject to pressures from all sides. A minority who refuse to integrate into our culture, and an even smaller minority who act with violence against us.

'Rather than helping clarify, the media has unfortunately played to hysteria and fear mongering. This inquest will help bring facts and impartiality to the debate, using a proven and independent system which has effectively delivered the same results in other situations.

'I call on every observer and participant to avoid extreme language, and to work with us all to find a common ground.'

The crowds cheered, then she went on.

'There is not, cannot be any racism in this decision, or the inquiry that it activates. Racism is discrimination based on a person's race, their genetic history. This is illegal in Australia and unacceptable in our society. Islam welcomes members from all races, therefore it is not a race, so there can be no racism.'

'I am also announcing the establishment of a formal Halal authority, with a ten-member board − half of which will be comprised of government employees, the rest will be open to anyone who wishes to apply, and applications will be assessed on merit. Any current Halal certifications will expire on 31 December of this year, and from that date only the official government halal certification will be accepted. This independent monitor will ensure that Halal certification is applied correctly, and the funds from certification will be invested in health care, education and infrastructure.'

'These steps bring clarity and oversight to the issues, and will help unite all Australians under Australian law and Australian values. Thank you all.'

'Prime Minister' called out the TV anchor for Channel 7, raising her hand to ask a question. 'Are there any concerns of protest or violence because of this ban on Islam?'

The PM's face became stern as she glared directly into the cameras. 'We are NOT banning anything' she declared. 'Anyone caught committing acts of violence or vandalism will be arrested and punished − regardless of their race, nationality or religion. Nobody is above the law.'

While playing the part for the media circus, she was privately thinking 'I fucken hope this works. If this doesn't cause a riot, and give us an excuse to clamp down and sweep up some intel, I don't know what will.'

Next it was a question from SBS: 'Prime Minister, will the government be providing counseling services to anyone who might feel upset by this inquiry?'

The PM laughed. 'No. Anyone is welcome to read the terms of reference and lodge a submission. The government is not responsible for hurt feelings.'

A few more questions, and the press conference was ended.

The effect was more dramatic than anyone could have imagined.

Within an hour, angry crowds had filled the streets around several mosques, not only in Sydney but smaller protests also took place in every capital city and some larger country towns like Bendigo and Young. In Lakemba, crowds of ten to twenty thousand were spread out below the TV helicopters, broadcasting a bird's eye view of the surging mass of humanity, united in outrage.

The warm weather normally drew people out of their houses anyway, to eat and socialize once the sun went down. But the news of the day – spun and twisted by a thousand different rumours into anything from Islam being banned to Muslims being deported – and every shade of rumor in between – swirled through the crowds. The Mullah had been expecting something like this and he was ready, rehearsed and prepared to deliver the most shocking news the country had ever heard.

Bilal had been managing an extensive social media presence since he began following the Mullah, and their Facebook, Twitter and Instagram accounts each had thousands of followers, including dozens of reporters for all the major news networks.

An update was immediately posted: 'Important - Mullah will make major announcement, FB Live in 10 min.'

This circulated faster than a wildfire, with followers sharing updates to friends who weren't necessarily following the Mullah, by the time the Mullah's live stream started, their following had almost doubled.

Bilal followed the Mullah up the tight, twisting stairwell inside the spire that rose high above the domed roof of the

Mosque. The Mullah set an incredibly fast pace, rushing ahead of him and Bilal's heart was pounding by the time they reached the landing.

Bilal's head swam as his eyes took in the view over Western Sydney from their vantage point, but he had no time to appreciate it. The Mullah looked over the simple PA system that the Muezzin used to broadcast the call to prayer, flicked it on and picked up the microphone.

Bilal took the Mullah's phone, and pulled out his own. He quickly logged in the Mullah's phone to their Facebook account, and turned on his own phone's video recorder so they would have a HD version as well. Stepping out onto the curved balcony that ran around the outside of the spire, Bilal confirmed that the Facebook Live video was streaming, looked at the Mullah to check he was ready, and nodded. They were live and recording.

The Mullah raised the microphone to just below his mouth, took a deep breath and gazed directly into the cameras.

'Allahu Ackbar!'

As his voice was amplified and broadcast out across the entire suburb, the surging crowds became still. People within visual range and earshot looked towards the spire, while thousands elsewhere clustered around glowing screens as they watched the live feed.

'Brothers and Sisters, Fathers and Children, Muslims! Hear Me!'

The Mullah paused in between each phrase, almost as if he was reading poetry. This gave the listener's time to process what he was saying.

'In the name of Allah, the Merciful, the All-Powerful,
and in the name of his servant,
Muhammed bin Nayef,
King of Saudi Arabia –
direct descendent of Muhammed and Protector of the Holy Shrines,

I bring great news of freedom to you all!'

'You have heard the words of the Australian Government.
They have declared that, according to their understanding, Islam is not a
religion. We accept this.
'We do not expect them to understand. We do not live according to
THEIR understanding!'
'We declare that there is only one God, and Mohammed is his prophet.
'Truly all the world belongs to Allah, although much is still shrouded in
darkness, sin and ignorance. Worship of Allah is the light that brings
peace and guidance.
'Will we respond in anger, to these insults from unbelievers? We will
not.
'That would only give them an excuse to further harm us and restrict us,
to spy on us and jail our sons and daughter. NO! We will not.
'Instead, I declare a Caliphate. A holy land. Our. Holy. Land.
'I declare that the suburbs from Campsie to Bankstown — all the land
between the Cooks River and the Georges River, all these lands
inhabited by Muslims are now separate. Holy. Free!
'I declare that the Australian Government has no power, authority or
jurisdiction in this Caliphate. Under the wise rulership of our Caliph,
all Muslims will live safely and peacefully, following the divine guidance
in the Sharia.
'Rejoice, brothers and sisters. Celebrate this day when we all unite to
protect our families, our businesses and our futures.
'I declare my allegiance to Muhammed bin Nayef, my Caliph.
'In the name of Allah, I ask you to do the same'
'Allah Ackbar'

The Mullah flicked off the microphone and Bilal cut the Live
feed, then the video recording. As he turned back to the Mullah
he heard the noise of the crowd cheering, rising like a storm
wind rushing through a forest of trees. Car horns honked all
over the city as Muslims began to celebrate.

Bilal finally had time to gaze out across the dome of the mosque, the crowds thronging the car park, the streets around and in the yards of all the surrounding houses.

He saw a sea of upturned faces, reflecting the light. He couldn't pick out individual people, but he felt surges of emotions wash over him as he saw and heard the singing, the dancing, the cheering of his people.

Bilal knew that they were all in uncharted territory. He felt immense pride that he had been selected to play such an important role in the declaration. He felt like a liberator, standing on a palace balcony as the people celebrated the end of a terrible war.

But he also knew that the war was only just beginning. He was impressed at the Mullah's choice of words – carefully avoiding any mention of jihad, guiding people away from violence and leaving open the option of negotiation with the authorities.

Would they get away with it? The Mullah had told him about the creation of Israel in 1948, brought into existence with the stroke of a pen – but only after decades of warfare by Jews against the British authorities.

But there was no internet in 1948, no social media; no politicians beholden to opinion polls and minority protest groups. There had been no oil wealth either, and Bilal knew that if the British had tried something similar in 2017, the results would have been very different.

Right there, standing beside the Mullah, Bilal decided he would dedicate his life to the Caliph. If the Caliphate succeeded, he would be powerful beyond his wildest dreams and if it failed, he would be better off dead.

Ever hungry for a controversial story, the Mullah's announcement exploded across the mainstream media outlets like a cow falling into a river full of piranha.

The news and media frenzy rapidly assembled a variety of characters to interview, from hardliner hate preachers calling for retaliation against racism and discrimination to tax accountants speculating on the effect on government spending. Daily TV pseudo-news 'infotainment' shows all had a 'moderate Muslim' on their panel of 'experts', all cut from the same cloth as the original. This particular host, Yusuf, was furiously trying to maintain a centrist position, being accused of apostasy from one side, yet worried about upsetting the producer's lefty ideology if he spoke out angrily against the government's position.

Sweat was beading on his brow as he shared the screen with the Sydney Sheikh.

'Let me clarify' he sputtered, sensing the danger he was in from the lunatic fringe. 'I'm not saying this is okay, at all. I'm not saying the government is right. What I'm saying is that the government has the right to form an opinion, and we all have the right to disagree with that opinion. If we want to…'

The Sydney Sheik glared back, breathing heavily as he tried to convey his anger at both the situation and this infidel-collaborating weasel. 'NO, NO!' he thundered. 'This is an unacceptable insult. Understand, we cannot, will not sit quietly under these conditions. Every Muslim has been slandered…'

The TV host knew he had no comeback but that his work was largely done, creating a sensation and boosting ratings. He wasn't paid – extremely well paid - to advance the cause of Islam in Australia, or convince the extremists to become moderate – his job for the TV station was simple – boost ratings while maintaining the left's ideology of consumerism, celebrity worship, feminization and superficialities. Serious debate and critical thinking were to be avoided at all costs.

Cutting off his guest, the host smoothly turned away, looked into the alternate camera and said lightly 'now, let's go to Amanda with the latest weather…'

The TV cut away from the Sheik in mid-sentence.

The only words transmitted to the control room, which were then edited out by the show's producers, were 'you will shortly see…'

–

Three days later, Senior Constable Zelinski and Constable Connor were setting up a speed trap on the Hume Highway when the radio called them to investigate a report of armed robbery in progress at a bank in Chapel Road – right in the middle of Bankstown. The lights and siren lit up and parted traffic as they raced their V8 Commodore through the narrow streets towards the Caliphate.

They slowed down to navigate some left and right turns, then the car came to a screeching halt as a small group of men blocked the road. SC Zelinski hit the siren again and hooted the horn but instead of clearing the road, the men surrounded the car, shaking their heads, holding out their hands, palm down in a sign that the car should stop.

The two cops glanced at each other, knowing what the other was thinking and understanding immediately that it wasn't good. If somebody got hurt today, they knew very clearly that they would be hung out to dry by the politically correct police hierarchy and crucified by the media. This was a no-win situation.

This was a minefield that nobody wanted to touch, yet the police were duty bound to follow orders and investigate a crime in progress.

One of the men approached the driver's door as the others stood in front of the car, waving their hands in a gesture that clearly meant 'go away'.

SC Zelinski spoke first. 'Sir, please clear the road. We are on urgent police business.'

'No, no, no' said the man lazily. He eyed both cops in their seats, then looked in the rest of the car before continuing. 'You go, no come here. We handle it.'

Zelinski heard the radio chirp with the operator asking if they were at the bank yet. He tried to remain calm. 'Sir, if you do not clear the road, you may be charged with hindering a police investigation…'

'No, no' said the man again, lazily shaking his head. 'This is an Islamic area now, no police. If dere is a crime, we will handle it. You, go. No come again.'

Shit, shit, shit. Connor got on the radio and asked for advice. There was no room to go around the group of men in the road, not enough space to run them over and still get away – and besides, that would only cause more trouble – neither cop wanted to be the ones that triggered an uprising in an already tense environment.

The idling police car in the road was attracting more and more people, coming out of the homes in the street to watch, surrounding the car with a shimmering tide that was both curious and threatening at the same time. Several people were filming the incident on their phones.

The radio operator advised them that they were to avoid conflict at all costs, reverse and try a different street to get to the bank. Zelinski looked at Connor and saw Connor looking at him with a set, taut expression on his face. Neither police officer moved a muscle, but they both knew that the other was thinking. Unwritten orders had gone around their police station – a directive right from the very top – that minorities and immigrants were to be treated with exceptional tolerance and awareness of cultural differences.

Neither of them wanted to be accused of stepping out of line. It would cost them their jobs and they would be utterly demonized in the press – trial by media was becoming the most popular form of police discipline for simple reasons: deniability from upper ranks, it was cheap and extremely effective. Any officer subject to media scrutiny immediately had their entire family reading all the comments on social media, instantly. Nobody was safe, and it not only affected the officers involved, it destroyed families as well.

Zelinski swallowed the hard lump in his throat, turned to the man outside his window and said slowly and clearly 'OKAY, we go. Please let us reverse,' jerking his thumb towards the rear of the car as he shifted the lever into R. The white reversing lights came on and both cops breathed a sigh of relief as the bystanders parted, allowing them to slowly reverse away. Connor turned off the lights and updated the radio operator that they had de-escalated and were trying a different route.

Both cops breathed a huge sigh of relief as the car was permitted to do a 3-point turn and leave the area, making a left at the next side street.

They turned left again, parallel to the blocked street, only to have the same thing happen again. It was obvious that word was spreading via text message and every communication medium that the cops were to be kept out of the area and everyone knew what to do, blocking the roads in crowds.

'Fuck it' said Zelinski. 'We're never going to get in. Every street is full of people'

Connor grunted in agreement. 'It's like a scene from Black Hawk Down. They're all on welfare, so they don't need to work, just sit home all day and get in our way.'

'Enough' barked Zelinski, the pressure of their predicament getting to him. 'Nothing we can do about it, no use getting a black mark on your record for being racist. Just focus on the job...' his voice trailed off as he wove the car through traffic and onto Stacey Street. The main road was still open to traffic – for now, but very slow.

Ten minutes later, the police car finally pulled up outside the bank and the two officers discovered that the thieves had gotten clean away while they were tied up in the suburban streets.

-

Fernand Maurice von Rothschild was in an unusually happy mood. A short, thin man with equally thinning white hair, a hatchet face and sunken, beady eyes, this was a marked change from his usual dour self. He danced around his spacious Vienna apartment with moves that resembled a jig, clapping his hands and chanting 'haha, haha' in excitement.

Fernand von Rothschild's story was not a sad one, but not an overly happy one either, considering his family line. Born in 1930 to one of the household maids, the illegitimate second son of Maurice Edmond Karl de Rothschild had been discreetly hidden away, educated at boarding school but firmly kept at a prudent social distance from the main Rothschild dynasty.

For over thirty years, Fernand watched from afar as his older brother Edmond inherited the family fortune from their father, who had served in the French Senate before dying in 1957 at age 76. Devoid of grief for a father he never knew, Fernand was instead consumed with jealousy as he saw his half-brother grow the family fortune beyond anything imagined by their parents, accumulating global power that culminated in him joining the Bilderberg Group Steering Committee.

Fernand accumulated a tidy fortune himself, cultivating many contacts in his family's social and business circles, working the system like any dedicated salesman – doing favors, offering opportunities and connecting investors with those who needed finance. Like the rest of his banking family, there was no moral limit to the business opportunities he financed – infrastructure development, drugs, even localized wars – but he was never able to reach the scale of his half-brother or cousins, the London Rothschilds.

When his rival died in 1997, Fernand's black emotions did not lighten. Years, decades of living in the shadows had taken their toll on his personality, leaving him permanently jaded, cynical - a human vulture.

Among the top names on the list of people he despised were the House of Saud, mostly the current king, Muhammed bin Nayef. Jacob Rothschild, King Nayef and George Soros often collaborated on the most profitable projects, and no matter how hard he tried, Fernand constantly found himself subtly frozen out of the deals. He felt it was like an invisible wall, a force field that his money, connections and effort simply could not penetrate.

He took it as a personal insult. And the feelings didn't dissipate with age, they grew stronger. By 2016, he had begun toying with his enemies from a distance. Supporting opponents of their plans, betting against and then sabotaging some projects, profiting financially and emotionally when the elites took losses.

And earlier this morning, he had a working breakfast with two contacts in his favorite eating place, the Justice Ministry Canteen. The hour-long meeting began at 7.00am when the facility opened, and the morning rush of lawyers, politicians, lobbyists and media whores ensured that the conversation, huddled together over some of the best coffee available in Europe, went undetected and unreported.

Fernand said very little, as the other two men reported on their findings. Efficient gatekeepers of information, Fernand paid them well to keep him informed of where the tides and rivers of money were flowing. In turn, the informers trusted

Fernand to never act rashly, so they couldn't be identified as the source of his information. Investing the money, he paid them in accordance with his advice had increased their wealth considerably, and all were keenly aware of the mutual benefits they created.

It was a business arrangement replicated a thousand times in every country, since the dawn of commerce. Money flowed to where it was treated well, and there were many people getting wealthy from following the money.

But the story that energized the elderly investor was not about money. It was about people. Two people. People whose names burned in his mind and his heart. George Soros and Mohammed Nayef.

The story of the imminent collapse of the Saudi economy, and George's offer to the King was absorbed by Fernand's brain without a flicker of emotion on his face or anywhere else on his body. As far as his colleagues were concerned, he reacted as if they had simply told him last week's interest rates. A major shift in geopolitical influence didn't concern Fernand at all, after all – he had profited from many of them over the past decades.

Only when the meeting was over, and he was safely back inside his apartment, did the old man release his emotions.

'So, the old pretender is bailing out while the going's good!' He cackled to himself as his brain ran through countless options, weighing investment opportunities, alternatives, resources required and return on investment.

'And George is helping him move to Australia…they will own the country in two years…less…'

Bringing his emotions under control, he sat at a large wooden desk beneath the open windows and quickly made several notes on a sheet of paper. Then he picked up the phone and dialed a series of brokers, bankers and associates, giving instructions to alter his investments to take advantage of the coming chaos in the Gulf.

It was during the last phone call, that the true genius hit him. He ended the call, lurched out of the chair and danced around the room in glee at what had to be the best idea of his life.

So much revenge to be had.

'Hah, you want to slink away to a neutral country? Like RATS leaving a ship?' His voice shook as his brain fitted more pieces together, taking a simple idea – sabotage the Caliphate – and refining it, adding actions and consequences, anticipating how the various actors would react, how the people and the media might be manipulated.

He picked up the phone and dialed again, this time to an intermediary he had never met. 'Yes? I need to meet with Viktor... Good.'

The intermediary was an agent for Viktor Bout, the code name for several arms dealers, mercenaries and similar problem-solvers for those who worked behind the scenes. The basis for the main character in the film 'Lord of War', one of the group had been famously arrested in Thailand in 2008, and was currently in prison in America.

But the rest were still operational. And willing to intervene – violently – in foreign affairs. Particularly when so much profit could be made if you knew which way the stock markets were likely to react to such events. Even better for those few people who initiated opportunities, rather than merely taking advantage once they had happened, the profits to be made exceeded those of the herd many times over.

Six hours later, a nondescript Mercedes pulled into the garage under the block of apartments and parked in the second car space of Fernand's unit. The driver got out of the car, pulled a wide-brimmed hat tighter on his head to conceal his face from any observers or CCTV and took the elevator to the top floor. Responding to a triple knock on the apartment door, Fernand opened it and let in his guest, inviting him to sit on one of the two ancient leather couches that faced each other over an antique French coffee table.

Fernand and 'Victor' sat and assessed each other silently across the table for a moment, then Fernand began his briefing. Leaving out very few of the details or people involved, he sketched out the requirements for a job he wanted done.

'Sydney, Australia. Has high social tensions around immigrants. The media constantly hypes up a fear of terrorism. Certain... investors are making a play into the market and while I cannot intervene directly, I want to turn the people against it. By playing on the social tensions and moral panic...'

The other man, tall and stocky with a deeply tanned face under a number 2 haircut nodded, squinting his blue eyes as he did his own mental arithmetic.

'We could bring down an airliner very simply, very cheap' he offered.

His employer shook his head. 'No, not airlines. My investments are already struggling with the cost of jet fuel, another crisis isn't desirable at all.'

'You want to turn the population against them?' The mercenary gave his assessment. 'How about a train bombing? That would shut down public transport for days, bring in draconian civil liberty restrictions... all kinds of consequences.'

The older man wagged his head from side to side as he weighed up the options, alternatives and consequences.

'Not a train line, because reconstruction is very easy. Something more substantial, that we can make real profit from rebuilding. A shopping mall...?'

The mercenary nodded. 'We've done it before, seven men, five vans. Bombs outside, going off once the gunmen get inside. It will be even more horrific in Australia because the paramedics aren't allowed to help people until the location is declared safe. So, the news crews can film people dying in agony, live on TV. Very visceral.'

'You'll get everything you need from the human panic, plus bidding rights for reconstruction afterwards.'

The older man nodded. 'Done. Half now, half on completion, as usual?' he asked.

'Actually, could I request a change from the usual? As a favor?' asked the mercenary. 'The payment terms can stay the same, just change the method to Bitcoins?'

'Of course,' said the older man, nodding. 'Everyone is trading in Bitcoin these days. Happy to oblige.'

'Da, good. Then goodnight' said the younger warfighter, as he rose and moved to the door. The two men shook hands, and then Fernand let him out into the hall, and closed the apartment door behind him.

He never knew or learned that he had just handed George a gift, instead of a poison pill. Turning the population against the Caliphate was exactly what George was hoping to achieve, and Fernand's actions would seal the fate of the Caliphate without anyone being able to link George to it.

Chapter 12

October

Castle Towers Shopping Centre

One of Australia's largest shopping centers sits in the hills in Sydney's North West. Topped by several levels of parking, capable of holding over 6,000 vehicles, it boasts three levels of shops, restaurants and a cinema - over one hundred thousand square meters of retail shopping space.

The cinema itself is on ground level, above two floors of parking, and adjacent to an outdoor Piazza, containing two levels of restaurants, a fountain and extensive outdoor seating. Most shoppers park inside the giant parking garages, then use the entry foyers housing escalators and travellators to move inside the shopping center.

One of the few exceptions is the Piazza – this open area allows pedestrians to walk from the street, into the shopping center near the cinema, then a right-hand turn leads to the main shopping levels, and another food court. It was just after dark, and the food court was packed with shoppers eating dinner.

This was the path Con had taken. Almost six-foot-tall, he was somewhat overweight, but his tracksuit and baseball cap exaggerated the effect, making him seem larger and more intimidating. He could offset the effect when necessary with a wide, open smile that gave him the appearance of a harmless goofball, and this came in quite handy as he could switch on the menace as required, although he usually only had to do it once, if one of his customers couldn't pay for the drugs they had bought.

If the menace wasn't enough, he normally only had to show the chump a glimpse of the Glock pistol he carried to motivate them to pay up. He had bought the 9mm Glock several years ago, after he tried to apply for his pistol license. Since he had no criminal record, he figured it would be the same as getting a driver's license – fill in some forms, maybe do a safety course, buy pistol.

So, he went to Terrey Hills and spoke to the man at the gun shop.

'Sure, I can help you buy a pistol' he had chuckled. 'First you have to join a pistol club. Some of them let you join right away, sometimes there is a waiting period until they get a minimum number of applicants.

'Then you attend a pistol handling course at the club. You get a certificate of completion.

'Send your certificate and license application in to the registry, and wait for them to send you a probationary license.

'You must then participate in three competitions at the pistol club, under supervision. Once you've completed the competitions you send the certificate to the registry and wait.'

Con's head was spinning already, but the man went on.

'Six months from the date of your probationary license, having completed the course and competitions you can then apply for a Permit to Acquire a pistol of your own. This has a further 28 day waiting period before the PTA is issued.

'You bring that PTA in here, and you can buy your pistol.'

Con shook his head and left the shop. He knew a friend of a friend who had imported over 200 pistols in their component pieces through Sylvania Post Office, so he made a few phone calls and within 24 hours had a brand new 9mm Glock in his pants pocket.

Unfortunately for Con, this importer was discovered and arrested shortly afterwards, so he had to buy an additional magazine from another contact. He was very pleased with the extra mag, since it ironically been intended for the NSW Police force, as they moved from revolvers to semi-automatics. An entire container of 1,500 Glocks had simply disappeared from the docks, directly into the black market where they were used to protect and enforce the ever-shifting territories in the drug war. Con loved the idea of using genuine police equipment to enforce his criminal activities.

Although Con knew basically how to use it, and had fired it a few times when he first got it, just to check it out and get a feel for it, he had never had to kill anyone with it – which was fine with him. If his business could operate with just the threat of violence, that was okay.

Saturday evening was one of the busiest times for the shopping center, and after buying a kebab with extra tabbouleh, it took several minutes of wandering around to find an empty seat. Finally, he could enjoy his meal while waiting for one of his suppliers to turn up. He flicked through the news feed on his phone while he ate.

UNEMPLOYMENT RATE AMONG NEW MIGRANTS DOUBLES

WHAT FILTHY TENANTS LEAVE BEHIND

TRUMP BACKTRACKS ON DEAL WITH AUSTRALIA

Con liked meeting in crowded public places like this. Even though there were few exits, the sheer volume of people made it very secure. Nobody would be able to overhear their conversation, and switching backpacks was a simple matter of dropping them under the table, then grabbing the opposite one when it was time to leave. His bag with the drugs, the supplier's bag with the cash.

It was a familiar routine he had used many times in the past, the only difference being the contents of the supplies. His customers' needs varied, from steroids, to Viagra, cocaine and heroin. He also did a small business in distributing tax free cigarettes, either stolen goods from Australia or imported through the wide, sandy borders.

Con had almost finished his kebab when he heard a series of loud explosions and the building trembled and shook as if it was about to come apart. Anyone standing was tossed to the ground in a screaming tangle of arms, legs, spilled food and smashed crockery. Screaming noises filled the air as fear spread like a virus through the crowd.

'What WAS that?' shouted several people nearby. Heads bobbed around as people began to panic.

'Was that a bomb?' Voices rose and overlapped.

'Shush. That's not funny.'

'I'm serious. Was that a BOMB?' the looks on faces turned from confusion to deadly fear.

People all around started scrambling to their feet, looking for a safe place.

Con looked around and saw absolute pandemonium as families, shoppers and staff began to run in every direction, knocking each other over in a desperate race to get to the exit near the cinemas, or running the other way, deeper into the shopping complex.

Con started to move towards the cinema, trying to get out of the cramped food court table maze, staying as close to the wall as possible to avoid being trampled, when over the screaming crowd he heard a noise that was unmistakable, the loud, metallic sound of an AK-47 firing short bursts on full auto.

BANG BANG BANG BANG.
Pause.
BANG BANG BANG BANG BANG
Pause
BANG BANG BANG BANG BANG

Con looked to his right and saw the shooter standing near the escalators on the opposite side of the food court, firing point blank into the crowds of people in the area. Bodies fell to the floor, some shot, some taking cover, all of them tripping over anyone who was still running. Dark blood pooled on the floor around the bodies, but Con's eyes locked on the attacker as if by magic.

Dressed all in black, with a black cloth hood covering most of the face, it was impossible to tell if it was a man or a woman. Con's brain stopped taking in more information, as without being aware of it, he instinctively drew the pistol and pushed his arm out in front of him, towards the black figure across the room. Time seemed to slow as his dominant eye naturally settled on the front sight, and his vision appeared to narrow to just what was around it. As the sight moved through the air, he saw the gunman swinging the rifle to the right, away from Con and towards the shoppers on the far side of the shopping level.

Con fired twice, and blew two smoking holes in the plastic ATM cover, several meters behind the attacker.

'Shit' he said aloud, head reeling as his body dumped adrenaline into his bloodstream. He didn't know it, but his fine motor skills were reduced, his heart rate slowed as his fight-or-flight responses primed his body for combat. Time and motion slowed as if he was underwater.

Alerted by the unexpected shots, the attacker swung the barrel back to the left, stepping back with their left foot to keep the rifle butt securely against their right shoulder. Con dropped to one knee and fired three times more – his second and third shots hitting the attacker in the chest and neck.

The black figure dropped like a string had been cut. Instantly, people started scrambling up off the floor, crawling, running, moving left, through the shops towards the exit near the cinema.

Ears ringing from the shots fired inside the enclosed space, Con jostled past the tables and forced his jelly legs to work.

Brain spinning, hands shaking, Con moved with them until the crushing crowd came to a screaming, bleeding halt. Another black-clad figure blocked the exit, swinging another blazing rifle back and forth like a hose. Tripping over a body on the floor, Con lunged left, cushioning his fall by sliding down the glass shop window at the side of the crowd. Lying on the floor, he pushed the Glock out in front again, lined up the shooter and fired twice more. At the second shot, a body fell on top of him and he couldn't see what happened next, but he realized that the distinctive hammer sound noise of the second AK had stopped.

Getting unsteadily to his feet, Con saw that his Glock's slide was locked back, the sign that the magazine was empty. His thumb pressed the mag release and the metal tube dropped out of the pistol. Fishing out the spare magazine from his pocked, he felt his heart skip a beat as he tried to push it into the gun.

It didn't fit.

He tried to reverse it, a voice in his head screaming to get it done, get it in, get it in...

It still didn't fit.

Con didn't know that the Glock was chambered in 9mm and the original magazine matched the gun, but the spare magazine be had bought was from the police shipment and a similar but different caliber - .40 Smith & Wesson. They weren't compatible.

Seeing their attacker fall, the crowd resumed pushing out towards the exit and safety.

Brain whirling, Con completely forgot about the empty magazine on the floor, stuffed the pistol and full magazine back into his tracksuit pockets and ran with the crowd, out into the Piazza and then spilling down the street – thousands of crying, bleeding, stumbling people trying to put as much distance between them and the terror as possible.

Heading downhill, he passed two blocks of shops and offices and then turned left into his street, blindly seeking the apartment block that he called home. Stumbling up the external stairs, he took out his keys but found his hand was shaking too much to fit the key in the front door lock. It took several deep breaths and both hands on the key before he could open the door, enter the building and collapse into the lift.

Seconds later, he opened his unit door, dropped his phone and keys on the floor and threw himself onto the sofa. He felt a burning pain on his thigh and instinctively thought he must have been hit by one of the bullets in the shops. But gingerly exploring the area, he soon discovered the truth – firing the pistol had heated up the gun barrel and while not red hot, the hot metal in his pants had melted the nylon and burned his skin when it touched his leg.

Con's head swam, he felt the walls of the room compressing in on him, and he fell to the floor, retching weakly. Crawling towards the bathroom, he made it as far as the shower when he retched again and vomited the contents of his stomach onto the tiles. His brain throbbed, stomach acid and half-digested tabbouleh burned his throat and nose as he threw up a few more times, then his stomach was empty, and he just lay trembling on the floor. Waves of shock washed over him as his body began to process the stress he had endured, physically purging excess chemicals by shaking it out of his muscles.

Crawling into the shower, still fully clothed and clutching the empty pistol, Con turned on the water and slumped against the wall as the warm water swirled the mess into the drain and washed the sweat from his body. He sat motionless as his mind raced; images, sounds and thoughts flashing through his mind's eye in a chaotic pattern. Eventually the storm subsided a little, and he stood up and got out of his wet clothes, dropping the pistol into the fabric. He washed his face and hair, rinsed out his mouth, turned off the water, stepped out of the shower and dried off. Mechanically dressing in fresh clothes, he checked his phone – no calls, no messages.

'Shit' he said aloud, trying to calm his mind to think and plan properly.

'Shit, shit, shit, shit, shit.'

'First, get rid of the evidence' he thought as he went into the kitchen to get a black plastic garbage bag. He stuffed the wet clothes from the shower into it, tied a knot in the top, grabbed his keys and went downstairs. The air was filled with sirens, three helicopters were clattering overhead but the street was deserted. Con knew better than to put the evidence in his own bin, so he walked next door and stuffed the bag into one of theirs.

Back in the unit, he saw the loaded magazine lying next to the sofa, picked it up, then went and got the pistol from the shower. The slide was still locked back, and it didn't move when he tried to release it – glued to the frame by molten nylon from his tracksuit pocket.

Turning the magazine over in his hands, he tried to figure out why it wouldn't fit. There was writing on the back of it – '.40 Restricted LE/Govt only.' He chuckled at the irony of how effectively the government prevented anything good from happening – sure stopped him reloading when he needed it.

For the first time, he noticed writing on the side of the pistol 'Glock 19 AUSTRIA 9x19' it read.

He thumbed up a web browser on his phone and searched 'Glock 40 9x19'

Wikipedia quickly educated him that Glock pistols were made to take a range of different ammunition. The pistol was chambered in 9mm – a very common caliber that he was familiar with from rap lyrics and movies he had seen. However, the magazine in his hand was loaded with .40 Smith & Wesson bullets – suitable for the NSW Police Glock 22 but incompatible with the gun in his hand.

Until now, he had no idea how complicated firearms could be, and it never occurred to either him or the guy who supplied the extra magazine to check that it fitted the gun. Con still felt ill, so he slumped back onto the sofa and flicked on the TV.

'…Witnesses are calling him 'the Castle Hill Angel'' came the voice of a news anchor, standing with her back towards the Piazza just up the road. Con's attention focused away from her face and devoured the activities in the background. Police, Fire Brigade and medics were running into the building and others were ferrying out bodies on stretchers. 'According to several witness statements, a man in the food court allegedly fired back at the attackers, killing two and allowing almost a thousand people in the Western half of the mall to escape. Without this man's efforts, the death toll would no doubt have been higher, as this brutal terrorist attack would have kept the victims pinned inside the center.

'At this early stage, we have no ID or CCTV images of the savior, who police believe to be either an off-duty police officer or security guard, but police are appealing to the man to come forward.'

Con snorted. 'Yeah that won't be fucken happening' he said to himself.

The camera cut to a studio where the usual talking heads began to discuss what they already knew (which was not much at all), and make wild and unsubstantiated speculations about the attacker's motives, damage done and the mysterious hero who had fought back.

The screen cut away to a press conference near the scene, where a man in a police uniform was speaking to a large group of microphones.

'…information that we have at this moment,' he was saying 'is that between five and ten attackers were involved. Car bombs were set off near each access foyer, except the piazza, after the attackers had gone inside.

'They proceeded to set off the bombs, then opened fire on the innocent shoppers inside the center. By starting at the exits, they forced their victims to stay inside the center, where they were systematically shot.

'I can confirm that one individual did engage two attackers with an unidentified firearm and allowed many victims to escape. I'm not at liberty to discuss the identity of this person, or the legality of shooting back during a terrorist attack. Our advice to anyone caught in an emergency is to remain calm, seek a hiding place and wait for the trained emergency services to arrive. We do not advise anyone to take the law into their own hands.'

'Dickhead' said Con, aloud. 'It's okay for you with armed guards, but we're supposed to just lie down and take it? Fuck off.'

On the screen, the police spokesman raised both hands in the air. 'I want to emphasize the position of the government and the police is NOT to take matters into your own hands. If there is an emergency, remain calm and wait for instructions.'

One of the reporters asked, 'Given the results of the Lindt Café inquest, which was damning of the police response, how confident are you that people will follow this advice?'

The spokesman looked uncomfortable. 'Anyone caught carrying illegal firearms or weapons to defend themselves will be arrested and punished accordingly,' he said. 'There is no need, in a civilized country, for untrained civilians to arm themselves. It is our job to protect you.'

Con couldn't believe what he was hearing. Sure, he had used an illegal gun, but the results were there in the people who were alive because of him. 'As if people are going to wait quietly to be slaughtered' he said to himself. 'This cop dickhead is just covering himself and his pay masters.'

The TV went back to the studio, where a blonde woman was saying 'my sister drives an armored car, and she can carry a gun to protect the money. But if she was to be attacked by terrorists, and used her gun to defend her life and the lives of others, she will go to prison. I don't think that is right, what about you?'

-

Across the city, citizens began discussing what could be done about the rising crime waves and threat of terrorist attacks. Some suburbs formed patrol groups, often incorporating veterans and licensed firearms owners who moved around their streets at night, communicating with each other via mobile phone or CB radio. Some used drones to provide a bird's eye view of their streets. A vigilante group from Europe called Soldiers of Odin opened several chapters in Sydney and Melbourne, bringing together local citizens to patrol their streets.

Almost instantly, the mainstream media went on the attack, criticizing these 'militia groups' as 'vigilantes, taking the law into their own hands' – when in fact these groups were not arresting or assaulting anyone, rather they were gathering important information that allowed the police to make legitimate arrests.

But the media never lets the facts stand in the way of hysteria, and they routinely ran footage of a press conference where the police spokesman had said 'we cannot stress enough the risks that go with it.' This advice was ignored by people who now knew the meaning of the proverb 'when seconds count, the police are minutes away' and when a couple of officers attempted to arrest ten people who were patrolling a street in Hurstville, they were surrounded by an angry mob accusing them of targeting the wrong people.

'Where were you when my home was robbed?'

'Took you 2 hours to respond to my home invasion – and then you did nothing, NOTHING'

'Why are you hassling us, instead of arresting the criminals who are making us do this?'

The officers made no arrests, and rapidly retreated to their vehicle and left the area, but mobile phone video of the incident immediately went onto the internet, and was picked up by the daytime TV shows, who ran it the next morning and brought on several social scientists and guests to give their opinions.

Following the lead story of 'Two men sentenced for shocking Sydney Terror Plot', the TV cut back to the studio, using emotionally charged language to hype up fear about what had happened.

'Terrifying scenes of mob violence against those sworn to protect us' began the TV show host as she introduced the video. 'But the question must be asked – are the police doing enough to protect us in our homes? Joining me today are Senator David Leyonhjelm of the Liberal Democrats; farmer, shooter & musician Steve Lee; and gun control expert Professor Philip Alpers from the Public Health Department at Sydney University.

'Senator, is there anything right about what we've seen in this shocking video?'

The bald man cleared his throat and spoke confidently. 'I understand their position, and their anger. In 1996, the government and the media convinced the public to give up their firearms and their legal rights to self-defense. This is allegedly part of an unwritten contract between the government, police and the public – that the public do not need a right to self-defense because the government and police will do it for them.'

'Well, times have changed, and the nation is a different place now. The courts are letting criminals off with a warning or a small fine, while charging and imprisoning otherwise law-abiding citizens for minor or technical infractions. Legislation changes create paper criminals – who were law abiding one day, but criminals the next, merely at the whim of a faceless bureaucrat in government.

The host turned to Steve Lee. 'Steve, you've been in trouble with the law about your firearms licenses, how do you see this incident affecting licensed shooters?'

'I don't see any connection' replied Steve. 'The only people in the video with firearms were the police, who probably don't have a license for them – only an exemption as part of their employment. No matter how much you over hype it, it's just not an issue.'

'My biggest concern is why you referred to Mister Alpers here as 'professor' – I'd like to hear about the qualifications he holds and why they would give his opinion any validity.'

The host was taken aback; this wasn't the direction the producers wanted to discussion to go. She knew nothing about the other bald man on the set – all she had done was read his credentials from the teleprompter. 'Well, let's hear from Professor Alpers – Professor?'

This was the question that Philip Alpers had always dreaded. In the past, he had always managed to dodge it because the hosts managed the discussion so well, but Steve Lee had just called him out before he had a chance to say anything. 'Yes' he said, trying hard to remain calm and fake a high level of composure. 'I'm an Adjunct Professor in the Department of Public Health at the University of Sydney.'

Steve Lee pressed further 'Adjunct Professor – so you aren't a full professor at all. Can you please tell us what academic qualifications you have to warrant the award of that title? What was the title and subject of your thesis?'

Alpers gave his stock answer, but he knew it would ring hollow 'I'm a researcher and policy analyst, I've published two books, four reports and contributed chapters to 3 other books about firearms.'

This time it was the Senator's turn 'You haven't answered the question. What are your academic qualifications? Where was your bachelor's degree awarded? What subject was your post-graduate thesis on?'

'An adjunct Professorship can be awarded independently of academic work, it's up to the discretion of the University' stammered Alpers nervously. 'There's nothing illegal about my title and my published research and books have been very well received.'

By this time, both Steve and the Senator were smiling at Alpers' discomfort. 'You don't have any qualifications, do you?' pressed Steve relentlessly, and then paused to let Philip squirm on camera.

After a few awkward moments of silence, Steve smiled thinly and said 'overlooking your lack of qualifications for a moment, you were also introduced as a 'gun control expert. Being an expert, can you please explain the difference between the selector switch on an AK47 and the one on an M-16A1?'

'Those are both assault rifles – highly dangerous' sputtered the fraudulent academic. 'The watering down of John Howard's courageous gun laws presents a clear danger to public safety.'

'You haven't answered the question' said David and Steve at the same time, then laughing together. Compounding Alpers' discomfort, the host laughed as well.

'I'll ask it slower' chuckled David. 'What is the difference...between the selector switch...on an AK-47...compared to an M16A1?'

'Do you even know? Answer the question' asked Steve, becoming a little hostile. 'How about...what is the difference between the Adler A-110 and an A-10 Warthog?'

Alpers was caught, pinned like a butterfly in a display case. 'No, I don't know' he admitted. 'But that's not the point. Mass shootings in America...'

'Stop, just stop,' cut in Steve. 'You are fear mongering. How many mass shootings have there been in New Zealand in the past five years?'

Alpers didn't say anything, so David answered the question. 'None' he said softly.

Steve continued 'Now, New Zealand didn't ban semi auto rifles or shotguns, like you are saying stopped mass shootings in Australia. They are readily available, if the purchaser has a license. It is wrong of you to focus on America and whip up hysteria, when our neighbors next door are much closer to our society, culture and history, yet remain very peaceful.'

The host saw an angle and stepped in 'So Steve, what are you saying – is there another explanation for why we haven't had any mass shootings in 20 years?'

'First, we have had mass shootings, but the gun control lobby and the media keep changing the definition to make it seem as if we haven't. Second, licensing is all that is required to minimize the risk of firearms getting into the wrong hands – note I said 'minimize' not 'prevent' because criminals will always be able to get illegal firearms.'

'So, are you saying that the USA should introduce licensing like Australia and New Zealand did, to curb their gun crime?' asked the host.

'No, I'm not saying that,' said Steve. 'I've spent a lot of time in America and from what I've observed; gun crime is very specific in two categories: gang crime and random spree shootings.'

'Gang crime is almost exclusively drug related, and explains the high numbers of young males in the data – many of these are called 'children' by people seeking to create hysteria about gun violence. There are four cities with high gun crime: Chicago, Detroit, New York and Los Angeles. If you were to remove these cities from the data, America is one of the safest places in the world. Ironically, these are the four cities with the strictest gun control laws in America, yet they have the highest gun crime.

'So that leaves spree shootings. The majority of these are copycat crimes committed by mentally ill people almost exclusively in Gun Free Zones. Personally, I lay a lot of the blame with the media for these zones, by hyping and publicizing the details and identity of the killer. Mister Gun Control here…' he gestured to Alpers, 'would argue that removing law abiding citizen's firearms would make them safer.' Alpers nodded vigorously, bobbing his head like a ferret or a squirrel but Steve went on 'the facts prove otherwise. Any time a shooter has attempted to kill people OUTSIDE a gun free zone, they are quickly stopped by licensed concealed carriers. The average casualty numbers when a concealed carrier stopped a mass shooting were 2.3 compared to 14.3 if everyone just waits for the police to arrive.' He paused, then delivered the final hammer blow. 'Gun control kills an average of twelve people every time there is a mass shooting, because it denies people their fundamental right to defend their own lives.'

David neatly segued into a closing statement. 'The police have our full support. But as they are inadequate to resolve these problems, then people have a right to feel upset that their social contract has been broken. And they certainly have a right to defend their lives and property against criminals.'

Having secured more than enough controversial footage to guarantee a social media storm, the host closed the interview. As soon as the footage went up on Facebook, the comments section filled up with people taking both sides of the issue, and the clickbait revenue climbed steadily.

-

Craig had signed up for the protest march at Parliament House as soon as he had heard about it. His house had been broken into twice, his car broken into and then stolen a week later. Each time he had done the right thing and called the police who were less than useless. Overwhelmed with work, chasing shadows and sticking to their politically correct script, they had taken so long to respond that his insurance company had denied his claim.

The government had ignored people like him for too long, he reasoned. Well, now he – and the thousands of others like him - would make them listen.

The plan was simple: anyone concerned that the government was not doing enough to keep the people safe was to meet at Hyde Park at 9am, then march down Macquarie Street to Parliament House.

One last time, he looked at the list of instructions on his phone.

'Bring as much of these as you can:
Padded jacket – motorcycle jacket if you have one
Protective helmet or hat
Gloves
Ear plugs or muffs
Gas mask if you can get one
Several bags of marbles or large ball bearings
Zip ties
Several bottles of water
Sound reflector
Milk in a plastic bottle'

He had all those items organized neatly in his backpack. He checked his face in the mirror, psyching himself up to step into battle with the authorities, then shouldered the pack and left his flat. The weather was cool but clear and as he walked to the bus stop he checked his phone to see if there were any changes to the plan published by the organizers.

'Update: We know there are agents' provocateur who will be in the crowd trying to discredit us. Anyone vandalizing property or attacking bystanders MUST be surrounded, apprehended and zip tied until they can be handed over to the police. Do not let anyone get away with vandalism as this runs counter to our message.'

Craig nodded as he read the update. The whole point of the protest was that the government and police were unable or incapable of keeping people safe, and the people should be trusted to defend themselves. Therefore, policing themselves efficiently would be an effective PR coup. He was aware that government agents had infiltrated other protests, both in Australia and overseas. These people had done a lot of vandalism and effectively turned public opinion against the protesters. Thankfully, it looked like people were learning from this and taking precautions.

Three hours later, despite the cool air, Craig was sweating under his protective clothing. His gloved hands were hot as he dashed forward, picked up another smoking tear gas canister and threw it back towards the solid line of police that stretched across the North end of the street. The canisters were very hot, due to the chemical reaction that created the tear gas, so thick welding gloves were required for those protesters who were tossing them back.

Patting his hands together gently to try to cool them down, he trotted back to the main body of protesters. This was marked by a ring of plastic milk cartons, which formed a sort of platform, so the organizers could see what was going on and a blonde man in a blue boiler suit would issue megaphone instructions accordingly.

It also contained a small aid station where milk was being used to flush the eyes of people affected by tear gas. Five or six black-clad, flex-cuffed agents' provocateur were sitting glumly off to one side. Trying to create damage in front of the media cameras to give the police an excuse to crack down hard, their plan had failed when half of the crowd had surrounded them and placed them under citizen's arrest.

One of the organizers was standing off to one side, giving a live interview for two TV camera crews. It was also being streamed on Facebook Live, to an audience of millions around Australia and the world.

'The police are making our point for us' she was saying. 'How is it possible to deploy such numbers and equipment against a peaceful protest, yet there are no resources available to protect our families in our suburbs?'

She waved her hand to indicate the riot police blocking the road. 'Why can't these police patrol our suburbs and do their job – stopping crime and arresting criminals?'

The interview was cut short by several whistles being blown from the milk crate command center. The police line was re-forming around a black Nissan Patrol that reversed into the middle of the road. Craig saw that instead of a spare tyre mounted on the back, there was a flat, gray disc about the same size. As his eyes focused on it, the megaphone behind him blared orders to quickly bring everyone into a block in the middle of the street behind the front line of protesters. The front line was about forty people wide, standing side by side as over a thousand people squeezed into line behind them.

Craig was in the third row from the front when his skin started to prickle as if he had a bad sunburn. His ears began to throb, and Craig suspected this was some kind of sound or microwave weapon – an LRAD maybe? The sensation grew more intense, spreading inside him and he could feel his internal organs protesting. Every fiber in his being began to scream at him to run, to get away but the crowd held him tight in its own panicked embrace. The megaphone called for them all to STAND TOGETHER, STAND AND WAIT.

The protester's ears were burning, an irritating sensation that threatened to overpower the instructions from the megaphone.

Then the megaphone cut through the noise in his head. 'Reflectors – OUT, marbles, READY!' it called, and Craig saw movement in the second row – just in front of him. People were unfolding pieces of cardboard covered in aluminium foil, assembling them into a shape like a hollow pyramid, or a box with three ends cut off. Within two seconds, the reflectors were ready and pointing back at the disc weapon in the middle of the street.

The sound reflectors were based on the same geometric principle that maritime radar buoys use to amplify their radar signature to boats or aircraft. Sound waves enter at the widest point, are reflected off the inner panel back in the same direction – a geometric U-turn.

Immediately, Craig's senses began to return to normal. He was a little disappointed that the sound weapon didn't burst into flames or blow up the police car like in the movies, but cheered with the others as the crowd realized what they had achieved.

Several blocks from the site of the protest, the police Response Commander was advised that the LRAD was broken.

'That's a million-dollar piece of equipment. Are you telling me they BROKE it? How the FUCK does that happen?' He bellowed into the radio.

'We don't know sir' it crackled. 'As soon as we turned it on, a few of them unfolded metal or foil panels and moved into the second row. That was right before the circuits fried…'

'I want those panels – get those people into custody. I'm going to charge each of them with destruction of government property' bellowed the police commander.

Ten seconds later, half of the riot police in the cordon broke away from the main body that protected the LRAD and charged towards the tightly-packed group of protestors. As they approached, the reflector-carrying protesters shuffled back into the crowd and the front two rows began throwing handfuls of marbles and metal ball bearings onto the roadway in between.

The effect was either catastrophic or hilarious, depending on whose side you were on. Half of the police slipped on the marbles and went down; the other half lost their footing while trying to dodge the marbles and collided with the crowd individually, instead of a cohesive formation. The shock of their attack was completely neutralized then turned against them as the crowd surged forward, over the top of the fallen officers who were cuffed with zip ties, dragged back to the milk crate command center and dropped beside their associates. Craig was astonished at how quickly the key people moved, and guessed they had planned and practiced for some time before the protest was scheduled.

Craig's cheering joined the other's as they closed ranks again, facing off against the now completely disorganized police. Singly and in pairs, the uniformed officers retreated into their own lines and a tense standoff ensued, each side watching the other but neither willing to move.

Craig looked around and saw that Megaphone Man was deep in conversation with the Interview Woman, who was holding a phone to her ear as she turned her back to the camera and the reporter. They spoke briefly, nodded to each other and then the news crew moved rapidly away from them towards the fence of Parliament House.

Megaphone man got back onto the platform and announced 'HOLD POSITIONS, EVERYONE. PREMIER'S COMING OUT, WATCH FOR TRICKS, HOLD POSITIONS.'

To Craig's right, the sandstone and iron fence of Parliament house stood between the protesters and the façade of the building. Two simple staircases rose from ground level to a large verandah that ran the width of the building, in front of two doors that led inside. One set of doors opened, and four uniformed security guards came out, scanning the area and spreading out on either side of the door.

Finally, a slim, brunette woman emerged and stood at the railing. Dressed in a neat business suit, her shoulder length hair tussled in the wind until she tucked it behind her ears. Flanked by security guards, she waited until a tall, stocky man with dark hair and glasses arrived and stood behind her to the left.

One of the security guards wheeled out a speaker on a small trolley, and rested it on the verandah beside the Premier. He handed her a microphone and then stepped back. The Premier took a deep breath, and raised the microphone to her mouth.

'Okay' she said. 'I'm here.' She gestured to the man behind her. 'And my Police Minister. You've got our attention. What do you want? I'm listening.'

Megaphone Man immediately responded for the protesters.

'Four items' he announced, and looked at a sheet of paper in his hand.

'First, let us defend ourselves inside our homes, cars and businesses.

Two, stop all immigration for one year until this crime wave is under control.

Three, stop welfare payments to the families of any immigrant convicted of a crime.

Four, stop the courts handing out weak sentences as it only encourages and emboldens the criminals.'

There were some cheers from the crowd as the megaphone fell silent, and Craig waited along with the others to hear the Premier's response. He realized he was holding his breath, and had to consciously breathe while he waited.

The Premier turned to the Police Minister and had a brief conversation. Then she turned back and raised the microphone again.

'What you are demanding is very broad, and covers different portfolios. I am willing to schedule meetings with your representatives, and the ministers responsible for those portfolios, to discuss options. It can happen, but not overnight.'

'I guarantee you that I am taking your concerns seriously and will schedule a public meeting in the Town Hall on Monday evening. We will also accept submissions in writing. Okay?'

Craig was concerned that the politician was simply telling them what they wanted to hear, but he cheered along with the crowd. He saw Megaphone Man consult with Interview Woman and then reply 'Agreed. Pull back the police and we will leave. You can have your officers back – unharmed.'

The Premier nodded to the tall man behind her, and he spoke briefly into a hand-held radio. The riot police moved away, falling back in twos and threes until the street contained only marbles and the silent metal canisters that had once held tear gas.

The protesters also began to drift away, walking west through the city streets or south through Hyde Park to the train station. Eager to help with the Town Hall meeting, Craig tried to catch up with Megaphone Man or Interview Woman, but they merged into the crowd and disappeared.

Watching the protesters disperse from the verandah of Parliament House, the Premier and the Police Minister stood in silence until the minister asked quietly 'are you really going to meet them at the Town Hall?'

'Don't be silly' replied the Premier as she turned to walk back inside. 'I'll get a work experience kid to take notes from whoever turns up, promise a Task Force to 'look into it' and 'report back with recommendations. Nothing's going to happen, nothing's going to change.'

The Police Minister raised an eyebrow. 'I hope you know what you're doing. There are always unintended consequences.'

The Premier bit back her initial confident comment. While she was aware of the general details of the government's plan, the Police Minister hadn't been briefed yet, and she would not leak details of the Caliphate or the Government's response. So she just shrugged her shoulders and said 'Well, if they riot again, it's your job to arrest them all.'

The Police Minister shrugged, thinking 'we don't have enough prisons to house them all' but kept the thoughts to himself.

-

Cruising home after the gym, Bilal thumbed open his news feed.

HORRIFIC SCENES AS RACISTS DESTROY CITY CENTRE

POLICE FEARED TORTURED AFTER BEING SIEZED BY RACIST MOB

COUPLE WAIT ALL DAY FOR POLICE AFTER HOME INVASION

SWAMPED 000 BEGGING FOR VOLUNTEERS TO HANDLE CALLS

He laughed aloud. It seemed that the Australian government was losing all control of the population. Surely the Mullah was correct, the time was right for him and his people to seize their destiny.

Chapter 13

November

Canberra

The PM met with the heads of the ADF departments. Combined, there were 17 people in the room, including not only the heads of the Army, Navy and Air Force, but also adjutants, assistants and secretaries.

The PM opened by saying 'Thank you for coming. As you know, we are reliably informed that the new King of Saudi Arabia plans to move himself and most of his family into Bankstown, and establish a Caliphate inside Sydney – using force if necessary - to create a new state.'

'Apparently, if it was good enough for Israel, then it's good enough for him' she added drily.

There was silence in the room as her words registered. 'This meeting is to decide what to do about it.'

The silence continued. Various bodies around the long wooden table squirmed.

'Let's start with the Army' she said, fixing the Lieutenant General with her gaze.

The Lieutenant General quickly realized that honesty was the best policy. 'Well, Prime Minister, the ADF recently concluded sweeping changes under Plan Beersheba. While the Army used to have separate brigades for tanks, APCs and light infantry, we've re-organized our three operational brigades so they all include some of each element. This allows them to commit to combat separately or together, but utilizing the combined strengths of armor, mechanized and dismounted troops.'

'Sounds good' replied the PM. 'Where are these brigades?'

'Err....Townsville, Adelaide and Darwin' winced the General. 'There are really no combat troops in the Sydney basin - certainly not enough to counter this Caliphate.'

The effect was instantaneous.

'The FUCK?' exclaimed the PM. 'Who the fuck took all our troops and moved them out of the biggest city in the country – and the one with the largest risk of a terrorist attack?'

'Ahh, nobody in particular.' replied the General quickly. 'It was done over a long period of time, several governments, both State and Federal. Holsworthy used to have artillery, commandos, APCs but since it's a Labour seat....' his voice trailed off, the implication clear. The Liberal State government had encouraged/ordered the ADF to re-locate any assets that might benefit a Labour seat, into marginal Liberal seats to boost the economy in those areas.

'Attack helicopters' said the PM. 'Are they Army or Air Force?'

'Army' replied the Lieutenant General. 'The Tigers are 1st Aviation Regiment' He paused, squirmed and said 'Darwin'.

The PM's expression went from sour to horrified. Sydney had been stripped bare and laid open - there was nothing available to oppose the Caliphate.

'There's still 2 RAR' he added quickly - 'They're being trained as our counterpart to US Marines, so we located them in Sydney to be close to the Landing Ships.'

'Surprising' was the PM's retort. 'Whose genius idea was it to locate troops near the equipment they're going to need to use?'

'Don't answer that' she said, turning to the Air Marshall of the RAAF. 'Please tell me you've got something we can use.'

The older man cleared his throat 'Prime Minister, I'll update you geographically. The closest airfield is at Holsworthy, to the south. There are no fixed wing aircraft there, only helicopters. None of these are attack helicopters; they are transport and surveillance only.'

'Of course not' sneered the PM. 'Why on earth would you station armed helicopters near the biggest terrorist threat in the country?'

'To be fair' he countered, the Australia crimes that caused the greatest loss of life were NOT done by Muslims... and given the media and political attitudes at the time...well, it was thought best to remove anything that might upset anyone.'

The PM didn't look any happier. 'Keep moving' she said.

'The next closest air base is Richmond - again, no armed aircraft, but this is home to transport planes - Hercules troop and cargo transports. These are what we can use to bring in troops and equipment from Townsville, Darwin and Adelaide.'

'Start making that happen - both of you' she said, nodding to the Army and Air Force reps. 'Now, what about something with bombs?'

'Williamtown has FA/18s – Super Hornets - a multirole fighter that can drop bombs accurately. Less glamorous but perhaps more effective would be the Hawk trainers of No 76 Squadron - also at Williamtown. There are 18 of these, which for ground attack could be equipped with 2 guided bombs and a quad 30mm cannon pod.' He paused to check that she was following, then went on. 'While the Super Hornets are very fast, since the Caliphate has no radar guided anti-aircraft capacity, we could safely use aircraft with a lower speed and extended loiter time. Provided the Combat Air Controllers are communicating properly, it would be routine to stack up the various aircraft so they can fly in and out of the target area without bothering each other.'

'Good, let's use both types' the PM responded firmly. 'What else?'

'Amberley in Queensland has more FA/18 Super Hornets' the RAAF chief went on. 'They also have a squadron of aerial refueling aircraft we can use when ferrying troops and equipment from around the country.'

'Navy?' asked the PM. 'We don't have any battleships any more, do we?'

'Ah, no Ma'am' stuttered the Vice Admiral. 'But we don't need them - we do have ships perfectly suited for both kinds of operation this situation needs.'

'Both kinds?' asked the PM.

'Well, to be blunt' replied the man in the crisp white uniform, 'Corvettes can be stationed offshore and used for accurate bombardment with 5-inch shells, called in by the same teams controlling the aircraft and helicopters. But once the target is soft enough, ground troops will be required to secure the area. Given that they will probably have destroyed all the land bridges into the area, insurgent forces will be expecting a ground assault from the north. We would recommend that the plan include a sea-borne assault from the southeast as well - a pincer movement, striking up from Botany Bay, linking up at King George's Road to cut the Caliphate in half.'

'Good.' The PM was cheered up somewhat to learn that someone in the room was thinking. 'But the issue remains - we just can't scrape together enough troops to eliminate this Caliphate. Years of cutbacks, political correctness and the resulting morale issues mean we just don't have enough bodies.'

'If I may disagree, Prime Minister' countered the Lieutenant General. 'ADF morale is as strong as ever, and our troops are respected as some of the best in the world. The Army has been fine tuned to address the global threats we faced - in the places we faced them, and we have used US, British and European assets in combined operations to very good effect. Australia simply hasn't been required to fight a full-on war in our own front yard.'

'Well, times have changed' challenged the PM. 'We need bodies, yesterday. Fortunately for you, I have a plan' she picked up the phone and murmured 'send him in.'

All eyes in the room locked on the door as it swung open and Colonel Mason strode into the room. As he sat in an empty chair he took a moment to process what lay on the table in front of him: there were the normal stationery supplies – a pen, a pad of paper and a glass of water but what stood out was a brightly colored box of crayons.

Col Mason's mouth broke into a wide smile at the joke as he picked up the box. 'Thanks very much' he laughed, as if admiring a box of expensive chocolates. 'They look delicious.'

As the laughter in the room died down, the PM continued: 'As of today, I am ordering you to re-activate the New South Wales Marine Corps and call for civilian volunteers. The details are in the red folders in front of you.'

The ADF chiefs looked at each other, initially in horror at the idea, then the General shrugged and said '2 RAR has had excellent experience training with the Marines, and it will take at least 2 months to transport, stage and organize the supplies and assets needed to attack the Caliphate.'

The head of the Navy didn't look convinced.

'Besides, we routinely find men and women coming from civilian life or the reserves and making excellent troops. The Cafe at the Australian War Memorial is named Poppy after one of those excellent examples' noted the General.

'Every conflict since Federation has seen Australian men and women step forward out of civilian life and become formidable and cunning warriors' David Pearce joined the ADF in his 30s - that's how he got his nickname because he was so much older than the other men in his troop.'

The Navy Commodore shrugged and mimicked an American Accent 'You call, we haul.' 'I don't care where you get 'em or how you train them - once they hit the ground they aren't the Navy's responsibility any more. Just do us all a favor and try to stop the Marines from licking the windows.'

The PM smiled thinly. 'Good. I'll leave you here with Col Mason to develop the plan. I want a Marine Corps ready to start training recruits on the first of January. The Finance department have completed their initial paperwork and advise the budget for this is $7 billion at most, but given the track record of most defense projects, please try to keep it under twenty'. Eyes widened, wondering where the funding was coming from, but nobody dared to question this gift from heaven.

'I know this task is the single greatest threat to our country now' she concluded 'but make sure you see your families as well. Don't work past 7.30 tonight.'

At the door, she paused, turned and said 'Oh, and Colonel Mason, please drop by my office on your way out...I have some...questions you may be able to answer...'

-

Forty minutes later, the PM was holding another press conference.

'I want to express my deepest condolences to the victims and their families. You all have the full support of this government, and I have ordered all available resources to assist with medical care, clean-up, insurance and most importantly, the criminal investigation.'

'Currently, we have no information about the attackers, or their motives. While this is obviously a well-planned terrorist attack, I am not, repeat NOT going to make any assumptions about who might be responsible. I am calling for calm, I am calling for everyone to wait for the results of the investigations.'

'Now is the time to grieve, to console each other, and to find out the facts. There will be a time for action, there will be a time for punishment of the guilty. But that time is in the future. Please remain calm and help where you can.'

She looked directly into the TV cameras and said 'This is no time for fear mongering, for speculation or whipping up hysteria. That includes the media organizations. I solemnly request that you honor the dead and our criminal investigators by avoiding any speculation until the facts are known.'

'Secondly, as part of the jobs and security package that was part of our election promises, I am announcing the creation of a new organization for domestic civil defense, border protection and first aid rapid response. The New South Wales Marine Corps was the first regiment to defend the colony that became Australia, and I am reactivating them as of today.'

'The regiment will be renamed the Australian Marine Corps and recruit training will commence in January. Our good friends in the United States Marine Corps will assist with training until our own staff can take over. Australian Marines will receive basic training, then deploy in a wide range of responsibilities, assisting with customs & border protection, domestic security, first aid, intelligence and so forth. Career opportunities also include vehicle maintenance, communications, catering – you name it. Any Australian aged over 18 is able to volunteer, though the entry requirements are stringent and not everyone can be accepted.'

'This new Marine Corps will provide jobs, security and a much-needed boost to our border security, in order to confront the increasing threats entering from overseas – drugs, firearms and illegal immigrants.'

'Third' the PM ruffled through her papers and held up two sheets of A4 paper. 'I am holding a full pardon for the Castle Hill Angel. We would like to know your story, and I hope that the promise of immunity from prosecution will help you understand that we are truly grateful for you saving thousands of lives. You may have used an illegal firearm to defend yourself. We all understand that. But the laws were written in a different time, and times have changed. We recognize this, and are prepared to act in the same spirit that you did – to defend our lives and those of our loved ones.

'I also have a commission in the Australian Marine Corps for you. If you complete basic training, I would be honored to commission you as one of the Corps' first team leaders. Now more than ever, this great country needs people who are willing to step forward and do what it takes. I look forward to meeting with you as soon as possible.'

The daytime TV weasel was back in front of the camera, this time stoking the controversy of gun violence. He had never seen a gun in real life, but his brief was clear: to make the audience afraid of guns, and promote gun control - laws that were intended to reduce violence in the community and make people feel safer. The more sensationalist the better, facts be damned in favor of ratings.

Tilting his head slightly into the camera, he winked and said 'Good morning, we're talking about what can be done about terror attacks like the ones in America, Paris, Nice and Castle Hill.

'Joining me today is Samantha Lee, chair of Gun Control Australia expert and Mark Squires - a spokesperson for Gun Rights Australia. Sam, what message do you have for the people of Australia, and particularly Castle Hill?'

'Thanks for having me' began Samantha. 'Our message is that we cannot relax any gun laws that John Howard put in place. Terror attacks like this prove that there are too many guns in Australia, which have no place in a civilized society, which is why we again call on the Government to ban the Adler shotgun, and all semi-automatic handguns.

The host shrugged, and turned to the other camera 'Mark, how would you respond?'

'All the licensed shooters of Australia express their deepest condolences to the victims and their families' he began. 'But none of us was involved, and none of us are responsible. Why should we be punished with further restrictions that didn't stop this atrocity?'

'The media are constantly telling us not to judge all Muslims by the actions of a few. Now, I'm not saying anything about the attack or who was responsible, I'll wait for the investigation to finish – but I am demanding the same treatment, the same courtesy. We do not hold all Muslims accountable for the actions of a few – likewise we must not judge all gun owners by the actions of a few.'

'Samantha, in case you hadn't noticed, the killers – like all violent criminals, broke existing laws against murder, theft and assault. They certainly aren't bothered by laws against having guns.

'Secondly, these terrorists didn't use an Adler or a semi-automatic pistol. They used AK47 automatic rifles which have been illegal in Australia for over 20 years. This clearly proves that criminals can obtain illegal firearms whenever they want to. John Howard's laws have not stopped illegal firearms from getting to criminals.'

The camera went back to Samantha 'Well, our research shows that most of the illegal firearms in Australia were stolen from licensed firearms owners. Therefore, if we reduce the number of firearms in circulation, this reduces the availability of deadly weapons' she said.

Mark laughed coldly. 'That is simply untrue. The recent Senate Inquiry into Gun Violence proved that less than half of one percent of firearms used in a crime were stolen from licensed owners. The clear majority come into the country alongside the shipments of illegal drugs that they protect. That's where police efforts should be directed – not harassing the most law-abiding citizens and treating them all like potential murderers.

Samantha squirmed in her seat 'If we are to increase public safety, we must remove weapons of war from our streets' she said.

'In case you didn't notice' responded Mark, 'criminals and terrorists have no difficulty smuggling in weapons – they simply aren't stealing them domestically. Besides, the man who saved thousands at the Castle Hill shopping center did so using his own semi-automatic pistol. You know what I think? I don't believe this guy was an angel. I think he was a FALLEN angel. Given the fact that he hasn't come forward, this tells me he isn't a police officer or security guard. I believe he was a criminal, carrying an illegal pistol, who acted to protect his own life, and at the same time saved everyone around him.

'If he was lawfully carrying a pistol, why hasn't he come forward and co-operated with police? I reckon he's scared, because although he saved thousands of lives, he was breaking these stupid laws that only serve to protect criminals.'

'Tell me, Miss Gun Control Laws Save Lives – what would the death toll have been without that angel and his gun? Disarming the innocent does not protect them.'

The camera went back to Samantha, who was now visibly sweating 'The evidence is clear – Australia banned semi-automatics in 1996 and we haven't had a mass shooting since. This increased violence means we must all take further action to remove guns from society. We don't want to become like America.'

Mark responded calmly 'I'm going to address your claims in order. First, Australia did not ban semi-automatics. While it is true they are in a restricted category, there are thousands of legal, registered semi auto rifles, pistols and shotguns in Australia right now. None of them committed this crime.

'Secondly, we have had mass shootings since, but the Gun Control lobby keeps changing the definition to maintain the lie that 'Gun Control Works' – first it was 3 or more unrelated victims, then 4, now we are up to 5. Since 1996 we have had the Millewa State Forest shootings, Monash University shooting, Hectorville Siege, Wedderburn, Lockart, gang and drug shootings in Melbourne, Sydney and Brisbane, the Lindt Café and Parramatta Police Station shooting. We have also had mass killings in Childers (the backpacker fire), the Quakers Hill nursing home fire and the Cairns mass child stabbings so to suggest that Australia's strict laws have stopped gun crime or mass killings is ludicrous - and a deceitful warping of statistics.'

'But…' Samantha tried to interject, but Mark ignored her and continued.

'Third, New Zealand had a mass shooting in 1997 and they did not ban or restrict anything. They haven't had one since either. Canada has legal semi-auto rifles, shotguns and pistols but extremely low gun crime.

'In 2011, Anders Breivik killed 77 people - mostly children, at a summer camp in Norway. He was given 21 years in prison as punishment, but Norway did not ban the Mini-14 semi-auto rifle he used.

'Finally, you really should get out more. You'd learn there are more countries in the world than Australia and America – so the choices we have do not simply boil down to 'I don't want to live in America' – I can name 4 countries with better gun laws that have lower gun crime – we could easily adopt their laws and see similar results without all the fear mongering.'

'In short, you cannot put toothpaste back in the tube. Criminals and terrorists will always be able to get firearms, bombs, axes, knives and bats. Prohibition of alcohol didn't stop people drinking, prohibition of drugs didn't stop people taking them, and prohibition of firearms is just the same.'

Mark knew that his calm, fact-based approach was contradictory to everything the TV show stood for, and he was pleasantly surprised they had left him to speak for so long. Anticipating the end of the interview, Tom said 'Before we go, I'd like to share two posts from my recent Facebook feed.'

'The first is from a young American woman who was out jogging, carrying a legally concealed pistol – just like the one used by the Hills Angel – the one Samantha Lee wants to ban. She carries the pistol because her area contains cougars and snakes but recently, a car full of young men pulled over in front of her while running along a remote country road.

'As soon as she lifted her shirt and touched the pistol, one of the men said, 'She's got a gun' and the car immediately drove away. Having a semi-automatic pistol saved that young woman from rape and possible murder.

'The second is from a father in North Carolina. He will never forget the sound of his back door being kicked in at 4.30 in the morning. He woke up, drew his legal Sig Sauer pistol and confronted a home invader in the hallway. Yelling at the invader to leave, the home owner saw the intruder also had a gun and was ready to fire when the home invader turned and ran.

'These are just two examples of honest, law abiding citizens, lawfully defending themselves against violent criminals. Just like the Hills Angel, they used a firearm to protect their right to life. More and more Australians in Melbourne and Sydney are finding themselves in similar situations.'

'I have a right to life, you have a right to life, and we all have the right to defend that life. Nobody has the moral authority to deny me or anyone else the opportunity to defend myself or my family against an attacker. You may choose not to – that is your right, but you have no right or moral authority to render law abiding citizen's defenseless in the face of evil, simply based on a 'what if?'

'Samantha, I'd like to seriously question who you are trying to save? What's the reason for this gun control crusade of yours? What - or who - in your past, maybe your childhood - are you trying to save?

Samantha, who had been trying to interrupt him for several minutes, was suddenly silent. All the blood had drained from her face and her eyes were wide, as if she was re-living past trauma. Her mouth moved, but no words came out.

The camera went back to the host, who was relieved to be able to change the topic. 'Now let's go to Sonia with the weather…'

Lisa had been watching the debate on the TV from her hospital bed, but angrily clicked it off with the remote. She felt so distressed at the opinions presented, and lay back in the hospital bed trying to calm her thoughts. They swirled through her head like flames above a roaring fire, the blood rushing through her ears hissed like lava flowing from an erupting volcano inside her.

Desperately trying to make sense of how she woke up in the hospital, Lisa searched her fractured memories, attempting to piece them together. Agony flared in her soul as each jagged piece came to life in her recollection. She remembered shopping at Castle Towers with her husband Brad and infant daughter Tilly. Brad was taking Tilly to the car when Lisa had remembered that she had to buy a birthday card for one of her friends. 'Meet you at the car!' she had said to her family, kissing them both before quickly walking back to the newsagent. She knew that Brad & Tilly had gone towards the car park exit because that's where the rescue teams had found their bodies – piled up in the foyer with a dozen others, people who had been walking in or out of the shops when the bombs went off in the car park just outside the doors. They were killed instantly by the pressure wave of the explosion.

Lisa herself had been walking out of the newsagent almost a hundred meters away when the explosions rocked the building, and had seen the black clad figure walking towards her up the arcade. The shopping center's power and lights were still on, but an immense cloud of dust and smoke billowed along the ceiling and progressively darkened the whole area.

Given the distance from the blasts, Lisa's hearing was muted, but she could hear the cries and screams mixing with the sound of glass shattering and debris falling from the walls and ceiling. She had looked around, trying to figure out what was happening when the figure in black came closer, raised a rifle and started shooting in all directions. Lisa had been hit in the knee and the head, spun around by the impact and she had collapsed on the floor. Covered in blood, she appeared to be dead so her attacker moved on, further into the mall as the carnage continued. She lay in the same position until the rescue teams moved into the area, sorting through the living and the dead and transporting the living to hospital.

The hospital chaplain and counselors had visited her extensively, working with the doctors who were monitoring her physical recovery. They were pleased with the surgery on her knee, and scheduled her for physical therapy as soon as she could get out of bed. Lisa was also using their techniques to process her grief at losing her husband and daughter, the guilt she felt at surviving when so many others had not, and the anger she felt at everyone involved. Some worked better than others, some didn't work at all but overall, they helped her deal with a surprisingly wide range of emotions that attacked her regularly.

And it was working. In the first few weeks after waking up in the hospital, her brain was a swirling mess of memories, pain, grief and unfathomable anger. Working with the doctors, her body was healing steadily and her mind was as well, although she felt the recovery was far less smooth. She learned techniques to calm her thoughts, to assess them and recognize the feelings that came with the images.

Lisa could tell herself that none of it was her fault. Intellectually, she knew it all along but the journey to educate her emotions, her subconscious to that reality was a difficult process.

Evaluating her options was painfully difficult. She had received some money from life insurance and her medical bills were covered by private health insurance, but she would need to support herself once discharged as the money wouldn't last forever.

-

The PM was being briefed on the progress and discoveries made by the Castle Hill investigation. Seated at the head of a large Jarrah table, she stared past a dozen faces on each side to where the NSW Deputy Police Minister was delivering the information.

Nobody in the room was very happy, least of all the Deputy Minister.

'The investigation results indicate this was a VERY professional job. The explosives were not commercially manufactured. Rather, they were made of common chemicals – quite inefficient, comparatively, but enough to do the job. The number of explosives required was in the hundreds of kilograms – a lot of work to make and keep stable, then set off at the same time.

We seriously doubt there are more than a dozen people in the world who could have achieved this - without us knowing' he concluded.

'How's that?' The PM asked. In response, the man nodded and flipped through a few pages of notes on the desk in front of him.

'Firstly, it is extremely difficult to manufacture, store, transport and detonate this quantity of explosives. We monitor the sales of certain essential chemicals, and any unusual purchases are investigated.' He shook his head, 'No unusual purchases inside Australia in the last 3 months.'

'Secondly, the manufacturing process is complex and dangerous. For instance, during The Troubles in Northern Ireland, the IRA bomb makers were professionally trained by military chemists in Libya, and even *they* managed to blow themselves up reasonably frequently – despite obviously taking necessary precautions.

'If this volume of explosives *were* made locally, whoever did it was extremely lucky. Of course, they could have been made elsewhere and smuggled in – there are a hundred ways these bombs could have gotten into the country.'

The PM nodded slowly, digesting the information. At last, she asked 'Any indications that this was done by Islamic extremists?'

'No Ma'am, we have two long-term sources very well connected inside the Sydney Muslim community and they report absolutely no evidence about this attack' he replied. 'One of those sources is in the absolute inner circle. If this was done by a religious extremist, they would have been working alone, without support or the blessing of the community – which takes me back to my point about the difficulty of doing something like this. No, Ma'am; we do not believe the evidence points that way at all.'

'What about the perpetrators?' she asked, looking around the table. 'Anything?'

Most of the others shook their heads and the Deputy concluded 'They all fought until killed, so we can't question them. No unique tattoos or identifying marks, DNA testing is being done – that might tell us what region of the world they come from but until the results come back there's little to go on.'

The Deputy Police Minister hesitated a moment, then thought 'fuck it if she can't handle a dose of reality.' He cleared this throat and plunged ahead.

'We still haven't caught whoever it was who bombed the Hilton hotel in 1978. Unless we get lucky with the DNA, or somebody gets careless, or talks...' his voice trailed off as he caught the eye of the PM.

The PM allowed some of the anger she was suppressing leak to the surface and she leaned forward in her chair to make sure everyone understood her emphasis. 'This is threatening to blow up into a complete civil war. No matter how we try to spin this, social media is already calling for reprisals, revenge attacks, deportation, executions, you name it - the lunatics are calling for it. Militias are already being formed by residents who are fed up with this. We need arrests, we need action. NOW, DAMMIT!'

'At the moment we have no information tying this atrocity to any group, religious or otherwise' responded the Deputy strongly. 'Any rash action risks unintended consequences and unpredictable results.'

The PM pressed her palms to her temples and tried to focus. 'OK' she said to the room in general. 'Ideas. How are we going to sell this to the press?'

-

The weather in the Caliphate was unusually cold, the air was crisp, and the wind blew off snow falling in the mountains. It swept through the western suburbs of Sydney, swirling dead leaves across the borders of the Caliphate, chopping up the waters of Botany Bay and Port Hacking.

The cold, gloomy turmoil was reflected in the property market, which had experienced major upheavals that nobody could have foreseen. Perversely, it rewarded those who wanted to move into the Caliphate, since the number of them was less than those wanting to sell, and property prices were falling substantially.

Within days of the Mullah's announcement, over half of the homes in areas around Hurstville and Padstow were for sale, with thousands of people desperate to leave. Real estate agents earned astonishing commissions, brokering sales between desperate vendors and those who wished to move inside the Caliphate's borders.

Other residents simply packed up and left, shifting to holiday houses up or down the coast, relatives in other suburbs or inland towns like Bathurst, Orange and Albury.

The collapse in property prices was a windfall for many Sydney residents who had been locked out of the market by inflated property prices. As the cost of homes fell from around a million dollars, more and more people moved into the Caliphate as it presented their first opportunity to get into the property market – no matter what they might have thought of the risks involved.

Then there was another category of buyers – the Sydney residents who supported the Caliphate, who saw this as a welcome addition to Australia's multiculturalism, and wanted to be "in on the ground floor" as a political statement. The economic effects of the Caliphate resonated throughout the entire Sydney property market.

-

The proudest moment in Bilal's life so far was the 20th August. That was the day they closed down the Police Stations in Campsie and Bankstown, in a bold operation planned by Bilal's new mentors, the Mullah and the Sheikh.

Bilal thought the plan was brilliant. First, the buildings were surrounded by crowds of people, all chanting and singing in support of the Caliphate. Then the Mullah had gone inside, announced in a loud voice that the building was inside the Caliphate, and therefore was claimed by followers of the Caliph. The occupants had been given thirty minutes to evacuate the building before it was to be burned, in order to purify the ground it stood on. With a flourish, he had stalked out to cheers from the crowd, who had watched his whole performance, and the shock on the faces of the uniformed officers inside, via live video streamed onto Facebook.

An hour later, the building was well alight, and the enormous crowds blocked the streets to prevent fire engines from putting it out. Bilal saw the smoke as the symbol of the prayers of the faithful, ascending to the throne of Allah in heaven.

The Caliph's followers had taken their first main step to secure power.

Within a week, the council and local government administration offices had been taken over, with announcements quickly following that all Australian government taxes were void for businesses and people within the Caliphate's borders, and Zakat offerings would continue to be collected by the local mosque. The economy was transformed overnight, with a rapid increase in barter, other currencies, drugs and services – anything that had value could be haggled over.

Bilal was starting to enjoy reading his news feed. His interest in politics and business was increasing, and he was learning how the media worked and how people could gain and lose influence by how they spoke to the media.

Some headlines caught his eye:

CRIME SURGE LEAVES POLICE IMPOTENT

POLICE MINISTER WARNS AGAINST VIGILANTE
VIOLENCE

NEW POLICE MINISTER BATTLES 'NO
CONFIDENCE' PETITION

Bilal laughed at the unnecessary problems endured by
Western politicians. The patriarchal system – the clan – was the
most ancient and efficient form of local government. He
believed this because he was starting to experience it. The more
he learned about politics, the more he understood how
inefficient, how problematic, how weak it was. There was no
strength in politicians any more. And that was why it would fail.
Strong men would take power from those who could no longer
wield it.

-

Driving home from work on a bright Thursday evening,
Jason bumped his work Ute off the Hume Highway and into the
access road that led to the subdivision where he lived. The
hourly news was on the radio and he was listening to the
announcer describing the Alpha Gang's rise to notoriety in
South Western Sydney. A derivative of the Apex Gang from
Melbourne, these criminals were believed responsible for a
string of violent home invasions, assaults, carjacking and
robberies outside their base in the Caliphate.

Jason laughed cynically as the radio aired the Police
Commissioner's sound-bite. Police were doing everything they
could and under no circumstances should the public take the law

into their own hands. 'Too busy handing out speeding tickets in school zones to take on real criminals' he thought bitterly.

The road curved left between a warehouse and an industrial unit before dividing into a looping driveway that connected all the townhouses. Steering the vehicle in the narrow driveway, Jason's heart sank as he saw the dark shadow where his white front door should have been. Jason knew immediately what it meant, and a shouted curse filled the vehicle as he slammed his fist on the steering wheel. The door had been kicked open, and this was the second time in a month that his house had been robbed.

Rolling the ute to a stop in his driveway, Jason shut down the engine and blew out a deep breath, readying his nerves for whatever he would find inside. Instinctively grabbing the mail from his mailbox on the way, he stepped onto the tiny porch where the front door swung half open in the breeze, pushed it open and went inside.

Just as he feared, the place had been trashed.

Everything from the bookshelves, drawers, cupboards in the lounge and kitchen covered the entire ground floor. Moving upstairs to the two bedrooms he found the same destruction – everything had been ransacked and he could tell that the typically easy to pawn items were missing. He had only just recovered emotionally and financially from the first robbery, and now someone had come back and nicked all the replacement electronics and valuables.

Then he opened the bathroom door. Less than half a second later, he was on his hands and knees in the hallway, vomiting up the remains of his lunch and a growing pool of bile. The smell from the small room had hit his senses as if he had been clubbed with a bat.

Wiping his nose and mouth on his sleeve, Jason waited for his senses to adjust and then gingerly pushed the door open. Whoever had been in his house had left three piles of human shit in his bathroom: one in the shower, one in front of the sink and another on top of the closed lid of his toilet. A dramatic statement, a final series of bullet points as to exactly what the intruders thought of their victims.

Jason felt something change inside him. It was bad enough to break into someone's home and steal their possessions, but what kind of people hung a shit just to mark their territory? He shook his head and started making phone calls to the police and his insurance company.

There was no joy from the police, who took a statement and some photos, then basically told him to do all the work, make a list of the items stolen and email it in to the officers. They would then try to match it up with anything they recovered in the future. Bugger all, basically.

A locksmith arrived and repaired the door jamb where the door had been kicked open. Jason paid him a few extra dollars to use longer screws than went right into the frame of the wall as an extra security measure. It wasn't much, he knew, but it would at least make life a little harder for anyone else who wanted to kick his door in.

A harried-looking forensics guy came and dusted for fingerprints but rushed off again after failing to find anything in his quick search. Jason asked him about DNA from the shit in the bathroom and he just laughed cynically, replying that there was no way such an expensive test would be done unless a murder was involved.

Eventually a professional cleaner from the insurance company turned up to clean the waste out of his bathroom. While that was happening, Jason finally had time to realize he was still clutching the mail he had grabbed earlier in the evening. He righted a chair that was lying sideways on the kitchen floor and sat down at the table, grateful for a familiar task to take his mind off the destruction surrounding him.

There were only a few pieces of paper to sort through: his phone bill, a glossy flyer from the local pizza shop and an A4 typed sheet that had been folded in thirds and stuffed in amongst the rest. It read:

COMMUNITY SAFETY MEETING

Discuss current increase in crime and what we can do to keep our families safe.

Unit 4
7pm Thursday Night

Jason's mouth twisted in a grimace of appreciation and he nodded his head gently as he digested this information. It looked like he wasn't alone, and someone was being proactive in looking for a solution. That was good. His mood improved immediately as he resolved to attend the meeting and he glanced at his watch – it read 6:25 pm. The cleaner advised that the bathroom was clean and Jason thanked him and wished him good luck as he packed away his equipment.

He left his unit just before 7.00pm and walked around the driveway to number 4. The door was open and he followed the sounds of loud conversation down a short hallway and into an open plan dining/entertainment area.

Chairs and sofas had been arranged in a semi-circle in the room, and a wide glass sliding door was open to an outdoor rear patio area, allowing fresh air into the room and giving extra space for people to stand. Jason waited near the hallway and looked around awkwardly. He didn't know anyone and the people all seemed to be talking in small groups. He was embarrassed to just go up and join into a group if he didn't know what they were talking about.

His concerns were eased when a short, skinny man with a bald head clapped his hands several times and waited for quiet. Dressed in dark casual pants and a light-blue collared shirt, he looked around and smiled a tense, thin smile at the group.

'Welcome everyone, thanks for coming' he began, voice shaking a little, then steadying as he became more confident.

'My name is Michael, Mike – I'm the owner of this unit, number 4.' He gestured to the chairs, 'Please, have a seat, wherever you like.'

Trying to be inconspicuous, Jason moved into the middle of the room and took a kitchen chair near the glass door. As the jumble of people settled down into a sitting position, Mike went on, 'can we just go around the room and introduce everyone? Who is in what unit, how long you've been here, that kind of thing? Let's start on my left and go clockwise.'

He gestured to the couple sitting on his left, who shifted in their seats at the sudden attention. 'Bill and Lorna from number 1, we were the first to buy off the plan, back when I retired in 1990. Been here ever since.' Bill's voice trailed off as he looked at the man sitting on his left, silently passing the group's attention over.

'Hi everyone, I'm Prabhu' he said. 'My parents moved to Australia from India in 1971, I was just a baby. I live in number 7 with my wife and our little girl – they are both at home, so it is just me here tonight. We've been broken into, about 4 weeks ago...' He looked around nervously but the young woman next to him jumped right into the conversation.

'I'm Lydia Rhiannon, number 6. I teach at the local school, lived here for about two years but I'm not an owner.' She giggled and went on, 'no way could I afford to buy anything in Sydney...'

Then it was Jason's turn. 'Hi, I'm Jason. This might be the first time you've seen me – I used to do work shift work so I'm usually asleep when everyone else is up, although I'm working business hours now. Moved in about a year ago and I've been robbed twice since then. Mum's been carjacked the last time she came to visit, yeah…. not good at all.'

His comment kicked off several people talking at once, until Mike clapped again and asked for quiet. 'We all have stories to share, but can we please just get everyone introduced?'

Jason noticed that Mike was writing down names and details on a pad of paper. This was a good sign; Mike seemed to be prepared and able to run a meeting. The other people in the room introduced themselves and most of them spoke angrily about home invasions or burglaries they had suffered. Finally, the last resident fell silent and then looked at Mike expectantly.

'Okay', he said, glancing at his notepaper. 'We all know why we are here. We've all seen the news, night after night – crime, robberies and assaults.' He looked at Jason and went on 'at least three of us have been robbed in the last two months…'

Jason spoke up: 'Twice!' All the heads in the room snapped around to look at him in amazement, and there were a couple of audible gasps.

Mike nodded to Jason, who took this as an invitation to say more.

'Yeah, ummm, they broke in, took my electronics – just the usual stuff, easy to sell - about 4 months ago. Then I got home from work this morning and they done it again, got all the new stuff my insurance paid for.'

Mike nodded in sympathy, as did some of the others. Then he took over the meeting again. 'So, to solve a problem, we need to define that problem. What do we know about these criminals?'

There was a moment of silence before everyone started talking at once.

'It can't be just one guy, has to be a group'

'Immigrants?' - 'That Apex Gang?'

'The cops are useless, just put it in the too hard basket'

'I haven't seen anyone, but I'm very concerned it will happen to me'

Mike held up his hands and called for quiet.

'OK, ok, let's take it in turns. Bill, you start and then we'll go around again. Please keep it brief and to the point.'

Bill looked uncomfortable at being put on the spot, and his wife jumped in early: 'I don't know much but I'm very concerned. We've never lived in such fear of being attacked in our own homes, never. I don't know what's happened to this country, but we are both over 60, none of us are a match for even one home invader, let alone more. Something has to be done'

The others in the group nodded.

Lydia the school teacher was next. 'I haven't noticed anything unusual or any strangers hanging around, but honestly, I wasn't really paying attention. I think we should set up a committee to build closer relations with the police, I'd be happy to be president...'

Mike didn't seem enthused by the idea of a committee, but didn't say anything, he just nodded to Jason.

'Well, there were at least three in my place overnight' he began. 'Seems to me these guys, whether they are professional thieves or just junkies, are as good at their jobs as we are at ours. It's their profession, so they are quiet, fast and know how to move around.'

'Hold on' said Mike. 'How do you know there were three? Do you have CCTV?'

'No, I can't afford CCTV, and life isn't an episode of The Bill where it magically solves everything. Even if you do get a good image of the person, they can just stand up in court and say, 'that's not me' and the judge believes them. CCTV is only a deterrent for opportunists, not organized gangs like we are dealing with.' He took a breath.

'I know there were at least three, because three people... went to the toilet...left a dump...in my bathroom...' his voice trailed off, partly in embarrassment to be talking about this in polite company, but also as he caught the shocked expressions on the faces around him. After a moment of stunned silence, Mike finally expressed what they were all thinking.

'Well...shit... Words fail me.' He shook his head and laughed sadly, then looked around the room. His joke had broken the stunned silence and got the conversation back on track.

'That gives you an insight into the mentality of these people. They aren't afraid of anything; they're marking their territory in the most basic, offensive way possible.'

'Even if the police catch these people, and in the unlikely event a judge convicts them, what will happen? They will go to prison, enjoy a comfortable holiday while joining a prison gang to learn more criminal skills for when they are released. Then they come back out, more dangerous than before. We have to find a better solution.'

Lydia spoke up again. 'I agree, a better solution is to build closer ties with the police, so they will attend faster if we have a problem.'

Jason didn't think that would work. 'Who in the police force would this committee work with, and do they have any influence over police response times? I mean, if we call and there's no police available because there's...I dunno...a riot or a prison break or something...we're no safer than we are now.' Lydia shot him a dirty look, but her reply was cut off.

'Well, if CCTV is expensive and doesn't really work, and the police aren't going to arrive in time...what CAN we do? Can we hold them until the police arrive?' asked Prabhu. 'No way will any of us be able to do that...'

Nobody appeared to have any answers, so Mike spoke up. 'There are several issues here:

'Firstly, we all need to be prepared to take responsibility for a share of defending our homes. None of us can do it on our own, we are either too old, too weak or not at home when a home invasion might happen. We need a kind of Neighborhood Watch or Safety House program, remember them? They were intended to share the burden of safety around all members of the community.

'So, we need a low-level amount of constant surveillance, a warning system, so that we can get on with our lives but still respond as a group when needed.

'We also need a communication system, so that when there is an emergency, we all get the message immediately.

'We also need to protect ourselves from the police or the criminals' lawyers. Nobody wants to be accused of something they didn't do...'

Jason had an idea what was coming, but preferred to hold his tongue and let Mike run the show.

'Firstly, we can install a motion sensing CCTV camera at the driveway, covering the front of all the townhouses. Connected to WIFI, it will stream footage when activated, so we will all know if someone is coming or going, as if we were all peeking through our curtains at the same time – no different. The hardware and wiring would be less than $200.00 to install. We can share the cost around, it would be less than $10 each...' he was cut off as Lydia interrupted.

'Sorry, but I just can't agree to being spied upon' she said, with false politeness covering angry emotions. 'It sounds to me like an invasion of privacy! I read in The Guardian...'

One of the others in the room spoke up – Jason had missed the lady's name in the round of introductions, but now she tore into Lydia.

'Don't be silly. Your blinds will be closed, nobody will be able to see into your actual house and anyway, the camera is only looking at the outside to see if a car pulls up - with people we don't know. And in case you hadn't noticed, some of us have had our privacy breached in the worst possible way – so wake up and smell the coffee!'

Lydia looked as if she had swallowed a wasp, but while she tried to get her brain and mouth connected, finally she said 'then why can't we install a dummy camera. Thieves won't know it's a fake, so it would have the same effect.'

Jason spoke up. 'Sorry Lydia, but that's not possible either. There was a case a few years ago, where a strata unit block put up dummy cameras and a 'CCTV IN OPERATION' sign. So, a young couple bought in, moved in, and the wife was raped in the carpark one night. The police went to the committee and asked for the footage, but there was none, because it was a dummy camera. The couple sued the strata owners for damages because they bought in, specifically thinking it had CCTV.' Several people in the room shuddered at the thought, including Lydia.

'If we put in cameras, they have to be real.'

Mike caught his eye as a signal to finish, and then went on as if nothing had happened. 'Secondly, communication. There is a phone app called Cell-411 which we can all download. It will connect us all in a group, and we can message everyone at the same time, so even if you aren't at home, you'll be kept informed.

'If you keep your phone on, and these apps running, you'll always be able to tell who is coming and going, and if any of us has an emergency, we can call for help right away.

'Cell-411 also allows you to stream video from your phone to a secure server. So, if there is an incident, we can all video what happened, and this video will be evidence in court. Even if a criminal breaks your phone, or the police confiscate it, the video is still on the server.'

There were several heads nodding around the room, and a few people pulled out phones and started downloading the app.

Jason did the same as Mike opened his mouth to continue, only to be cut off by Lydia.

'OK, so you can play with your phones' she sneered. 'What are you going to do if you actually catch someone? Are you going to ask them nicely to wait for the police to arrive?' She was beginning to breathe heavily as her emotions boiled up.

'No' replied Mike calmly. 'I'm going to hold them at gunpoint until the police arrive.'

There was a stunned silence in the room as his words were processed. The mention of guns seemed to bring a new dimension to the discussion, as if nobody was serious before, but now they truly appreciated the gravity of the situation.

'Guns?' asked Lydia, her voice ratcheting up a level and becoming shrill. 'I can't believe what I'm hearing. Guns? Guns are dangerous. Guns kill. Guns don't belong in a civilized society! We have the government to keep us safe, we shouldn't take the law into our own hands!' Her head swiveled around as she sought approval from the rest of the room.

Anticipating objections, Mike held up a hand. 'First of all, we aren't living in a civilized society, we are subject to repeated, random violence and burglary. I'm a cop, I believe in the rules down to my bones. But unfortunately, even in a civilized country, there comes a time when the rules just don't work anymore, and each man & woman has to be responsible for their own safety.'

'Secondly, I'm a retired Detective and former Army Reserve officer. I've had a firearms license for the past thirty years and I train many times more than any police officer is required to.' Mike's calm demeanor and the soothing authority in his voice seemed to calm the room, and Lydia's face returned to something like normality.

'On that point' continued Mike, 'does anyone else have a firearms license?'

Jason put up his hand and was surprised to see that the older woman who had rebutted Lydia earlier also put her hand up. 'My dad was John Murphy. He won Bronze in the 1966 Commonwealth Games – it was the first-time shooting was included, ever. So, I've grown up with professional shooters and shot competitively all my life.' Her face smiled as good memories surfaced in her mind, taking her back to a time filled with fun and family.

Jason noticed that Lydia was looking at the speaker with her mouth agape, as if she couldn't process the fact that this elegant, older lady was more familiar with firearms than a police officer. He smiled at the thought of the education that the naïve school teacher must be getting.

Mike turned to Lydia and calmly went on: 'I understand you may be afraid of guns, because your only exposure to them has been via the news and social media, am I right?' She nodded, suddenly meek and attentive to him now she realised he had been an officer and a detective. His authority instinctively compelled her obedience.

'Let me ask you a question,' continued Mike. 'We all know that cars kill far more people than firearms do, right? So why is it that you drive a car, why aren't you more afraid of your car than my gun?'

Lydia thought for a moment, then said 'I suppose…because I learned to drive it…' Her voice trailed off as she saw the smile on Mike's face.

'Exactly!' he said calmly. 'You learned about it, and the knowledge took away your fear.'

'It's not the same' retorted Lydia as her fears rose again. 'Guns are only designed to kill people – cars are not.' She shook her head, 'no, no, no, I'll never agree, that's never okay, no guns…no…' her voice trailed off and so Mike took over the meeting again.

'Okay, I note Lydia's objections but I'm going to call a vote. Raise your hand if in favor of installing the motion cameras?'

All hands went up, including Lydia's.

'Good' said Mike. 'Hands up who needs help installing Cell-411?' A few hands went up, and Mike noted those people for later assistance.

'Finally, who is prepared to stand up to these criminals, and help us hold them until the police arrive?' More than half of the group raised their hands, each receiving a withering glare from Lydia, but the matter was settled.

Mike nodded his thanks to everyone for coming and formally closed the meeting, inviting anyone who needed help with Cell-411 to stay behind. Not knowing what to do, Jason waited at the back of the room while the rest of his neighbors either left early, or had their phones sorted. He used the time to download and install the app himself, and it wasn't long before he and Mike were alone in the room.

Jason introduced himself again, just to make sure Mike knew who he was. 'Thanks very much for hosting this meeting – good idea to get everyone together.'

'Yeah' said Mike. 'Good to know who will work as a team and who…won't' then he laughed with Jason.

'Are you really an ex-cop?' asked Jason. 'You don't seem the type.'

Mike laughed again, and then said quietly 'No, I'm an accountant. But these Leftist types, they need an authority figure in their lives. You saw how the idea of armed citizens scared her – she's already barely coping with life and her own insecurities. But by assuring her that I have state-sponsored authority, I fit into a pre-approved category in her mind and she isn't worried anymore.'

'Did I lie to her? Technically yes. But the good of the community is more important than her fragile belief system. Both of us are trained more highly than most police officers, and neither of us is going to risk losing our gun licenses by being idiots. At the end of the day, Lydia and all her neighbors will sleep soundly in their ignorance, just like they did yesterday.'

He smiled at Jason. 'Ninety percent of getting results is knowing how to deal with people, what their motivations are' he said. 'Lydia here, if it was her door being kicked in, would be screaming for you, me, and anyone to come and help her. But what are we going to do against 3 or 4 motivated, armed, younger attackers, like the guys that did over your place? People like Lydia don't understand what it takes to keep them safe in their little bubble.'

Jason nodded, glad that Mike seemed more and more competent with every passing minute. 'Jack Nicholson in A Few Good Men,' he quipped, and Mike immediately nodded.

'Exactly. 'I resent it when someone who rises and sleeps under a blanket of protection that I provide, dares to question the manner in which I provide it..."

Jason offered his hand, and Mike shook it. 'I'm glad we met, just not under these circumstances. What guns you got?'

Mike shook his head. 'Not so fast. Let's call together the volunteer group tomorrow night and do a proper plan. What we need, who has what, and who can get things we need, that sort of thing.'

Over the next few weeks, the group met, cooperated and welded into a solid team. Jason got to know his neighbors well. They all chipped in a few dollars to purchase the CCTV camera equipment, which Mike had cleverly hidden where it covered the driveway and the front of the houses, but was unable to be seen until you were right in front of it.

Jason was impressed at the video quality on his phone, and the ability of the app to stream video from the camera as soon as it was motion activated. They soon became used to the buzz from their phones, and a simple glance would let them know which of their neighbors was coming or going. The team had also agreed on how to deal with a threat if it arrived, where to meet and who would do what. It was a simple set of rules that were easy to remember.

Days passed, and they settled back into their usual routine. Mike and Jason had met with the other volunteers, unlocking their gun safes and discussing each other's firearms. Jason had learned that the elderly lady who had argued with Lydia was called Mary, and he was amazed to see that she had an Adler A-110 lever action shotgun in her safe.

'Wow, rapid fire and hyper-lethal' he had quipped, mocking the media hysteria they had recently endured from gun control advocates. Mary laughed and said 'oh yes, a deadly Adler. I never had much use for a lever, but with all the fuss, I just had to go and get one.'

Jason was impressed - 'I see you've put on a barrel extension.' In Australia at the time, it was illegal to import a 7-shot version of the Adler, however in a bizarre twist, there were other 7-shot lever action shotguns that were legal to import, made by Pardus, Chiappa or IAC. It was also completely legal to buy a 5-shot Adler and upgrade the magazine to take 7 or more shots. The import ban was completely meaningless.

Such was the ridiculous state of gun control laws in the country. But the illogical gun laws didn't end there. This lady was licensed to own a 7-shot, 12-guage, lever action shotgun but was prohibited from having pepper spray, a taser or even a suppressor for hearing protection. She could blast clay targets with a shotgun all day long, but not carry anything in her purse for self-defense when she went to the shops.

As the conversation broke up and they each went home, Jason checked his News Feed:

NEW POLICE MINISTER RESIGNS OVER CIVIL VIOLENCE

CEASE FIRE? CALIPHATE PROMISES PEACE FOR LEGAL STATUS

HOUSE PRICES TO STABILISE: EXPERT

Later that week, Jason had gone to bed when his phone buzzed, and he knew something was wrong. Normally, he would hear a door open or a car approach, and then the phone would buzz as the camera picked up the movement and streamed the footage to his phone, but this time, he hadn't heard anything.

He checked the screen and felt his heart flutter as he saw a large sedan stopped in the driveway, with the doors open but no sign of people standing around. Something wasn't right. He dressed quickly and took his unloaded shotgun out of the safe. He grabbed a handful of shells from the separate ammo container and slipped out the back door, stuffing them in his pocket and making his way to the agreed meeting point in Mike's back yard.

Mike had already checked the CCTV footage, assessed the situation, and gave quick instructions to the team.

'There are four of them. All wearing hoodies, looks like some kind of Alpha gang. They've gone into Lydia's place.'

Jason was surprised. 'Lydia's place? Any idea why?'

'None' said Mike. 'But after her comments at the meeting, there's no way I'm going to risk anything for her unless she asks for it.'

Jason laughed cynically. 'Good idea,' he said, nodding to Mike that he was ready to move.

'Prabhu, you're with us on the camera. Make sure you don't let any of the guns show on the tape, just to be safe. Mary, you take the back door of Lydia's place. Stop anyone coming out.'

Everyone nodded, loaded their firearms, set the safeties on and then the group split up. Less than two minutes had passed since the gang's car had arrived.

Mike paused for a few seconds to let Mary get in position at the back door, then with Prabhu filming from the side, approached Lydia's front door just as the sound of breaking glass and hysterical screaming came from inside the townhouse.

Mike used the flat of his palm to hammer on the front door, right next to where it had been levered open by a crowbar, and then latched shut from the inside.

The sounds from inside the building stopped, and an eerie silence fell over the area. Mike broke it by bellowing at the top of his lungs

'LYDIA? IT'S MIKE. YOU OK?'

Heavy footsteps could be heard thudding towards them from inside the townhouse, as Lydia's face appeared at the upstairs bedroom window. The abject terror on her face was apparent even at a distance, and Jason saw her looking at their guns, then back over her shoulder. Her eyes were so wide with fear that Jason thought they would fall out.

'DO YOU WANT US TO COME IN?' Mike called to her. She nodded in panic, and Mike snapped the shotgun up to his shoulder as the door was jerked open from the inside. Prabhu took a step to the side, keeping the camera pointed inside the house (and away from the shotguns) as the looming shadow in the doorway suddenly stopped and recoiled at the sight of two large shotguns. Two hands went up in the air, and a large, curved knife clattered to the ground as they turned palm out in a gesture of surrender.

Mike kept his voice the same volume - loud. 'DOWN, DOWN ON THE GROUND. GET DOWN' he screamed, bobbing the barrels up and down to emphasize his words. Even from his position behind Mike, Jason could see the intruder's eyes follow the looming death that lurked inside the black mouths of the shotgun. As the intruder stepped out into the light, Jason could see it was a man, mid-20s and from his skin color Jason would have bet he was an Alpha gang member. Eyes blazing and mouth snarling defiantly in surrender, he slowly kneeled and then stretched out prone. Mike produced a pair of plastic cable ties and cuffed the man's wrists and ankles, then followed Prabhu and the camera into Lydia's house. From upstairs came the sounds of splintering wood and Lydia's hysterical screaming.

Passing the front door, Jason guessed that the layout was identical to his own townhouse. The lounge and kitchen were on the left, garage through a door on the right and the bedrooms upstairs. The three men took only a few seconds to check that there was nobody else on their level and were approaching the stairs when all hell broke loose.

Two more intruders bolted down the stairs and almost fell over when instead of seeing their comrade; they were confronted by the three residents and two large shotguns. The first intruder stopped as if stunned by the sight, and the second ran into his back, throwing them both to the floor in a tangled heap. Just as a third man ran down the stairs, pivoted on one foot and raced to the back door. Yanking it open, he took three steps before his brain processed the sight of another shotgun pointed right in his face. Arms wind milling as he desperately tried to reverse his direction, he skidded on the grass and collapsed onto the ground at Mary's feet.

Sixty seconds later, all 3 intruders were cuffed and Lydia was sitting on the lounge, head in her hands and shaking uncontrollably. Mike said to Mary, 'Why don't you put on a cup of tea and have a chat with Lydia while we wait for the police to arrive?'

'Good idea, I could use one myself. All this excitement' said Mary, handing her shotgun to Mike. 'Put this away for me, would you?' she asked and Mike and Jason both nodded. Mike pointed the shotgun at the ground, and worked the lever to eject all the shells. Then he checked the safety was on, and slung it over his shoulder.

The three men went into the lounge room and Mike sat in a chair facing Lydia. Jason nodded to Prabhu and they backed away into the hall, still present in the room but giving Lydia space so she didn't feel threatened by them crowding her.

'Lydia?' Mike started. 'You're safe now, OK? Mary is going to stay with you for as long as you need, and the police are on their way. No idea how long they will take, but the three of us are going to tidy up. Mary can call us if you need anything more, OK?'

Lydia drew a deep, shuddering breath and looked at Mike. Jason thought there was something different in her eyes, the set of her jaw maybe, but then again, given what she had just suffered, maybe he was reading too much into it. 'Mike…thank you.' Lydia stammered. 'I know I was opposed…at the meeting…but now…I can't imagine…' her voice trailed off but instead of lecturing her, Mike just patted her hand and said 'I'm glad you're OK. Let us know if you need anything, OK?'

Lydia nodded, and then asked, almost absent-mindedly 'w-w-what am I going to tell the police?'

Mike grinned a little sheepishly, and then became serious. 'Tell them the truth' he suggested. 'You were asleep, the noise of the break in woke you up, they tried to get into the bedroom, but something must have startled them. By the time you got downstairs they were tied up but nobody else was here. Mary heard the noise and came to investigate, found them like this and called the police. Maybe it was Batman?'

Mary entered the room with two steaming mugs that smelled like Peppermint. She set them down on the table and Mike took the opportunity to leave.

'You're safe now' he reassured Lydia. 'Talk to Mary if you have any questions about how to handle the police, OK?'

Lydia nodded again and Mike hoped he had done enough – Lydia might need counseling after the shock she had received. Everything she believed about her own safety and the evil of guns, had been proved false in one terrible incident. He knew they had all been very lucky.

Outside, he and Jason and Prabhu all shook hands and slapped each other on the back. The adrenaline was still pumping through their bodies, so Mike suggested they lock the guns away, then meet back at his house to run through what happened, what might have happened, and what they could do differently next time.

Because they all knew, there would definitely be a next time.

-

The weather outside Parliament House was perfect for a Press Conference – the sky was clear and there was no breeze to interfere with the audio or the PM's hairdo.

The PM stood at the microphone, flanked by the Premier and the Attorney General, both looking dour and serious. With a well-rehearsed show of earnest regret and salesmanship, she played to the cameras.

'Regrettably, our efforts to find a peaceful solution to the Caliphate have come to nothing,' she said.

'We have invested considerable resources in trying to accommodate the needs of ALL Australians, however the people making the decisions in the Caliphate reject that description, and defiantly declare that the land is no longer part of Australia.

'We will therefore be launching action in the High Court of Australia, to determine our legal options. This is expected to take 6-9 months, and until that happens we will not, we cannot recognize the Caliphate or any independent borders, trading partners or legal jurisdictions. The NSW Police will retain jurisdiction over ALL of NSW, all taxes and government charges will continue to apply.

'Nobody is above the laws of the Commonwealth and the State of New South Wales.'

Watching the broadcast Live on his phone, Bilal laughed and immediately began posting a picture he had found, one that had become very popular on social media in Sydney in the weeks leading up to the Cronulla Riots. It was a simple map of New South Wales, with 'Under New Management' written across it. The colors used were green, white and red, the same as the Lebanese national flag.

Thumbing across to Twitter, he laughed when the hashtag #UnderNewManagement began trending strongly, liked and forwarded by thousands of supporters in Sydney and across the world.

-

Bilal's heart was filled with pride and joy as he drove west down the M4 towards Penrith. His car contained two other lions, his new friends Mazen and Khaled. It was also crammed with camping equipment, clothes and food supplies for two weeks training near Dubbo. After months of book learning, working the delivery route and helping the Mullah with everything from stacking shelves to delivering money, Bilal and his companions had been selected for the real thing: actual war training.

Finally, they felt they were doing REAL work. Men's work.

The afternoon was warm, so the car windows were down and the stereo was loud – with Bilal's playlist pumping from his phone via the Bluetooth connection. The young men joked with each other, ate snacks and yelled song lyrics as the car ate up the road towards the setting sun.

Steering the sports car down the wide, smooth freeway, Bilal's mind drifted back to his last meeting with the Mullah, when he was given this mission. Once the religious instruction and memorizing the Koran was finished, the Mullah had asked Bilal if there were any questions.

Bilal asked about Xanthe. He liked her; liked her a lot. She seemed receptive to the idea of converting to Islam, and Bilal asked the Mullah for his opinion about whether he had a chance of marrying her.

The Mullah's eyes and face smiled widely at the question, but he knew that the only chance of keeping his army intact and fighting for a place in heaven was to make sure they never learned that heaven was to be found on earth - in the arms of a loving woman. Depriving the young men of meaningful relationships, while promising eternal pleasures in the world to come, was a powerful control mechanism practiced by many religions all over the world, and the Caliphate's rulers knew very well the power of such control.

So, the Mullah warmly and kindly responded to Bilal's nervous question. 'Bilal, truly you are becoming a great man. Wonderful things, riches and many beautiful wives lie in store for you. I have seen Xanthe a few times, and I agree, if she were to convert to Islam, she may make a fine wife.'

Then his expression turned serious, and he leaned in towards Bilal and spoke softly, conspiratorially, emphasizing that these words were for Bilal alone: 'Submission to Allah means total submission of mind, body and soul. Right now, Allah has called you to greatness, and you do best to focus on things that are eternal, rather than temporary.

'Your eternal reward comes from victory in our struggle here. Yes, fine wives and riches are surely a temporary, earthly reward, and they will come, in time. But only if you secure success in establishing the Caliphate between the rivers.'

He looked Bilal directly in the eyes. 'Hold your thought of Xanthe. Once the Caliphate is secure, you will be even more valuable and attractive to her as a husband. But the needs of a wife will distract you from success, and then you risk having neither riches now, or eternal pleasure in heaven. Understand?'

Bilal nodded. 'Short term pain for long term gain,' he said.

The Mullah smiled even wider, and embraced Bilal like a son. 'Exactly' he said. 'You are already growing wise beyond your years. Truly you will be a great and wise warrior for the Caliph. A prince among your people. *Inshallah.*'

After a few hours of driving, Bilal pulled the EVO into a petrol station. His eyes and brain hurt from navigating the steep hills and twisting road that had taken them far away from Sydney. He dragged his body out of the driver's seat and stretched, moving his arms and legs - sore from sitting so long.

Khaled and Mazen also stepped out of the sports car and looked around. It was a standard Shell service station on the Great Western Highway, like thousands which dotted the highways and towns all over the country. A signpost said, 'Magpie Hollow Road' and 'Lake Lyell' – neither of which meant anything to the three men. Bilal jerked the nozzle out of the petrol pump and began to fill the car. He nodded to Khaled 'Must be nearly there – check the map, bro.' They had all left their phones with other trainees back in Sydney, so as far as anyone tracking them would know, they were sticking to their old work, gym and home routines. *Taqiya.*

Khaled pulled the paper tourist map out of the side pocked in the car door and spread it out on the bonnet. 'What're we in now?' he asked Bilal.

'Almost in Lithgow' he replied and watched as Khaled put his finger on Dubbo and moved it across the map towards the ocean. His finger wavered around as his eyes roved over the map looking for 'Lithgow.'

'Wellington, Mudgee, Molong, Orange, Bathurst…we bin through Bathurst? How long ago we go through Bathurst?'

Bilal couldn't remember going through any of those towns. He frowned, hanging up the nozzle and then stepping over to the bonnet beside his friend. He put his finger on Sydney and moved it across the map, mentally ticking off the places he was certain they had been.

'Penrith – yep, Katoomba – yep.' His finger moved another centimeter across the map and stopped at 'Lithgow.' Bilal was horrified, his brain trying to comprehend the distance they had travelled in the car, compared to the tiny amount of the map they had traversed. His eyes ran out to where Khaled's finger rested on Dubbo, then back to Lithgow, and finally to Sydney, struggling to comprehend the size of the country they were crossing.

He looked at Khaled, who had visibly paled, and shook his head. 'Dis can't be right. How long's it supposed to take to get there?'

Khaled shrugged. 'Dunno – nobody told me'.

'F…' Bilal bit back the swear words that rose into his mouth. It was going to take hours. Hours more than the hours they had already travelled – they were barely a quarter of the way.

Khaled folded up the map as Bilal went into the shop and paid for the fuel. He returned to the car with two plastic bags bulging with snacks, chips and energy drinks. The three men got back into the car, fired it up and continued west.

It was less than an hour before Bilal's body became resistant to the ever-increasing doses of sugar and stimulant he was guzzling from a can and he realized it was dangerous to continue. Mazen agreed to drive for a while and so Bilal slowed the car and looked for a place to pull over. This presented a serious problem, given the low clearance under the sports car, but eventually he was able to move left and pull over on the side of the road. He opened the door, stepped out into the chill night air and shuddered involuntarily as his senses registered something primeval that he had never experienced before.

He lacked the words to describe what he was seeing and what it imparted to his subconscious. The blazing expanse of the

Milky Way above lit up the sky in a way he had never seen before, and could never have imagined, growing up in a city surrounded by artificial light. The air was still and menacing, there were no buildings around to reflect sound back to him so the whole experience drummed into him that he was small, insignificant. Trees set back from the road broke up the horizon a little, but Bilal felt that if he stepped away from the car, he would be swallowed up by the landscape, squashed into nothing – like a fly on the car windscreen. He felt as if there was a monstrous force in the night sky, tugging at him, and if he lost his footing he might be snatched away, never to return home.

He knew there were people around – they had driven through towns and little hamlets – but out here, you might walk for a day without seeing another person. He felt true doubt gnaw at his confidence. The Caliph may be secure Between The Rivers in Sydney, but how on earth would they be able to control a country as big as this?

He shook his head to clear such doubts. Surely, it was the will of Allah and therefore it would be miraculous when it happened, as it surely would. The gravel crunched underfoot as he walked past the motor – still running – and got into the passenger seat.

But the feeling of unease got into the car with him, and hugged him for a long time, driving away sleep & comfort and torturing him with an endless series of 'what if' scenarios.

After several more hours - with Bilal back behind the wheel - they reached Dubbo, and crawled through the main street of town at 60km/h instead of the 120 km/h they had averaged on the highways. The road passed the now-familiar string of petrol station, car and farm machinery dealers, Chinese restaurant and a couple of pubs – all eerily still and silent under the cool gaze of the waning moon. Bilal slowed as the road curved slightly to the left before they came to a bridge over the Macquarie River. He pressed the small button on the trip meter beside the fuel gauge and zeroed it, then pulled out the slip of paper with their final directions.

Heading south-west on the Newell Highway, they drove for 16.9km and turned Right onto Tinks Road, which veered left and became Springvale Road. Bilal winced as the black asphalt gave way to dirt and he heard the constant dinging of rocks underneath the car. Now he understood the patronizing smiles on the faces of the people who had been out here before, when he declared – somewhat defensively – that the EVO would be fine. He had been insulted that they dared question his car, mocking it and therefore his masculinity for buying it, but now he realized the country was far different to anything he could have imagined. It was a hard lesson for him to learn.

After almost another hour, they arrived at the marked gate and drove through, closing it behind them. The road continued into the bush, curved to the left between two hills and then burst out of the trees into a large clearing, illuminated by a glowing campfire, several 12-volt lights and the spectacular stars frozen in the sky above.

They had passed their first training exercise – getting here. Now their military training would begin in earnest. Bilal swung the car onto a patch of grass next to an old F-100 and shut off the engine. The silence rushed into the car as he opened the door and stepped out into the menacingly empty night. His skin crawled again – just like it had earlier that night. He felt like the sky had a magnetic field that was tugging sound, warmth and his very being up into the empty nothingness beyond.

Three car doors broke the silence as the boys shut them, and again the noise seemed to be eerily absorbed by the unfamiliar landscape.

The campsite was deserted.

Bilal looked around, squinting as he tried to make his eyes see in the dark. He turned to the others, only to find them looking at him. He shrugged. 'I wonder where everyone…' he started to say, but the rest of the sentence didn't leave his mouth.

On the far side of the campsite, four sets of car headlights suddenly burst into life, shocking the three into petrified statues as an amplified voice boomed 'POLICE. FREEZE.'

Oddly, it was the alien, disembodied, almost mechanized voice that broke the spell. Bilal was already turning as he yelled 'Run' to his fellows and broke into a sprint, back the way he had come. The noise of the blood pumping in his head and the air burning his lungs drowned out the noise of pursuit, so he couldn't tell if anyone was chasing, or how close they were. He couldn't even tell if Mazen or Khaled were following, he just dashed blindly away from the police, running headlong down the road until his heart sank further.

Headlights were approaching – another car moving in behind to cut off their retreat and close the trap.

Bilal noted it, processed it immediately, considered giving up, decided against it and veered to the right, off the road and out into the unknown. Crashing through knee high bushes, narrowly dodging around trees that loomed out of the night like sentries, he glanced around once and saw Mazen and Khaled trailing him, with two sets of headlights approaching some distance behind.

Buoyed by the knowledge that his friends were still close, he desperately tried to plan a way to escape. They were miles away from the closest town, with no water, no map, no phone service, nothing. Hiding and waiting for dawn wasn't an option. Shit! Shit! Shit! – what could they do?

Still running as fast as possible through the night, Bilal hadn't thought of anything when the ground suddenly disappeared underfoot, and the three runners fell headlong into a deep gully that ran diagonally across their path. Crashing into the sand at the bottom, the softer sand didn't absorb much of the impact and each of them let out a deep moan - a moose call, as all the air was knocked out of their lungs and they fought for breath.

Panicked and desperate, Bilal forced his limbs to work, crawling a few meters down the gully until torchlight blazed over them all and several shadows crowded around, grabbing them off the ground, pulling black hoods over their heads and hauling them back up to ground level.

Wrists zip-tied together, the three fugitives were marched back towards camp. Bilal was thrown onto the ground near the fire – he could hear the sound and feel the heat on his body, and he heard the other two being dragged further away until the noise faded, and he was left alone with the soft crackling of the fire and the icy void forming in his stomach. The fear grew up into his throat, choking him and paralyzing his body and his mind, threatening to suffocate him. He decided he wouldn't say anything, no matter what. Defiance was one thing he could hold onto. They could never take that away.

It seemed to Bilal that hours had passed when he heard the scrunch of boots across the ground and his captors returned. Wrists still cuffed behind his back, he was hauled to his feet and thrown backwards into a soft camp chair. Wriggling a little in discomfort, he found that he was unable to sit forward enough to get out of the chair, and he heard the others laughing at him wriggling like an eel as he did so.

Then the questions started.

'What's your name?'

'Where do you live?'

'Who were you meeting here?'

'Do you know, or have you heard of the following people: Khalid bin Mahfouz, Alfred Hartman or Shaikh Mohammed Ishaq?'

Bilal remained silent and motionless, refusing to even wiggle in case they interpreted it as an answer.

'What about Melina Roberge?' it sounded like a French name, pronounced with a long 'rrrghe' sound. Bilal stayed silent. His fears ratcheted to a higher level even though he had no idea who these people were – it sounded like the police were trying to tie him to them and that was definitely not a good thing. At all.

He grunted aloud as a heavy hand cuffed him on the side of his hooded head. Unseen and unexpected, the blow shook him to the core. Pain exploded across his ear and his skin felt as if it was on fire. He barely heard a second voice ask 'What'ssa matter? Cat gotcha tongue?'

'Fuck this' Bilal said. 'You can't treat me like this. I got rights.'

All he heard in return was laughter. Then another blow landed, harder than the first, rocking his head on his neck and making him see stars. It was the simplest kind of rebuttal to his protestations, telling him a lot of things without saying a word. Bilal decided to never make another sound until they killed him.

Then the questions started again. 'What's your name?'

'Do you know Melina Roberge?'

'Your friends have already told us everything, so we will know if you lie to us. What is your address?'

Bilal sighed inwardly. Now that the shock of the chase and captivity had worn off, he was beginning to think about the implications of his situation. His life was over. Captured by the police, he would likely spend the rest of his life in jail. Gone were his business plans, his car, his friends – he wondered how they were coping.

Eventually, the sun rose and he began to sweat inside his nylon tracksuit and suffocating hood. There was pain in every part of his body, from his hands cuffed underneath him, his shoulders aching from hours in an awkward chair, his eyes, nose and mouth itching from the hood and his brain throbbing from several slaps around the head. His mouth was dry but every time he was offered water, he shook his head, determined to deny his captors any chance to mess with him.

Thinking about jail, he consoled himself with the idea that some of his friends and relatives were in there already, and he would no doubt be taught how to live and prosper in that environment. He would learn. He would adapt. He would survive.

His captors became increasingly aggressive and physically abusive, until the beatings reached a crescendo and the first voice said 'Forget it, he's never going to break. Just kill him now and dump the body.'

Bilal almost shat himself, but then some part of the Mullah, rising to the surface of his mind, cooled his fear and calmed his thoughts. If he was to die, Inshallah, then he would be in paradise. He had fought hard against the interrogation, he hadn't given the infidels a thing, and he knew Allah would reward his devotion once he left this world.

He didn't resist as he was hauled to his feet, thrown forward to his knees and felt the hard, cold barrel of a gun pressed against the back of his head. 'Last chance!' Rasped the second interrogator. 'What is your name?'

Bilal stayed as still as he could, his body felt as if it was burning in the fires of hell itself, hot from the sun and his nylon clothes, barely able to breathe inside the stifling hood and bruised all over from the beatings. Inside his head however, it was a different story. He kept his thoughts focused on the Mullah's lessons, the teachings of the Holy Scriptures, and the glory he knew awaited him in Paradise.

'All right, dead man,' said the voice behind him, and the pressure on his skull eased as the gun was drawn back. Bilal's body tensed involuntarily and then jerked reflexively as there was a sharp 'CRACK' sound.

But there was no pain. He was still conscious.

What the fuck was happening?

Suddenly the hood was ripped off his head and all he could hear was laughter – he opened his eyes, blinking rapidly and squinting in the harsh sunlight and saw a group, maybe ten people standing around laughing at him as hard as they could.

He then noticed that none of them were wearing police uniforms, they were mostly in jeans and T-shirts; some even wore the traditional dishdasha and sandals. Someone fumbled with his hands and he felt the zip ties being cut away. Then the blood started to flow back into his hands and it was agony.

Trying to speak, he moved his jaw and mouth but nothing came out except a croaking sound. The crowd laughed harder, but Bilal began to detect humor rather than spite, and gratefully accepted a water bottle, which he drained. He was finishing the water as he heard the first interrogator's voice say, 'very good.'

Turning his head, he saw the voice belonged to a short, thick man who looked about forty years old. He had short, graying black hair which merged on his pudgy cheeks into a wide, thick beard. Although he looked fat, Bilal could tell by the way he moved that there was a lot of muscle underneath, and this guy was very powerful, very dangerous. Bilal decided to keep his mouth shut.

'Bilal, welcome!' the man went on, embracing him with a traditional kiss on both cheeks. 'Congratulations on passing your first test, with flying colors!' The man gestured to the others, who broke into applause and crowded around him, saying their congratulations and slapping him on the back and shaking his hand.

Bilal's face broke into a grin as the situation became clear to him. 'There were no cops, then?' he asked sheepishly. The whole thing had been a trick to see if he would break.

The crowd roared with laughter again, and he saw Mazen and Khaled, looking as disheveled and uncomfortable as he felt he must look. They greeted each other and stood together in front of the older man.

'You did very well, my sons. Very impressive, none of you gave up a thing, even when threatened with death' replied the man. 'My name is Hamad, Hamad Al-Aqua. You will get to know the others...' he waved his hand around...'over the next few days. But now, let's eat...after we pray, yes?'

Bilal nodded. Now that the adrenaline had worn off, he realized he was starving. After their familiar morning ritual, the crowd broke up into smaller groups who began preparing food and organizing the campsite. Bilal and Mazen unloaded the food they had brought while Khaled and a few others set up their tents.

Once they had eaten, the three friends were introduced to the man who would dominate every waking second of their lives for the next two weeks – and a great portion of their sleeping nightmares. Bilal hadn't seen Deng since the lunch in Lakemba after Xanthe had broken him out of Villawood. Now he was dressed as if he had raided the bargain bin at an army disposal store. Old black boots, faded green camo pants and a tattered, long sleeve shirt were topped with an equally faded green boonie hat. In one hand, Deng carried a bamboo staff about the size of a broomstick, leaning on it like a walking stick as he showed them around the area, using it to point out the toilet area, generator and fuel, exercise equipment and so on.

Bilal looked over the exercise equipment and wasn't impressed at all. There was no gym, just a chin-up bar tied across the branches of a large tree, and some rusty free weights on the ground below. He tried to focus on what Deng was saying, but only caught the last part.

'...two weeks. So we train every day, get your mind an body ready for protectin' de Caliph and 'is lands. Lissen good now, you tree must be closer than brothers. We train you together, understand? Together. You stay together, you eat together, one stand guard while two sleep, understand? You watch each other's backs, help each other? OK?'

The three nodded, and Deng pointed with his cane at a large, blackened tree that stood out against the horizon. Bilal guessed that it had been hit by lighting, or deliberately burned by fire, 'Now, we run dere to dat tree, run back, ok?'

He looked at the three, who nodded. 'RUN' he called, and set off towards the tree in the distance. The others dashed after Deng, caught up and then slackened off to keep pace with him.

The ground wasn't like a road or playing field that Bilal had used for school sports, and he hadn't run more than a few meters in the past year – the only exercise he had been going was heavy weight training in the gym. So while his legs were strong, he was constantly trying to keep his footing among the tussocks of grass that dotted the undulating ground, scoured and cut by centuries of flooding rains and decade-long droughts. His lungs burned, and the blood roared in his ears as he grimly forced himself to keep up with the nimble trainer.

Deng reached the tree first, slapped it with his hand and then waited a few seconds while the others did the same. Bilal felt sicker than he ever had in his life – the combination of running, dehydration, nylon tracksuit and morning heat had given him a pounding headache, and he was gasping for breath as well. Sweat was pouring from his head and face, down his back, making the tracksuit pants stick to his legs. He turned to Deng, who hadn't even started to perspire, and asked:

'What we running so much for? Aren't we gonna have cars and shit in the city?' The others, looking as wrecked as he felt, nodded and turned to Deng. What was the point of so much running?

Deng's face didn't change at all, he simply swung the cane quickly through the air and hit Bilal in the thigh. There was a sharp 'CRACK' sound but Bilal didn't hear it because the pain exploded up his leg as if he had been shot. He cried aloud and tried to hop on his good leg, but Deng grabbed his arm and got right up in his face.

'You bin shot by de police – now what you gonna do' he screamed into Bilal's face, the words and the emotion they conveyed going right into his soul.

'You gonna wait for dem to catch you? Torture you? Drug you so you tell dem everyting?' Bilal's face contorted with pain and he couldn't answer. Deng was right up in his personal space, screaming.

'Yes? NO? You gonna even try to get away?'

Bilal nodded, humming and gritting his teeth at the pain. 'RUN', he managed to gasp, and Deng nodded.

'Yes, RUN' and he turned to Mazen and Khaled – 'Him shot by police? You help him, now. RUN.'

Then he set off back towards the camp.

Bilal grunted as his friends grabbed an arm each and half dragged, half supported him back towards camp. By the time they reached Deng, Bilal's leg had stopped hurting as much and he was able to limp on his own. They jogged up to Deng and he looked at them with a menacing eye.

'You unnerstand now?' he asked, looking at all three in turn. 'No excuses. You keep fighting no matter what. You never leave your brother, you drag him away if necessary. Understand?'

Chests heaving for air and drenched in sweat from their exertions and inappropriate clothing, the three volunteers could only nod and squint against the sun in their eyes. They followed Deng over to the weight training equipment to begin the next set of exercises – all designed to train their minds to overcome any resistance, boredom or objection and work together to finish the set tasks.

-

Senior Constable Zelinski and Constable Connor were out doing a safe storage inspection. Every time a firearm is legally purchased in Australia, the owner is required to declare the physical address of where the firearm will be stored. The local police use this information to do a random annual inspection, to make sure all the legal firearms are where they are supposed to be.

The two police officers liked this kind of job, because the legal firearms owners were all polite, well-behaved and generally happy to help get the intrusion out of the way. This time was no different, and Bill, the gun owner, greeted them at the door, opened his gun safe and passed over the selection of rifles and shotguns so that Constable Connor could check off the serial numbers against the sheets of paper printed off by the Police Register. One by one, the numbers were checked until Bill passed over the last one, an antique double-barrel shotgun.

Admiring the work of art, Connor pressed the lever to open the gun and almost wet himself when two red shotgun shells popped out, narrowly missing his face. Flaming with anger, he turned to Bill angrily, 'You handed me a loaded shotgun? I could have killed myself!' His hand instinctively went to his notebook in preparation for charging Bill with firearms offences. The junior police officer's personal shock translated easily into bureaucratic power, and he was looking forward to taking Bill's cherished firearms and watching them be crushed.

'They're snap caps. It's not loaded...' Bill said calmly – while his facial expression said 'What are we, in kindergarten? Why don't you know this?'

Picking the plastic items off the floor, Bill explained, 'Storing a shotgun like this, when it's empty places a strain on the firing spring. And dry-firing can damage the firing pin. Anyone with this type of shotgun will store it with inert snap caps in it. I'll show you.' Gently taking the shotgun from the shaken officer, he pointed the firearm towards the ground and demonstrated.

'Look at the snap caps – they are just a piece of plastic. There is no primer, no ammunition. It's just a chock to avoid damaging the working parts.'

'First, you open the breech, and check it's clear. Then you put in the snap caps, and close it.' Bill snapped the shotgun closed with a practiced swing of his wrist, and noticed the officers wince as the firearm suddenly appeared more dangerous now that it was closed.

'Relax,' he said. 'Remember, it's not loaded. Less dangerous than a hammer or a machete,' before finishing the lesson. He squeezed the trigger and the gun made a metallic SNAP sound as the firing pin was released into the plastic cap.

'Finally, you release the mechanism on both barrels,' he moved the selector switch and squeezed the trigger again, making the sound a second time. 'This gun is now completely safe, and it's not putting any strain on the firing mechanism. You want a try?'

Connor shook his head but Zelinski took up Bill on his offer. Bill walked him through the procedure and praised the officer upon successful completion. Watching his fellow officer do it seemed to calm Connor down, and he then accepted Bill's offer of a lesson.

The tension in the room broken, Bill was glad he had been able to educate the officers. He hoped that their experience would help them in future dealings with his fellow licensed shooters. As they turned to leave, Connor's eyes fell on a perfect opportunity to get even. Sitting on top of the gun safe, almost out of sight and certainly out of reach of children was a cardboard sheet with a plastic toy rifle attached to it.

Shaped like an Austeyr, the service rifle of the Australian Defence Forces, the child's toy could be deemed a 'prohibited item' because it looked substantially the same as a real, prohibited firearm. Picking it up, Connor turned triumphantly to Bill and said 'I'll have to confiscate this. It's a breach of Section 3(A)(1) of Schedule 1 of the Weapons Prohibition Act.'

Bill felt a cold weight settle in his heart. It was a harsh contrast to the good feelings he had about the way the snap caps episode had ended, and he was hoping the officers were leaving on good terms. He desperately tried to think of a reason why his son's Christmas present should be left alone, but instead was horrified at the words that came of out of his mouth. His mouth ran away without any connection to his thought process, and all he could do was listen to himself.

'Ahhh, that's a pity, it's a Christmas present for one of the refugee kids at the LGBT women's shelter… but if it's the law then I guess you'll have to seize it.'

He became philosophical, asking 'I wonder how your desk Sergeant will go about explaining it to The Project or Today Tonight once they hear about it?' Bill shut his mouth as quickly as he realized what he was saying, and waited to see if the upstart young officer would arrest him for interfering in a police investigation. Mentally he was kicking himself for disrespecting the one person who could really cause serious trouble in his life. He could be in serious trouble.

To his surprise both Connor and Zelinski went pale, and looked at each other. An unspoken understanding passed between them then Connor simply put the toy back on top of the safe and said 'Thanks for your time, Bill. Appreciate the info about snap caps.'

Bill managed to swallow his astonishment and escorted the officers out of his home. Once the door was closed behind them, he sagged onto the sofa and let out a deep breath. 'Jesus, Bill' he exhaled. 'Mouthing off to the cops, what's got into ya?'

Thinking about the reaction of the police officers to his sarcastic remarks, he wondered what kind of politically correct bullshit the front-line coppers were subjected to. Given the rubbish he knew was pushed by the daytime TV propaganda shows, he guessed that the politically motivated senior cops would be extremely sensitive to anything about refugees or sexual politics.

He almost felt sorry for the young coppers. Almost.

Lisa was running through the dawn, pushing her body and her mind towards the goal she had settled on weeks before. Hearing the PM's announcement of the Marine Corps had lit a fire inside her that was completely new, and surprised her by its intensity. Despite her emotional trauma, she had seen the opportunity to serve her country, to travel and save some money at the same time as a healing process.

Her therapist had been skeptical, when Lisa first brought up the Marines, but after discussing her progress and the opportunities she saw, they agreed that she should apply. Lisa understood that the Marines may reject her application, due to her personal history, but she was determined to give it her best shot.

As her lungs burned in the crisp morning air, Lisa's mind drifted off the pain in her body, back to when it was so strong she felt she would pass out. Her physical therapy had been grueling, painstakingly putting her body through increasingly difficult stress to regain her muscle tone and motor skills.

She found that having a concrete goal, and minimum fitness requirements to meet for recruit training gave her a lot of incentive, and improved her mood and motivation. The freedom of being able to exercise out in nature, rather than the more claustrophobic therapy rooms in the hospital gave her something to look forward to every morning.

Thinking of the therapy rooms made her remember a funny incident that stood out amongst what was generally a depressing and painful experience. Lisa and the other patients were sitting in chairs, a small weight or a bean bag on their ankle, systematically lifting and lowering the injured limbs as they worked on the muscles.

One day, the door burst open and in hobbled a thin, blonde and very tanned man, wearing sandals, shorts and a blue singlet. He introduced himself as 'Joe', threw himself into a vacant chair, put a bean bag on his ankle and proceeded to crank out his exercises while striking up conversations with everyone else in the room. His energy was infectious, and the other patients were pleased to join in and share their stories.

But it was Joe's story that caught their imagination.

Joe was an environmentalist, a full-time student who basically lived on the dole and spent as much time as he could climbing mountains. He had fallen off a cliff, high up on a mountain in South America –the kind of situation that was normally a death sentence. In an amazing story of survival, Joe had crawled back down to safety and managed to get home with Simon.

Following several operations, the doctors told Joe he would never walk properly again, but he proved them wrong by his determination and pig-headed refusal to accept the odds against his recovery. He pushed ahead with therapy, eventually regaining ten degrees movement in his knee.

With his therapy progressing well, Joe and some mates were out at the pub to celebrate an engagement. Late in the evening and roaring drunk, Joe stepped out of the pub door, misjudged the step and collapsed back on his weak knee. There was a sickening, grisly crunching noise and everything went black.

Joe woke up in bed the next morning with his knee the size of a pumpkin. Explaining to his doctor what had happened, the doctor replied, 'You've performed a manipulation on yourself. Normally we would knock you out for something like that, but congratulations, you've now got thirty degrees movement in your knee.'

Joe seemed to have something – a magical energy that carried him through life and gave him what it took to survive. Through some combination of luck, bloody minded determination and alcohol, he had somehow survived something like Lisa's experience.

Thinking about what had led Joe to their therapy room, and his positive attitude towards recovery – and life in general – gave Lisa what she needed to push hard against her own challenges.

A chime in her earphones told Lisa that her 5km was finished, and she dropped into a series of pushups, sit ups and stretches. Although her body didn't meet the minimum standards for the Marines yet, she was well on her way and confident that she would be ready when her time came.

-

Bilal opened the apartment door and stepped inside, calling out to see if anyone was home. Only silence responded – his mother and everyone else were gone for the day. Xanthe followed him into the living room, taking off her hijab and hanging the material on a hook near the door. She shook out her blonde hair and caught Bilal looking at her as her body wiggled. She was wearing a long sleeve dress that reached almost to the floor, but it was made of a silky material that clung to every curve like liquid. It was completely in accordance with traditional dress codes yet screamingly sexual.

Frozen like a statue, unsure of what to say or do, Bilal felt Xanthe take his hand and lead him to the staircase that led up to the bedrooms. As her bare feet moved up the stairs in front of him, a small gold chain on her tanned ankle drew Bilal's attention. His eyes moved up her legs, flexing as she climbed the stairs and completely defined by the smooth fabric that clung to her skin. Bilal felt his heart pounding as if it would burst, until his eyes rose further, and he saw there was no panty line under the dress. That was when his heart stopped for a full beat and he almost tripped down the stairs.

Xanthe tilted her head and looked down at him, a smile lighting up her face with amusement at his predicament. She winked at him, opened his bedroom door and pulled on his hand, yanking him into the room before pushing him backwards onto the bed.

Lying on his back, with his knees bent and feet flat on the floor, Bilal craned his neck to look up at Xanthe. She shut the door, then pressed her hand to his head, easing him back onto the mattress.

'Shhhhh, my love' she whispered, 'relax and let me.'

Bilal felt his heart about to burst as Xanthe kneeled in front of him. His pulse roared in his ears and he was afraid of doing or saying something that would spoil the moment. But that fear exploded into mindless terror as another face loomed over him.

A man's face. Bearded, swarthy and purple with rage.

The Mullah. His mouth opened like the caverns of hell and Bilal felt hot breath on his cheek as the Mullah bellowed 'HARAM!'

Haram was forbidden. Religiously unclean. Defiling.

Bilal jerked awake, covered in sweat and tangled in his bed sheets. He shook his head, trying to mentally sort out his burning lust for Xanthe, his religious obligations, and his great desire to please the Mullah and be an obedient student.

It was a long time before he could fall back to sleep.

Chapter 14

December

Now in a delivery truck of his own, Bilal waited in the hot sun for his turn to unload his delivery at the Sydney International Cruise Terminal in The Rocks. He idly thumbed through his news feed as he grew bored of watching the forklifts scurry back and forth, feeding pallets into the hungry ship.

CLERIC: 'SAYING 'MERRY CHRISTMAS' WORSE THAN MURDER

TERROR RAIDS AND MORE CELEBRITY DEATHS

NEW MARINE CORPS RECRUITS BEGIN TRAINING

MULLAH: BAN ON NYE ALCOHOL WOULD REDUCE VIOLENCE

He looked up from his phone in time to be waved through. He put the truck in gear, pulled into position and opened the rear shutter to allow the forklifts access to the pallet inside. Once his load was delivered and signed for, nobody was paying any attention to him, so he quickly double-parked at the side of the terminal building, taking care to make sure the truck was in the shade. Leaving the truck locked and hazard lights flashing, he ran around the corner and joined the crowds of passengers milling outside the terminal. Jostling through the mass of people and luggage, he found his delivery contact waiting beside the escalators that led up to the taxi rank on the upper level. The young woman was wearing a yellow shirt, as per Bilal's arrangements, and her green trolley suitcase had a yellow strap around it. She also wore a hiking daypack and a bored expression behind her reflector sunglasses.

'Hey, I hope you haven't been waiting more than five minutes' said Bilal, carefully choosing the number he used in the greeting. The woman's response would give him vital information about the situation – if her response, when added to his number, brought the total of the numbers to today's day in the month, he would know it was safe. If the number she gave was too high or too low, he would know to either walk away and meet at another time, or that he was being followed and he would need to shake off a tail.

'No, no – only two minutes' she replied with a smile. 'No problems at all.' Bilal breathed a sigh of relief. Today was Thursday December 7. All was well. He nodded at the green suitcase.

'All there?' he asked, but she just smiled at him and said 'I haven't opened it at all. I just lived out of my backpack for the whole week.'

Bilal hovered awkwardly for a moment, then took hold of the suitcase. He nodded to the anonymous young woman and she said, 'have a nice day' as she turned and disappeared into the crowd. Just another bronzed Millennial who had spent a week at sea. Ferrying her suitcase through customs had been a simple task for the young actress. She considered it part of her job and had trained hard to match all the innocent mannerisms of the normal traveler, avoiding any of the telltale signs that the customs agents were scanning the crowd for – looking for a guilty traveler. It was a skill set she was happy to invest in, since the twenty kilograms of cocaine, steroids and other drugs stashed inside the bag by Bilal's contacts on the ship ensured she was well paid. Her Bitcoin account was becoming very healthy. If she ever needed more cash than her waitressing job paid, she could use any of the Hawala exchangers to sell Bitcoins for untraceable local currency, precious metal coins or credit with any of the dealer's other trusted customers. And a regular cruise was just part of the job – nice work if you can get it.

Pushing the suitcase through the crowd, Bilal also appeared to be nothing more than a traveler eager to get home. He moved back to his truck and put the suitcase in the passenger foot well. Then he climbed in the driver's side, started the engine and drove out into the afternoon weekday traffic. Most of this delivery would be gone by Sunday, sold and snorted at parties all over the city, with his own Bitcoin account replenished by the profits, and then the process would start all over again with the next cruise ship. Although his operation was very small by comparison, Bilal was basically running an international smuggling operation with nothing more than a Bitcoin account, a burner phone and a hundred free Wi-Fi Hotspots all over Sydney. Just twenty years ago, an operation of this size would have required significantly more investment in people, security, bribes and computerisation, but now the same resources were available online, at a fraction of the cost.

Chapter 15

January, two years from now

Australian Marine Corps Recruit Training Depot Holsworthy

Lisa had survived Hell Week.

Looking in the mirror, she barely recognized herself. While she had lost weight, gained a tan and cut her hair off, the main change was in her eyes. She knew that she wasn't the same person.

The bags of sorrow and pain underneath her eyes were gone. The woman who had cried for entire nights, lost in blanketing clouds of loss didn't exist anymore. Lisa had stepped off the bus with 45 other volunteers, signed the necessary paperwork and by the time she sat in the barber's chair, the old Lisa had started to disappear. Recruit training protocols helped the process even more - she now referred to herself as 'this recruit' – screamed at the top of her lungs – part of the scientifically designed transformation process used by the Marines to train the best small unit fighting troops in the world. Other recruits were 'that recruit' or 'those recruits.' Apart from 'Sir, Yes Sir' and 'Sir, No Sir', there were few words she and the other recruits were permitted to utter in the presence of the Training Staff.

Lisa's mind was refreshed because she was generally getting 8 hours sleep per night. The terrors of the past months had been banished from her dreams and replaced with rehearsals of drill movements, complex instructions reduced to acronyms and the other military concepts she was learning. The daily pace was hectic, deliberately set high to simulate the chaos of battle, and acclimatise the recruit's brains and bodies to thinking, moving and communicating rapidly and clearly. By the time the recruits fell into bed at the end of a day spent running, climbing, crawling and doing martial arts, none of them had any trouble falling asleep.

Outside the barracks where she was currently brushing her teeth, piles of equipment, rifles, ammunition, radios, vehicles, parts, food and medical supplies were being stacked, sorted and distributed in a non-stop dervish of noise and movement. It blended into the background of aircraft overhead, training platoons doing PT and vehicles moving troops and equipment across the base. The already overstretched and under-resourced NSW Police were further strained by the requirement to escort convoys of container trucks from Kingswood to Holsworthy, bringing in tonnes of ammunition, grenades, flares and other explosives from the stores there. As those stores became depleted, more convoys had to be organized to bring in supplies from further afield, from Eden on the south coast, and a little place near Parkes called Bogan Gate.

Over the past 3 months, three US Navy ships had arrived in Port Kembla, unloading tones of equipment which was then trucked north to Holsworthy. This included crates of M-16 rifles, ammunition, uniforms, MREs, compasses – a thousand different pieces of technology necessary for fighting a modern war. It was obvious to anyone observing that the US was selling off their old inventory to Australia at current prices, making room in the warehouses for fresh supplies. Moving against the Caliphate wasn't just boosting the Australian economy, it was also a gift to arms suppliers and manufacturers in America as well, generating profits for the shareholders in a time when many other areas of the economy were suffering and shrinking.

Lisa had memorized the serial number of her rifle and had spent hours taking it apart, cleaning and then putting it back together. Although she hadn't fired it yet, hours of familiarization had changed the object from something strange and frightening into a well-known friend. Having spent every waking and sleeping hour connected to it, she now felt as if it was an extension of her arm, and felt incomplete, startled, if she wasn't carrying it. The Marine and her rifle were becoming a single, unified being, operating without a separate, conscious thought process.

Even though she had watched Full Metal Jacket as a teen, she had still been surprised and disturbed by the behavior of the instruction staff. Most of the recruits were adults in their mid to late twenties, yet the drill sergeants were carrying on as if they were teenagers, or babies. During a quiet moment while cleaning their equipment for the hundredth time, Lisa asked the other members of her squad about it.

'There's several factors involved' explained Tim, a sandy-haired young man who had read a lot about the military. 'They need to know what we're capable of, that we will obey stupid orders, reflexively. That's a big part of it.

'But there's also self-preservation. Think about it – these guys are sergeants, squad leaders. Each of them must be ready to take over if their officer was killed. So each of them need to know we are the best we can be, and that we're not going to get them killed by doing something stupid.'

Lisa nodded. That made a lot of sense. She sure wanted to kill the bastards who had killed her family, but she wanted to do it right. There was no sense in going off blindly. She worked hard to keep her emotions in check, storing them away in a room inside her mind, only cracking the door open if she needed help completing the obstacle course or the last few hundred meters of a timed run.

Several times now, she had been face down in a muddy puddle, desperately trying to push her body up and take a breath, with the training staff standing over her screaming 'encouragement.' Letting out those powerful emotions would often push her body beyond the limits her mind imposed and help her complete the tasks required.

To all appearances, Lisa was a professional - strong and fit, polite and keen to learn. When the time came to learn marksmanship, she was surprised at how quickly she was able to learn the fundamentals. The advice given by the instructors was clear, simple and effective:

Steady Position
Aiming
Breath Control
Trigger Squeeze

Shooting wasn't a matter of luck, zen or growing up on a farm. All the recruits had to do was follow the instructions and they would hit the target.

Although some of the other recruits in Lisa's platoon were shooters from various gun clubs who had volunteered for the Marines, Lisa found that the instructors were able to coach all the recruits – many who had never shot before - to a high level within two weeks.

When the time came to shoot for score, Lisa found her nerves disappeared, despite sweating in the full summer sun for hours, and she walked off the line with a 230 out of 300 – a score that qualified her for 'Expert' rifle badge. For various reasons, some of the more experienced rifle shooters didn't score as highly, but the Range Officer gave her a 'well done, Ma'am' as she packed away her gear and got ready to re-join the platoon. She didn't show it, but Lisa was ecstatic and very proud of what she had achieved.

Three months ago, she had been a shattered, broken wreck. Now she could feel the weight of her pain was lifting, shrinking, dissipating. She was ready for whatever the future held, no matter how far she had to travel.

Chapter 16

February

News Corporation Sydney Office

Just before 7am, Patrick stood at the head of the conference room table, waiting for the rest of the day shift to arrive. Outside the morning summer sun was lighting up the city windows, sparkling and reflecting in a dazzling light show but Patrick's mind couldn't appreciate the beautiful sight.

Average height, with sandy grey hair above hooded blue eyes and a wide nose, Patrick had worked hard, gotten lucky and played his cards right. Aged forty, he was essentially the editor in charge of the city's main newspaper. There were over a dozen people who directly reported to him, and over a hundred more below them, gathering, collating, spinning and presenting news and opinion from all over the globe.

Patrick was good at what he did, a team player who rewarded results. He knew the crucial position that newspapers played in shaping the nation, and felt strong professional pride in shaping a team that helped keep the city informed, influenced and distracted at the right times.

While truth was indeed the first casualty in war, Patrick knew the power wielded by the papers, even more now that paper was being replaced by online devices. In Australia, that power was first wielded by Rupert Murdoch in 1975 when he destroyed the Whitlam government, and secured behind-the-scenes control of every subsequent government, using the same unspoken threat. Murdoch himself was on record as considering himself a 'change agent' – actively shaping public opinion on issues from immigration and the environment to taxation and foreign policy.

By remaining in the corporation, Patrick had demonstrated his loyalty, and his hard work showed that he was one of the 'true believers' in their mission to change the world. Now, he had his instructions, and while he may not agree with all of them, he was a man well paid to ignore his moral compass in favor of corporate interests.

He collected his thoughts as the rest of the team members drifted into the boardroom and their 'start of work briefing' meeting began.

'Right,' began Patrick. 'Today marks the beginning of a substantial shift in our narrative.

'We will begin to subtly turn away from supporting the Caliphate and the Greens. Our aim is change public perception against the Caliphate within 6-12 months.

A dozen pens scribbled onto notepads.

'We will also begin to soften our opposition to self-defense laws, and then slowly begin to call for a relaxation of them. Let's find some examples of people defending themselves and support them – basically the opposite of the way we handled Batterham, understood?'

The Batterham story was unique and Patrick acknowledged that the media had taken a risk in the way they had spun it – and the public backlash had been substantial. A man called Batterham had found a home invader in his house, fought with him and in the struggle, the invader had died. It turned out that the invader was a serial criminal and rapist, but instead of just shaking his hand and thanking him for doing their job for them, the police had followed procedures and arrested him.

So far, this was normal – the police do not have much discretion and prefer to arrest everyone and let the lawyers sort it out – a convenient arrangement that suits the law makers, lawyers and authorities at all levels.

But where it all got out of hand was the media spinning the home invader as the victim. They had interviewed his family members, drumming up a real sob story about how they were so sad they would never see him again, and ignoring the fact that the home owner was the victim of a home invasion. This went on for over a week, with the media pushing the criminal's family as the victims, but the social media response broke records. Thousands of people commented on the story, criticizing the media spin and defending the home owner – saying he did the right thing, and it was wrong of the government to deny people the right to defend their families inside their own homes.

Patrick could tell that the room was divided. Some people didn't care, they would write what they were told to write and didn't get personal. These were the mercenaries, the true believers.

Then there were the minority who felt opposed to the left-wing, appeasing, impotence promoting stance that the media had pushed in the last decade or two. These were obviously relieved at this announcement and relished the thought of pushing back against the emasculation of society.

But by far the largest group were those journalists incapable of thinking beyond the mainstream propaganda they had grown up with. Terrified of guns and the idea of defending their own lives, these people would rather be dead or raped than take the risk of fighting back against an attacker. Most of them believed in their hearts that only the police and military should have guns, that if they were even in danger, a phone call to the police would ensure they were safe. The fact that most of them lived in comfortable suburbs with low crime reinforced the idea that they had no need to change the narrative, and the idea of other people taking the law into their own hands seemed offensive.

If pushed to answer, many of them would be forced to admit they would rather be defenseless and dead when attacked, than take a chance and fight back. Being unarmed guaranteed they would lose any fight, and perversely this was appealing to their mindset, since it would mean they were right after all. They might be dead, but since their plan was to be defenseless and die anyway, their plan would have worked and their conscience would be clean, because their intentions had been vindicated.

Emma had nowhere this level of introspection or self-awareness, but being born a city girl and having lived her whole life in a protected bubble, had little idea about firearms or self-defense either. The idea had never seriously entered her mind until given this new assignment by Patrick. She knew the other reporters would be visiting hospitals and calling friendly police officers for story ideas, but she felt drawn to another angle to the usual heart-rending human-interest story.

She remembered a story about a female journalist who was charged for carrying pepper spray in New South Wales where it was banned – although she had purchased it in Western Australia, where it was legal. She sipped at a bottle of spring water and Googled a few search words like 'woman,' 'pepper spray' and 'charged'. She immediately found it – wincing as she noted it was in the competition newspaper - and scanned the story.

It wasn't really a story of self-defense; it was more about the immoral and inconsistent laws in Australia. The reporter had been hiking in Western Australia, where pepper spray is legal and women are encouraged to carry it as a deterrent. Potential attackers who know there is a chance that a victim can defend themselves are proven to be less likely to 'take a chance' than rapists who know their victims are defenseless. The writer had left it in the bottom of her backpack when she moved to New South Wales, where it is prohibited, alongside body armor, machine guns and collapsible batons. The story began with her putting the bag through a metal detector when attending court as a journalist. It followed the disproportionately heavy-handed approach taken by the police and prosecutor who had her up in front of a judge facing weapons charges as if she was Al Capone.

Fortunately, the judge threw out the case, but the writer raised interesting questions about the morality of laws 'for our own good' which conflict with reality. Regardless of the eternal questions like 'why do women need to defend themselves anyway, can't we just teach men not to attack them?' the facts are that one in three women will be attacked in their lifetime, and by then it is too late to think about self-defense. Emma thought about the issues for the first time. Even though she was one of the women who had never experienced violence, she didn't like the feelings that reading the story had provoked in her. She had been through court security scans enough times – imagine if there was a law she was unaware of, and she wasn't as lucky as the pepper spray owner – she could lose her job, lose her apartment – everything.

Not a good feeling at all. The world took on a shade of menace that hadn't been there before, a shapeless danger that now tinted everything she saw. While nothing in the world had changed apart from her own perception, she was now aware that she was vulnerable, rendered weak and helpless against an unknown number of people who wished her harm – not because of anything she had done; it was simply the way they were. No, she definitely did not like this feeling; a feeling of being cheated of her innocence, robbed of the comfortable bubble that she had existed in.

The sound of her phone pinging snatched her back to reality. She shook the gloomy thoughts from her head and checked the screen.

BONNIE: Coffee?

Her friend from the art department, Bonnie was checking their usual 10.30 Cappuccino meeting was still on. 'Yup' she texted back, set her 'Out of Office' notification on the computer and went downstairs.

The pair chatted while waiting in line to place their orders, then collected the coffees and sat at a small table away from the door. Emma sat on a wooden chair with her back to the room and Bonnie sat on a padded shelf that ran along the wall.

'So, the paper's pushing in a whole new direction' Emma was saying to Bonnie, trying to convey her frustration and confusion without sounding like she was bitching. 'The whole ideology. Instead of calling for more tolerance and education, we're supposed to be shifting towards more self-defense.' She blew at the froth on her cappuccino, not noticing Bonnie's facial expression, and added 'I guess it's a bit scary to think about – rising crime, violent assaults – I mean, I write articles about them all the time, but I never thought about...it happening to me...' her voice trailed off as she caught the look on Bonnie's face. 'What's the matter?' she asked.

All the color had drained from her face and something like icy stone or a stormy ocean had set in her eyes. It was a haunted face, staring off into the distance while reliving some past trauma. Soldiers call it 'the thousand-yard stare' but it can affect anyone – not just people in a war zone. Bonnie's mind had shifted off the spot where her eyes were focused.

Emma reached out and gently placed her hand over Bonnie's where it lay on the table between them. 'Hey?' she asked gently, 'are you all right?'

Bonnie shivered violently, then shook her head and focused on Emma's face. 'Sorry, I just...' Her voice seemed strained, and she had difficulty finishing the sentence. She swallowed and then said, 'You just reminded me of a horrible experience I had – not your fault.'

Emma's emotions flipped around like a Ukrainian gymnast. She felt sorry for upsetting her friend, concerned for her well-being but also, as a journalist she had a mercenary desire to tap into a story, and this just might be a great one to take to the editor. She desperately tried to balance out her love for her friend and nailing a brilliant story, so she put it onto Bonnie, rather than asking directly.

'Oh love,' she said. 'Sorry if I upset you. Don't have to talk about it if you don't want to...' her voice trailed off as she passive-aggressively led Bonnie towards wanting to talk about whatever was bothering her.

'No, no, it's okay – it's just a very personal story. I've never shared it fully before.' She took a sip of her coffee and looked down at the table.

'At the time I was so ashamed I just ran home instead of reporting it to the police.' Emma's heart settled like concrete into her stomach at this news – it sounded horrible, but she stayed quiet and waited for Bonnie to continue.

'It was in 2009, I was 19 and living on the Gold Coast. I had just left a club in Surfer's Paradise – about 1am, I suppose. I'd had a few drinks, but I wasn't smashed, I was just tipsy.' She looked at Emma and took a deep breath to steel herself for the rest of the story.

'I walked along the beach, since that was the quickest way home. About halfway this guy came into view, walking towards me. He was dark, but I couldn't tell what nationality he was. When I walked past, he wolf whistled me and asked if I wanted to chat.

'I just said 'No thanks' and continued on, but he started walking back towards me, faster, he asked me 'what's the matter, don't you like me?''

Emma felt Bonnie's body trembling through the hand she was still holding on the table. She gave it a gently squeeze of support and encouragement.

'I just said I was tired and I was on my way home, but he reached out and grabbed my arm. I yanked it away and tried to run but he was on me before I'd gone more than a meter. He put his full weight on top of me, his strength was incredible – I was completely overpowered, I couldn't move but I just started to scream for help as loud as I could.'

Emma was horrified. She had been to Surfer's many times but only had great memories of great food and fantastic parties – she hadn't imagined that such a fun place could contain something so evil at the same time. The only words that came out of her mouth were 'oh my god.'

Bonnie twitched, 'It gets worse. He covered my face with his jacket and was getting out of his pants – he let go of the jacket for a second and I screamed as loud as I could. I can't describe the feeling – part of me was dead inside, part of me was so angry, so helpless, so outraged at how wrong it was, and I couldn't do a thing to stop it.'

She shuddered again, and Emma covered her mouth at the horror she imagined her friend had been through – not only that lonely night but every day and night since.

'I was saved by a couple walking their dog on the beach' Bonnie said. 'The guy and his wife were ready to call the police, but I was so frightened, so scared and ashamed, I was in tears and I just started running home, I didn't stop until I got home.' Bonnie's words tumbled out in a jumble as the intense emotions interfered with her brain's ability to speak. She raised her eyes and looked at Emma. 'I've never talked about it to anyone until now.'

Emma was still processing the shock. 'How awful. And you've carried that with you ever since...' She moved around and sat beside Bonnie on the sofa, draping an arm around her and hugging her friend tightly. Bonnie was taking deep breaths, trying to calm her body enough to keep talking.

'Sometimes, all I can think about is...what if that couple hadn't been there? Then I wonder...how many times he did it, before, after me? And I know he's not the only one...'

'I got away, but how many others didn't?'

Emma reached over the table to move her coffee mug closer, and asked 'had you thought about self-defense before then?'

Bonnie jerked away as if stung by a bee, then relaxed 'I'd never given it a thought. I suppose, if you had asked me before… I would've probably said it didn't bother me either way – I certainly never felt the need to be protected.

'After it, I was a wreck. Being that defenseless is a scary thing. I lost a part of my soul that night – and I don't want to imagine what would have happened if he hadn't been scared off.' She shuddered again. 'That Jill woman in Melbourne…oh god…what did she suffer before she finally died?' Both women felt their brains attempt to process the horror, but knew that no matter what they thought, the reality would be much worse.

'I definitely support carrying items for self-defense, pepper spray, a gun, whatever.' She paused again and looked hard at Emma. 'I never, EVER want to experience it again' she said, and her voice trembled as if a choking hand was wrapped around her voice box.

Emma's head spun, and she fought for control. Her friend's revelation had taken her earlier thoughts about self-defense and smashed them beyond repair. Snatches of questions whirled around inside her head but she felt unsure of where to start. She also didn't want to appear to be feeding off her friend's trauma.

'What would you say to a woman who opposes carrying pepper spray or a gun, saying you're more likely to have it taken off you and be harmed with it?'

Bonnie's face hardened again, and her voice cut Emma like a gravel rash. 'When one person denies another the right to practical self-defense due to 'possible' outcomes – one of which is successful getting away, or preventing it in the first place. It's selfish and it's ignorant. I'd just hope they never have to experience what I went through.'

She paused, then added 'Here's the thing – self-defense is all about risk. There's a scale on both sides, which changes with each situation.

'The attacker is weighing up the victim against his own strengths. In my case, a woman much weaker than him, it was dark, few people around – so he took a chance. Turns out he was interrupted. But he took the chance knowing that it's illegal for a woman to carry something to defend herself. The law empowered him – a criminal, a rapist. At the same time, it took away what little power I had.

'If the law was changed, and it was legal for a woman to carry a gun, or even just non-lethal - pepper spray or a Taser – that would change the risk profile of every potential victim. Even if I wasn't carrying, my attacker would have to factor that in when deciding whether to go ahead with it. The risk to his crime would be higher.

'All of life is about risk, and if we were trying to eliminate it completely, then we'd just stay home wrapped in cotton wool. But the risk of me being harmed with my own pepper spray, or accidentally shooting a bystander while I'm defending my own life – that's a risk everyone should be able to decide on their own. And I'll tell you this – the risk of that is far lower than the risk of being attacked by a criminal who knows you are defenseless. Changing that risk assessment won't put anyone in danger.'

Half an hour later, Emma stumbled back to her desk feeling like she had been run through a washing machine. She sat limply in front of her computer, trying to summon the words to express what she had just experienced.

Who, What, Where, When, Why & How. Suddenly her old journalistic friends seemed so corny, insultingly trivial. She sensed an impossible task, a chasm yawning at her feet. If she went down this rabbit hole, would she ever be able to return to her happy, youthful self? Or would she change forever, having seen society's dark underbelly and forever unable to escape her newfound knowledge?

Worse, was the feeling that exploiting her friend's trauma might not end up as a decent, powerful article. Instead, Emma was afraid it would be stripped of everything important and turned into clickbait – the paper had lately grown a substantial bias towards tabloid sensationalism as opposed to investigative journalism.

-

Cris was tall and skinny, with a shaved head that protruded over sunken eyes and a broken nose. He felt as if he had been watching his country spin out of control for a decade. In his mind, he had watched impotently as wave after wave of immigrants arrived, took jobs away from Australians, got on welfare and started crime gangs. As Sydney had grown, the problem in his mind had increased as well, to the point where it was all-consuming.

Something had to be done.

Every day he noticed more litter in the streets, vandalized cars, graffiti on walls and fences. Rent went up, the cost of living went up, but Western Sydney hadn't improved at all. Traffic was a mess; it took forever to get anywhere on a weekend, the city had taken all his money but given him no return on investment.

To Cris' mind, the only people who benefited from the past 10 years had been the investor class and the unemployed immigrants – anyone who didn't own a home by 2001 was basically screwed.

And Cris knew who was to blame. Immigrants. Taking jobs away, clogging the roads, overwhelming public transport. Breeding. Draining social security with large families while he couldn't even get a second date with a woman.

As soon as the Caliphate was announced, Cris knew he had to do something about it, but he had no idea what to do. He was one man, alone, but he felt a strong and supernatural calling that he couldn't explain. It just felt like his destiny.

With his Facebook feed stuffed with racist and right-wing propaganda, he was constantly fed a media diet of extremist alarmism, much of which was fabricated - but he didn't know that. His own confirmation bias filtered out conflicting thoughts, and his Facebook news feed did the rest.

As soon as the Soldiers of Odin set up a Western Sydney chapter, he went along to the meetings and became involved. He had high hopes for the Soldiers, but was disappointed to learn they were strictly a local, defensive group for each neighborhood.

Cris saw their point. There was a need for neighborhood watch, but he wanted more. He wanted to strike back, to express his anger at everything he felt wronged by. He wanted an army. Some of the people in the Soldiers were receptive to his rants, but it didn't take long for him to be labeled a troublemaker and asked not to return.

Cris stayed in touch with those who felt the same way he did, drinking and sharing his steady supply of weed with them; building a sense of community and feeding each other's paranoia. His news feed, automatically tailored to his paranoid fears only served to feed his illusions, giving him the sense that far more people shared his views than was really the case. News items were recycled, some from decades ago, but each time they popped up in his feed, his brain registered it as a new threat, dosing his system with fight-or-flight chemicals, a process repeated with every 'like' and 'share' at his fingertips.

On Friday afternoon, Cris and his mate Mal were leaving their local Coles, loaded up with chips, snacks, some bottled RTDs and a few goon sacks in preparation for a good weekend when their metaphorical death warrants were signed.

Plastic bags rustled as they rode the escalators down to the underground car park and exited the glass sliding doors. They were coming around the corner past the trolley bay when Cris ran straight into another man who had dodged around the corner without looking. In the confusion, Cris dropped the plastic shopping bags he was carrying, and he heard a glass bottle break.

The first phrase out of Cris' mouth was something like 'What de fuck?' But as he lifted his eyes from the bags at his feet to the dark, skinny man in front of him, then to the turban wrapped around his head, something snapped inside him, and Cris suddenly felt ice-cold all over.

'FUCKOFFBACKWHEREYACAMEFROM, FUCKEN MOOZIE! TERRIST. I'LLFUCKYAUP.'

The skinny man took a step backwards and put out both hands, palm out.

'Sorry, Sorry' he said very quickly in a heavily accented voice. 'I was in a rush' – but Cris was beyond reason.

'YAFUCKENDOG!' He took a step towards the skinny man, closing the gap and pressing his chest against the out-turned palms. He screamed again, blood rushing into his face as his brain dumped FIGHT chemicals into his bloodstream. 'FUCKENMOOSLIM, FUCKOFF! ALLAYAS!'

The skinny man took another step backwards and shook his head as words babbled out of him. 'No, no, no, I'm not a Muslim, NOT a Muslim, I'm Sikh.' While Cris heard the words, he lacked the education to make the connection. All he saw was a dark man with a funny accent and a head covering.

'Sick, FUCKYA, I'll make ya sick orright!' All he saw was a dark man with a funny accent and a head covering. He stepped forward again and drove his left fist deep into the man's stomach, right on the belly button. As the air was forced from his lungs, the man doubled over, bringing his head down and Cris' right hook took him under the chin, sending the man flying backwards to crack his head on the concrete floor.

The man twitched once, then lay still.

Mal grabbed Cris' arm, 'fuck, mate, what the fuck?'

Cris turned to his friend, still breathing heavily, beginning to realize what had happened, and it was serious. 'Get the fuck outta here!'

Leaving their victim on the ground, they split up, walking quickly out opposite ends of the car park then met up back at Cris' house.

Mal collapsed on the couch as Cris paced around the living room, alternating drinking from a Rum & Cola and popping pills from an unlabeled prescription bottle. His brain was spinning as he tried to absorb the consequences of what he had done and the drugs in his system felt like they were helping, when they were doing the opposite. Then suddenly, he saw everything clearly. He knew exactly what he had to do. It was as if clouds had parted, and a ray of warm sunshine lit up his brain with exactly what was needed.

'Cops'll be coming – woulda seen the CCTV, someone from the shops'll recognize us, dob us in. FUCK, FUCK' he said, only serving to drive himself and Mal further into paranoia. Cris' brain, reeling from the effects of stress, alcohol, narcotics and a regular diet of racism, xenophobia and outrage developed a messiah complex, where he believed he was the only one able to 'save' society from its problems. He knew that most of society felt the same way he did, they were just too scared to act, to start the cleansing that the country desperately needed. He knew there would be thousands of followers, once there arose a leader who took the first step. All he needed to do was light the fuse.

Suddenly sure of himself for the first time in his life, Cris grabbed his car keys and hustled Mal out of the house. He drove them south east, down Rodd Street, then down Auburn Road into the heart of Yagoona and Bankstown.

It didn't take long to find the object of his rage and terror. Two women were walking on the footpath beside the road, covered from head to toe in fabric. One wore a black niqab, the veil covering her whole face except for her eyes. The other wore a blue burqa, where the face veil was part of the head covering, with a mesh strip covering even her eyes. Cris knew the meaning of his life was now crystal clear – to liberate these women from their oppressors, and to become a shining leader to others who would follow his example.

The car shuddered to a stop as he jammed on the brakes, and said to Mal 'you, drive.' He jumped out of the driver's seat, raced over to the kerb, screaming obscenities as he confronted the two pedestrians.

'Fucken terrrists. GO BACK WHERE YA CAME FROM,' he bellowed as he crashed into them, knocking them over in a flurry of billowing black and blue. Foaming a little at the mouth, he rolled to his feet and delivered several hard kicks to each. Then he grabbed at the veils, one in each hand, ripped them off and ran back to the car. He dived into the passenger seat, expecting Mal to speed away, but Mal just sat there with his mouth open, unable to process what he had just seen.

'Move, fucken move!' screamed Cris, punching Mal in the arm and shaking him out of his trance. Mal released the handbrake and hit the throttle, speeding away from the scene of the crime. Cris began cackling in glee, clenching the fabric veils in his fists and ranting incoherently. Terrified of what had come over his mate, Mal drove automatically, trying to get back home, but Cris was insistent. 'No, left, left fuckya' he screamed, pointing the car towards another woman, wearing the niqab and walking with two young children.

Again, the car stopped but Cris was on them faster than his earlier victims, since he was on the passenger side. Again he pushed, kicked and left the woman without her veil and her children lying terrified and bleeding on the ground, as the car zoomed off, seeking more victims.

Next time, Cris thought he had hit the jackpot. A small group of shops beside the road held an outdoor café, and several black-clad women were sitting at the tables. Again, the car screeched to a stop and Cris continued his crusade, mindlessly swinging feet and fists in his attempt to save the world.

He had driven two of the women to the ground and was kicking, hard, when he thought he heard two car doors slamming, hard. He whirled around, but all he could see was his own car, with the passenger door open, driver's door closed and Mal behind the wheel, staring at him with gaping mouth and eyes wide in horror.

Then the pain welled up in his chest.

Pressing a palm to the pain, he looked down and was shocked to see bright red blood pumping around his fingers. Strength drained from his legs and he staggered into a chair, staring up at one of the women standing in front of him, clutching her black handbag in one hand and the black handle of an evil looking pistol, gaping at him with a large, smoking barrel.

As the life drained out of his eyes, the last thing Cris saw was a moving crowd of people clustered around his car, dragging Mal out of the driver's seat. Then the rising darkness reached his eyes, and he slipped away into the black.

His body was cold and stiff by the time Emma arrived. She had tried to talk her way through the roadblocks surrounding the Caliphate, only gaining access after handing over $500.00 in cash to the sullen guards who never took their eyes off her figure.

Emma's resentment at having to bribe her way into part of her own city burned inside her as she drove towards the scene of the killing, but evaporated when she saw there were no other reporters on the scene, although the lack of police puzzled her. Parking the car and approaching the small crowd, she wondered if she should have brought a scarf to put over her head. 'Too late now', she thought as she stepped up and had a look at the body lying on the ground.

It was the first time she had seen a dead body in real life, and she was surprised at how she didn't recoil. There was supposed to be a shock, a horror when you saw a dead body, but to Emma, it just looked like a supermarket display. The only emotion she felt was a burning need to get the story before other reporters arrived.

Some of the people in the crowd were snapping photos with their phones, so she joined in, taking shots from different angles but avoiding the selfies that some of the teens were doing.

Horrific pictures were good, she knew – but on her first real assignment, Patrick would need her to bring back the full spectrum story, something that could go out immediately. She needed comments, terror, horrific eyewitness statements that could be quoted. So she thumbed her phone over to the 'voice recorder' app and turned to the people closest to her.

'Hi, I'm Emma, NewsCorp. Can you tell me what happened here? What's your name?' she asked a young woman. But the woman just shook her head. 'Didn't see anything,' she replied. 'I was in the shop, came out and found him like this.'

Emma spoke to several of the women, growing increasingly desperate but the story was the same. Nobody had seen anything. Emma was also vaguely uneasy that there was no sign of police anywhere. A dead guy, covered in blood and what looked like two bullet holes in his shirt, but nobody had called the police...

Emma turned to the last woman, only to see her walking rapidly away, closely followed by the rest. Emma whirled around to see a battered Hilux Dual-cab pulling up in the car park. The doors opened, and four large men got out and strode up towards her. Emma swallowed her fear and stepped forward with a confident step she didn't feel.

'Hi, I'm Emma, NewsCorp – the newspaper' she said. 'Can anyone tell me what happened here?' She held out the voice recorder as if it was an award trophy.

But the men ignored her, looking at the body, then calling to the cafe owner in Arabic. Emma had no idea what they were saying, and made a mental note to learn the language in future.

After lots of shouting and arm waving, the cafe owner came out waved at the body, then the men, and even Emma could tell he was telling them to get rid of the body. One of the men went to the vehicle and came back with a blue tarpaulin, then the others bent and helped slide the body onto it.

Emma stepped back and took several photos, including one of the bloodstains that she thought was quite artistic. But she was snapped back to reality when two of the men picked up the tarpaulin and carried it around to the rear tray of the vehicle. They grunted as they lifted the body and dumped it in the tray as if it was a bag of cement. Time running out, Emma was desperate to get a comment, anything. She turned to the man who had been driving.

'Please, anything?' Emma was getting desperate. 'What happened here? Was this man involved with the Caliphate?'

The man stopped and studied her, dark eyes flashing as he evaluated what he saw.

'Nahh' he grunted. His voice was deep and Emma internally shrank away from the powerful emotions she sensed. But she was determined to press on. The man gestured around with his hands. 'Dat guy just gone crazy. Started attacking women. Kicking dem on da ground. Crazy guy.'

Emma's brain kicked into gear. Abandoning the mental theme she had been operating on, the assumption that this was a gangland execution, this was now something she had been thinking about for a while – self-defense. She concentrated as the man went on, his words running together as the story seemed to well up and pour out of him.

'My wife, she saw it all. She was 'ere, she called me. Her sister shot dis guy before he kill someone. He was crazy. She called me to clean up da mess.'

Emma's reporter brain kicked into gear. She smelled a bigger story than the now-tired 'yet another gangster slain in Western Sydney' line and she stepped closer. 'Has the election of One Nation caused women to fear for their safety and carry guns? Does the Caliphate have a self-defense policy different to the National Firearms Agreement?'

The man paused and looked at her, studying her again. 'I dunno anyting about da Caliphate. But I can take you to guys who do. You wanna ask dem?'

Something in Emma's brain fired up, trying to warn her that she was alone in a separatist area teeming with different cultures, but her reporter training squashed it before it could register properly. She nodded and pulled out her car keys. The man did the same, turning back to the dual-cab which now had the passengers back inside the cab, watching Emma. The man asked, 'you follow me in your car?' and Emma nodded. She rushed back to her car and began to follow the blue tarp in the growing afternoon traffic.

Pulling out her phone, she dialed the office, asking to speak to Patrick. Predictably, he was on the phone, so she spoke to his voicemail.

'Patrick, its Emma. The shooting in Bankstown wasn't gang related, it was a crazy white guy attacking Muslim women. One of them shot him in self-defense. I'm not sure how you want to spin it, but that's the witness statement. Possible One Nation voter.' She paused, then pressed on with what she hoped was a victory speech, getting forgiveness rather than permission.

'One of the witnesses has a contact in the Caliphate. He's taking me to meet them, I'll call you back as soon as I have anything more.'

She hung up the phone just as her guide pulled up at one of the Caliphate's roadblocks. Emma recognized it as the one she had come through earlier. She watched through the windscreen as the driver spoke to the paramilitary guys manning the roadblock.

Another car eased up behind her and stopped, in the checkpoint queue, but Emma didn't notice. She saw the driver waving his hands, and the guard look back at her, then nod his head. The guard pulled out a wad of money and counted out several notes, handing them over to the driver. The rest of the checkpoint guards walked casually back towards her, their rifles held carelessly at their sides. Emma rolled down her window, ready to ask the men about the Caliphate and was horrified when they suddenly ripped her door open, slit her seatbelt and wrapped a fist into her hair, dragging her out of the car and into the dirt. Emma's world consisted of only one thing – the pain in her head and she was incapable of thinking, resisting, or even thinking about remembering where she was being taken. Her world turned upside down twice as she was rolled in the dirt.

A black cloth was pulled over her head and the pressure on her hair stopped, before she was thrown inside the back of a small delivery van that smelled like rotten seafood. Her captors bound her wrists and ankles with tape and then the vehicle jerked into motion.

Emma's day got even worse when she realised that her phone, purse, everything was still in her car parked at the roadblock – if it was still there at all. Worse, it was probably her own money that the guide had been paid for delivering her to her captors. Nasty karma.

Would anyone find her? Emma wondered desperately if her dead body would even be discovered, or if she had simply disappeared from the face of the earth.

Chapter 17

March

Samantha Lee from Gun Control Australia was back on TV, trying to spin her argument that firearms were bad because they were used to kill people, but archery was okay because it was only a sport and had no military value. Unfortunately, she hadn't been able to speak first, and the other guest – Tom Steele, immediately dominated the narrative.

'It is patently obvious that our gun laws are not stopping criminals and terrorists from getting guns' said the other guest on the program. 'We already have laws against murder, assault and theft which criminals are not obeying – why would this be any different?'

'We do not want an American Gun Culture here in Australia' she said earnestly.

'We don't have one. What we DO have, RIGHT NOW is a militant Islamic Caliphate on our doorstep. One which is already attacking people – and police officers!' he replied. 'I want you to tell me right now, what are our citizens supposed to do, when confronted by armed terrorists?'

Samantha stuck to her script. 'The risk of terrorism is much lower than the risk of gun violence spilling out into our streets. There is no reason for ordinary people to own guns. Instead, we need to remove guns from society, to stop gun violence. The more guns in a suburb, the more chances they will be sold to criminals by licensed gun owners.'

Tom wasn't rocked by the outrageous accusation, but he feigned outrage at such a lie. 'No licensed owner can sell a firearm to a criminal' he said. 'And I'll prove to you that it just doesn't happen...

'Let's say that somebody does sell a licensed firearm to a criminal. That criminal owes the seller nothing, and if they are caught by the police, would give up the identity of the person who supplied the firearm. Goodbye license, hello prison for the license holder.'

'Now what is going to stop the criminal coming back a month later, and demanding they provide more firearms, threatening to dob them in to the police if they fail? Nobody in their right mind is going to sell a legal firearm to a criminal – the risks are just too great.

'The penalties against the law abiding are quite sufficient to stop them doing the wrong thing – particularly when there is no need to. There are no queues of criminals trying to buy licensed firearms from people – because they simply import them along with the drugs, cigarettes and other prohibited items. Banning something only makes it more valuable to the black market.'

Samantha changed the subject. 'High powered and high capacity killing machines have no place in a modern society. In the interest of public safety, all these weapons should be destroyed.'

Tom smiled, she had walked right into his trap, and now he sprung.

'Samantha, can you please explain to me – in your own words – what the definition of high powered is?' He sat back in his chair, cocking his head to the side as he waited for her reply.

In a stressful situation, some people feel that a day is like a week and a week goes by like a month, but on live TV - a second can last a lifetime. Tom waited while the camera stayed on Samantha's face as she desperately tried to think of an answer to the question.

Tom cleared his throat, and the red light on his camera came back on. 'How about an easier question – as an expert on gun control and firearms, can you explain the difference between the selector switch on an AK-47 and an M16A1? Or even just name two firearms invented by John Moses Browning?'

Samantha squirmed and began to perspire again. This had moved way off the script and she was completely clueless about the technical details of firearms. She desperately tried to take control of the discussion again. 'We've moved off topic, Tom – the fact is that more people feel unsafe today than in 1996 when John Howard bravely introduced strict new gun control laws. These laws have been watered down over time...'

She was interrupted by the host saying 'Hold on Samantha, even I know that none of the gun laws have been watered down. Instead, there have even been more restrictions brought in since 1996.'

Before she had a chance to answer, Tom questioned her credibility again. 'Sam, could you please establish your credibility by answering my basic firearms questions. I believe that you have no idea what you are talking about, therefore have no right to be contributing to this conversation on national TV.'

'No, I am not going to answer these childish and immature questions, which are off topic,' returned Samantha evenly. 'I was invited onto the show and I am entitled to be here.'

'No, your lack of knowledge proves that you have no value here. Any opinion you may have about firearms and public safety is automatically invalid because you have no education about the subject. If you don't even know basic facts about firearms, then you are not entitled to have your uninformed opinion broadcast around the country.'

Tom was starting to enjoy himself, since he had found something to pin down the anti-gun lobbyists; but the host cut off anything further by saying, 'and that's all we have time for. Coming up, let's hear from a group of mothers concerned about celebrity body-shaming and the effect it is having on their sons...'

Chapter 18

April

The night was overcast, a tiny sliver of moon barely peeking above the horizon as Bilal drove his EVO down the Bangor Bypass and into Kirrawee. He nosed the sports car into Greys' Point, wincing as the car scraped on the uneven roadway, and parked in front of the Swallow Point Boat Ramp. The ramp itself and the carpark were deserted, but moored to the pier – lying almost motionless in the cool air – was a giant 50-foot fishing cruiser. Bilal tucked his phone under the driver's seat of the car, locked it and walked down towards the water.

Bilal's eyes were wide as he closed the distance, finally reaching the end of the wooden pier and comprehending the size of the boat in front of him. He noticed movement up on the deck and a moment later, Sargon's voice said, 'cast off.' A shadowy arm pointed fore and aft at the ropes holding the boat to the bollards. Bilal unwound the thick, heavy ropes and threw them aboard, then climbed over the side into the boat as the engines rumbled into life.

The boat moved slowly downstream as Bilal climbed a few steps and found Sargon standing behind the pilot's chair. Bilal didn't recognize the man at the controls, and knew better than to ask questions. Since he had never been on a boat before, Bilal took the opportunity to look around. The small room they were in housed a chair for the pilot in front of a dashboard like the one in his car, but the resemblance ended there. The windscreen was huge, connecting to side windows that ended only at the end of the platform that supported the chair. Even seated, the pilot had 360-degree views all around the boat.

Bilal took a closer look at the dashboard instruments – some of them looked familiar, others were unknown. From the corner of his eye, the pilot noticed Bilal's interest and offered a quick lesson.

'Fuel, speed, engine revs' he said, pointing at the three dials in sequence. 'Heading' was indicated by a glowing square screen that looked more like a GPS than a compass, 'depth and fish finder' described the final square screen, which was currently black.

The pilot turned to Sargon and joked 'don't need it for this trip – it's a different kinda fish we're after, huh?' Sargon just grunted and opened a bag he had stashed near his feet. He drew out a laptop computer and plugged in a large, bulky phone, and switched them both on.

By the time the computer had booted up and the phone was connected, the boat had picked up speed, entered deeper water and was passing Bundeena, heading out past the Royal National Park and into the Pacific Ocean. The pilot held the direction dial steady on E, and pushed forward two levers that Bilal guessed were the throttles. The noise and vibration from the bowels of the boat increased, and the speed picked up noticeably, Bilal had to grab onto a rail that ran around his side of the wheelhouse to steady himself. He flexed his thighs to stay upright as the ocean swell moved the boat around.

Several minutes passed, with the boat nosing into the swelling waves, rolling a little and Bilal felt his stomach turn. He noticed a small pain growing on each side of his jaw, and combined with the acidic churning feeling in his stomach he knew that he was about to be sick. He reflexively stumbled down the stairs to the main deck and managed to get his head over the side before the first heaves sent his dinner, lunch and what felt like breakfast into the ocean.

He collapsed onto the deck, wiping his mouth with the sleeve of his tracksuit as the nausea began to settle down. After a few minutes, he managed to pull himself upright and steady his body against the rail. He felt a hand on his shoulder and Sargon said 'sort yo'self out. Work to do.'

Clutching the rail, Bilal followed Sargon forward, passing the base of the wheelhouse and onto the front deck of the boat. They were moving fast, fast enough that the bow was high, out of the water and the motion through the swell was even worse.

Sargon passed Bilal a pair of binoculars and said, 'orange or green light in the water – find it', then opened a box on the deck and drew out a long pole with a wickedly curved hook on the end. Bilal was afraid of the weapon, but took the binoculars and put them to his eyes.

He couldn't see a thing.

Moving his head, he realised that the binoculars were pointing into the ocean right in front of the boat, so he looked further out, turning his head from right to left as he searched the ocean for the lights Sargon wanted. Nothing. There wasn't even a distinction between the ocean and the sky, everything was the same shade of black.

Bilal put the binoculars down for a moment, oriented himself against the boat's movement and then scanned again, tracking across the front of the boat but there was nothing in the water. He looked at Sargon.

'Keep lookee.' said Sargon, anticipating his question. 'We heading right for it.'

Bilal put the eyepieces back on his face and resumed searching. 'What are we looking for?'

Sargon explained. 'Empty ship coming into Kembla to get coal for Japan. Our men onboard dropped off de bags an hour ago wid a GPS trakkah. Laptop in dis boat pickin up da signal but de range is only about twenny meters. So just before dey drop de bags, dey crack a coupla light sticks tied to de ends. You be able ta see em any minnit now.'

The boat had slowed, and Bilal felt the deck tilting under his feet as it changed direction in the swell. The pilot was zigzagging to keep the nose pointed towards the signal emitted from the GPS tracker and continuously reduced speed as they got closer. Bilal panned the binoculars left again, and registered a faint orange glow further out. He moved the binoculars and located the orange light, then a green one a little further away. He gave a shout, and pointed his arm in the direction of the light.

The pilot must have noticed, because the boat slowed almost to a stop, and turned in the direction Bilal indicated. Sargon cheered, slapped him on the back and then thrust the hooked pole over the side and fished a length of rope out of the water. Bilal set the binoculars on the deck, grabbed one part of the wet, salty rope and pulled it into the boat. At the end of the rope was a foam buoy about the size of a soccer ball, white with an orange stripe painted on it. Glued to the middle of the buoy was a clear ziplock bag which contained a cream coloured plastic square about half the size of a credit card, and a green glow stick used at kid's parties all over the world.

'Dere's the GPS trakkah – give it me' said Sargon, so Bilal pried it off and handed it over. Sargon opened the plastic box and pulled out a SIM card identical to the one in Bilal's phone. Bilal wondered which kid in Singapore or Nigeria's name was on the account registered to the device. Such thoughts were cut short as he pulled in the rest of the rope and felt it go taught as something heavy bumped against the side of the boat. Sargon moved closer and helped him pull three large waterproof bags over the side of the boat. Each was about the size of a household rubbish bin, and very heavy.

'Fuck this' grunted Bilal as he and Sargon struggled with the bags, getting drenched with salt water and slipping on the deck. Finally, the last bag came over the side, followed by a length of rope and a buoy identical to the first one, except the ziplock bag only contained an orange glow stick. Dragging the bags into line in the middle of the deck, Sargon waved to the pilot who turned the boat back towards shore and increased the speed. Sargon put the boathook back into a locker, and pulled out two lengths of wood, laying them next to the three bags on the deck.

Bilal felt as if he was getting used to the ocean, since the return journey seemed to pass more quickly, and he wasn't feeling the urge to throw up any more. He watched as Sargon went back upstairs to pack up his laptop and the satellite phone, and came back down to Bilal just as the boat was slowing down and navigating the channel markers they had left just hours before.

Taming the urge to talk about something, anything, just to fill in the quiet time, Bilal looked out at the lights of the houses slipping past in the dark. Each of those houses was worth over a million dollars, and Bilal wondered about the families who lived there. Doctors, lawyers, and business people – he thought about what connections they would have needed, to set up a career or business and generate the wealth to repay a loan of a million dollars plus the interest. A twinge of anger arose, as he thought about the few opportunities available to him and his school friends – an entire community of second class citizens, spread out from Hurstville to Cabramatta. Cheap labour, comprised of desperate people fleeing wars that the Western powers had started. People who worked their hardest to build something of a life in a new country, only to discover the deck stacked against them every time. He resolved then and there to never play by their rules, never to pay tax, always to work to undermine their influence in his community.

The boat eased back up the river and then made a wide turn to the right, the pilot expertly bringing the side of the boat to meet the jetty. Bilal jumped over the side and looped the hawsers over the bollards, reversing the jobs he had done when he arrived. Still on the boat, Sargon pulled the ropes tight and wound them around the bollards on the deck, securing the boat tight against the dock as the pilot shut the engines down and descended to the main deck. He and Sargon then slid the two pieces of wood over the side to make a ramp down to Bilal's level, and dragged the first bag down the timbers to where Bilal could slide it onto the dock. The second and third bags followed, then Sargon clambered over the side and went up to the carpark.

He returned a minute later, driving the DIMO Food truck, and reversed it as close to the dock as he could. Then he opened the roller shutter on the back of the truck, took out a hand trolley and came back to where Bilal was standing. Bilal helped him ferry the three bags into the truck, then watched as Sargon went back to the pilot. They shook hands, and Sargon passed an envelope to the pilot, then came back to Bilal and said 'follah me in yo car.'

Patting his pockets for the keys, Bilal walked back to the EVO, pulled out his phone and thumbed it on. No messages, no emails, no voicemails. Good. Starting the car, he did a U-turn and followed Sargon away from the water as he headed north into Kirrawee, and took the Bangor Bypass. Crossing the Alfords Point Bridge into Padstow, the tiny convoy crossed the train lines at Wiley Park, then slowed and turned into a mechanical workshop close to the Lakemba Mosque. The security roller shutter began to close as soon as Bilal's car was inside, and he carefully parked next to the DIMO truck so his car wouldn't block access as they unloaded.

Bilal shut off the engine and got out of the car to find Sargon and one of the guys he recognized from the gym opening the back of the truck. The older men were much stronger than Bilal, and working together they quickly had the three bags out of the truck and lying on the floor next to a long workbench. Although there were some tools on the bench that Bilal recognized – hammers, screwdrivers and a spanner, most of the bench was clear.

'OK' Said Sargon, straightening up from the last bag. 'Imma takin de truck back.' He looked at Bilal and said 'Help Ninos, learn. Do whatevah he say, K.' Bilal nodded, to Sargon and then to Ninos. He opened the workshop roller door for Sargon to reverse the truck out, then shut it again. The garage became quiet, Bilal noticed the smell of oil and exhaust from the truck.

Ninos motioned to the bags on the floor and said, 'time to get to work.' Bilal helped him cut through the plastic on one end, and lift out several plastic boxes. They were all different sizes, but whatever was in them was heavy.

Ninos grabbed one and lifted the lid, grunted at what he saw and pointed to the middle of the bench. 'There' was all he said, but Bilal understood and heaved the box onto the bench where indicated as Ninos looked in the second one. Bilal had to put this one on the left of the first, then the third beside it.

By the time the three bags were empty, there were over a dozen open plastic boxes on the workbench, placed into an order that only Ninos understood. Each box contained a number of metal parts that Bilal didn't recognize, and he had no idea why Ninos wanted them arranged like that.

The final box immediately unlocked the mystery in Bilal's mind, and an icy hand squeezed his stomach as his eyes fell on the contents. Instead of metal, the last package was full of wooden blocks formed into two shapes. The first was an irregular lump about the size of his forearm, but the second type was unmistakably a rifle stock.

Ninos seized one and commanded Bilal 'watch, learn,' then proceeded to the first box of parts. He took out the metal receiver and showed Bilal how to attach it to the stock. Then he moved on to the next box, adding more parts as he moved down the production line, humming softly in between showing Bilal what to do. Before the last few items were assembled the iconic shape was clear and Bilal let out a low whistle. 'Fucken A' he breathed. 'AK-47. When you absolutely, positively must kill every last mutherfucker in the room, accept no substitute.'

Ninos glanced at him, looking annoyed. 'No, it's not an AK-47' he said. 'It's a Type 56 – Chinese version. Different.'

Bilal felt angry at being corrected but held his tongue. He didn't want to piss off a guy who obviously knew a lot about and had access to highly illegal firearms. Ninos' eyes noted the struggle going on inside Bilal's mind and cut in, 'Now you do it.'

Bilal took another stock and went to the start of the row. Ninos moved beside him, occasionally nodding and grunting 'good' as he assembled the rifle correctly, and pointing out changes if he had forgotten. When they got to the end of the line, Ninos took the rifle, pointed it at the floor while he pulled back on a lever on the side and then squeezed the trigger. The rifle made a sharp click, and Ninos smirked and nodded approvingly at Bilal. 'It works, well done. Now do another one.' He took the two completed rifles, wrapped some rag around the end of the barrel and placed them inside a metal drum at the end of the bench. Pointing down, the wooden stocks came about two thirds of the way up the side of the drum.

Bilal went back to the start, and worked his way through the list of parts again. This time, Ninos was behind him, starting on a fourth assembly. Bilal made the final adjustments and turned to copy what Ninos had done, pulling back on the lever on the side of the rifle. As he did so, the rifle barrel moved up away from the floor, pointing at Ninos but Bilal's attention was focused on the unfamiliar mechanism and he didn't notice.

In a flash, Ninos pushed the barrel away from him and pinned Bilal against the bench, pressing his forearm into Bilal's throat and choking him. Bewildered and disoriented by the sudden attack, Bilal struggled, shaking his head but Ninos was too strong. Bilal's head swam and he let go of the rifle, barely aware that it didn't fall to the ground because Ninos was holding the barrel.

Suddenly, the pressure released a little and Bilal could draw a shallow, shuddering breath. His brain was screaming 'WHAT

THE FUCK? WHAT THE FUCK?' but he paid attention when Ninos spoke.

Ninos' voice was quiet but hissed venomously like a snake. 'Never, ever, point a gun at anyone you are not going to kill.' He pushed against Bilal's throat again to emphasize his point.

'Always assume every firearm is always loaded. Never point it at anyone. Understand?'

Bilal nodded, and the pressure on his throat released again. His heart was pounding and his ears burning, flushed with exertion, shame and confusion.

'What the fuck, man?' he asked, once his tongue started working again. He looked at Ninos, who appeared to have calmed down somewhat. 'Fucks sake.'

Ninos stared at Bilal. 'You scared the shit outta me. Didn't anyone teach you the rules?'

Bilal shrugged and shook his head. 'I never touched a gun before this.'

Ninos grunted as he understood. 'Sorry fo being rough, then. But it's a lesson you need to learn good. Too many good men dead because the people around em weren't careful.' He looked at Bilal, to make sure he followed. 'If you're a moron, and you die in a gun accident, it's better, ya know? Better than if a good man is killed by a moron – the moron stays alive, but we lost the good man, ok?'

'Fuck yeah, I get it' said Bilal. 'It's serious'

'Deadly serious' said Ninos, then he paused. 'Sargon didn't tell me you were a noob, so it's really his fault. If I'da known, I'da given you the lesson first.'

'First, always assume every gun is loaded.' He looked at Bilal, 'most accidents happen becuz the operator didn't think it was loaded. Never make that assumption, be safe instead.'

Ninos held up the rifle in front of his chest and pointed at the barrel. 'Imagine a laser beam is always shining outta the barrel, always gonna slice and burn anyone it touches. Like a

Darth Vader lightsaber. Never, ever point a gun at something you're not ready to shoot.' Bilal nodded and Ninos concluded 'This is called Muzzle Discipline. Keep the barrel pointed at the ground.'

'Next, trigger discipline' the lesson continued. 'Keep your finger off the trigger until ready to shoot, until the kill decision has been made and the sights are on the target.' Ninos pointed his trigger finger down the side of the rifle, above the trigger but close enough that he could fire in a moment. 'You show everyone around you that you know you're safe by pointing the finger like this, understand?'

'Finally, be aware of the target and what is beyond it.' Ninos explained that it wasn't good enough to shoot an enemy, if there were friendlies or innocents behind them that would be hit by stray bullets. 'Dis also includes penetrations,' Ninos added. 'House walls, fences, stuff like that. Gotta be careful of what's behind the target, through walls, car doors, anything.'

'It's super simple stuff but you need to be safe' Ninos said. 'I learned this shit soon as I could walk, it just becomes a way of life. I keep on about it because if you dumb-kill yourself that's bad enough, but if you kill me too…,' he shook his head.

Bilal shrugged, vaguely interested but he didn't see why this would be relevant to him, it wasn't as if he – or even Australia - was going to war. Sure, Australia was already at war, but the fighting was going on overseas, where people had been fighting since before the invention of fire.

'It's early,' said Ninos. 'Get back to work.' They found a rhythm and in just over an hour, there were 50 rifles assembled, lightly oiled and stacked neatly inside the empty oil drum.

Ninos went to another bench and picked up a large metal pan and brought it over. The pan had a flat bottom like a soup pot, and a flared rim around the top. Ninos pushed the pan inside the top of the oil drum, where it fit snugly, the flared rim matched perfectly to the rim of the oil drum.

Pouring in a few liters of motor oil, it was impossible to tell that the drum contained anything else, especially when Ninos fastened a lid over the top and secured it with the appropriate hoop & latch. Together, the two men grunted as they tilted and rolled the drum away from the bench, into a storage room at the back of the workshop. They set it down next to a dozen other identical ones.

Bilal followed Ninos to a wash basin where they cleaned the dirt and gun oil off their hands, then back into the main workshop area. Ninos turned off the lights and said to Bilal 'go home, I see you next week, yeah?'

'Fuck yeah, OK' said Bilal, fishing out his car keys. It would be good to sleep in for the rest of the day.

Chapter 19

May

Bilal knew his part in the plan, but waiting for it to kick off was almost unbearable. He was in the back seat of his own car, which Ninos was driving. They were following Sargon in a stolen car north up St Hillier's Road, leaving the road blocks on the border of the Caliphate and heading into enemy territory.

Sargon had been sent a text message that told him roughly where to expect a police operation – either a radar speed trap, license check or RBT so while they knew the general area, leaving their phones at home meant they could not receive updates – this was a one-stop mission. The two cars cruised around until they saw their target – a single police car with the officer standing beside it with a radar gun, tracking the oncoming traffic. They pulled the cars into a side street and quickly took the license plates off the vehicles. No words were said, they all knew their jobs and were too hyped up to bother with small talk. This was serious.

Sargon left first, opening a gap between the two cars while Bilal settled into the rear seat behind the driver. He broke open the shotgun, two long barrels resting side by side, and pushed in two red and brass shells. He left the gun open, resting across his knees and pointing the barrels safely into the passenger foot-well. He watched through the windscreen as Sargon's car shot ahead, screaming past the police car at double the speed limit.

The reaction would have been comical if Bilal wasn't so focused on what he was about to do.

The officer sprinted to the driver's side of the car, yanked open the door and dived inside. The tail lights flashed as the cruiser started and went into gear, then shot forward as the siren and lights came on and Sargon's car turned left, off the main road and disappeared. The police cruiser followed, and Ninos slowly approached the intersection and turned as well, both spotting the police car a few hundred meters down the street, with Sargon's car stationary in front of it. Driving close, Ninos timed it so they approached just as the cop was walking from his car towards Sargon. Bilal knew that Sargon had dropped the driver's seat back as far to the rear as it would go, lying with his body almost horizontal and concealed by the tinted windows.

Ninos slowed their car as they approached the cop, rolling down the rear passenger electric window at the same time. Time seemed to slow for Bilal as he raised the shotgun and clicked it shut, thumbing off the safety in one fluid movement, just like he had practiced a dozen times. The shotgun barrels were so long that the end of the gun was barely inside the car as they slowed alongside the cop. Bilal slumped with his back against the door to brace his shoulder, making sure the shotgun was angled up, out the window so he didn't hit Sargon. He wasn't sure if he screamed 'ALLAH ACKBAR' but it made no difference, the noise of the shotgun firing was deafening inside the car. He thumbed the little lever to select the other barrel, sighted on the black leather jacket that filled the window and squeezed the trigger again. Ninos put the car in second, his foot floored the accelerator pedal and the car shot away from the scene of the crime. Blood roaring in his ears and head spinning, Bilal sat up as the window went back up, looking out the back as Sargon's car became smaller and smaller. He saw the driver's door open, but the speeding car he was in turned a corner before he could see any more.

He knew that Sargon would be grabbing whatever equipment he could from the fallen cop, then sticking Deng's time bomb between the front tyre and the wheel well wall of the police car before following them back home. When the bomb went off, the car would be wrecked – denying the police yet more resources to use against their Caliphate. It would also cost the state government a lot of money to replace their equipment, so the government would be hurting, as well as the police.

They met up in the house near the Mosque, Sargon arriving about ten minutes after Bilal and Ninos and embracing them all as the adrenaline was wearing off. The Melbourne Mullah was there to meet them: 'Lions of Allah, how did you go?'

Bilal's pulse had returned to normal, but he was still suffering a massive stress reaction from the killing. Literally getting away with murder was nothing like in the movies.

'We got him,' said Bilal, looking the Mullah in the eye, even though his hands were still shaking. The Mullah smiled and nodded his approval.

'Good, good. Truly you have struck a blow against the great Satan and your names are recorded in Allah's book of the blessed.' He moved over to Sargon, who had placed a backpack on the floor between himself and the Mullah and gave his report. 'I got his radio, gun and badge. But no time to get his jacket – it was a big mess. I just set da bomb and went, just like you said.' He opened the bag and handed over the items, which the Mullah set on the floor beside him.

'Truly, Allah is merciful, and He will be merciful to you,' intoned the Mullah. His manner was almost hypnotic, and Bilal felt his sick feeling fading away, being replaced by the blessed peace of God.

The Mullah continued the conversation, debriefing the three men, calming their fears, praising their dedication and describing the rewards that awaited them. Bilal was less concerned about the rewards in heaven than the more immediate rewards the Mullah could provide him – import connections, smuggling opportunities, anything to get him the cash and legitimate cover story he needed to get ahead in life. The Mullah looked at him said, 'First I saw you, I knew. I knew you were a prince. You deserve to be honored with a high place in the Caliph's court. Inshallah, it will happen soon.'

Bilal could barely believe his ears. Here was this educated, holy, powerful and connected man telling him exactly how he was going to help him achieve his dreams. He resolved then and there that nothing would stop him from carrying out the Mullah's orders. A prince in the court – yes, that was exactly where he wanted to be, and he was prepared to do anything in order to get there.

'Peace' said the Mullah, handing over three envelopes stuffed with cash. 'Even in nature, the lion needs to rest once it has taken the prey.'

'Rest now, sleep and I will see you at morning prayers.' They were dismissed.

Bilal went home and fell into a dreamless, refreshing sleep.

-

Talking heads were back on TV, further stoking the controversial positions that had neatly split the commentary arena in two. On one side of the debate were the supporters of the Caliphate, who said that everyone had the right to self-determination, the right to feel safe in their own homes, and be free from bigotry or racism. If the Caliphate was the only way for Muslims to feel safe, then they should be allowed to proceed.

They were countered by a larger group who supported the PM's position, that this is Australia, we already have a functioning democracy which guarantees freedom of worship. Therefore, there is no need to change anything. The opinions and commentary flowed back and forth while the hosts tried to maintain an image of concerned moral aloofness.

One overweight woman with frizzy black hair and stylish glasses said 'While it is true that there are extremists in all religions, even the IRA came to the negotiating table and formed a political party. If the Islamic community wants to participate in democracy, they can form a party and take it to elections.'

'Are you mad, or just ignorant of history?' responded a thin man with a red face, flushed with anger. 'The British fought a full-on war in Northern Ireland, with armored vehicles, spies, the SAS – everything. The IRA fought has hard as they could and killed hundreds of soldiers and civilians. We are already seeing the same thing here – a violent faction that you are ignoring at your own peril. India is still fighting a low-level war with Pakistan – they've been fighting for eighty years, including four full on wars – over a million casualties.

'But we've learned from the overseas experiences,' opined another. 'Surely the Caliph will need to impose law and order once the borders are agreed upon. We must be tolerant of other ideas and ways of life.'

'Tell that to the victims, the police, their families,' responded the thin man. 'Or better yet, go to Saudi Arabia and have a good look at how law & order is going to work in the Caliphate.' He paused to let the cameras focus on the confused looks on the other guests' faces, then went on, pointing specifically to the woman. 'Let me ask you a serious question. Honestly. What do you think is going to happen to feminists and the LGBT community inside the Caliphate?'

She frowned in confusion. 'What do you mean?' she asked.

'Well, the Caliph will install Sharia law and Sharia courts' said the thin man. 'Under sharia, women's rights are severely restricted, and we've all seen the footage of gay men being thrown off buildings, watched by crowds of 'moderate Muslims' who do nothing to stop it. So, answer my question. Are you willing to sacrifice the freedom of women, and the lives of gay and transgender people, for what? To feel happy that you are being tolerant?'

'I don't understand what you are asking' said the woman obtusely. 'Why would their lives be any different? Look, our national anthem specifically says, 'for those who've sailed across the seas, we've boundless plains to share' - so why aren't we sharing them?'

The thin man threw his hands in the air in an expression of resignation. 'Their lives will be OVER. The people who practice sharia law believe it is their duty, their obligation to oppress women and kill anyone who doesn't conform to how they think it should be... And yes, whatever moral authority the national anthem may have – it says 'boundless plains' - not city suburbs that become ghettos. Our anthem calls immigrants to settle into the regional towns and cities out beyond the Great Dividing Range – adopting Australian culture and assimilating – not overcrowding urban ghettos and demanding that we change laws and a society that has served us perfectly well for over 200 years...,' his voice trailed off as he realised the camera wasn't broadcasting him any longer.

-

Checking her news feed, Virginia was pleased to see the main headline was

MORE COPS KILLED – CRIME OUT OF CONTROL

Less cops in her world meant less chance of her being arrested.

Virginia's problems had started when she was a baby, and had been given a name that every school kid could nickname 'Vagina the Whiner.'

In a spiral replicated a thousand times a year, low self-esteem brought low social standing, leading to low grades, which led to her being put in classes with other kids who didn't want to learn. By the time she was fifteen, Virginia was a regular drug user and dealer, desperate to try any substance that would ease her creeping self-loathing and insecurities.

Virginia had done well for herself, her wits and cunning keeping her out of jail for three years since she left school at sixteen. But now, business was hurting because Sydney was being flooded with cheap drugs from all over the world. Regularly breaking the Golden Rule of drug dealing, Virginia was addicted to the peace that a high brought to her, helping her forget the pain that underlined the entirety of her life.

And to make matters worse, it had been a while since she had scored, and the landlord had taken the last of her cash to pay some of her arrears. For a couple of days, she had simply existed, lying on her bed and feeling the despair of withdrawal. The physical symptoms – runny eyes, diarrhea, dehydration and physical pain were bad, but the mental symptoms were worse. Anxiety and panic attacks battled each other inside her head until she was convinced that she had gone insane.

But didn't that mean she wasn't insane? If she was insane, she would feel normal. Wouldn't she?

So when her some-time flat mate, fellow junkie and general dead-beat dad Jim had shown up and dragged her outside into the night air, she felt relief that there was something different going on. Something to distract her brain from the war going on inside it. She felt a little better but was still completely occupied with the problems inside her.

They left her tiny flat in Glebe and headed towards the airport in his ancient Datsun 180B. Cruising slowly through the crowded industrial streets of Zetland, they eventually arrived in the newly-developed residential areas; where towering blocks of shiny white and grey apartments glistened in the moonlight above and the street lights below.

Not that Virginia was looking, her twitching body was hunched in the passenger seat, eyes twisted shut as she tried to control the shakes. 'Where we going?' she asked Jim.

'To see a guy' was all he would reply. He pulled out a sheet of paper, checked an address on it and then pulled the car over into an empty spot on the side of the road. 'Come on, I need you – back me up' he said, cajoling her out of the car as he slung a small backpack over his shoulder and led her up to the smooth white concrete wall of a block of apartments. A black steel gate was set menacingly into it, but Jim pulled out a key, twisted it in the lock and pushed the gate open. He turned and smiled at her, gloating. 'Ta daa…' he said, waving his hand to invite her to enter.

Virginia walked slowly into the courtyard of the unit block, looking around at the clean, expensive and well-maintained apartments. It was like being in a real-life Disney film, where the clever but disadvantaged gutter-kid is invited to see how the rulers live.

Except this was real. As real as the fire ants burrowing under her skin, behind her eyes. Virginia reflexively pulled out her phone again, but Jim snapped 'put that away, watch my back.'

'Why? What are we doing?' she asked again, as they approached one of the brightly lit entry doors to one of the towers that rose above them, sprinkled with lights like a Christmas tree. 'I told you, meeting a guy' snapped Jim, using the key again to open the door. They entered a sterile, tiled area with mailboxes on one wall, a noticeboard opposite and a set of gleaming silver doors in the middle. Jim pressed the call button for the lift and they waited nervously while the equipment hummed.

Virginia's paranoia got the better of her. 'CCTV?' she asked him but he just shook his head. 'Nahh, builders are too tight to put 'em in and de owners are so new they can't afford them. Perfect target.'

'Target?' asked Virginia. Her skin began to crawl even more as she felt Jim was leading them into danger. But he managed to avoid the question as the elevator doors opened with a PING and they went inside. He pressed level 5 and the doors closed, trapping them within the shiny metal coffin. Virginia's eyes began to water, and she felt like she was about to throw up. She screwed her eyes tight and rubbed her temples, trying to hold onto normality as long as she could.

'Don't worry,' soothed Jim quietly. 'This guy owes my mate, so we're just claiming what's ours. Besides, he's probably still at work, we'll be in and out in 5 minutes'.

The indicator numbers crawled up to 5 and the doors opened with another muted PING, allowing them out into a carpeted hallway, anonymously grey and white like a thousand similar unit blocks all over Sydney. Jim found unit 54 and then pulled a small crowbar out of the backpack. Setting it into the door, he turned and whispered to Virginia 'know why this guy is so unlucky?'

Virginia shook her head and he replied 'Chinese numerology. Fifty Four means "I love death",' he cackled softly, then leaned onto the metal bar. He pushed the door enough to break the flimsy lock and Virginia's long experience in burglary took over. She gently opened the door and took two steps inside then stopped to listen. Jim stepped out of the hallway and paused. Silence. Nodding to each other, Virginia took another step as Jim eased the apartment door closed. It was statistically unlikely that anyone from outside would notice anything, and even more unlikely that they would do anything about it if they saw something unusual.

Jim took another, empty backpack out of his one and handed it to Virginia. Ignoring the bulky TV, she went to the cabinet and unplugged the game console, stashing it and the controller in her bag. She checked the books on the bookshelf and the fittings around the power points, looking for hidden valuables, then went into the kitchen and did the same in the pantry cupboard. People often hid jewelry and money behind the power point, in fake food tins or books.

With long experience, Virginia and Jim were as good at their jobs as any white-collar professional was at theirs. They had learned from others – both in and out of prison - how to defeat CCTV, how to move without leaving evidence and what items were valuable – and where they could be found. Corporations spend millions of dollars a year in training their staff, yet thieves like Jim and Virginia had much more incentive to learn from the training they received around a shared bong or six-month prison term. Pooling ideas and information kept them out of jail – or the grave.

Virginia was finished in the kitchen when she heard a muted THUMP from the other side of the unit. Moving down the short hallway past a bathroom, she was suddenly attacked by a grotesque figure, grabbing at her with frenzied, bleeding arms and groaning a bubbling, moaning cry that tore at her soul.

Recoiling, Virginia involuntarily took a step back, but the figure was too fast, bumping into her and sending her sprawling down the white wall of the apartment, leaving a red blood trail as they went. Heart pounding and a layer of red hot terror smothering her underlying withdrawal symptoms, Virginia kicked and struggled to get free.

Then she realised it was Jim.

He was covered in blood – his own blood. Virginia looked closer and saw that his head, face and arms were all bleeding from deep cuts, and his shirt was slashed in several places, scarlet blood pooling from deep inside to soak onto her clothes. Jim made another last gurgle and then went limp, collapsing onto her legs and pinning her to the ground.

A light clicked on at the far end of the hallway, washing Virginia's living nightmare with a glare that struck deep into her eyes, stabbing into her brain. Squinting against the pain, she saw a young Asian man step toward her. He was completely naked, but Virginia's eyes were drawn to the short, curved sword that swing idly and confidently from his hand.

Shrinking away from the terror overloading her badly misfiring brain cells, Virginia tried to wiggle backwards, to put distance between herself and this terrifying menace. She struggled as hard as she could but Jim's dead weight was simply too much for her. Then the man stepped forward, looking around with a scowl at all the blood and spoke aloud.

'Gonna have to replace all the carpet now. Fuck.'

Then he looked down at Virginia, swung the sword viciously through the air and with a SNICK, Virginia's life was snuffed out.

Chapter 20

June

Samantha Lee was beginning to regret going on TV. Previously accommodating hosts had begun to show ambivalence, to turn against her arguments, and the guest position ratios had changed. Where once she was normally teamed up with two or three anti-gun guests, now she was the lone voice calling for more restrictions, as more and more people realised that criminals and the Caliphate would never stop getting weapons, and began feeling the need to arm themselves again violence. The number of dead and wounded police officers was increasing, and their vehicles were regularly sabotaged or rammed, stretching their resources even more thinly across the city.

The mood in the city was subdued, even taking into effect the winter weather. Society had lost its innocence, people realised that terrorism and violent crime weren't just ideas they saw on TV, that happened 'over there' in poor suburbs or dusty countries - it was happening to their families, their neighbors and workmates.

After Friday prayers at the Mosque, Bilal steered his yellow EVO west along Punchbowl Rd, then turned right up Cosgrove Road, heading towards the Hume Hwy. Cosgrove Rd ran through several industrial estates, parallel to the train lines on his left. The night air was cold, so he had the windows up and the music high as the sports car ate up the black road below. He was familiar with the road and the industrial scenery, having taken this short cut many times.

Idling along in the traffic, he thumbed over to his phone's news feed.

MORE BACON LEFT IN BANKSTOWN HOSPITAL PRAYER ROOM

POLICE ADMIT THEY STRUGGLE TO RESPOND TO 000 CALLS

OUTRAGED RESIDENTS PROTEST OUTSIDE PARLIAMENT

Shifting out of third gear and into fourth, he wasn't really paying attention to his surroundings when he had to brake suddenly as a large tractor-trailer loomed out of the darkness into the field of his headlights. Aware of the Mullah's routine warnings against getting into trouble, he braked the car behind the truck instead of recklessly pulling out onto the other side of the road. He couldn't miss the giant blade on the grader sitting on the bed of the transporter – right at the same level of his head as he drove behind.

Orange indicator lights flashed on the left-hand side, and the truck pulled out into the right lane to give it room to turn left into the large goods yard beside the train line. Relieved that the obstruction had moved off his path, he shifted back into second, dropped the clutch and the EVO shot forward, picking up speed as he looked left, into the open gate where the truck had gone, expecting to see the normally empty yard.

It wasn't empty any more.

Parked in neat rows, silently glistening in the sulphur yellow glare of the night floodlights, was a diverse group of construction and earthmoving equipment. Giant Tonka dump trucks, excavators, front-end loaders, graders mixed with cement mixers, generator units and portable flood lights.

Bilal took all this in with a flash as the car shot away from the gate, but the unexpected image stayed with him, the emotion attached to it causing it to stay in his mind's eye long after the road darkened behind him. He wondered if the State Government had finally sold off the goods yard - it would make a great development site, he thought ruefully, disappointed that he didn't yet have the capital or the connections to get in on the construction action booming across Sydney.

One day. One day, he would rule it all, taking a cut from all the business done in his part of the world.

A few moments later, he pulled the EVO onto the side of the road and stopped behind a brand new C63 AMG. He silenced the engine and got out into the black night, hunching his shoulders at the chilly air as he looked about, making sure the street was deserted.

The interior light in the other car lit up briefly as the driver got out, zipping up his Adidas tracksuit jacket as Bilal strolled around to the rear of the EVO. He popped open the luggage compartment and took out a small backpack. Walking around to the front, he dropped it on the ground between the two cars and then stood over it, facing the other driver, who had pulled out his phone. He nodded in greeting and said 'Bilal.'

Bilal nodded his own greeting. 'Tony. Peace be upon you' he said, taking out his own phone.

'Allah Ackbar,' said Tony, jokingly. The two had known each other from school, and Bilal's couching had grown Tony's minor, weekend and part-time drug supply operation into a decent player, running drugs into several social networks all over Sydney. Except for Cabramatta – they never went near Cabramatta, with good reason. In the late 1990s, growing Lebanese crime gangs had been spreading all over Sydney, operating across the whole crime spectrum with heroin, other drugs, prostitution, car rebirthing, extortion, counterfeiting and politics. They intended to "own" the entire city, but when they tried to push into Cabramatta, their people simply disappeared. When the police eventually found the mutilated remains of the dealers, the message reached the top levels very quickly: Cabramatta was already under 'management' and new operators were not tolerated.

The two criminal elements had settled into an uneasy truce, avoiding each other's territory and effectively dividing up Sydney between them.

On their phones, both men opened their Bitcoin apps, and Tony transferred the value of the drugs in Bilal's bag into Bilal's account. There was a ten second delay as the confirmation email arrived in his inbox, then a PING as Tony's phone advised a text message had arrived from the merchant. Tony put the six-digit code into the app, releasing the value from his own account into Bilal's.

While he waited for the confirmation, Bilal swiped across his news feed:

GOV PARALYSED BY CALIPHATE NEGOTIATIONS

DOZENS OF POLICE SLAIN IN HORRIFIC MURDERS

MARINES ORDERED TO NORTH QLD TO BEGIN OPERATIONS

The news feed was interrupted by a PING of his own. A glance at the app confirmed that the value of his bitcoin had increased, and he stepped back, thumbing his phone off and slipping it into his pocket.

Their business over, Bilal asked 'How you bin, bro?'

'Yeah good,' replied Tony. 'Business is hectic, might go overseas for a bit.'

Bilal nodded, then changed the subject. 'Hey, beside the train line, on Cosgrove Road, you seen all the equipment there?'

Tony nodded, 'Not just there, mate. Lots of em all over. Chipping Norton, Homebush, back of Strathfield station...'

Bilal nodded as if he knew all along, but inside he was intrigued. Some developers must have pooled their resources for something major, but he couldn't figure out what it could be. Hopefully it was so big he could find a way to invest and get a foot in the door before it was finished.

Mindful of the time, and both their security concerns, he nodded to Tony and bid him good night.

'You too,' said Tony. 'Inshallah.'

Bilal shook Tony's hand and got back into his own car as Tony picked up the bag and fired up the V8 twin turbo AMG. The two sports cars left the area in different directions, and Bilal drove slowly back past the construction equipment on Cosgrove Road.

One day, he thought – one day, he would be the one placing the orders for massive construction jobs.

One day soon.

Chapter 21

July

'No, no, no, NO!' a chubby man shouted at the PM. The man was almost as wide as he was tall, with several gold rings on his fingers and a broad moustache that reminded her of Saddam Hussein. He was agitated, angry and frightened, desperately trying to make the authorities understand the implications of their accusations.

'How many times? How can we say it so you will understand? These criminals are NOT Muslims. They have NOTHING to do with us. We do not support them, we do not support their Caliphate. We want them GONE.'

'No Australian Muslim wants death and destruction. We just want to be left alone.'

The PM was meeting with leaders and elders from the Islamic community all over Sydney. It wasn't going well, for anyone in the room.

She fixed the man with her trademark glare as he ended his rant, then overruled the others in the room by raising her hand and pointing at him, jabbing her finger at each of the rest as she emphasized her words.

'Listen carefully to me,' she said slowly and clearly, the warning clear in her voice. 'You all, and my government, are in an impossible situation. We share the same fate, but the outcomes won't be the same.'

'I understand that this is not a religious matter. My ancestry is Irish, so I appreciate that the IRA were not fighting a religious war - even if some of them tried to paint it that way. It's all about politics.'

'Most of you just want to be left alone, to run your businesses, raise your families and worship in peace.'

The men in the room nodded.

'You all like living in this country. You have opportunities that do not exist anywhere else. We all admit that the authorities overlook a lot, and if we expanded the recent inquiries into other areas, there is a lot of dirt we could dig up that would destroy everyone in this room's standing in their community.' The mood in the room changed as she went on, an invisible charge of electrified emotion focused their attention on her message. This was personal to each one of them.

'But right now, this situation is intolerable.'

'The people of Australia want action. They are calling, writing, and visiting every day, demanding retribution - for the Lindt Cafe, for Castle Towers, for falling property values - everything. Right now, YOU ALL are being blamed for every misfortune.

'If this government is unable to present a workable resolution, we risk losing control of the population. I cannot, cannot, stress enough how dangerous that would be. No matter how hard you think you may fight, two percent of the population - you have no chance.

'They will burn your Caliphate to the ground and thousands of innocent people - Muslims, Australians, it won't matter how you identify, and there will be blood and I WILL NOT HAVE THAT.' Her voice snapped in the electrified air like a frozen lake cracking underfoot.

'The Caliphate. Cannot. Continue.' Every eye in the room was fixed on hers. 'Nobody in this room wants a crusade - YOU most of all.'

'Right now, we all have options,' the PM continued, more calmly. 'But if this crime and violence continues, I will have no option but to begin very strong measures. I do not control the media; however I will do everything I can to stop calls for a crusade.

'But understand this,' she went on coldly, 'these terrorists make war in the name of Islam, so it does come back to you, no matter how hard you deny it. There is a public perception that you must, MUST consider - if you ignore it, you will all die. You and I MUST work together to isolate and remove these criminals - but it comes back to you. Right now, every crime victim isn't thinking 'I was attacked by a criminal', they are thinking 'I was attacked by a Muslim.' Just look at the Facebook comments on any of the news stories and you'll see what I mean.'

'I know it's not fair, I know it's not right, but that is the reality we are living with. If you want to survive, you MUST help us root out these people. Listen to my warning. If this continues, I will be forced to recognize these crimes as a declaration of war.' She paused to give full effect to her words.

'Control your people. Full co-operation with our intelligence and security forces. We are under a microscope here and any further crime – anything – and I will be forced to act. Understand this – if forced to act, there will be nothing left of the Caliphate. We will destroy homes, businesses and infrastructure. I do not want this. You do not want this. Innocent lives will be lost if it goes there. But you are responsible for keeping the war away, is that understood?'

All the heads in the room nodded. They knew from the experiences overseas that none of the local people really won a war. Even after the fighting was over, local conditions were usually worse than they were before.

Leaving the sour meeting, the PM's next meeting was a private lunch with The Englishman. Eternally jolly, he chatted about trivialities for a few moments and until the PM told him to cut the bullshit.

'Quite. Well. Here we are,' he said calmly. 'Initial loans comprising $17 Billion have been approved, broken up into several different packages to keep them under anyone's radar.'

Eyes shining with excitement, the Englishman produced an A3 sheet of paper and unrolled it on the table. The PM saw a map of Sydney, marked with a shaded area right in the middle.

'The Caliphate, I know…' she started, but the Englishman cut her off.

'No, no, this isn't the Caliphate,' he said. 'This is the future.'

'I've just come from a meeting with the development consortium. Architects, builders, electricians, planners – all sworn and signed to secrecy, naturally.

'They've all been very eager to earn some of this funding, and they've given me this concept art – to give you an impression of what they see, once the dust has settled…'

The PM grunted her understanding. The vampires were already salivating over the profit to be made from destroying a section of the city.

'Let's start with infrastructure,' continued the Englishman. He laid a manicured finger on the map just west of Campsie train station.

'The main railway line splits here, the north-west line is a freight line to Chullora but the western line goes to Belmore, Lakemba and Wiley Park.

'Once those areas are…well…levelled, the line will be dug up and moved underground. A trench will be run two point one kilometers between Belmore and Wiley Park.

'Just like the Cross City and Harbour tunnels, but a train version. Into the trench will be run water, electricity, communications, and surveillance - everything you'll need to run a modern community.'

Over the top of the map he laid another sheet, this one a cross section with color coded levels, from deep below ground to a hundred stories above.

'On top of the train line, but still below ground will be the car parks, waste disposal access points, loading bays, emergency vehicle access points – all the infrastructure required to supply and support what goes on above ground.'

'At ground level, there are three bus interchanges, commercial shops, restaurants, groceries, medical facilities and police stations.' His finger moved higher up the page as he outlined the plan.

'Above the shops, there would be three or four levels of commercial office space, leaving the rest for residential units of all kind – tiny cupboards to luxury penthouses.'

'You should see the strata managers fighting over how the management will be divided up' he smirked. 'I think they might be greedier than the developers, since they stand to make long-term profits from the ongoing management and commissions…'

While still shocked and disgusted at the plan to manipulate and kill so many people, the PM had to admit the result would relieve a lot of problems faced by that area of the city.

'Traffic congestion reduced, easier delivery of food and removal of rubbish, fire measures brought up to modern standards…' she mused aloud.

The plan did have merit, albeit at a horrible cost.

'How has this worked overseas?' she asked.

The Englishman cocked his head to the side as his brain compiled a list, compared data and summarized it for her.

'OK, take Vukovar for example. In August of 1991, the city of 25,000 people was attacked by about 35,000 JNA troops. After 87 days of fighting, where an average of 12,000 artillery shells a day were fired into the city, the conflict was over and every building in the city was badly damaged, if not destroyed.

'After integrating into Croatia in 1998, the city has been progressively rebuilt. The iconic water tower has been left as a memorial, but a modern tourist would find little other evidence of the past obliteration. Crime is low, and tourism is a major source of income for the city.

'Now, while the number of people in Vukovar compare to the Caliphate, that city is ten times the size of the area we are looking at. This gives us more control over the battlespace, and the reconstruction should be faster, due to the smaller footprint.'

'Capacity-wise, we will be replacing thirty square kilometers of low to medium density housing with medium to high-density, allowing far more people to reside there, in better quality homes, closer to better services than were available earlier. Walkable. Efficient. Green.'

'All we have to do is kill half of them' retorted the PM.

'Not at all' replied the Englishman smoothly. 'By the time people start dying, they will be enemy combatants who chose to stay in an active war zone. We already have plans taking shape to house over 20,000 people in regional NSW towns, and anyone who wishes to take advantage of temporary relocation will have a complete security screening done to make sure any of the rotten apples don't leave.'

The Englishman cleared his throat and leaned forward earnestly. 'Please, Madam Prime Minister, set your mind at ease. The people I represent have been doing this for centuries, and have learned valuable lessons and insight every time. Agincourt, Austerlitz, Waterloo, Verdun, Leningrad, Stalingrad, Warsaw, Saigon, Mosul, Fallujah, Aleppo – the very best minds on the planet, imbued with two hundred and fifty years of combined experience. Documented, analyzed, interpreted, enacted, evaluated. You'll notice that Eastern Ukraine is in a similar situation, a little more advanced than yours, in that their shooting war has already been going for some time. After the shelling does enough damage, we'll let the Russians take responsibility for their territory on the condition that we can lend them the reconstruction funds. It's all under control, all exceedingly profitable and you will be handsomely rewarded for your part.'

'Now, the first batch of Marines have finished basic training and are almost through their combat arms training. The media will be told they are shipping off to Far North Queensland to support operations against illegal immigration, but in reality they will be diverted at the last minute and encircle the Caliphate.'

He turned back the map and drew several lines across it in broad, sweeping strokes. 'The basic plan has been extremely effective in the past, surround the enemy, cut off their supplies and then reduce their territory, one block at a time. As the Marines secure an area, it will be cordoned off with construction hoardings which are already being stockpiled. Insurance assessors will then do their work on damaged buildings in the outer rings, however we expect damage to be slight and incidental. Many of the residents in the outer suburbs will be able to return to their homes fairly quickly.'

He then drew a line down King Georges Road, then another one across the M5 and a third along Canterbury Road. 'The Marines will cut the Caliphate in half, then in half again, then continue along the major roads. Armored vehicles will provide mobile fire support to the infantry, who will clear the houses, remove weapons caches and hand over any personnel to the Military Police and ASIO for processing.'

The Englishman circled the area between Campsie and Wiley Park. 'As I covered earlier, this is the heart of the Caliphate, which we expect to be hard fought over. Air and artillery resources will be used against enemy personnel, but keep in mind the big secret – the whole point of the exercise is not necessarily to kill everyone, but to demolish - to rebuild.'

He looked the PM in the eye and finalized his sales pitch. 'Once the residents move back in, you will be hailed as the saviour of Western Sydney.'

The PM held his gaze with her own, filled with contempt. 'Just because I realize this is the only way, doesn't mean I like it' she said, but the Englishman maintained eye contact. A tiny smile twisted the edges of his mouth and his eyes were shining with megalomania – or perhaps outright insanity. He rolled up the map and packed it into the small briefcase at his feet, then pushed back from the table and stood up. 'You'll have a briefing from the ADF brass about all this next week. Do try to act surprised.'

Having accepted the deal with the devil and the role she had to play, the PM simply glared at him as he turned and left the room.

Two hours later, the PM was in a TV studio, sitting at a curved bench along with a university professor, a Catholic priest and a female author who was also a Muslim. The smug, greying and somewhat overweight host sat in the middle, holding court and playing to the TV cameras and live audience alike.

The inner-city, latte-type crowd were mostly hostile, and the female writer was finishing up a long tirade about racism, xenophobia and government oppression of minorities. The crowd cheered and applauded, and the host had to call for quiet, so the PM was able to respond. She took a deep breath and plunged into the debate.

'I reject all these emotional and baseless allegations,' she began. 'Our government is not racist. We are not xenophobic. We have repeatedly stated that we will welcome all refugees, once our homeless – and especially our homeless veterans – are looked after.'

'There is no social justice in taking resources away from Australians, born in this great nation, who have answered the call to protect and defend us all, only to be denied basic living standards when they return. A refugee has rights. A refugee deserves protection. But a refugee has not yet contributed to our nation and our society like our veterans have. The fact that there is a single homeless veteran on the street tonight should be a source of shame for all of you, all of us. It is for me, and I am doing something about it.'

The crowd jeered, and someone shouted, 'torturing people on Manus Island.' More cheers and jeering. Both the PM and the host had to hold up their hands so she could proceed.

'Anyone on Manus Island is there only because we cannot verify their identity. We have interviewed all the refugees, and where possible we have validated their stories and identities. Those who have cooperated and been vetted are now in Australia.

'But if someone refuses to give us details of who they are and where they came from, or if the authorities cannot confirm that what we were told is true, then we have an obligation to all Australians to keep them safe, by holding unknown persons until we are certain they do not mean to harm us.'

'And it's not hard. Some years ago, a French national was arrested in Dubai on false charges and managed to escape on a sailboat, even though the Dubai authorities had his passport. He sailed to Mumbai, went to the French embassy and identified himself. He said he had lost his passport, could they issue a new one?'

'Sure, they gave him a list of questions to answer, faxed them to Paris and the people in Paris did a background check – verified that the details he gave matched what was in their system. Twenty-four hours later, he had a new passport and was on his way to America.'

'The same thing has happened with most of the refugees that come to Australia. We verify their identity, issue them with a visa and they are allowed in. That is fair, that is right. But there is no justice in letting in a person we do not know, who has lied to us about their past, their identity, if they harm an Australian.'

The crowd was silent, her arguments about justice were making them uncomfortable. Sensing victory, the PM pressed on.

'I have been informed of allegations of abuse from the authorities at the camps. These have shocked and angered me, as well as all my staff. I have ordered a complete investigation, and if anyone is proven to have broken the law, they will be punished. That is justice. But I will not punish those who are keeping us safe, based on mere allegations from people who may have another agenda. That is not justice.'

'Anyone in the camps, who believes our immigration system is unbearable, is welcome to go home. They are welcome to go to any of the six or seven countries they travelled through to get here. None of those countries are at war, many of them have the same religion as the refugees.'

'I have no interest in being constantly attacked over offshore detention. If I could do anything to get people out of there – without risking the safety of Australians, I would do it immediately.'

'But I will not risk our safety on a "maybe" – if there were to be an attack, it would be me, not you all, speaking to the victim's families. I have a responsibility to put the safety of Australians above that of refugees who may not be completely honest with us.'

Chapter 22

August

Midnight.

Bilal and Sargon were back on the boat. Launching from their usual jetty at Gray's Point, the pilot sailed out from Bundeena but then turned south, parallel to the coastal cliffs of the Royal National Park. This time, the boat was towing a small black inflatable behind it - the kind of zodiac boat that Bilal had seen the lifeguards use, but those ones were red, this one was black and bobbed along obediently behind the larger cruiser.

The sky was overcast, eerie and the ocean calm, cold and menacing. An ominous feeling made worse by Bilal's lack of knowledge of their mission. He didn't know exactly what they were after, but if they were caught, life in prison would be the very best outcome they could hope for. He tucked the thought away and focused on the mission.

The boat cruised slowly down the coastline, past the towering cliffs where sloppy waves churned over jagged rocks. The cliffs were sliced open at intervals with gullies, ravines and even open beaches. Bilal knew that some of the beaches could be accessed by road, but many of them could only be reached by boat or on foot via the many walking tracks in the National Park.

Bilal checked his news feed, looking for trends that might indicate investment opportunities now that his wealth was starting to grow.

CALIPHATE DEFIANT TO PM's DEMANDS

CRIME WAVE PARALYSES NEIGHBOURHOODS

VIDEO OF SICKENING ATTACK ON HOMELESS MAN

MARINES TO LEAVE SOON FOR QLD PATROLS

The boat slowed as the pilot altered course at Sargon's instructions, nosing in towards one of the sandy beaches between the cliffs. After jockeying around with the throttle and rudder for a few minutes, the pilot said to Sargon 'No closer.' He gestured at the water and the waves surging at the rocks nearby and Sargon nodded that he understood.

Bilal knew what he had to do, and pulled on the tow rope to bring the inflatable close to the larger boat. He held it there while Sargon climbed down into it, then stepped in himself. He immediately felt the physical change as the smaller boat rocked in the swell, but also the emotional charge of going beyond the point of no return. He was committed now, no going back. Inshallah. God willed it.

Bilal was surprised at how quiet the motor was - much different to the noisy two strokes that the Cronulla lifeguards used. He asked Sargon about it who whispered 'Electric. No more talk.'

His curiosity satisfied, Bilal held on as the boat crept towards the shore. The incoming tide rushed them the last few meters as Sargon ran the boat up onto the sand. Both men climbed out and dragged it further up the beach, away from the rising water. Bilal hammered a stake into the sand and tied the boat to it.

From the bottom of the boat, Bilal then unpacked a shovel, tarpaulin and some rope while Sargon pulled a Ziploc bag out of his jacket pocket. The bag held a head torch, Silva compass, a topo map of the area and a single sheet of greaseproof paper.

The two men sat on a rock where the beach ended and looked at the papers. Written on the transparent sheet were some numbers, a cross and a circle. Bilal had no idea what was going on, so Sargon explained.

'Find da grid reference. Den you put the cross on it, and the circle tell us where to go.'

He traced his finger across the numbers that ran down the sides of the map and across the top and bottom. At last he grunted and lay the baking paper on top of the map like an overlay. Squinting in the light of the head torch, Bilal saw the spot indicated by the circle - two tracks met in a sort of crossroads. He nodded to Sargon and they moved off, sharing the equipment load between them.

They struggled uphill and through waist-high bushes for almost half an hour – although it felt much longer. Scratched, bleeding and covered in sweat, Sargon finally arrived at the spot where two tracks joined, dropped his load and looked around, stretching his shoulders and back. Bilal joined him, waiting for instructions.

Sargon moved around the area, checking the trees until he found one with a small metal disc nailed to it about waist height. Bilal looked at it – it seemed innocent enough, just the metal lid off a Milo tin or something similar. Sargon waved the torch around until they saw the light reflect off another identical one nailed to another tree about three meters away. Sargon walked to a spot half way between the two metal disks and said 'here, we dig. Carefully.'

Bilal grabbed his shovel and dug it into the sandy earth. Although it was mostly sand, there were a lot of large rocks that had to be dug out which made it slow and frustrating work. The shovel struck each rock and jarred Bilal's arms, then he had to dig around to try to loosen it, lever it up so Sargon could lift it out of the hole. Bilal piled up the sandy soil on one side and Sargon dropped the larger rocks on the other side while the hole in the middle grew deeper.

Finally, the shovel hit something that wasn't rock with a 'donk' sound. Bilal thought it sounded like plywood and by scraping around with the shovel, he proved his thought was correct. As more dirt was removed, it uncovered a plywood sheet about a meter square, then as he scraped around the sides, it revealed the plywood was the lid of a wooden box like a packing case. Sargon brushed away most of the dirt from the lid and then used the shovel to lever it up, off the main part of the box which remained trapped in the ground.

The light from the head torch danced around crazily as Sargon climbed into the shallow hole and then centered on the contents of the crate – an unremarkable black mass covered in a fine layer of dust as their exertions settled in the cool night air. Bilal heard the rustling of plastic as Sargon reached into the box and lifted out one of the items it contained and lifted it over his head, so Bilal could reach it.

Dropping his shovel, Bilal grabbed it with both hands and set it on the ground. The black plastic bag was tied shut, but he could tell that it held a heavy tube about a meter long. He turned back to Sargon just in time to receive another bag-wrapped tube, laying it beside the other one. In less than a minute, the box was empty, and five packages lay on the surface. Sargon climbed out of the hole and slid the lid back onto the box as Bilal tossed the rocks back on top and then shoveled the sandy earth in after.

Once the ground was filled in, they piled the cargo and their tools onto the tarpaulin and used the rope to tie it up in a bundle they could carry between them. All up, the five tubes and their tools weighed close to twenty kilograms, and they stumbled back the way they had come as the rising moon cast a bitter, pale glow over their route. Bilal could see the coast and their boat long before they reached it, and the sight of their destination, tantalizingly close but separated by rough ground covered in sharp bushes played on his mind, every step jarring his knees, shoulders and arms as the muscles burned and the rope cut into his skin.

After slogging through the scrub, they descended the rocky slope to the sandy beach and staggered through the soft sand to the zodiac boat. They carefully put their burden into the middle of the craft and then carried and dragged it back towards the water. Bilal was saturated by the time the boat was in the water and he was able to climb inside, as Sargon started the electric motor and pointed the bow towards the cruiser waiting offshore.

When they were bobbing alongside, Bilal awkwardly clambered onto the larger vessel and pulled the zodiac right up against the hull, Sargon cut the electric motor and carefully moved around so he could pass the bagged tubes to Bilal, one at a time. When all the bags were safely aboard, Sargon tossed the tarp – still tied to the shovels – over the side where it silently sank out of sight. Then he climbed onto the main boat and smiled at Bilal, breathing out a huge sigh of relief.

'Good work, got dem all.' He said, but Bilal was still nervous.

'We aren't home yet, let's get outta here' Sargon grunted agreement and nodded to the pilot who started the diesel engine and turned the bow north, back towards Sydney.

Once the cruiser reached the jetty, it was a simple matter to carry the black bags off the boat and load them into Bilal's EVO. As Bilal drove slowly back to Ninos' workshop, he pondered whether he should ask what they were carrying. Eventually, he decided that he had earned Sargon's trust but played it cool, rather than coming right out and asking.

'Seems cool,' he started. 'Drugs wouldn't have been buried out there…' he let his voice trail off in the hopes that Sargon would fill in the silence.

Instead Sargon looked sideways at him, obviously weighing up in his own mind how much Bilal deserved to know. At last he said 'Wizz Bang. Rocket launchers, just in case ting's get outta control.'

'Rocket launchers?' asked Bilal incredulously. 'What the fuck?'

'Yeah' grunted Sargon. 'Army guy called Shane Della-something stole em, sold em to Eddie Darwiche, who sold em to Mohammed Ali Elomar. Did de Mullah tell you about dat?'

Bilal remembered the Mullah's lesson about using the mobile phones to decoy the police away from their true location. It was amazing that something which had been the subject of such intense searching, legal work and media publicity was now riding in the back of his car. Bilal truly felt connected to great and important events, surely the Caliphate held the promise of riches and respect beyond imagining.

But then his stomach turned. If these rocket launchers were to be used, what would they be shooting at? Tanks?

'Don't worry' said Sargon, reading the expression on his face in the green glow of the dashboard lights. 'Dis govment and media won't allow tanks or anyting to be used against us – be only police in dere cars and 4x4s – we hit one of dem, then dey run away and leave us alone forevah...'

Bilal wanted to believe that, but the news on his phone didn't seem to be in line with what Sargon was saying. Six months ago, sure, all the media were in favor of tolerance, communication and against Islamophobia but recently the mood seemed to have changed. Support was dwindling and even though the Mullah and the Sheikh were obviously very well connected politically, Bilal sure hoped it wouldn't come down to open warfare in the streets. He wasn't a coward, he had already pledged to lay down his life for the Caliphate, but he knew that if a large enough area of the city was destroyed, it would be difficult to grow his business.

Chapter 23

September

'Atten-SHUN!'

The spring day was warm and bright as Lisa snapped to attention with the rest of the platoon on a small concrete parade ground in the vast training area south of Holsworthy. Beside the platoon stood three other platoons in their training Company. In front of them, sprawling across almost a square kilometer lay a training town, a mock village of streets, houses and unit blocks. Occupying some high ground between Dingo and Kallibucca Creeks, the terrain had been graded flat and turned into a somewhat realistic version of the Caliphate's suburbs.

The platoons had spent the past two weeks in sustained training for MOUT – Military Operations in Urban Terrain. Lisa and her team had practiced clearing houses, providing security and overwatch for other teams, vehicle transport and all their communication and co-ordination protocols. Testing all the skills the recruits had been taught, the exercises culminated in the Crucible – a week-long endurance exercise that added starvation, sleep deprivation and exhaustion to the challenges and obstacles.

The Crucible finalized all their training, and the recruits were ready for deployment. Unlike other ADF recruit training, they had spent the past few months in a complete media blackout – no phones, no news, completely focused on learning the business of broad spectrum warfare. Everyone was looking forward to two weeks' worth of leave, before they reported to their next assignments.

Squinting in the sun, Lisa kept her head still but used her eyes to look around at the troops assembled beside her. They were all covered in mud and grass, with dark rings of sweat under their armpits. But they all stood straight, confident, and proud of what they had achieved.

Movement to the front of the formation drew Lisa's attention, and she saw several uniformed officers line up in front of the first row of Marines. As they came to attention themselves, the Marines all saluted smartly, then dropped their arms as one of the officers stepped forward and called 'at ease'.

Lisa shifted her position in time with the other Marines, and listened to the officer introduce himself as Major Robert Ross, congratulate them on completing one of the most modern and rigorous military training programs and welcome them to the Marines.

Lisa's heart soared as the officers moved down the rows, shaking hands and passing over their unit insignia – a black metal badge with a wreath surrounding the NSW cross. When it was her turn, Major Ross shook her right hand, placing the coveted badge in her left. She was hoping for some word of congratulations, or acknowledgement of her hard work but instead he said, 'You're not finished yet.'

Keeping her face expressionless, Lisa accepted this as a compliment in line with the same austere standards of the US Marines they were modeled after. She took a second to glance down at the small metal shape that represented the incredible changes in her that had taken place. The Marines had transformed her from a shattered wreck into a lion, and she wondered what else lay in store for her.

After a few minutes, all the Marines were confirmed, and the officers moved back to the front of the formation. 'Congratulations. You've passed the bare minimum to become Marines. Now, you are going to be tested beyond anything we've been able to throw at you.

'You've all been operating under the assumption that Marines will be supporting operations against illegal immigration in

North Queensland. This is partly true.' A murmur of surprise ran through the assembled troops, and the Major continued:

'You will be supporting operations against illegal immigration, but the location has been changed. While you were in training, several Sydney suburbs seceded from the state and declared themselves an Islamic Caliphate.' This statement shook all the Marines to the core, and dead silence fell as they processed the news.

'Naturally, the Federal and State governments are negotiating with representatives of the Caliphate, however there are few positive signs of progress' continued the Major. 'We have been ordered to integrate with and support regular Army and Air Force units, training and planning for operations to clear the area, and kill or capture insurgent personnel found there.'

He paused for a moment, to allow the stunned Marines to process what was happening to their city, their families, and their homes.

'We have confirmed all your families are safe' resumed the Major. 'Anyone living inside the Caliphate has been relocated – either with family or to a town outside the Sydney basin. Given the progress of negotiations, we expect this to be over by Christmas, and most people will be allowed to return home.'

The Marines groaned as the Major dropped the next bombshell. 'All leave is cancelled, you will now report back to Holsworthy for assignment to active units. You can call your families, but total operational security applies from now until rescinded. Understood?'

'SIR, YES SIR' shouted Lisa, in unison with a hundred other voices. Her mind was spinning with conflicting emotions – fear, curiosity, ambition. But most of all, she wondered if she was going into battle against the people who had killed her family.

Bilal left Friday prayers at the Mosque feeling like he was on top of the world. From being a nobody, a stranger, a kid, he was now recognized and greeted by many of the men – even the older, wealthier men, those who had the family and connections that Bilal so desperately wanted. They now saw him as a player, on the radar, with some growing respectability. People asked him for help & favors now, and he did everything in his power to help, spreading around money, effort and time to grow his social status and influence.

Even the women looked at him differently. The younger women & girls his own age no longer ignored him completely, and the older women – those with teenage daughters of their own, regarded him as a possible son-in-law. Everyone knew he was tight with the Mullah, a trained member of the security forces and a man with broad business interests. If they could get the Australian Government to recognize their claims to territory – if they could just pull it off – Bilal knew there was wealth, fame and many wives in his future.

These thoughts were bustling around in Bilal's mind as he parked the EVO outside Ninos' workshop. He didn't bother locking it – everyone knew who it belonged to and the damage that would be done to anyone foolish enough to touch the car.

The parking area outside the workshop area contained a large delivery truck. DIMO CARPETS & FURNISHINGS was painted on the white exterior in fading, chipped black paint. Two Philippine employees, dressed in dirty blue boiler suits and work boots were busy unloading boxes and cartons, stacking them inside the shop. Ninos greeted Bilal and asked him to help. The boxes were heavy, and there were a lot of them.

Sweating in the warm evening air, Bilal asked Ninos 'delivery from overseas?'

Ninos grunted as he carried the other end of a long wooden box. 'Yeah. Ten forty-foot containers on the Carolina from Dubai via Mauritius. Most of 'em were legit carpets, tables but two of dem – the back half was full of AK parts, ammo, grenades, RPGs and chemicals for Deng.'

'Deng?' asked Bilal. He hadn't seen or heard of the enigmatic little man since their training camp out in Dubbo. 'What's he doing now?'

'The Mullah's Chief of Security, that's what' grunted Ninos. 'He's connected to the Caliph himself, goes way back with the royal family, fought for them all over the place. He been doing strategy, helping negotiations with the Government, making all kinds of bombs, training all the security forces. He's a Sahir – a wizard.'

Bilal felt upset that the Mullah hadn't allowed him to know this information, but he remembered the training from his lessons in the house near the mosque. Compartmentalization of any organization helped with security. If one of them was captured and interrogated, they simply didn't know anything about the rest of the people involved.

Knowing the contents of the containers made Bilal uneasy. He had seen Black Hawk Down, and he knew what RPGs could do to helicopters and armored vehicles. But he also knew that the enemy had a vote too, and the infidels would have learned a lot from those experiences. He hoped the Mullah would be able to negotiate a peace treaty, but it looked as if they were preparing for a full-on war.

Burning up in the hot sun, Bilal took a rest break, but his news feed held only puzzles as well:

RSL OUTRAGED OVER THEFT OF DISPLAY CANNONS

SCHOOL WELCOMES FIRST NON-BINARY GENDER TEACHER

MORE MARINES DEPART FOR NORTH QLD

He had seen the old World War 2 cannons outside several RSL clubs, and he and his friends had often made penis jokes, climbing on them and taking selfies. But surely they would be useless to defend the Caliphate, since the maze of streets would make it impossible to land shells onto enemy troops, and they didn't have any high-tech equipment to fire back at Australian artillery.

So, who had taken the guns and why didn't he know about it?

And how could he diplomatically ask the Mullah? Without coming across as a whining upstart?

His brain was working hard as he went back to physical work.

-

Williamtown Air Base had been a hive of activity for several weeks, with a major new program of exercises pushed through by the new Government. The base itself is not large, but it employs 3,500 people including 765 contract staff with salaries totaling $28 million. Not all of these people eat at the cafeteria or two mess halls (one for enlisted, the other for officers), but it still serves almost a thousand meals a day using a wide range of local foods cooked into regular meals as well as Kosher and Halal options.

Now the exercises been cancelled, and all operations staff were briefed on the situation.

Most of them already knew what their job would be, having followed the news over the past year. They had tracked the media narrative as it cycled from supporting the Caliphate's claims and demanding tolerance and understanding; to reporting the increasing stories of violence and retaliation as the city adjusted to the new reality; and finally ramping up support for the government and the Marines as they began deploying in the surrounding neighborhoods. It was the same in every ADF operation – a cover story would be 'leaked' to the media, something like joint exercises in Townsville or Darwin – then at the last minute the exercise would be cancelled, and the troops would head off to Timor, Afghanistan or wherever.

Anyone surprised that the exercises were being cancelled didn't belong in their units, because they obviously hadn't been paying attention.

Surveillance aircraft had been loitering over the area for weeks already, feeding back live video and electronic intercepts to the Joint Tactical Operations Centre, and relaying orders, information and updates to the teams on the ground. These PC-9A E-7A Wedgetail aircraft had returned from long deployments in the Middle East and were crewed by veteran personnel who knew their jobs inside out. They could even anticipate the needs of the officers on the ground to some extent, which gave everyone a tactical advantage, having information pushed to them instead of pulled just made everything run smoother. It also contributed to morale; the more vulnerable men on the ground felt much better about their jobs knowing there were guardian angels hovering out of sight above them.

Air Commodore Anthony Grady was in his office when the new orders came through, and he immediately knew that this operation would need to be handled differently to the others. He picked up the phone handset, pressed the intercom button and called for the SADFO. Then he leaned back in his chair, clasped his hands behind his head and closed his eyes for a moment, letting his brain do what it did best without any interruptions.

The Senior Australian Defence Officer is the liaison between the senior officers and the heads of department. It took several minutes for Robertson to arrive in the CO's office, and by that time the Aid Commodore had already run mental scenarios about how best to present the ugly news to the rest of the base. Saluting and then taking his seat, SADFO Robertson looked expectantly at his boss. He knew better than to ask anything; he would listen to what he was given and then ask any questions he needed.

Leaning back in his executive chair, the Air Commodore breathed out deeply and composed his thoughts. 'Change to the mission scope,' he said evenly. 'In addition to surveillance and co-ordination, we will be assisting ground forces as they re-locate the civilian population of the Caliphate.' He paused, but the SADFO had no questions yet.

'A substantial education program is underway to advise civilians that the government will not allow the Caliphate to remain. Anyone wishing to leave the area will receive assistance, with a deadline of 1 November. Nobody is going to say it aloud, but after November 1, anyone living within the borders of the Caliphate will be declared hostile. You know what that means.'

The SADFO's lean, tanned face paled somewhat, and he also leaned back in his chair as his brain processed the information – and the implications.

After a moment the two men locked eyes, and nodded as they both understood their mission. Their facial expressions told each other that neither men liked the task they had been given, but they had resolved to do their best and honour the oath they had sworn to the nation. Ultimately it was no different to any other foreign power seizing control of part of the country where Australian citizens were helping them establish a beachhead.

Eventually the CO spoke his orders. 'SADFO, arrange to incorporate close air support for ground operations in Sydney commencing zero hundred hours 1 November 2018.'

The SADFO nodded grimly, haunted by the thought of killing his own countrymen. No, he countered it - by the time the planes were overhead, the only people in the Area of Operations would be enemy fighters who had sworn loyalty to a foreign power and attempted to steal part of Australia away from its people. He saluted, turned smartly on his heel and left the room.

Two hours later, there were a dozen people seated in his briefing room, but instead of the calm professionalism he normally felt at a briefing, the SADFO found his stomach uneasy and his throat sore. 'Stiff upper lip,' he thought, directing his thoughts away from his body and out towards the other people at the table. These were the officers in charge of the various departments which would be involved in combat operations: Officers and staff responsible for the actual aircraft:

No. 3 and No. 77 Squadrons (F/A-18 Hornets),
No. 76 Squadron (Hawk fighters),
No. 4 Squadron (Pilatus PC-9 trainers)

Also at the table were the officers responsible for the thousand and one other tasks required to get aircraft into the air with what they needed to carry out the mission: supplies of fuel, ammunition and ordinance, engineering, personnel, base security, communications as well as liaisons to the local council and government and the media. They had to cover every possible eventuality, going so far as liaising with Sydney Airport Air Traffic Control and the NSW Police to provide escorts when transporting bombs and ammunition from the Kingswood storage facility to the base.

It was noted ironically that the time taken to drive the bombs and rockets from Penrith to Newcastle was far longer than the time it would take to fly them back almost to the same place and drop them into the Caliphate. Then they got back to business.

After an hour's debate, it was agreed that the air base could support round-the-clock air operations against the Caliphate, since it was so close that there was no need for aerial refueling.

Planes would take off and fly south down the coast, making a starboard turn over the airport itself before diving into the Caliphate and delivering whatever had been requested to the spot indicated.

Finishing up his spiel, the SADFO felt his mouth going dry from speaking so much, and decided he should let some of the other officers talk for a while. He looked down the table at the row of faces and found himself having to squint and focus his vision.

'Err…Jim, can you take over for a bit…' He wiped a hand across his forehead and found it running with sweat, yet his mouth and throat were dry.

Jim cleared his throat, and put a hand up to his head. 'Sorry boss, headache just came on. Where were we…fuel stores – currently at 78 percent of capacity…' his voice trailed off and he sprang to his feet with the others as the SADFO's body missed the seat he was trying to collapse into and hit the floor. Jim tried to move and help his boss, but his legs refused to co-operate, and he fell to his knees as his stomach heaved and emptied its contents onto the carpet. Head pounding, he tried to stand but instead his arms and legs turned to jelly, he fell back into the puddle of vomit and passed out.

-

He had no idea how long he had been unconscious when he finally came to, opened his eyes and looked around, then quickly shut them again as his head felt like it would explode. He felt awful, and was somewhat relieved to see that he was in a hospital, hooked up to a drip. Rolling his head to the side, squinting against the pain in his skull, he could see Jim in the bed next to him, and moved his foot to get his attention. Jim rolled his head towards him and looked him over. 'Morning Sir' he whispered hoarsely. 'Good to see you're awake at last.'

The SADFO grimaced and blinked to try and concentrate. 'What the hell happened?'

Jim shrugged. 'They don't know yet, but we all suspect food poisoning. Botulism maybe?'

'Jesus, the food – do they know…how many?'

Jim shrugged again. 'A hundred and twenty, in various stages,' he said. 'Evenly split between officers and other ranks – which makes it look like the food supplies to both messes and the canteen, rather than just one of them. No deaths – yet, but the base is not operational now.'

Robertson groaned. 'Just as we are ramping up for major operations…' his voice trailed off as the implications fully registered. 'That means…'

Jim nodded, 'I'm sure the investigators are looking at the catering people, but nobody's been in to update us yet. All we can do is wait for the doctors to come around…ah!' His voice trailed off as not one, but two doctors stepped into the room, an elderly blonde woman and a younger, dark skinned man with black hair and a white smile.

They both looked at the Officers with interest and the woman spoke first, while the male doctor plucked a chart from the bed and flipped through it.

'Gentlemen, good to see you are awake' she said, as she checked the bags attached to the SADFO's drip. 'I'm Doctor Creedmore, this is Doctor Tan. How are you feeling?'

'Headache, nausea, very weak,' whispered the SADFO. 'Did you say food poisoning?'

Doctor Tan nodded. 'Yes, test results confirmed you've all had botulism poisoning. Can be fatal but we caught it in time. In the past, we treat it with Trivalent which has quite a good success rate, however recovery takes weeks as the body slowly adapts. In your case, the ADF has authorized us to test a newer treatment on you. This one uses a synthetic adaptation of naturally produced human globulin which seems to be working much faster – the fact that you can move a little and speak is amazing of its own.'

He noticed the looks on the patient's faces and said, 'Sorry, I'm getting a little excited, seeing it work in front of my eyes.'

Dr Creedmore took the chart and leafed through it, then shrugged and asked, 'any questions?'

SADFO Robertson was concerned that he was essentially a guinea pig for medical experiments, but at the same time he was glad the treatment seemed to be working. 'How long? How long are we going to be out of action?'

The two doctors looked at each other, then Dr. Creedmore said 'Hard to tell. Based on how you're feeling, I'd say you need a few days for observation but we're getting daily test results and as long as they're fine...' she looked at Dr. Tan and waited for him to add anything. He simply nodded in agreement - 'A couple more days, but no longer than a week.

The SADFO looked relieved, and he looked over at Jim, who nodded.

'Get some rest' advised Dr. Tan. 'You don't have anything urgent on, do you? Surely you can have a few days off?'

'Yeah sure' grunted Jim, and the two doctors left the room. Once they were out of earshot, the two men laughed weakly. 'Nothing urgent, no, nothing at all...'

-

The midday sun blazed out of a cloudless sky over the southern border of the Caliphate

Lisa's platoon had completed their mission objectives, settled into a perimeter and Lieutenant Barrett put together their situation report. The rest of the Marines took the opportunity to drink, check their weapons and equipment and take some weight off their feet as the radio squawked back and forth.

'Rhino, this is Rhino Two One. How copy?'

'Rhino Two One, this is Rhino. Send traffic.'

'Our location:

Five Six Hotel Lima Hotel

Two Two Two Six Six

Four Two Four Zero Two.

Everything south of the M5, west of King George's Road - clear.

No contacts, friendly or hostile. 'It's a ghost town, they can start bringing in the barriers.'

'Two One, Rhino copies all. Will relay. Stand by for more. Out'

Lt Barrett turned to the platoon. 'Ok folks, we just cleared everything south of the M5. Good work.' There were a few smiles and Lisa exchanged high-fives with her buddy as the Lt continued: 'Engineers will be stringing out the rest of the barriers through here any minute, take five while we wait for further orders.' He found a spot in the shade of a gum tree, sat down and drank from his canteen as the radio crackled into life again.

'Rhino Two One, this is Rhino Actual.'

'Actual, this is Two One, copy'

'Move East Two Zero Zero meters. Join Rhino One at the roadblock on King George's Road over the M5. How copy?'

'Actual, Rhino Two One. Good Copy, we are Oscar Mike now, out.'

The platoon instinctively got to their feet and moved into a loosely spaced patrol formation. Barrett updated everyone with their new orders and put Lisa out on point. She headed up the hill slowly, with the Lieutenant and the rest of the platoon spaced out behind her, covering each direction as they moved.

The sun was hot, directly overhead as Lisa led the platoon up the steep little hill that led from their position up onto King George's Road where the other platoons – call sign Rhino – were located. Challenged by the sentries, she gave the day's response and asked where Rhino One was. The sentry pointed north. 'See those three ASLAVs? On the other side.'

The sight of the ASLAVs was both reassuring and terrifying at the same time. The size of a tank, they drove on eight giant rubber wheels and instead of a long anti-tank cannon, sported a smaller M242 Bushmaster chain gun. These vehicles had been tried and proven in Afghanistan with great success; the locals reportedly referring to them as 'the great destroyers.' The ASLAVS would be doing the main reconnaissance and security work, but they were vulnerable to anti-armor and IEDs, so infantry was needed to screen them.

Lisa knew the ADF had learned a lot of lessons not only in Iraq and Afghanistan, but from the Russian experience in Chechnya as well. Sending armour into a hostile city was a death sentence. The Afghans and Chechens had perfected the art of waiting until a column of vehicles were moving down a city street and then disabling the first and last one to create a trap. Their fighters would then pick off the trapped soldiers from the buildings above and basements below, or burn them out using Molotov cocktails.

Eyeing off the hulking machines as they walked into their shade, Lisa knew that they were a symbol that the operation was changing. Soon they would be stepping up a gear, from clearing empty homes in relative safety and moving into an active combat zone. She shivered involuntarily, both in apprehension and excitement that her training would be put into practice.

Lieutenant Barrett called the platoon to a halt while he went forward to report and discuss their mission with the Officer in Charge. Lisa and her family sat in the shade, resting against the black rubber wheels of the ASLAVs, eating, drinking or resting their eyes as they waited – taking their part in a military ritual dating back beyond recorded history.

Lisa looked around at the lean, tanned faces of her platoon. Ordinary Australians, born into a time of peace and prosperity, who had seen their country change before their eyes, and stepped up when the time came. Most of them were from Sydney, a few from country towns and cities who had joined the Marines partly from a sense of duty, partly for the money and a chance to get a head start in the city – all of them eager to help their country. Lisa was surprised at the lack of crazy talk – blood lust, the Full Metal Jacket style stereotyping of the enemy – 'I just wanna blow shit up' talk. The Marines in her platoon didn't talk like that at all, and she made a mental note to ask the LT about it when she had a chance.

Lisa closed her eyes for a moment and thought fondly of her family. She used her counsellor's advice and focused on the good memories, letting those feelings wash over her instead of the pain, anger and frustration that lurked on the fringes of her mind. The rage would always be there, but she had been able to create an oasis of calm and peace, and centering herself there. The more she practiced, the larger her mental oasis grew, and it was a part of the healing process that Lisa was finding greatest success with.

Her thoughts were interrupted by the return of the Lieutenant. He called the platoon into a circle around him and spread out a map. 'Ok, we are here, on top of the M5 on King Georges Road.'

'ASLAV call sign is War Pig – their mission is to push north five kays to the Hume Highway, we are going to support them and screen both sides of their advance.'

'Humint indicates the main base of the Caliphate is in Lakemba. The further west you go, the less influence they have. We are going to take away access to half their territory by fixing them east from here to the Cooks River. First Marines has all the water access sealed off and covered 24/7, so once we control this road, Third and Fourth will go through everything to the West and ferret out any weapons, drugs, that kind of thing. We expect that to take seven to ten days – during which we can expect sporadic attacks all down the line as the Caliph's forces probe for weak spots. Will they find any?' he asked.

'NO SIR' sounded the platoon enthusiastically. The ASLAVs, with their powerful weapons and thermal sights would look after the platoon at long range, and the platoon would scour the ground and buildings around to keep the vehicles safe from enemy attacks.

That covered the Commander's Intent – the first of five parts to a set of orders. Lt Barrett went on to cover the Situation, Mission, Enemy, Administration and Communication – each of these 5 had up to a dozen sub categories that dealt with how they would move, estimates of enemy numbers and weapons, how to communicate and what to do if separated, ambushed or loss of radio contact.

During training, Lisa and the other recruits had practiced these orders routinely, often running to a dozen or more pages and at the time she had wondered why the exercises were so detailed – there would be no time for such paperwork in combat. 'That's the point,' had replied the training staff. 'In combat, there won't be time so each of you needs to understand it implicitly – any fuck ups and you'll end up getting people killed.' Now, she saw the wisdom in such rigorous training – most of the order elements were commonly used all the time and kept deliberately simple, or reduced to acronyms so they could learn and remember them better. A simple mistake in calling for artillery or air support, for example, could land high explosives on their own position as easily as onto an enemy. Yes, it may be onerous and catered to the lowest common denominator, but that was done for good reason – keeping allied troops alive while neutralizing the enemy as efficiently as possible.

Lt Barrett explained that the mission would be done in two phases. The first would be a three kilometer push north to Punchbowl Road – adjacent to the heart of the Caliphate. An outpost would be established there, with several Observation Points, a Command Post and a supply dump. Six ASLAVs would be stationed at the top of each hill, along King Georges Road, roughly five hundred meters apart, each covering the others with electronic sensors.

'We will move in a tactical column, keeping pace with the ASLAVs' continued the Lieutenant. 'The good news is, our platoon is on the western side, away from the Caliphate's center but make no mistake, from the moment we step off we are effectively surrounded in hostile territory. Cover each other, keep your eyes open and take no risks. If you see something, call it in – better safe than sorry, OK! Questions?'

He raised his eyes and looked at each of the faces in his platoon. Lisa was comforted by the human connection, terrified at walking willingly into a war zone so she closed her eyes for a moment and cracked open the door in her mind to where the anger and the rage lived, letting a little of it out into her conscious mind. She knew why she was here. It was right for her to be here. Action – reaction.

There were no questions. The ASLAVs moved out, and the Marines moved with them.

Chapter 24

October

Bilal was feeling naked without his phone. Even after weeks of operating 'sterile', years of growing up with a phone always within arm's reach had left a deep psychological impression that was taking a long time to overcome.

Making it worse was the lack of news about what was going on. He hadn't seen the Mullah for a week, and was steadily losing contact with many of his friends and associates. Nobody seemed to know what was going on, only that the government had refused to recognize their Caliphate, and instead had encircled the Caliphate with troops.

Bilal remembered the Mullah laughing when he had asked him about the Australian Army. The Mullah had said that the Australians were good fighters, well respected by their enemies. But there were few of them, and most of them were overseas, sharing America's war in the Middle East.

'You see the brilliance of our plan?' The Mullah had asked. 'Their best fighters, all their equipment, it's overseas. Meanwhile, we rise up and seize what is ours, right from under their noses!'

Bilal had to admit the plan was good. Audacious, but if they could pull it off and secure their borders before the Australian troops could be brought home, they would be safe. And if the Australian's left the Middle East, then Allah's warriors would have the advantage handed to them. Either way, it would be advancing the cause of Holy War across the globe.

He remembered the glorious days of the earlier months in the year, when he and thousands of others had paraded through the streets, dressed in black and green, waving and smiling at the crowds of cheering onlookers. There had been weeks of partying, feasting and dancing at night while his business and wealth grew by day.

The crowds were gone now. There were no more parades and people ate quietly in the dark, the mood was tense, hostile and everyone was jumpy. There were only a few people that he could trust, and nobody was using phones to communicate any more. Instead, kids would carry messages between checkpoints, running through the streets that were increasingly empty as the population and economy of the Caliphate declined.

The past few weeks had seen increasing levels of combat, skirmishes between checkpoints and Australian Marines as their defenses were probed and each side learned about the other. Bilal was impressed at the Mullah's skill in directing the battles, never using the same techniques twice. Normally, whenever a checkpoint came under attack, they would retreat as the Mullah ordered fighters from a neighboring checkpoint to circle around and attack the Marines from the side or the rear. Most of the Caliphate's soldiers used an AK47 or some variant – the 7.62mm bullets were readily available, reloadable and packed a powerful punch at the short ranges that the battles involved.

They had several long-range rifles, Dragunov sniper and Remington hunting rifles with long range scopes, set up in all the high buildings around the Caliphate, reporting on enemy activity and occasionally engaging in 'shoot and scoot' – hitting Marines and then running to another building before accurate return fire or artillery could be brought in.

His heart pounded as he relived his first real, balls-out firefight against the Marines. Just before dark, a preteen messenger boy had run up to the checkpoint that Bilal, and seven other lions were guarding. The kid blurted out that Marines had been moving into position nearby, and they were to light bonfires all around their position, to wash out the Marine's night vision equipment. The Mullah would send an ambush force, but Bilal was to hold on to the position and keep the Marines pinned down until the trap could be sprung.

Traditionally, the high-tech armies had owned the night, with thermal and infra-red equipment that insurgent armies could never afford to purchase. But every conflict involves learning on both sides, and many ideas had been tested to overcome the technological advantages. With hot fires blazing on both sides of the street, in both directions, the Marines would be forced out into the light before they could see the Caliph's waiting soldiers. It would be the kind of fight all soldiers hated – a fair one.

Sending the messenger back to the Mullah, Bilal dispersed his fighters in pairs, scraping shallow fighting holes close to the fires, hidden from the light and the night vision cameras. Settling backwards into the recessed doorway of the unit block closest to the checkpoint, Bilal had looked over the scene and felt terribly exposed. He had trained hard with these young lions, but waiting for the Marines to approach brought up icy strings of doubt and fear into his brain. Would they hold? Could they hold off the Marines? Or would the Marines turn the tables, and just call in a bomber to end them in one fiery blast?

The seconds seemed to drag into long, dreary, agonizing hours until he spotted movement at the most distant fire. A pair of Marines were approaching, crouched, on the far-left side of the road. Bilal mentally ran through the names and abilities of his young lions, and decided Mazen was the best marksman. He would be the one to shoot first, triggering the rest of the *lions* to pick targets whenever they saw them.

But before he could speak, Bilal spotted another pair sneaking down the opposite side of the street. If Mazen shot at one side, the opposite Marines would spot the muzzle flash and return fire. They needed the Marines to come in closer, so the flanking force could roll up behind them.

Bilal made a decision. 'Mazen, Seyed' he hissed, and two heads turned towards him. 'Mazen, the left pair. Seyed, on the right. Wait until they reach the second fire.'

Both heads nodded, and they leaned back over their rifles.

The next ten minutes were the longest of Bilal's life, and probably aged him ten years in the process. Waiting for the Marines to slowly and systematically approach, while remaining still and hidden was almost too much to bear, but Bilal's mind churned with the Mullah's instructions. The Mullah wanted him to hold the checkpoint, so they would hold, or die fighting.

Eventually, finally, the two pairs of Marines reached the second fire that had been set about a hundred meters past the checkpoint. Bilal couldn't hear anything, but he saw Mazen's mouth move as he quietly counted to Seyed. Two thumbs pressed down the selector switches, from SAFE to AUTO and then to SEMI. Then both rifles cracked twice, then the two young men rolled in opposite directions, away from where the muzzle flashes had been.

Bilal's nerves were stretched to breaking point as he strained his eyes to see if they had hit anything, then it seemed as if the earth opened and swallowed him right down to the depths of hell.

The Marines hadn't bothered trying to target the individual shooters, instead they had lobbed two M-203 40mm grenades into the middle of the road, and the concussion threw him against the brick wall of the building as income gunfire roared past his head. Chips of brick and burning hot metal fragments peppered his face and hands, as he struggled to his feet to try and see what was going on.

After the 203 grenades had exploded, the Marines had rushed forward, expecting to exploit the confusion and trusting that the shrapnel would have wounded many of the fighters defending the position. Snug in their holes however, none of the lions had been hit and the shrapnel had gone harmlessly over their heads.

Now, they all screamed 'Allah Ackbar' and poured fire back at the Marines. Fighting in pairs, each lion would fire several bursts at the moving shadows down the street, while his partner reloaded. At the Dubbo training camps, they had all learned how difficult it was to wait, letting the others shoot, instead of jumping into the fight all at the same time. Bilal suppressed the strong desire to rush out, guns blazing, because Deng had taught them that such actions were suicidal. Smarter fighters were the ones who had battlefield discipline, doing what they were told. Those were the ones who would live gloriously, which was much better than dying gloriously.

Bilal's position on the steps, rather than being dug into the grass, gave him a better view of the situation, and allowed him to call out targets to the others. He tried to keep count of the Marines who fell, but the chaos of battle took over and events moved faster than he could adapt. His vision blurred and sparkled as tracer bullets flew in both directions. In modern, urban combat, there were threats everywhere but as he used the sights of his rifle to find targets, they were very rare and usually moving fast, bopping up and down. It was maddening.

Then Seyed was shot in the head, killed instantly as he was changing magazines in his Type 56 rifle. Mazen kept firing, but moved back towards Bilal, emptying the magazine as he collapsed beside his friend. They looked at each other, covered in dust and sweat, eyes wide with terror and adrenaline. Mazen changed magazines as Bilal saw another of his crew jerk violently as he was struck by several bullets at once. The two crumped figures on the ground jerked Bilal back to reality and he realised that there was nobody covering the left-hand side of the road.

Deafened by the gunfire and knowing Mazen would be the same, he tapped Mazen on the shoulder, put his mouth close to Mazen's ear and screamed 'follow' as he fired random shots towards the Marines, then darted across to a vacant hole on the left-hand side of their position. Skidding into the ground, he fired again and again at shadows, flashes, sometimes even nothing at all. Using the training that Deng had drilled into them, the fighters fired either single shots or short bursts on semi-auto, conserving their ammo and increasing accuracy at the same time. They knew that the recoil from anything more than 3 or 4 rounds would cause the barrel to rise, sending the rest of the bullets flying over the target.

But the Marines pressed in, and after several magazine changes, he knew he was running low on ammunition and the others had been shooting longer than he. Everyone would be almost out and at that point, they would all be dead. Desperation took over as he wondered where the Mullah's counter-attack was.

The Marines were very close, shooting and crawling when Bilal was blinded by a sharp, bright explosion in front of another unit block on the far side of the road. Squinting in that direction, he saw movement in some of the upstairs windows, and then two more explosions cracked open the ground next to the Marines. The sounds of gunfire surged but all Bilal could hear over the battle was faint cries of 'Allah Ackbar' and he involuntarily screamed the same thing in reply. His lions kept shooting, but also cried out; verbalizing their joy as they understood that the trap had been sprung. The Marines were now under attack from two sides, trapped against the fences and buildings opposite this new threat, and taking fire from the upper floors.

Gradually, the rate of fire from the Marines slowed, as they pulled back in groups, taking turns to keep shooting at the checkpoint while others ran back a few paces. Bilal's rifle bolt locked back on an empty chamber, and when he reached for another magazine, there were none. He kept his head down for a few more seconds, but the rifle shots he heard were all AKs – outgoing. There were no bullets coming towards him from the Marines – they had all pulled back when attacked from the side.

Bilal shook his head as the memories faded and he came back to reality. He had seen a lot of combat since those early days, lost good friends and learned a lot about the infidels and their tactics. Many times, it was only sheer luck that had saved his life.

No, not luck. The Mullah had said it was clear that Allah was protecting him, like a shepherd – guiding him towards the glorious future that awaited.

-

Lisa's platoon had spent a week clearing houses and then had been relieved for some much-needed rest. While they couldn't leave the Area, even a few hours away from the front lines did a lot of good for the Marines' mental health and stress levels.

The platoon had showered at the FOB on King Georges Road and changed into fresh uniforms, then queued up for hot food. Settling into a ring of camp chairs, the Marines were able to relax, joke around and eat something more nutritious than the constipating MREs they ate while on operations. Someone had painted a crude sign on a piece of plywood and hung it over the entrance to the area where the food was served. It was a tropical island scene, with palm trees and a sandy beach under the words 'ALOHA SNACK BAR.'

Lisa found herself seated next to Lt Barrett, and after polishing off half her plate of rice, meat and vegetables – almost in a single mouthful - she leaned back in her chair, drank several gulps of water and let out a sigh of contentment. Lt Barrett noticed and chuckled.

'For a Trooper, happiness consists of food and sleep' he commented cynically. It wasn't his usual type of language, it sounded scripted, like a quote from a book.

Lisa nodded. 'Sun Tzu?' she asked – the quote sounded familiar, but the word Trooper didn't fit with ancient Chinese. The Lieutenant laughed.

'No, better – Robert A Heinlein,' he said. 'From his book 'Starship Troopers'; '– an excellent book absolutely ruined by Hollywood when they made the movie,' he added.

'Food and sleep…' Lisa nodded. 'I couldn't agree more!' She was about to go on, then stopped, unsure if she should continue. The Lieutenant noticed.

'Something on your mind?' he prompted. Lisa smiled.

'Nothing really, I was just looking around the Platoon and wondering why there were no Rambo types…'

The Lieutenant laughed. 'Yeah, they all wash out early in basic training.'

Now it was Lisa's turn to prompt him to go on. He became serious, his plate of food forgotten.

'The shrinks have been working on it for years, and they still don't know why some people make it and others don't. They've looked at everything, and there's just no way to predict who has what it takes – who lives and who dies.'

'But the Rambo types – most of them are compensating for insecurity. They project a certain image because deep down, they either fear or know they don't have it. Look around – these people made it because of what they had inside. In here:' he tapped his head, 'and in here,' then tapped his heart. 'The security of knowing that you can handle a challenge, that you're capable of handling whatever life throws at you – my opinion, that's what counts.'

'Nobody can tell how they'll behave until it kicks off, but I know this – someone who's all show, acting tough, nine times out of ten they're just acting and when the heat is on, they'll fold. First Phase of training is specifically designed to weed out those who definitely haven't got what it takes.'

Lisa thought about what he had said. It made a lot of sense, and agreed with some of the things that her counseling sessions had covered. It also made sense that the military would put a lot of effort into trying to figure out how to determine who would make a better soldier.

Maybe one day they would unlock that mystery.

-

Maryam woke to find the house falling apart around her. Like many of those who stayed in the Caliphate, she had feared that this day would come, but had remained anyway.

At times, she had thought about the reasons why she didn't leave, particularly when she had scrolled through her news feed and seen the media and comments turning strongly against the Caliphate, when they had initially been in full support of their self-determination. Every time the fear had risen in her, she thought of her family, her friends, what they would think of her if she abandoned them. How would she start again, outside the neighborhoods she had known since birth, in a country that had firmly rejected their desire for a separate state?

Every time, she had convinced herself that staying was the right decision. It was her duty.

Now, she knew she was going to die.

All through the winter and spring, the artillery and bombs had been falling, but always in the distance, never close at hand. The fighting had been terrifying and exciting at first, but had soon faded into the background noise as people went about their lives and businesses, importing food and goods through the border checkpoints, trading, praying and eating as life went on.

She saw less and less of her male relatives, as many of them had joined the Lions and gone off to keep the border secure, but the women rallied together, as all their ancestors had done in times of war, making do with what they had.

The shells that had woken her up hadn't hit her unit block, but they were close. Maryam threw on day clothes, grabbed her bag of essentials and ducked down the stairs, moving with other panicked people as they went out into the street, trying to figure out where the next shells were going to hit, so they could run in the opposite direction.

Nothing happened. The wind blew eerily through the crowd, moving clothes and hair but not doing much to disperse the smoke.

The small crowd moved about aimlessly, staring at the smoking ruins of the abandoned bakery across the road. Some people stood quite close to the wrecked building, hoping that the shells would never land in the same place twice.

Suddenly, a loud truck horn sounded. Everyone jumped towards the buildings on either side of the street as a large truck thundered past, covering them all in a layer of dust. It was the type used on construction sites, for removing earth and rubble - Maryam glimpsed the high metal sides and the fabric cover drawn over the top to stop debris falling out.

But as it roared past, she noticed that the back of the truck had been modified – instead of a full rear door, the metal plate at the back only reached half way up. She thought she saw people inside, but then the truck was gone, and she had other things on her mind.

She checked that her clothes were okay, dusted herself off as best she could, and set out on foot to find the rest of her family.

Chapter 25

November

Bilal could tell the ring was closing. His section had been attacked briefly a couple of times in the past week, but they didn't see anyone. It was just a few shots in the night that made the teams scramble into position, then everything went quiet. He felt reasonably secure, being in the middle of the defensive line that ran from west to east across the northern border of the Caliphate. Their position was strong, dug in deep into the ground, reinforced with concrete road dividers and a series of corrugated iron roofing to defeat the infra-red scanners.

That wasn't what was worrying him.

He hadn't heard from the Mullah or the Sheikh for over a week.

-

Seventeen kilometers to the south-west, the Joint Control Centre took a Priority Call For Fire relayed from the FOB in King Georges Road. Two squads blocking the railway tracks were taking accurate sniper fire from several unit blocks in Bellevue Ave and the air support had returned to Williamtown for resupply.

'Coral Base, this is Rhino Actual. Call For Fire.' The radio operator in the ASLAV worked through his checklist.

'IMMEDIATE SUPPRESSION. TEN DIGIT GRID.'

'FIVE SIX HOTEL LIMA HOTEL'

'TWO ONE NINE ONE FOUR FOUR NINE SIX'

The number of guns requested was deliberately omitted, to let the Battery's Fire Direction Controller make the decision. A SNAPS description of the target followed:

'ESTIMATE 5 ENEMY SNIPERS. STATIONERY. INSIDE UNIT BLOCKS.'

'DANGER CLOSE.' This told the FDC that the enemy was within 500 meters of friendly forces.

'HE. QUICK. 3 ROUNDS.' The Marines wanted 3 High-Explosive shells per gun to fall, exploding on impact to cause the most damage to the buildings as possible.

Several seconds - that felt like an eternity to the pinned Marines – passed as the artillery battery became a hive of activity. Plots made on paper maps became electronic commands checked and punched into computers. Electric motors whirred as the M777 howitzers were oriented onto the target. Loaders rammed HE shells into the open breeches, followed by several bags of propellant. The heavy breech assemblies swung closed and locked into the interrupted screw threads inside the barrel, creating an airtight seal and arming the spring-loaded firing pin.

Aimed and loaded, the gunner at No. 1 gun clipped the lanyard to the firing mechanism, stepped backwards to the limit of the cord and then muttered 'Aloha Snackbar, motherfuckers' as he pulled on it. The ring popped off the breech, allowing the firing pin to snap forward, detonating a small charge that flashed into the breech, igniting the bags of propellant and creating pressure of over 50 KSI. In a microsecond, the interior of the breech had gone from normal air pressure at ground level, to something resembling the exhaust from a jet engine.

Something had to give.

The shell, a complicated mix of chemicals in a steel case, nestled snugly on a bed of explosive propellant, responded immediately.

Lifted by the incredible expanding pressure, it rose up the barrel, rotating in the rifling grooves until it blasted out into the air, through the sound barrier, freed from any restraint but the laws of physics and aerodynamics. The physical shock of the howitzer cracked over the dusty Holsworthy ground, raising a cloud of dust to mix with the smoke blasted from the muzzle.

The FDC passed word to the FOB. 'SHOT. OVER.'

The FOB acknowledged: 'SHOT. OUT.'

Still spinning while the earth rotated below, the shell's trajectory peaked, and it nosed over, diving back to earth faster and faster, like a hungry predator who smelled prey. Or a Greyhound, rounding the final corner of a racetrack, hungry for the rabbit that was always just out of reach.

The sound of an approaching express train was incongruous to the Marines huddled on the side of the railway tracks. They knew the line was closed to trains, and there was no vibration from the rails that would indicate a goods train approaching, but the screaming sound from the air grew piercingly until the shell impacted well to the North, on Lakemba Street, demolishing a church hall and sending debris flying into the air.

The Marines called back on the radio to the FOB:

'SPLASH. OVER,' and the FDC acknowledged 'SPLASH. OUT.'

With that shot, a baseline was established for bringing the full firepower of the battery to bear on the Caliphate. Quickly referring to their own maps, the trapped Marines fed correcting data back to the FOB and the FDC.

'ADJUST FIRE. LEFT FIFTY, DROP ONE HUNDRED. FIRE FOR EFFECT.'

The commands were relayed to Holsworthy and the gun muzzles danced in unison as they corrected their aim. This time, the four guns in the battery barked in series, one after the other, shaking the ground and rattling the teeth of everyone within earshot.

Each gun fired three rounds in 90 seconds and then fell silent. Smoking gently in the afternoon air. The dust settled and an eerie quiet fell over the whole area.

In contrast, the centre of Western Sydney had become a scene right out of hell. The Marines cheered at first, then fell silent as the enemy's position was obliterated, blasted into a choking cloud of stinking dust that settled over everything. The dust cloud spread south and east as more and more Marines called in artillery and air strikes all over the Caliphate.

The Holsworthy FDC was kept busy all through the rest of the afternoon and into the night, directing artillery onto houses and unit blocks in an area of thirty square kilometers, from Bankstown to Earlwood.

The artillery continued firing at targets marked by the individual Marine units as priority, but fire missions were also scheduled in between, so the guns fired at a steady pace, to maintain a continuous rate of fire but minimize wear and tear on the barrels. The lower priority targets were drawn from a list provided to the FDC directly from the Regiment HQ – who knows how far up the chain the document originated, but that was not their job to know.

The artillery moved steadily across the Caliphate, randomly shelling streets, buildings, parks and infrastructure. While he knew it wasn't his job to ask, the FDC was puzzled at the low intensity of the bombardment.

It was almost as if the intention of the HQ was to cause structural damage to a large number of buildings, instead of bringing maximum firepower onto as small an area as possible. Ordinarily, the artillery tried to be as target specific as possible, minimizing collateral damage – but this seemed to be the opposite. He guessed it was to make as many buildings in the area uninhabitable, denying sanctuary to enemy fighters.

In that sense, it was a solid plan. He hoped there was a method behind it, too many times he had refrained from rolling his eyes at the instructions coming down from the politically correct robots with stars and eagles on their uniforms.

Chapter 26

December

From his vantage point in the bedroom of an abandoned house in Albion Street, Bilal watched the ASLAV moving slowly down the street towards him, screened on both sides and ahead by the Marines on foot. His eyes switched between the approaching machine and a stormwater drain opening in the kerb.

The rest of his team were waiting in ambush, three houses further down the street, but they dared not show themselves until the ASLAV was destroyed – it would cut them to pieces before they could get off more than a few shots. So, they had laid one of Deng's special bombs in the stormwater drain, set the radio detonator and then hid in a vacant house that gave him a clear view of the site where he would start to ambush the Marines when they arrived.

As the hulking machine reached the stormwater drain, Bilal flipped up the red cover of the arming switch and flicked it on. The tiny red light glowed, and he pressed the second button to blow the bomb.

Nothing happened.

He had no idea that the Marines and ASLAVs all had the REDWING system.

The REDWING system has two versions: Greengum was the name for the infantry version, able to be carried alongside the radio and ammunition pouches on the Marine's chest rigs. The Greygum system was larger and mounted inside the vehicles. Both systems broadcast on a radio spectrum to prevent the detonation signal from reaching booby traps and IEDs. They had saved countless lives in combat in the Middle East, and were automatically included with the Marines' equipment.

Bilal tried to remain cool as he reversed the process, closing all the switches then trying again. Armed, activated, but still no explosion from out in the street. He muttered a curse in Arabic, dropped the useless handset back into the pack at his feet and drew out the M72 Rocket Launcher. Fumbling in his haste, he pulled the inner tube back from the outer housing, feeling it click as the shoulder support locked into place. Kneeling, checked the view through the open window, brought the tube to his shoulder and pointed it out the window at the ASLAV – it was so close he couldn't miss.

His fingers naturally curled around the trigger mechanism as he took a deep breath, centered the sight on the side panel of the ALSAV outside and then pressed down hard on the button.

He was expecting a 'whoosh' sound like in the movies, but instead it just went off with a CRACK like a loud rifle shot, right next to his ear. He knew that to wait around meant certain death, so Bilal immediately dropped to the ground, grabbed his pack and crawled to the door. He struggled to his feet, bolted out of the house, down the back steps and ran as hard as he could, climbing over fences and running through the suburban yards to find the other lions. They would then decide how to attack the foot soldiers, once their ASLAV had been put out of action.

Out in the street, Lisa had heard the CRACK of the M72 fire, and dropped to one knee as she called what she heard and saw to Lt Barrett. She had no way of following the small rocket with her eyes as it raced across the open space – one second there had been a CRACK from inside that house, the next instant there was a DONG from the steel plate on the ASLAV beside her, and the crumpled remains of the rocket dropped to the ground beside the giant black wheels. It took Lisa a second to process what had happened, that the rocket was a dud and that she had been so close to being killed instantly.

'Contact Right Five Zero Meters,' the scream left her mouth before her brain caught up with the words. In one smooth motion, Lisa raised her rifle, nestled the butt into her shoulder and welded her cheek to the comb. Her brain was dumping adrenaline into her bloodstream, but the weeks of relentless training paid off and her body moved reflexively, checking the range, releasing the safety, moving the selector switch from SAFE to SEMI and calling to her squad mates 'watch my tracer' just before she squeezed the trigger.

The first three rounds in the rifle's magazine were tracer, after that there was a tracer every third round, until the last three rounds which were all tracer. In theory, this manner of loading the magazine would enable her to correct her aim using the first three rounds, then fire a succession of 3-round bursts which the individual tracers would help adjust her aim. The final 3 rounds would help tell her the magazine was almost empty. In training, this had been extremely effective, allowing all the Marines to deliver fast, accurate fire during their relentless drill sessions.

Which was good, because it all went out the window when the shots were fired in real life. Before she realised it, Lisa's rifle was empty and she was reloading, almost deafened by the noise of a dozen rifles and light machine guns firing in unison. Only half the platoon fired at any one time, their partners taking over as their magazines emptied and they had to reload. In this manner, for almost 20 seconds, the volume of fire did not slacken at all.

That was the amount of time it took the turret of the ASLAV to rotate towards the target house, smoking and splintering from the small caliber rifle rounds. Then the 25mm Bushmaster chain gun opened, and Lisa felt like the sky was being torn apart right over her head and she was showered with what felt like red-hot meteors.

With a sound like a giant zipper being opened slowly, the Bushmaster spewed three M791 sabot rounds a second into the house Bilal had just vacated. Unlike most rifle and cannon ammunition, the 25mm M791 is not a solid 25-mm projectile. Instead, it is a much thinner tungsten-carbide dart, surrounded in the cartridge by metal wings to bring the diameter up to 25mm. When fired, the 25mm unit leaves the barrel, after which the wings separate from the dart and fall to the ground, leaving the smaller, faster dart to deliver a devastating, armor-piercing impact, utilizing the maximum kinetic energy possible.

The stream of supersonic projectiles cut through the house like a chainsaw, blasting a foot-high swathe right through the walls and disintegrating everything inside. The walls collapsed, and the roof caved in, blowing a cloud of dust and insulation into the air.

Lisa couldn't hear a thing, and she missed most of the impressive sight as she was scrambling away from the falling sabot parts, still burning hot as they fell on the road beside the ASLAV. Her pulse was racing, and all her senses seemed on high alert. At the same time as the active part of her brain was getting her body settled into a new position, checking her sector for targets and conducting a self-assessment to see if she was burnt from any of the falling brass, she also knew that it was unlikely they had hit anyone – nobody could be stupid enough to stay in the house for a moment longer than they were discovered. They would have legged it as fast as possible in the opposite direction. All these thoughts poured through Lisa's mind in a landslide, and she just didn't have enough brain capacity to get in touch with Lt Barrett and warn him.

Gasping in air and blinking her eyes, Lisa scanned the other houses and tried to get herself under control. She shook her head and tried to focus but her brain seemed to be running in slow motion.

She knew her hearing was starting to return as she heard Lt Barrett on the radio, calling in the F/A-18s onto their position. As if he had read her mind, he estimated that whoever was in the house wouldn't run far, then they would re-group for another attack a few houses further down the street.

He wasn't about to let that happen.

'Cobra Two Five, this is Rhino Two One, Requesting Airstrike. How copy?'

Lisa's radio was on a different frequency, so she couldn't hear the Weapon Officer's replies, but she heard enough from Lt Barrett to follow what was going on.

'Confirm you can see my IR laser?' Lt Barrett pointed his rifle up in the air, shining the Infrared laser pointer so the aircraft systems could see it.

'I am marking the target. Be advised target is Danger Close.' Lisa was glad that LT Barrett was telling the aircrew there were friendly forces within 500 meters of the target. Barret's rifle was pointing down the street, its energy only visible through night vision devices, or the instruments aboard the F/A-18.

Barret ran through the rest of his checklist, feeding data to the aircraft about what direction to approach from, the type of ordnance to drop and exit route to keep the jet over friendly forces for as long as possible.

Scanning the sky, Lisa couldn't see the jet, but she heard the whine increase as it dropped out of the sky, then an accompanying whistle grew louder and louder as the bomb came down, tiny fins guiding its sensors into the point designated by Lt Barret's laser. Lisa and her platoon crouched in their defensive perimeter, hunched against the shock wave they knew was coming.

The sound cracked through the Marines on the ground, rattling their teeth as three houses in the row in front of them simply disappeared in a shower of dust and flying roof tiles. They cheered and high-fived as they celebrated the hit, grateful for the utterly reassuring show of protection they knew hovered unseen overhead.

Then it was back to business. Lt Barret pushed out teams on both sides of the road, checking houses while the ASLAVs slowly moved forward, then paused, then moved again, scanning the road ahead and keeping pace with the Marines on foot. They found Deng's bomb, which Bilal had hidden in the storm water drain, called it in and marked the location so the EOD bomb disposal techs could find and neutralize it, then moved on to secure the rest of the street. Two teams swept the wreckage of the bombed houses, but didn't find anything resembling human remains.

Lisa's heart rate remained high for the rest of the patrol. Experiencing the bombing run at close range had changed something inside all the Marines present. This wasn't something they could train for, it was just an experience that you had, or didn't have. Calling in bombs on Australian homes was far removed from the rifle range or the drills they had done in training. There was no going back now, and Lisa knew that even after this war was over, she would never be the same.

-

Two hundred meters away, Bilal crouched behind the flat tyres of a Ford Falcon parked in the driveway of another abandoned house. Dust covered his face, but his eyes sparkled, and a giant, cheesy grin split his face. Truly, Allah was powerful and wise, he thought, recalling the events that had kept him alive through the infidel's rain of bombs.

He had dashed out of the back door of the house and climbed the fence very awkwardly, the pack on his back throwing him off balance in every way possible. He heard the ASLAV's Bushmaster fire, and was puzzled because it should have been destroyed. Still thinking about the ASLAV, he slipped when going over the third fence and fell straight onto his head. Stunned but conscious, he lay on the ground, moaning softly and holding his temples with both hands as the F/A-18 soared overhead and bombed the house next door to the one he lay beside. The blast wave cracked overhead, sucking the air from his lungs but the walls of the house shielded him from the impact and the debris.

Unable to fully process what had happened, his brain screamed only one idea at his muscles – to put as much distance between himself and the infidels as possible. He rolled over, settled the pack on his back and ran at right angles to his original path, crossing the back fence and then ducking down a side passageway to get into the front yard and access the street which ran parallel to the one the Marines and the ASLAV were in. By the time the Marines arrived and searched the area, he was out of sight on the other side of the block.

Now, he crouched in the shadows, checking around just as Deng had trained him. Only when he was sure the street was deserted did he move, making his way steadily back towards his teammates. It took almost fifteen minutes, and by the time he snuck into their hiding place, the Marines were in sight, just down the road.

Reaching their position, they updated each other in rushed whispers. Bilal told them how neither Deng's bomb nor the Bazooka had taken out the ASLAV. Mazen told Bilal that he was lucky – there was a woman in the group of Marines, and he would have gone to Hell if killed by a woman.

They all laughed at Bilal's lucky escape from the falling bombs, and then Mazen grew serious. 'I want to kill the infidel woman.'

Bilal looked at him skeptically. 'And how?' he asked. 'You won't get within ten metres of her.'

Mazen quickly outlined his plan. 'Look, they are almost at the brick fence, with the bomb crater in the other side of the road. I'll hide behind da wall, and you three get into da house next door - behind the crater. De woman is out the front, so you all shoot a few rounds once dey go past. Dat will distract them long enough for me to run out, grab her and drag her inside the house.

'Nobody will see me, dey will all be looking – in the wrong place – for you.'

Bilal shrugged, he wasn't convinced and Mazen put the pressure on. 'C'mon bro. An Infidel, and a woman… you always going on about propaganda. This will strike fear into all dere hearts. We all be famous.'

Bilal looked at Mazen, saw the light shining in his eyes and he knew Mazen was on a mission, nothing he said would change Mazen's mind.

'Ok, *Inshallah*. Two clicks when ready.' He said, and the team split up. Bilal took the other two around the back of the houses, circling towards the Marines approaching down the street. Settling into position, he eased his eyes around the corner of the house and saw the Marines were directly in front of his position, the ASLAV slowly moving down the street as Marines checked out the empty houses on either side.

Positioning himself between the other two, he turned his head to the right and whispered 'the one on the far right.' Acknowledged with a nod, he turned his head left and whispered, 'third from the right.' Another nod confirmed his instructions, so he settled his sights on the second Marine from the right, grasped the radio handset and pressed the PTT button twice, telling Mazen he was ready.

In his earpiece, the radio static hissed twice, confirming Mazen was ready. Bilal's heart was thumping in his chest, and he wondered what Mazen was feeling, about to charge directly into battle like the heroes in the stories that the old men told young children.

Bilal had timed it right, and the house they were hiding behind had just been cleared, so the Marines were surprised when three AK-47s opened fire from a supposedly secure flank, spraying the troops with gunfire and dropping two Marines into the road, screaming for help.

Twice in one day, Bilal didn't wait to watch the effect of his actions. He sprinted back the way they had come, shepherding the other two until they reached their hiding place. Sliding into cover, Bilal saw that the first part of Mazen's bold plan had worked: The ASLAV turret was blasting the Bushmaster into the empty house, and the Marines were looking at the destruction as Mazen sprinted the few meters from his hiding place and grabbed the woman from behind. Just like they had been taught at the training camp, he covered her mouth with his left hand, wrapped his right arm under her chin in a choke hold and then started dragging her backwards as fast as he could.

Lisa was out on point, checking the road in front of the Platoon for signs of more IEDs when Bilal's diversion grabbed her attention. She swung her body to the left, raising her rifle and sighting in on the source of the gunfire.

She managed to get off three or four rounds when she felt strong hands wrap around her, cover her mouth and pull her off balance.

Half stunned by the speed that her circumstances had changed, Lisa instinctively forgot her rifle and grabbed at the arm that was choking her throat, desperately trying to pull it free but it refused to budge. Under a mortal threat and losing oxygen, Lisa's subconscious mind decided she needed all the help she could get, and opened the memories of the attack in Castle Towers. The overwhelming grief and anger at losing her family fired up her entire body, focusing all her energy and rage at the man holding her – as if he alone was responsible for the murder of her husband and child.

Immediately, Bilal could tell something was wrong. Assessing the woman's size and weight, Mazen hadn't counted on almost fifty kilograms of body armor, ammunition, water and other equipment that the Marines carried. Mazen managed to drag the woman a few steps before Bilal's worst fears came true before his horrified eyes.

Lisa's mind screamed obscenities as it tried to translate her emotions into words, but the hand over her mouth silenced her attempts to speak or breathe. Channeling the rage into her body, Lisa's muscles twitched violently as she let go of any control and allowed herself to be consumed by pure, fiery anger.

The woman had instinctively dropped her rifle and grabbed at Mazen's choking arm when she was taken, and it dangled from her chest rig on a short sling. Off balance, toppling backwards and losing oxygen, she suddenly pushed backwards, twisted inside Mazen's grip and in one fluid motion, drew a knife and plunged it deep into the young man behind her.

Pushing her attacker off balance, Lisa used her right hand to draw the KABAR bayonet that was strapped, handle down, in the center of her chest rig. Dropping her left shoulder as far as it would go against the restraint, she stabbed the steel blade as hard as she could into the soft flesh behind her left hip.

The blade moved in her hand as it glanced off bone, so she twisted, withdrew it and stabbed again.

And again.

Literally mindless with grief fueled rage, she stabbed again, rewarded by oxygen filling her lungs as the grip on her throat released.

'FUCK! FUCK! MOTHERFUCKER.'

The words burst from deep in her anguished soul as her feelings became sounds.

'THIS IS FOR BRAD! AND TILLY'

Trapped behind a mound of rubble beside the road, Bilal could only watch as the woman stabbed again and again, screaming a long string of sounds that made no sense. Mazen collapsed to his knees in the road and the woman whirled to face him, gripped his dishdasha in her left fist and then drove the knife right into his pelvis.

'YOU WANT ME TOO? NOT JUST TILLY? ME TOO? EAT SHIT, FUCKER. NOT TODAY!' The woman snarled as she slowly killed Mazen, spitting in his face as his mouth opened wide in a horrified scream. She twisted the blade inside him, then drew it out and stabbed again.

Twisted with grief at the thought of his friend killed by a woman, and worse, emasculated, Bilal saw Mazen struggle as the knife rose and fell in chorus with her swearing, then fell still. Dark blood pooled around his body as the other Marines approached, stunned at the scene they had just witnessed. Lisa had literally gone berserk, losing control in front of their eyes.

Bilal knew they had to get out of there while the Marines were occupied with Mazen's body. He wiggled his hand at the other two and they wriggled away, taking cover behind ruined houses as they made their escape. There was no hope of recovering Mazen's body or giving him a proper funeral, they knew they would barely escape with their lives.

Stumbling back the way they had come, Bilal's mind worked overtime to try and process what he had just experienced. Three times they had to throw themselves flat as infidel planes roared overhead, dropping bombs around the various Marine platoons as they fought their way down every street.

Twice he heard the familiar WHOOSH – BANG as rockets were fired, but he couldn't tell which side they were from.

Deep down, he didn't really want to find out.

-

Two weeks later, Bilal knew that the end was drawing near. He knew that the Marines had systematically cut the Caliphate into sections, ever closing a steel ring around him until the Caliphate consisted of Parry Park, from Roberts Road, east to the Mosque but not much further. Marines had seized the goods train line and dug in, creating an anvil upon which the attackers would smash the defenders.

Bilal and his two team mates had roasted under the midday sun, standing at the concrete barricades across Punchbowl Road. They had a clear view across the park to their north, and east-west along the roadway. Their right flank was secured by the unit blocks to the south, but Bilal knew they couldn't hold out much longer.

The artillery worked across the Caliphate constantly, blasting buildings and roads into rubble and making travel exceedingly difficult. Not only was there the constant danger from steel rain, but the damage and rubble meant that a secure path one day could be impassable the next.

To his great relief, the Mullah had delivered some food, ammo and the last M72 rocket launcher, which Bilal hoped would work better than the last one he had held, just before Mazen had been killed.

The horrible scene replayed in his mind as the setting sun dazzled him from the west, squinting his eyes and probing the horizon for signs of movement. There were none.

The three young men shared a nervous meal, rotating the sentry position between them so there was always someone alert. The other two cleaned weapons, chatted and generally avoided talking about what was really on their minds: the inevitable final attack by the Marines to finish them off. Bilal secretly expected it to come after midnight, but given his experience with the cunning of the Marines, he feared they would know this and attack earlier in the evening – possibly before dusk as the defenders would be blinded by the setting sun.

Taking his turn as sentry, Bilal stretched his neck and shoulders, moving his head around to work out the knots in his muscles. He checked the sky, noting that black storm clouds were rolling in from the east. He hoped that was a good sign, if the weather was bad enough, it would prevent the infidel aircraft from bombing – and it was doubtful the Marines would attack without air support. His part of the world was quiet, but instead of soothing him, he felt it was too quiet, and his nerves were even further on edge than before.

Alternating between watching for Marines on the ground or aircraft in the sky, Bilal heard the planes approaching before he spotted them, and his heart sank as he saw what was happening.

In front of the storm, dropping out of the blackening east sky came a stream of jet engine noise and flying metal. Wave after wave of F/A 18 fighter bombers screamed in from the sea and unloaded bombs into an area 1.5km long by 2.5km wide. Everything between Lakemba Street and Parry Park transformed into a choking inferno of exploding buildings and flying shrapnel.

Trapped on the far end of the Caliphate, Bilal and his team could only huddle in terror as the ground moved underneath and around them, overloading their senses and driving their bodies to huddle on the bottom of their fighting hole.

Driven by anger, Bilal forced himself to his feet and peered over the lip of their refuge, slack mouthed as the scene hitting his eyes failed to register in his brain.

Parry Park, which last Ramadan had held thousands of praying faithful, was churned into a wasteland of smoking craters. Stunned and horrified, Bilal knew this was the end, a fiery half-symbolic ending of all the hopes he had, to fill the Caliphate with loyal followers.

Hauling the other two to their feet, he pushed them up, out of the hole, then climbed out onto the ground beside them. None of them could hear a thing, but they could feel the ground vibrating under them and they knew the Marines were on their way. Working quickly, they spread out, ducking behind the white concrete traffic dividers they had used to block off the road. They shared out their combined firepower between them, a pitifully small arsenal compared to what was rumbling towards them.

Each man had an AK-47 or Type 56 rifle with ten 30-round banana magazines. They also had an imported M-249 SAW, which they had been feeding with ammunition scavenged from killed Marines. The drum round magazine underneath held a bit over half of its 200-round capacity.

In addition to four grenades and the last M-72, that was all they had. Bilal looked at the others, holding eye contact with each and they all knew this was the end. Quickly peeking over the barriers at the still deserted street, Bilal guessed that they had just enough time to prepare themselves for paradise.

Turning to face Mecca, the three began to chant. Haltingly at first, then with growing confidence as their resolve hardened into a fanatical embrace of their own coming death:

'La ilahah il-lal lahu Halimul Karim;
La ilaha il-lal lahu 'Aliyyul 'Azim;
Subhana 'l-laha Rabbus samawatis sab'i
Wa Rabbul ardhinas sab'i;
Wa ma fee hinna wa ma bayna hunna
Wa ma fawqa hunna wa ma tahta hunna;
Wa Rabbul 'arshil 'azim;
Wal hamdu lil-lahi Rabbis 'alameen.'

Settling back into a crouching position behind the smooth, white concrete, Bilal sought out a crack between two of the blocks and his heart leaped as he saw the first ASLAV pull out of Roberts Road and head straight toward him. Glued to the tiny portal, he saw dozens of Marines on foot follow the same path, tucking in behind the giant steel monster as they rolled in to finish off the Caliphate.

Never taking his eyes from the gunner's hatch on the looming ASLAV, Bilal whispered to the others 'Inshallah! I'll use the rocket first, knock out the ASLAV. The infidels will spread out and try to get around beside us, wait until they get in close, then we use the grenades, two in front, one on each side. After that, I'll empty the machine gun, use your rifles. Single shot only, make it count. K?'

Jaws set in defiance, they all nodded to each other. Bilal blew out a deep breath, grabbed the M-72, extracted the tube and settled his eye into the sight. Then in one smooth movement, he bobbed his shoulders up over the barricade, sighted, fired and ducked back down again.

Although it was old, and had been buried in the sand for almost a decade, the rocket's effect was devastating. Missing the main frontal armor by pure chance, the warhead impacted just below the Bushmaster gun, right on the ring supporting the rotating turret. There was no visible flash outside the vehicle, but the explosion drove a jet of plasma inside the hull, killing everyone inside instantly and setting the interior on fire.

The giant vehicle lurched to a stop, smoke pouring out where the overpressure had burst the hatch seals. Peering through the barricade again, Bilal saw the Marines spreading out on both sides, running forward to meet them.

Gripping the first grenade until his hand hurt, Bilal watched and waited, excoriatingly holding himself below the concrete wall as the Marines rushed closer. 'Ready' he muttered to the others, then finally 'NOW!'

Two grenades landed in front of the Marines approaching from the middle of the street, then a second pair were thrown out onto the flanks. Several Marines were hit, and the momentum of the whole attack was disrupted as the blast waves knocked others to the ground, tangling yet more in a flail of limbs and rifles.

By the time the noise had stopped, Bilal and the others were back up, barely visible above the concrete wall, firing their rifles at the Marines as they frantically sought cover.

Bilal picked up the M240, slid the long barrel over the barricade and leaned into it. Confident now, that his death would send him straight to Allah, he slipped off the safety catch and screamed over the noise of the rattling weapon.

'ALLAH ACKBAAAAAAAAH!' he screamed, firing the machinegun as if it was a rifle, taking aimed, short bursts of 3 or 4 rounds each. The muzzle flash lit up the looming darkness around them as he hosed down groups of infidels as they tried to re-organize.

Although his words couldn't really be heard over the gunfire, it fired up the others and they also screamed defiance as they fought their attackers. One by one, they ducked back into cover to swap empty magazines for full ones, as Bilal kept the machine gun firing over their heads.

The sight of a second ASLAV nosing around the burning wreck signaled the end of their defense of the Caliphate. Bilal's heart sank, and his courage faded away - he knew they had nothing left to defeat the armored vehicle, but that was the last thought that went through his conscious mind. The second Bushmaster fired, chewing the barricade into pieces and one of the flying chunks hit him squarely in the head.

Bilal slumped backwards as everything went black.

His part in Saudi Australia was over.

For now…

I hope you enjoyed this story as much as I enjoyed writing it.

Reviews are the life blood of any writer, so please leave a review on Amazon or Lulu for me. Thanks in advance.

If you're concerned about contemporary social issues, you should also check out Dragons in the Coral Sea: the looming war with China.

I've also written an expose of the Port Arthur Massacre – based on the actual witness statements and court documents before the media distorted the message. The 2nd Empty Chair: The Port Arthur Paradox reads like an action thriller, with footnotes to the evidence supporting the plot.

Both novels are available from Amazon or Lulu.com

The future will not be like the past. Good luck!